THREE *to* TANGO

THREE *to* TANGO

EMMA HOLLY

LAUREN DANE

MEGAN HART

BETHANY KANE

HEAT | NEW YORK

THE BERKLEY PUBLISHING GROUP
Published by the Penguin Group
Penguin Group (USA) Inc.
375 Hudson Street, New York, New York 10014, USA
Penguin Group (Canada), 90 Eglinton Avenue East, Suite 700, Toronto, Ontario M4P 2Y3, Canada
(a division of Pearson Penguin Canada Inc.)
Penguin Books Ltd., 80 Strand, London WC2R 0RL, England
Penguin Group Ireland, 25 St. Stephen's Green, Dublin 2, Ireland (a division of Penguin Books Ltd.)
Penguin Group (Australia), 250 Camberwell Road, Camberwell, Victoria 3124, Australia
(a division of Pearson Australia Group Pty. Ltd.)
Penguin Books India Pvt. Ltd., 11 Community Centre, Panchsheel Park, New Delhi—110 017, India
Penguin Group (NZ), 67 Apollo Drive, Rosedale, Auckland 0632, New Zealand
(a division of Pearson New Zealand Ltd.)
Penguin Books (South Africa) (Pty.) Ltd., 24 Sturdee Avenue, Rosebank, Johannesburg 2196,
South Africa

Penguin Books Ltd., Registered Offices: 80 Strand, London WC2R 0RL, England

This book is an original publication of The Berkley Publishing Group.

Collection copyright © 2011 by Penguin Group (USA) Inc.
"dirty/bad/wrong" copyright © 2011 by Lauren Dane.
"Just for One Night" copyright © 2011 by Megan Hart.
"Flipping for Chelsea" copyright © 2011 by Emma Holly.
"On the Job" copyright © 2011 by Bethany Kane.
Cover photograph of threesome © Claudio Marinesco; cover photograph of three chairs with frame: SOMMthink/Shutterstock.
Text design by Kristin del Rosario.

PRINTING HISTORY
Heat trade paperback edition / May 2011

Library of Congress Cataloging-in-Publication Data

Three to tango / Emma Holly, Lauren Dane, Megan Hart, Bethany Kane.—Heat trade pbk. ed.
    p. cm.
    ISBN 978-0-425-24093-9 (trade pbk.)
    1. Triangles (Interpersonal relations)—Fiction. 2. Erotic stories, American. I. Holly, Emma. Flipping for Chelsea. II. Dane, Lauren. Dirty/bad/wrong. III. Hart, Megan. Just for one night. IV. Kane, Bethany. On the job.
    PS648.E7T478 2011
    813'.01083538—dc22

                                                    2010036499

PRINTED IN THE UNITED STATES OF AMERICA

10 9 8 7 6 5 4

CONTENTS

CONTENTS

dirty/bad/wrong

LAUREN DANE

One

Ava saw the *Welcome to Petal* sign and sighed. *Home.* No matter what, it always called to her. She'd left, promising herself to never look back. And for the most part, she hadn't. Built a good life for herself in Los Angeles.

Ten years and she'd grown comfortable in her skin. It had taken a long time to wash the stench of that three-room shack from her life. A long time before she didn't cast her eyes downward every time she entered a store or restaurant.

A long time before she could give herself permission not to come back for holiday dinners soaked in too much alcohol and loathing. She'd choked on it her entire life. It had become second nature to feel inferior and ashamed.

And now it was over. Or so she hoped. Her father dead five years and her mother now gone just a few days before. The funeral would be in two days, which is what had brought her back to a place filled with too many memories and a place her heart had always thought of as home despite the bad ones.

She wasn't close to her mother. Hadn't spoken to her for longer than a five-minute phone call a few times a year. In truth, Ava had pretty much considered herself as having no parents for most of her life. Just adults who she tried to avoid as much as she could.

Her assistant had asked her why she was traveling all the way to Petal for a woman who'd never lifted a finger to stop the beatings, and Ava hadn't really had an answer for it other than it was what she was supposed to do. She had no idea why it mattered.

It just did.

And a not so very small part of her had come back to see the few people in town who'd mattered to her. Who she mattered to.

She needed to drop off some papers at the funeral home and check in to the small hotel at the southeast corner of town, near the cutoff to the highway.

Begley's Funeral Home was on Main Street, just down from the courthouse. The door was set back from the street, behind a lush garden that separated it from the noise and traffic. She sat in her car, hands on her keys.

The shame was there, as always a slick sort of second skin. She *knew* it wasn't hers to own. Logically, she understood her father's violence and addictions to anything that made him a worse human being had nothing to do with her. Just as her mother's public scene making, addiction to other people's husbands and alcohol were not hers to be responsible for. And yet, she would always be The Rand Girl to a lot of people in town.

So, she thought as she pulled the keys from the ignition of her rental car, she would do the right thing for herself. The memorial service wasn't for Marlene Rand, horrible, abusive woman who died after she wrapped her car around a tree trunk while driving drunk. It was for The Rand Girl.

She needed to close the door without slamming it and she needed to stop letting her memories get the better of her. So she put her keys in her bag, checked her lipstick and hair and reached for the door.

The blast of heat that hit her when she opened the door to step out served a sharp reminder that it was summertime in Georgia.

Despite the heat, it smelled strongly of roses. Roses from the planters all up and down Main Street. She smiled as she stood on the sidewalk, taking in the street and blocks of colorful flowers. Not every memory of Petal was a bad one, she thought as her gaze took in The Honey Bear at the other end of the street.

First things first.

The entry of the funeral home was suitably quiet. Classic and subtle, though the rug at her feet showed some wear. She'd never been inside. Seeing all the velvet and leather would have sent the younger version of herself into sensory delight.

On her way toward the door marked *Office*, Ava allowed herself the luxury of a caress of the deep green velvet on the back of a chair, the burnished wood on the corner of a table and the nap of a lampshade to the right of the door.

An owlish man she figured had to be the junior Begley came out into the entry. "You must be Ms. Rand. I'm sorry about your mother." He held out a hand for her to take, which she did.

He couldn't have been more than seventeen, but he had the same calm air his father had when she'd spoken with him on the phone two days prior.

"Yes, thank you." She pulled an envelope from her bag and handed it to him. "This is everything you said you'd need."

He placed the envelope in the pocket of a file marked *RAND*. "We have your mother here. If you'd like to see her, I can arrange for that."

"No. Thank you." She forced it back into the box. She would

not show them any weakness. She'd last seen Marlene five years before on a brief visit to the hospital in Shackleton, some thirty miles away. That had been enough.

He bent to look at the papers on his desk. "Everything for her service is set up. You said sunflowers, yes?"

She nodded, wondering if her accent had ever been as thick as his. Probably worse. She'd ironed it from her voice as much as she could. Ruthlessly destroying her connections, even something as simple as an accent, to this past.

"Yes. Sunflowers. Coffee. Tea both hot and cold. I can't imagine that more than three people are going to bother to show up, but please be sure to have enough food on hand. Can the excess be donated anywhere?"

"We have an agreement with the three local churches. It goes on a rotating basis."

She'd probably benefited from leftover memorial-service food in her childhood.

"All right then. Three p.m. on Wednesday. The obituary you provided ran in the paper today. I did receive some calls about a service."

"You did?" She couldn't quite disguise her surprise.

"Polly Chase. She's sort of the town matriarch." He frowned a moment. "I suppose you'd likely know that if you grew up round here. Mrs. Chase called for details. Asked about flowers and that sort of thing."

"I do know her. Yes." Polly Chase had never shown her pity, never looked at her with suspicion in her eyes. She'd come to Ava's classroom once or twice to talk about town history. Freshly pressed, big giant hair, sharp, pretty eyes. She'd smelled of Chanel No. 5. What a fine thing it would be to have a mother who smelled of something as feminine and fancy as Chanel No. 5.

He blushed, meeting her eyes. "Nice lady."

"Yes, very much so." Ava held her bag close to her side. "If there's nothing else, I'll be back shortly before the day after tomorrow. I'm at the Petal Inn if you need anything." She shook his hand again and made for the door. "Thank you."

The heat slapped her back into place when she walked out onto the porch and down the front steps.

On autopilot, she managed to get down to the hotel and check in. The place was clean and kept up well. Not luxurious. Not modern, but the bed was very comfortable and they had breakfast and free Internet.

She called work to check in and was assured for the millionth time that things were just fine and to forget about work and deal with the funeral.

She thought about a nap but rejected it. She needed some food and to go see Jasper and Maryellen. It occurred to her she could walk back into town. Then she remembered how hot it was and went back to change into something cooler, pulling her hair up into a ponytail while she was at it.

Late afternoon had settled in, casting shadows on perfect squares of green lawn as she walked down Miller Lane to cut over Sycamore to Main. Weeping willows shaded her every once in a while. Insects chattered and hummed. The air was thick with moisture and the heady, cloying scent of magnolias and . . . ah, star jasmine.

People looked up from porches and gardens as she passed. She'd had very few friends in town. Mainly the other kids who lived out near the railroad tracks in the strip of crappy little houses where she grew up.

She'd had friends there. One or two. Angelo lived a few hours away in Atlanta. In a big house she'd only seen pictures of, though he had invited her to stay several times. Some of the Murphy kids who lived in a trailer across the way from her house on Riverbend.

A few of the daughters had been close to her age and Ava had had a mighty big crush on Nathan, one of the older brothers, as they were growing up.

And Luca . . . it was complicated, but one thing was totally, utterly certain. She counted him as a friend and someone she cared deeply for.

The Honey Bear Café and Bakery loomed ahead, the familiar bear wood carving on the sidewalk just outside. Memories tightened her throat.

The place looked pretty much exactly the same as it had when she left a decade before. The linoleum on the floor had seen better days, but it was clean. The tabletops were new. Shiny red to go with the red-and-white-striped chairs and booths. Lost-dog fliers still shared space with garage-sale announcements on the corkboard at the entrance. The bells rang as the door closed behind her.

She hesitated as past and present swam in her vision, disorienting her with a wave of memory so very strong and sweet. Her first days there when Maryellen had ever so gently tapped her shoulder each time she found her looking at the floor.

She'd said, "The good Lord did not mean for you to be ashamed of yourself on account of what other people do. You are not your parents, Ava Rand. Hold your head up and be proud."

It'd been a difficult habit to break, one she never fully let go of until she'd lived in LA for a few years, but Maryellen Proffit had been the beginning and Ava had never forgotten that.

The customers already inside looked up, most looking back down, but a few were wondering if they recognized her.

A few did, including Luca Proffit, who'd just walked in from the back, where he'd been visiting with his parents. He'd been surprised to hear Ava was on her way and had only had time to make a quick call to Angelo to relay the news.

He paused, just taking her in. She stood there, far more confident than she had been the last time he saw her. She'd been young then. Barely out of high school. She'd been . . . gangly. Yes. Had walked as if she was not at home in her own skin. Gaze always turned to the floor, though his mother had made it her job to try to break that habit with stuff Ava hadn't known, like love and encouragement.

He knew she had fire inside her. Had admired it. Four years older than her, he'd been away at college for most of the time she'd worked for his parents. But it wasn't until those last few months she was in Petal that he'd realized that more than admiration, he had a raging case of the what-would-she-look-like-nakeds for her.

Four months. He'd seen her stripped bare and had never forgotten it. Innocent really, compared to most of the women he'd been with in the decade since. But she'd marked him with her jittery nature and her sad blue eyes.

The Ava of today didn't resemble the one who grew up here. Hair color and a good salon tamed the now deep auburn curls she'd captured into a ponytail. She wore small, black-framed glasses and very little makeup. Her skirt, well, lord above, it looked like something a wicked librarian would wear. Black, thigh length. The material flared as she'd moved. A white blouse with little red hearts as buttons added to the bad librarian look, and he liked it a lot.

"Mom, Dad, I think you two should come on out here," he called out as he moved toward her. "Ava?"

She caught sight of him and blinked several times, blushing wildly when she recognized him. But the warmth in her eyes was just for Luca, and some edgy part of him eased back and relaxed.

"Luca. It's good to see you."

He moved right in and hugged her. He'd surprised her, felt her body tighten and then relax as she hugged him back. "Good to see you, too."

"Ava!" Maryellen came out, wiping her hands on a towel. "We were all just talking about you. I was wondering when you'd make the time to bring yourself around here. Jasper! Come on out here and see Ava. Start up a cheeseburger and bring cobbler."

Ava grinned. "You remember."

"Cherry cobbler and a cheeseburger with extra-crispy fries. Luca, get her into a booth for goodness' sake. I'll be back with some tea."

"I was sure sorry to hear about your mother, Ava." Luca motioned her into a nearby booth, taking the opportunity to slide in next to her.

Ava had struggled with whether or not she should pretend to be sad about her mother's death. She was, in her own way. But she'd vowed to never shed another tear for her parents as she'd headed westbound on a bus out to Los Angeles.

Instead she just shrugged. "Thanks."

Jasper came out with a ridiculously huge plate of cobbler and hugged her. "It's mighty fine to see you, Ava." He sat with Maryellen, across from her. "Burger will be up in a few. Figured the cobbler would take the edge off." Jasper grinned, and she couldn't help but respond.

"You said two days ago you'd call. We've been worried." Maryellen looked her over. "You look pale. You need some rest."

The mothering smoothed Ava's jitters as she took several bites of the cobbler, sure she looked totally sexy inhaling it as if it was oxygen or something. Still Luca flustered her. He shouldn't. She was light-years away from the girl he'd bedded a decade ago. But it had been pretty remarkable.

At the lake, under the shade of an oak tree, he'd put his mouth on her pussy, had coaxed and kissed, licked and tickled her to a powerful climax. It had been the first time anyone had gone down on her. He'd been her first for most everything.

At the memory, a full-body blush hit, heating her cheeks as she bent over the cobbler, hoping he wouldn't notice. Though how he could miss it as he sat there next to her, far closer than he had to be, she wasn't sure.

"I know and I'm sorry. I've been on a crazy deadline for a presentation. I thought I'd be able to fly in yesterday, but I had to finish it all first. I'm tired. I guess I'm getting too old to stay up all night." She laughed. "But now it's finished, and I think we did a great job. Luckily the hotel has comfortable beds. I'll probably conk out by six thirty."

Maryellen's disapproving snort was enough to bring her attention back up from her plate. "You must be tuckered out, sweetie. You're staying at the hotel? Oh no. I told you to stay with us."

"I know and I appreciate it." As she'd assured them several times already. "But I have to be up at all hours and have my equipment running. It's too much to ask." Plus it would take up a great deal of space. And they didn't have air-conditioning. As much as she adored the two of them, it was August, and she hadn't lived in the deep South for a decade.

Luca stole a fry when the cheeseburger arrived, and she nudged him with an elbow, sending him a playful glare.

"Ava, I have room at my house. It's on the lake, so it's quiet. I have a home office if that helps."

Maryellen grabbed on to that quickly. "It's a big old house, Ava. Enough out of town that you won't be bothered."

"He does always have that fancy coffee I bet you like, too." Jasper winked. "We'd feel much better if you stayed with Luca." The man had gone with her to the bank in Riverton where she opened her first savings account. He was more of a father to her than the one she was born to, that's for sure.

"I can help you get your stuff from the hotel and get you settled in," Luca, ever so helpful, chimed in.

"I already paid and everything." But they sensed her weakness, and she knew it was a done deal.

"Lynell is a cousin on my daddy's side. I'm going to call him right now." Jasper stood, off on a mission to call the hotel's manager. "I'll tell him you and Luca will be over after you finish eating."

And that was that.

Two

Ava sat on the bed with its handmade quilt folded at the foot and sighed. The room was cool, shaded by a huge weeping willow just outside the window and the marvelously efficient air-conditioning she thanked heaven for.

She lay back and tried not to think about how close Luca kept getting to her over that afternoon. He'd sat right up against her at the café. And then he'd stayed to help her move her things, touching her, crowding her and generally making her as skittish as all get-out.

He'd kept the conversation light enough, but she hadn't failed to notice the way he watched her put her underpants back in her suitcase. So much remained unspoken between them, even as their back and forth had come fairly easily.

He'd been . . . so much to her. Everything at one time. The way she'd left it wasn't the best, she knew, but she didn't know how to bring it up.

She'd wanted to take his hand and tell him how those times

with him and Angelo had thrown something inside her open wide. How understanding her sexuality wasn't some horrible, shameful thing had freed her. They'd both shown her she was beautiful and worth love and respect.

But then she got embarrassed just thinking about it and left it unsaid. After all, he might have a girlfriend or a boyfriend, or maybe he looked back on those times a decade before through a different lens.

The last time she'd seen him, some seven years before, he'd been a man. Someone else's man, though no less sexy and desirable. The scent of him drove her crazy. The solid wall of his chest, the way his forearms looked with his shirtsleeves folded up, his hands—lordy, she did love the look of a sexy pair of hands, and he had them in a big way.

She rustled around, trying to find relaxation so she could sleep. He'd left her in the sleek and elegant spare bedroom about twenty minutes before, and now she lay on the bed, the ceiling fan lazily cooling her skin, filled with all sorts of filthy urges and no one to fulfill them.

The heat had leeched the small bit of energy she had left, and so she lay there, tired and emotionally frazzled and feeling exposed. Bone-deep exhaustion sapped her will after all the air travel and the details of her presentation, and this sort of up-close examination of her past didn't help. Her eyes hurt and a steady throb beat at her temples. Her mother was dead, and she couldn't find any part of her that felt empty because of that fact. This made her far more sad than the actual death.

She needed to make it all disappear for a few hours. Claim unconsciousness and find the sort of rest she couldn't get until she conked out. But sleep would not come. Probably because she was so horny.

Only one way to deal with that. She headed to the shower.

* * *

Luca had stood at the bottom of the stairs leading up to his guest room for a very long time.

The last thing he needed to do was start something with Ava Rand. Ava with her big, beautiful eyes. The years had been very good to her. Time, the sunshine and most undoubtedly the distance from her parents had fleshed her figure out. Her legs were long and shapely, rather than the skinny ones she'd left Petal with. Her tits, well, they'd been nice back then, only now she wore them in a pretty bra made to keep them mounded just right over the top of her blouse.

She'd had a ton of computer stuff with her. She'd told him she worked for a midsize software company. That had been unexpected.

Everything about that day had been unexpected, he supposed. Ava just popping up, looking so beautiful, and now, like a dream, she was in his house, just a few stair treads away.

He got all the way out to his favorite chair overlooking the water before he pulled his phone out and dialed the familiar number.

And of course got voice mail for the second time in a day. Cripes, Angelo really needed to listen to his damned messages every once in a while. Luca left a brief update and hung up, looking back at the house.

Skittish. She'd been nervous around him, and at first it had hurt. But then he realized she was uncertain, unsure of what they'd mean to each other all these years later, and he relaxed and gave her a little bit of space, which seemed to relax her as well.

Then they'd sort of clicked back into how they'd been before. And that, he thought, sweating because he'd begun to pace in the sun instead of sitting in his shaded chair, had disconcerted *him*.

Only Angelo shared that space in Luca's life, that sort of effort-lessness of being with someone you trusted completely.

She'd left. He'd woken up to find her gone, leaving behind nothing but a note begging for forgiveness because she had to get out of Petal or die.

He'd understood. They talked about her leaving, but he and Angelo hadn't wanted her to do it. He came from good people. From a family who'd loved and cherished him. He had a bright future. To him, Petal was a town filled with possibilities because he wanted to take his place in it, build an adult life there, have a family and do all that great stuff.

To her, it had been a place of contradictions. The kindnesses of people like his parents were contrasted by the way many judged her for her parents. It had been a dead end for her in many ways. He'd known it, but hadn't wanted to face her not being there.

And one day she was simply gone.

But his feelings for her, feelings he'd carefully boxed away, had never gone, and the shadow of her had remained. Like another person in the room each time he'd gone out with other women.

He still wanted her. Wanted the woman she'd become. He brought her to stay with him to have her near, and he couldn't find the energy to deny it to himself.

With a sigh, he stopped pacing and headed back toward the house.

She didn't answer when he knocked. His heart kicked with worry. She'd been pale, clearly tired. He shouldn't have even come back, but now that he stood there, worried, he had to be sure.

"Ava?" he called out as he opened the door.

She walked out from the bathroom on a puff of steam, wrapped in a towel.

A towel that slipped to the ground when she saw him and screamed, jumping three feet into the air.

"It's me! Ava, it's Luca." Feeling helpless and more than a little like a dumbass, he held his hands up. "I knocked and you didn't answer . . ." God her body was beautiful. He nearly lost his mind when he caught sight of the tattoos and pierced nipples.

How totally unexpected. He liked it. Especially his cock. Energy built as they stood there—her naked, hair slowly drying and beginning to curl. He remembered her taste, the feel of her skin against his lips.

She remembered, too. Right there, she stood and remembered it the way he did. Her pupils swallowed the color of her eyes, her skin pinked. That knowing passed between them, heavy and sticky.

It hung there with a delicious ache until the dryer sounded that it was done, the noise breaking the tension.

She bent to grab the towel and then sent him a raised brow. "Oh. Shit, sorry." He turned away while she rustled, getting dressed.

"I was taking a shower." She sighed. "You can turn around now. Not like you haven't seen it all before."

When he did she was in jeans, rolled up at the hems, and a pale yellow T-shirt. She wore no bra.

"I have, yes." He'd said it, meaning to tease, but once he took her in totally, he stood there without speaking.

Nothing like a totally silent moment to make a girl more nervous. It would have been worse had she not taken in the rather impressive line of his hard-on, pressing against the zip of his jeans. She was only human after all. The denim was so well used and faded it'd gone nearly white in some places. Threadbare glimpses of his thigh only added to the overall effect. No shoes. Just a pair of low-slung jeans, a slice of sun-kissed belly when he reached up to run his hand through that mass of golden hair. That downy trail of hair leading from his navel inside the waistband of his jeans led to places she'd never forget.

He was beautiful right then, but naked, well, he did naked really well, too.

Ava couldn't make him leave. Didn't want him to. She lost her exasperation and put a hand at her hip. "Why did you come in?"

"I was worried about you. You were tired and pale, and I had a brief moment of panic that you'd hit your head or something and I came in."

She rolled her eyes. "Why did you come back to my door to begin with? Is everything all right?"

"I tried to stay away. I stood outside in the sun, sweating and having a vicious argument in my head about why I needed to just keep moving and leave you before I did something."

He seemed nearly fierce as he began to pace. The sun behind him seemed to light him in gold. Against the fine hairs of his arms, exposed from mid-biceps down. His shirt clung to his body just right. A lot like his jeans did.

His hair had always reminded her of honey. Currently it was just a bit too long. But with the practiced scruff of his beard and the sleepy, big brown eyes, the package was one of a kind of sexy. Mature man sexy. The kind of sexy that drove women crazy. *This woman for damned sure.*

Luca had always been that boy all the girls had crushes on. The bad boy who was a good guy under the skin. Raced his car and rode a motorcycle, but he opened the door for a lady. He was intelligent and articulate, funny and generous.

Her ovaries were doing cartwheels just being in the same room with him.

"Do something like what?"

In two steps he was on her, pulling her to the very solid wall of his chest. His mouth found hers as she gasped in delight. Her fingers slid into his hair, as she'd wanted to do ever since she'd seen him just hours before.

His tongue slid into her mouth, dancing along hers. The shock of memory hit her. She'd had this with him before, had been marked by it in some way and she wanted more. Wanted it right then and now.

She arched against him, tugging on his hair when he made an attempt to break the kiss. He hummed his satisfaction, and she eagerly swallowed the sound. He sucked her bottom lip, nipping it until she shivered at the edge where pleasure slid into pain.

He broke the kiss, resting his forehead against hers. "Something like that."

She laughed. "For future reference, I'll go on record to say I approve of something like that."

"You wanna come out for a drink? Relax a little? Catch up?" He licked his lips, as if to taste her again. Her fingers twitched, wanting to touch him again, but she forced her hands into her back pockets to keep from hauling him closer and grabbing a handful of cock.

Still, he'd surprised her by asking. The tentative nature of his voice relaxed her a little. He was as uncertain as she. "I do. But it's two days before the funeral. It would look bad. Everyone will only say how much like her I am." She shuddered.

He caressed her cheek, sliding his palm down to cradle the side of her neck. When he spoke, his voice was gentle. "You're nothing like her, Ava. That you're here, that you're actually thinking about how your actions might affect others shows that. But I understand your discomfort. We can stay here. I can make dinner and drinks. Or you can sleep."

"My internal clock is off. I'm dead tired, but not sleepy. I'm going to try to stay awake until at least nine or I'll be all wonky tomorrow." She'd been hoping an orgasm would help make her drowsy, but his presence lit her up like a Christmas tree.

His smile was crooked, his eyes lit with something more than general amusement.

"I can think of things we can do here."

"That so?"

He kissed her again, his mouth warm and hungry as it settled over hers. She moaned, arching into his hold, which tightened around her, keeping her snug against him. Her hips jerked forward of their own accord when he sucked her tongue.

Her nails dug into his shoulders as she opened to him, to the kiss, to the direction the day was taking.

"I want you, Ava. Can I have you?" he panted as he broke the kiss.

"God yes."

He smiled, sliding his hands along the edge of her pants, along her waist, leaving goose bumps in his wake.

"You feel good," he murmured, kissing her neck. "Smell good. Taste good." As he spoke, he backed her against the dresser. "I've been hard since the moment your name came up earlier today."

Huh? "It's very hard to follow what you're saying when . . ." Oh yes yes yes.

He slid a hand down the front of her jeans—thank God they were loose—and into her panties. She gasped when he slid the pad of his middle finger along her labia and then between, against wet, sensitive, already swollen flesh.

"You drive me crazy. You know that? Widen your stance, baby. Yes, like that so I can get at your pussy better."

Hoo boy.

He petted her clit and she hissed, her hips jutting forward. "Mmm, you need this don't you? Shhh, let me give it to you. Take the edge off."

"I just had it," she murmured, letting him lever her back a little so he could pull her T-shirt up, exposing her breasts.

"Pierced. I need to see up close." He licked over each nipple, all as he continued to finger her. "You just had it? What does that mean? God I love these." He worshipped her nipples as she struggled to form a coherent sentence.

"An orgasm. But this is better." She gasped when he bit her nipple, moaning when it was hard enough to bring the edge of pain. And then he squeezed her clit between slippery fingers. Anything else she was going to say was lost as the roots of another climax dug in, took hold.

"Impatient." He chuckled against her skin as he twisted his wrist, sliding two fingers into her, his thumb flicking over her clit until she nearly screamed with the force of her climax. Instead she leaned forward, putting her head on his shoulder, her teeth finding the muscles of his shoulder.

Feeling returned slowly with the sharp press of the dresser's edge at her back. "As hospitality goes, I think this is the most welcome I've ever felt as a guest."

He righted her, slowly pulling his hand free, and then to her delight, he licked his fingers. "You taste like sin dusted with powdered sugar. Good and very bad all at the same time."

"That's really good." She laughed, reaching for the button of his jeans. "You need to get naked so I can ride you like a pony."

Surprise flitted over his features along with a mischievous smile. Whatever he'd been about to say was swallowed by the sound of the front door opening and closing and then a bellow of Luca's name that dulled into a softer inquiry as to his whereabouts.

They both froze. She'd recognize that slow, honeyed drawl anywhere. She wouldn't be alone of course; Angelo Bennett's voice and his ruggedly handsome face were on television from time to time, especially during football season.

"Angelo?" Ava murmured.

"I called him a while ago," Luca said as he went to the door, opening it to find Angelo standing there. "I secretly suspected you did indeed listen to your voice mail more often, but you just ignore it."

Angelo cocked his head. "Smells like sex in here," he said as he walked into the room, stealing the rest of the oxygen. His gaze settled on her like a physical thing. "There she is. Rumpled and flushed. I think you looked like this the last time I saw you, too."

He said nothing about her blush, instead sweeping her into a hug.

"Course the last time I saw you, you neglected to say you'd be leaving before dawn to move all the damned way across the country."

She knew it needed to be said. "Yeah. I'm sorry. It was shitty of me. I know it. But I had to go. I had to." She *had* contacted them both when she arrived in Los Angeles. Had apologized for leaving the way she had. But she did leave them both, exhausted from a long night before filled with sex and laughter.

He took her chin, tipping it up to meet his gaze. Angelo was big. Like six-and-a-half-feet tall, broad-shouldered big.

"I know you did. More than most anyone, I understand."

Angelo grew up on that same barren bit of land near the tracks she had. But he'd had his size to propel him into sports. Football. He'd been one of the golden people and had done his best to keep away from home.

He'd always been kind to her. Had even hauled her father off her on two different occasions. And then he'd gone off to college to play ball at UCLA while Luca had headed east to go to school.

"You can make it up to me with sex." He winked. "Luca, well now." With a smirk, Angelo turned to his best friend, looking him over as well.

Her body remembered those months they'd spent as lovers. Her pulse sped and her nipples, already at attention from Luca's presence, throbbed in beat with her clit.

And then Angelo strode over, leaned down and kissed Luca, leaving her rooted to her spot. Goddamn they were so fucking beautiful there, Angelo so big and braw, Luca long and lean, mouths fused, though she got the occasional flash of tongue, bringing a gasp she hadn't intended on making.

Angelo broke away, licking his lips. "Now, that's much better. Though I'm surprised your lips taste like pussy already. How long have you been back in town?" Angelo sent Ava a raised brow.

"I got in this afternoon. What are you doing here? I mean, I'm happy to see you and all."

"Damn, Luca, you're fast. As for your impertinent question, I live here."

She tried not to give in and be amused by him, but it was a losing battle. "No, you don't. You live in Atlanta."

"If you ever came to visit instead of hiding out in LA, you'd know Ramona still lives here." Ramona was one of his sisters. "I was at the JV baseball game. My nephew plays third base. They lost. We had pizza and soda. And then I listened to my voice mails." He paused and kissed the tip of her nose and then looked back at Luca over his shoulder. "Sorry. I know how bad I am at that."

Luca cleared his throat. "I was just trying to convince Ava to grab a drink. It'd be good to not agitate her straight out the door and back to Los Angeles."

Angelo's gaze on her face was knowing. "That what the kids call it today? Grabbing a drink is the code for tug job?"

"Ha! There was no tugging. You lumbered in before we got that far," Luca interjected, tossing himself back on the bed.

"Not *yet*. I was grabbing for his cock when you barged in." She hid a smile as she looked back up at Angelo's fallen-angel face.

He tucked her hair behind her left ear. "Still so pretty." He said it just for her, turning her knees to jelly, like he always had.

Angelo's attention turned back to Luca. "Town'll be buzzing about Marlene Rand's daughter boozing it up, and this right after her momma done up and got kilt by driving drunk." Angelo turned up the Southern. "Probably not the kind of attention our Ava wants."

"We went over that, too. My next sentence, if you ever let me get a fucking word in edgewise, was that I have tequila and that I'd make dinner here."

Ava turned her attention back to Luca, moving toward him. Angelo caught her, pulling her against him, her back to his front.

"I'm sorry about your mom." He slid his hands up her arms, and she tried not to swoon.

She sighed, tipping her head back to look up at him. "It's okay. I wasn't surprised when I got the call."

"Why didn't you call to tell me you were coming to Petal?" They'd spoken on and off over the years. She sent holiday cards. He sent lavish flowers at random, with little notes of invitation in them that she was never quite brave enough to accept. Still, they had something. A connection she'd never lost. He understood her in ways no one else really could.

What could she say to that? "I didn't know if you'd care."

His features darkened briefly. "Why wouldn't I?"

"I don't know!" She threw her hands up, flustered. "It was ten years ago, and I was a bitch to leave the way I did."

"You had to go to survive. I get it. You matter to me." He said it like it was obvious, and she supposed it was.

"And to me." Luca spoke from his place on the bed.

"Luca already got to show you how much." Angelo kissed her neck. "You're not wearing a bra."

"Are those sentences even related to each other?" Luca unzipped his jeans, pulling his cock out.

Hello, gorgeous.

"Do they need to be? It's a thing I noticed as I was staring down at her tits. Like you didn't look."

Luca fisted his cock, pumping it a few times, sending her train of thought right off the tracks. "No, no they don't need to be. Just wanted to be sure I wasn't missing something. Sometimes your logic escapes me."

Ava laughed. "I'd forgotten what the two of you were like together. Like old married people."

"Come on down here, Ava. Let's remember what the *three* of us were like." Luca waggled his brows, but her laugh caught in her throat as she caught sight of the shiny bead of pre-come on the head of his cock.

"Pretty bird, undress me first." Angelo spun her, leaving her breathless. The raw need on his face didn't help. "Since Luca got started before I'd even arrived. Rude." He sent an arched brow toward Luca, who snorted his response.

Ava ran her hands all over Angelo as she pulled his shirt from his body. He'd first called her pretty bird back when she was in middle school. But after they'd . . . after they'd been together, the tone of it, the way he'd emphasized the words, had been different, sexy.

Luca broke into her thoughts as he teased back, "Her taste is still in my mouth, as a matter of fact. Do I need to run that by you, too?"

Angelo cocked his head at the retort and each of them positively oozed testosterone.

"Both of you have big, giant cocks and fuck like rock stars," she droned, her voice dry. "Jeez, you two need a cookie or a gold star or something?"

Angelo barked a laugh, kissing her. "If cookie is pussy and I can eat yours, I'm on board with that plan."

Well, what on earth was there to argue about with that statement? She kissed up his side, pausing at the bar in his left nipple. "I like this." She tugged on it with her teeth, pulling just shy of pain. He arched into her with a snarled hiss of pleasure.

"Guess that works. Let's see what else does."

Luca groaned. "You're taking too long. How about we get her naked, too?"

Angelo mock-pouted at Luca. "What, you don't want to see me naked?"

Luca got to his knees and rolled from the bed, stalking toward Angelo. "Oh yes. Yes, I do. But I can multitask." Luca kissed her shoulder as he moved past.

She flushed. Before, when they'd all been together, the two of them had jerked each other off, but there was so much more between them now. The day was looking up!

"I'm going to be right back." Luca jogged from the room, and she turned back to Angelo.

Angelo arched into her touch, delighting in the feel of her mouth against his side, across his ribs.

"I've missed you," he couldn't stop himself from murmuring to her. No more than he could stop the way his heart swelled when she simply put her arms around him and held on.

She got to him. Had always gotten to him with those big, startled eyes of hers, usually turned to the floor. Nervous as she tried to remain unnoticed at school or in town. Especially at home.

She'd soaked up his kindnesses like thirsty ground, and he'd ruthlessly shoved all his desire for her away. Locked it down. Went to school, fucked women who weren't broken and sweet. Women who were of age, for God's sake.

None of them were her. In the years since he could still say the same.

He'd come back to Petal after he'd been drafted. For the time before training camp had started, and she'd been there. Legal. Beautiful. *And his best friend's girlfriend.*

He'd ached for her. Had watched her with Luca, jerking off to the memories of the way they'd touched each other. His presence was welcomed in their relationship, and he knew he hadn't been imagining the rising sexual tension between the three of them.

It all started when Luca had pulled on her hair and she'd reacted.

He shivered, thinking back to the ragged need in that sound, the awakening of something else inside him, and then he'd whispered in her ear and everything had changed.

"Does it make you wet? That little bit of pain?" he'd whispered like a stranger to himself.

She'd paused, and nodded slowly, her eyes wide with revelation, surprise, a little bit of fear and a lot of desire.

And then he'd been with both of them. Luca was the one who initiated it, leaning toward her, pulling her ponytail to bring her to his mouth. When her back was arched, Luca pressed her body into Angelo.

That kiss had been a breath away from his mouth, and Luca had said, "Baby, Angelo is here. I think we should invite him to stay."

And he had. That first time had been exhilarating. Teeth and nails, biting, sucking. He'd been drunk on her, bingeing on how fucking good she felt against him at last. And then Luca . . . he hadn't expected that upswell of desire, though he'd always had an attraction toward men and women.

He'd never felt so connected to anyone the way he had with them. He'd tried other threesomes. Had tried other men, but it had never been the same.

"I missed you, too. But I do get to see you on ESPN during football season." She grinned up at him and he laughed, kissing her soundly.

"But you're not on my television. I can't touch you." He pulled her shirt over her head, and Luca came back with condoms, lube and music sounding through the speakers embedded in the ceiling.

"I put some steaks in a marinade. When we're finished . . . with the first round at least, we can have some dinner."

Luca, beautiful, golden boy, grinned at both of them, and Angelo couldn't deny his lips turning up in response.

Ava walked around his body, pressing herself to his back. "I love this ink." She petted over the Samoan tattoos on his shoulders and down his spine. His mother had loved the homage he'd paid to her heritage with those tattoos. Seeing her so happy in those last months of her life had been worth the pain of getting them done in the traditional way, which took twenty days, though it's not so bad when you get to lie on your belly with the ocean just feet away.

Luca took his place on the bed, watching them both. Long limbed and toned, he'd taken his pants off and reclined, totally naked, stroking his cock as his gaze ate the two of them up.

Ava slid her palms down Angelo's belly, and he sighed, content. "Such a hard belly. God, it makes me wet." Her voice was barely above a whisper, but he heard it as it played back against the memory of that first time.

"Something else hard for you to touch, too."

Her cheek had been resting against his back, and he felt the swell of her smile.

"Like this?" She unzipped his jeans slowly, drawing her nails over his cock through the material of his boxer briefs.

"The very one."

Luca's gaze slid down his chest and to the place where Ava had pulled Angelo's cock free one-handed while shoving his pants and boxer briefs down with the other.

She circled again, stopping when she faced him. Her eyes weren't startled anymore. He realized that although she'd been open with him and Luca, this Ava was self-assured in a totally different way.

"What made you decide to get ink and piercings?" he murmured, walking her back to the bed.

She shrugged. Sliding graceful fingers up her side over the petals and ivy, she paused at the word written there—Fly.

"This one was the first. It was . . . painful." Her pupils flared and his heart kicked in his chest as he realized she liked that part.

He ran his hands up her sides to cup her breasts. After he

pinched the swollen nipples, he pulled on the rings, watching her face to gauge just when to stop.

"Lookit that, Luca. I remember how much our pretty bird likes a little pain with her pleasure."

Her eyes still held a glazed look, but her mouth broke on a smile so sensual and raw it shot straight to his already rock-hard dick.

"Is that why you got your piercings?" Luca moved to them.

She nodded her head slowly, licking her lips and driving Angelo crazy for her.

"Baby, you're so sexy." Luca licked up her spine, meeting Angelo's eyes. "But you're still partially dressed."

"Luca, why don't you help with that?"

"My pleasure." Luca knelt before her, unzipping and pulling the jeans from her body. The panties were a small scrap of bright red with tiny white polka dots. He pressed his face to her mound and breathed her in.

Angelo watched her fingers convulse in Luca's hair as she held him to her body.

Tom Petty's "American Girl" came on, and she tossed her head back and laughed. "I love this song."

Luca surged to his feet and pushed her back to the mattress, grabbing her panties and tossing them over his shoulder.

"My favorite," she murmured up at them. "Hot and cold running cock."

Angelo crawled over her, stopping when he got close enough to kiss her again. "You're a dirty girl."

She quirked up a smile. "I am. Is that a problem? Just so you know, I like it dirty and I don't like it guilty. I stopped apologizing several years ago. I like what I like."

"You say that like a challenge."

Her hand on his cheek was gentle. "Not with you." She looked to Luca. "Or you."

"I like dirty." Luca kissed her neck.

"Me too. So we've established that. Let's fuck."

She reached down and grabbed a cock in each hand. "All right then. Who's fucking who? Well"—she smirked and leaned forward enough to lick over the head of Angelo's cock and then Luca's—"I know I'm *getting* fucked. What order, how, when?"

Angelo's skin itched with the need to be in her. So much need that his hands shook as he rolled the condom on.

"Hands and knees, Ava. Face Luca and suck his cock while I fuck you from behind."

Any worry that she'd not be on board with the way he spoke to her dissolved as she closed her eyes for a moment, taking a deep breath. And then turned onto her belly and obeyed.

Christ. It nearly felled him to see her that way. Luca took in the long, pale line of her back, the ink there—the symbol of infinity with tiny purple flowers and vines all around. Her breasts hung heavy, the silver rings gleaming. Her eyelids were at half mast, lips open, glossy from her tongue as she'd swiped over them only moments before.

He scrambled into place as she crawled to him. First to kiss—the sweetness of her lips against his. And then to deliver licks and nibbles down his body until she reached his cock with a sexy, knowing, half smile.

"I've missed your taste, Luca."

Angling his cock, she licked around the crown and then across the slit.

Angelo's face relaxed, Luca realized, the moment he got all the way inside her pussy. Her moan, made with his cock in her mouth, vibrated up his spine.

So. Fucking. Good. So good it was nearly possible to ignore the sense of rightness. That part scared him a little.

She took him into that hot, slick mouth, using her tongue to massage all his sensitive spots. The sounds she made as Angelo fucked her rushed through his system, pushing him to come.

But he wanted more. Didn't want this part to end.

Even as he tried to think about what tax deductions he needed to take next year, she cupped his balls, pressing the pads of her fingers just behind them. His cock jerked, along with his hips, at the wave of sensation that brought.

Her hair had tumbled forward, veiling her face as she moved. It was cool and soft against the skin at the top of his thighs. He sifted his fingers through it as he looked up to meet Angelo's gaze.

He wore the same expression Luca was sure he had on as well. Wonder. No small amount of lust, satisfaction, need.

Her hand left his balls, reaching back to her pussy. He smiled up at Angelo, both of them amused by the way she took what she wanted. But her hand didn't stay. Instead the now-slippery fingers slid down past his balls, toward his ass.

He stilled, willing himself to relax as she stroked gently against his asshole before pressing inside.

He groaned as she stretched him a bit before finding her way to his prostate. "Fuck," he bit out as she began to stroke over it while taking him as deeply into her throat as she could. His cock was harder than he'd ever been. He ached with the need to come, with the need to drown himself in the pleasure she was giving him.

"I think he likes that, pretty bird." Angelo ran his hands over every inch of her skin he could reach. The relish on his face brightened his eyes when they met Luca's briefly before returning to her again. "Your cunt is so hot and wet. I never. Ever. Want to leave it."

Luca found himself in the clenched fist of climax, back bowed, his fingers in her hair tight, urging her closer as he thrust into her mouth.

She continued to nuzzle and lick until he was totally soft. With a kiss at the head, she turned her face up to his. "Yum."

He groaned. "You're a fucking menace with that mouth. On both levels."

Her smile lifted his heart.

"Now that Luca's cock isn't in your mouth I can move you a little. Can you kneel back? Keep my cock inside you. I'm not leaving any time soon."

She pushed herself back and then up, essentially sitting on Angelo's thighs as he banded an arm around her chest to hold her up. Each time he thrust, her tits bounced quite delightfully. Her eyes went sleepy and dazed as Luca's gaze slid down to watch Angelo's cock disappear into her pussy over and over.

He was sated enough to be satisfied simply watching as he caught his breath. The two of them, his oldest friend and the woman he always thought of as the girl who got away, fucking. Muscles bunching and relaxing, the hue of Ava's full body flush, the inky black rope of Angelo's hair against her very pale skin.

Her breathless gasps and Angelo's grunts played against the wet slap of cock to cunt. Beautiful.

Just when Ava was sure she was done coming for the time being, Luca stirred from the place where he'd been watching her and Angelo, crawling toward them with a smile on his face. He caught her in his gaze, and she couldn't have looked away, even if she'd wanted to.

Angelo's cock continued to fill her and retreat, lighting up all sorts of nerve endings deep inside. He was so *big*. His hands on her, putting her exactly where he wanted her, however he wanted her. His voice a rumble in his chest as he gave her instructions in that calm, in-charge voice.

Drove her crazy.

And Luca with his pretty face and tanned skin, those big sexy eyes and that sinful mouth. A mouth he latched on to her knee and then to the inside of her thigh. Ava held her breath, her gaze snagged on him as he licked down the crease between thigh and body.

"Such a pretty cunt," he murmured, spreading her open and pressing a kiss to her clit.

Angelo angled his head to watch as well, his chin resting on her shoulder.

Luca made long, slow licks through her pussy, pausing to include Angelo's cock as he pulled out. She gasped at the sight.

"Christ," Angelo hissed, losing his rhythm for a few strokes.

And when Luca's mouth found her clit, his tongue playing over it ever-so-lightly, just a ghost of pressure, she lost her hold, falling into climax with nearly mindless ferocity.

Angelo didn't wince when her nails dug into his thigh. He was too busy not screaming from the intensity of the squeeze of her cunt around his cock as she came. She squirmed, undulated and writhed, pushing him right to the edge in seconds. His resolve to make it last wisped away as he grabbed her hip with his free hand, holding her down on his cock as he came so hard he saw lights against his eyelids.

Even after he'd come, his muscles jumped, his heart raced and he didn't want to let her go, afraid that he'd come back and she'd be gone again.

But his knee wasn't what it once was, and the position wasn't one he could hold forever, so after a time, when he trusted his hands not to shake, he kissed her shoulder and helped lay her down as he pulled out and left briefly to get rid of the condom.

Standing in the bathroom, the purple light of sunset painting the walls, he looked at himself in the mirror before splashing water on his face and putting himself back together so that by the time he came back into the room and saw her there, so fucking beautiful in Luca's arms, a smile on her face, he could grin and join them.

Three

"**I** do believe I'm hungry." She stretched, put her arms above her head as the two men bracketed her.

Luca kissed her chest, right over her heart, his gaze locked with Angelo. "You sure you don't need a nap?"

"I was exhausted earlier. Now I'm just tired. Funny how sex can do that." She sat up. "Three orgasms in ninety minutes does a body good."

It was Luca who spoke, though Angelo liked to think he would have if Luca hadn't, "Baby, your mother died. A mother you had . . . mixed feelings about. But she was still your mother. And you came back here for the first time in years at what you admit was a crazy time work-wise. Is it too much to think that you needed a little bit of TLC?"

She blinked several times and shrugged, clearly holding back tears. Angelo pulled her to stand. "Take a long, hot shower. Let us feed you and ply you with alcohol and then you can sleep."

"Two pretty boys waiting on me? Feeding me and getting me drinks? Well, all right. That sounds like a very good offer." She made an effort to keep her words light, but Angelo heard the strain in them and gave her the space she so clearly needed.

She rustled through her suitcase, grabbing a handful of clothing, and after a kiss for both of them, disappeared into the bathroom.

Luca rolled from bed. "You can use the shower in my bedroom if you like," he called over his shoulder as he left the room.

"Are you all right?" Angelo asked as he followed Luca down the hall toward the large master suite.

"Yes." He answered quickly but then paused as he grabbed a towel, handing it over. "Shower. Let me get the steaks on."

He soaped up and thought about how a seemingly simple thing like fucking a beautiful woman was actually the most complicated thing he'd ever done.

Fucking was the easy part.

What he'd just done wasn't only fucking. The moment he'd seen her, had allowed himself to touch her and . . . fuck . . . *feel* for her again, he'd allowed himself to also think about the what-ifs.

He didn't do what-ifs. What-ifs were like pinning your hopes on winning the lotto. Angelo was a realist. What-ifs weakened a man. Hadn't they weakened his own father? Reduced him to a series of shitty, dead-end jobs and sad stories about his time on the rodeo circuit. A life he'd never have, and because of that, his father never felt happy about anything.

Angelo had no intention of being that person.

Luca put the steaks on the now hot grill, enjoying the sound and scent for long moments. He'd washed his face and hands, though he'd been reluctant to part with her scent.

He heard her voice as he sliced up cucumbers. Singing in the shower. Happiness bloomed through him at her presence. God-damn, he'd missed her. Funny to think he could have formed an attachment to her when they'd only been together for a handful of months. But he *knew* her.

In the time after he'd returned to Petal after graduation, they'd gotten closer. She'd opened up to him, talking about her dreams for the future. She'd been the first person he'd confided his interest in architecture to. His desire to abandon his plans to attend law school and pursue design instead.

The fall into a romance had been deliciously slow until he found himself with his hand up her shirt and his mouth fused to hers. What they'd had then had been incendiary. He couldn't get enough of her, spending every waking moment he could with her, helping out at the café just to see her more.

He'd known she had wanted to leave. Had known she'd been scrimping and saving every extra penny she'd earned working at The Honey Bear. Every moment they had had made him hungry for more.

And then Angelo had come back before he went off to training camp. She and he were already friends from childhood, and their energy together, instead of making Luca feel excluded, made him feel welcome. It had been so sexy to watch the two of them flirt, though she hadn't really known it. It was probably part of the lure originally for Angelo, the way she didn't fawn over him because he was *the* Angelo Bennett.

And they'd ended up, God, the first time had been in his parents' bonus room. They'd been there on an afternoon. It had been midsummer, so she'd had on these tiny shorts and a threadbare T-shirt. Her hair was brownish blonde then, and longer, so she'd often worn it in a braid. He'd reached out to touch it, pulling on it, and her eyes had widened as she made the sexiest groan he'd ever heard.

Everything had changed when Angelo had murmured something in her ear and she'd nodded, her eyes still wide.

Christ, he'd never been with anyone like that before. Or, hell, since. It had been wild, rutting, licking, biting. He'd fucked her while Angelo had watched, but then, he'd been there, his hands all over both of them, his cock in Ava, but then it had been in Luca's hand.

A new something had been born that day. A new bond with Angelo and, God help him, the seeds of the love he'd already begun to feel for Ava bloomed into something else, something deeper and less sweet than it had been before.

There had been other times, but it was the last one he remembered most. At a hotel in Riverton, just the three of them. All night long they'd loved and fucked and laughed, and when he woke up, she was gone. Nothing left behind but a note on the pillow for each of them saying she had to leave or she'd die in Petal, always being seen as The Rand Girl.

He'd moved on. Had even spoken to her briefly now and again. He most definitely always considered her a close friend because of what they'd been to each other. He'd nearly married once, though thank God he'd finally admitted to himself what a monumental mistake it would have been and called it off.

And now she was upstairs and he'd touched her. Her taste lived in him again. He would never be able to go back to what he was before he'd walked out of the back of the café to find her standing there looking lovely and sad.

He heard Angelo amble down the stairs and into the kitchen. "Smells good."

"I've got some mixed greens and tomatoes for salad. Oh, and cucumbers." He knew he babbled but couldn't seem to stop.

Angelo retrieved the tequila and some limeade from the freezer. "She gets to me. Takes me back to a place I thought I'd forgotten." He paused as Angelo used the blender. "I don't think I'm putting it into the right words."

"She makes me want things." Angelo poured the margaritas into a pitcher and salted the rims of the glasses.

Luca knew there'd be nothing more, though he waited patiently as he sliced the bread. Angelo had been raised to believe wanting things was a waste of time.

Luca heard her moving around, coming from the guest room toward the stairs. "It's more, Angelo," he said softly before she entered the room.

"My stomach just growled so loud it startled me." She bussed his cheek before grabbing a slice of cucumber. "May need those tomorrow morning."

"I think I can manage to make you eggs and pancakes. That what they do out in Los Angeles? Eat cucumbers for breakfast?"

She laughed, surprisingly close to a giggle. "No, silly. To put on my eyes to combat the dark circles I'm likely to wake up with. Though one of the writers I work with drinks wheatgrass every day instead of coffee." She shuddered.

"Margarita?" Angelo asked from behind them.

She turned. "Yes, please."

He drew the glass closer, luring her to him, and she stopped laughing when he kissed her. His fingers tangled in her hair, yanking enough to get her attention and drag a groan from her lips.

"Mmm." Ava licked her lips and then tasted the margarita. "Delicious. Margarita's good as well."

"I'm glad you're here. Sorry for the circumstances, but so fucking happy to see you."

Pleased and surprised, she smiled up at him. "Thank you. I hadn't, well, I guess I didn't know what to expect. I knew I'd see Maryellen and Jasper of course, but I . . ." She lifted her hands, not saying more.

"Drink up, baby. Let us take care of you." Luca pulled a chair out for her at the kitchen island.

Damn it, this whole trip had been . . . unexpected. She sure as hell didn't know why being taken care of should make her want to put her head down on the counter and weep.

She watched the two of them move in unison, in that rhythm they had that she used to be jealous of. But after a while she'd come to appreciate the beauty of being that connected to someone else.

Luca slid a tray of buttered bread under a broiler while Angelo put plates along the bar. He paused, kissing her neck as he passed.

That had been definitely unexpected. She had come back to town and hoped she'd see them, wondered if they'd still have that level of attraction. She hadn't expected to be swept into a threesome with them only hours after being back in Petal and she surely hadn't expected this . . . this sort of, *gah*, well, this sort of intimacy. As if she'd never left.

It befuddled her. She liked certainty, and this was chaotic. Wild. It felt so good her rational mind questioned it.

"Medium rare okay with you?" Luca looked up from the grill, and she nodded.

Moments later she was facing a plate heaping with salad, garlic bread and the perfect steak. Oh, and a hot man on either side.

"Score." She smiled after she said it, sipping her drink.

"Tell us about your life." Luca began to eat.

She told them about her job writing computer code, trying to avoid the boring details. Luca's attention was totally focused on her in that way he had of making her feel like no one else existed but her.

Angelo ate in a ruthlessly efficient way. Like a machine. It had always fascinated her, was part of the reason she'd stare at him when he wasn't looking back when they were kids.

Now she got to look her fill at him, and he didn't seem to mind at all.

"What about you?" she asked Luca.

"Well, we took on another partner two years ago. The economy has slowed our plans to bring on another architect, but there's plenty of work for us, thank God."

"He designed this place and my house in Atlanta," Angelo put into the silence.

"It's beautiful. The rooms are all so bright. The way you've positioned the house is perfect to get a view from every room I've been in so far. It's comfortable but still very classical. Masculine." She'd eyed the design, had seen it from her own perspective, of numbers and angles.

He blushed, and she couldn't help herself, she leaned over and hugged him. "You're amazingly talented, Luca."

She thought back to something her assistant had said. He'd said it in that way he had, self-deprecating, cutting and, yet, insightful. *Ava, darling, you don't realize this, but I must tell you how much it sucks that no one takes you seriously when you have a face like this.* With a shake of his head, he'd straightened the front of his shirt. *Oh, sure, everyone wants to take us home from the clubs, but no one seems to think we can add up a tip or balance a spreadsheet. It's a spreadsheet. It does the adding for you anyway.*

She had laughed at the way he tossed his hands up. *Ava, pretty boys need some love too. We get lots of fucking, I'm not gonna lie.* He'd winked. *But we need more love.*

She'd snorted, kissed his forehead and given him the rest of the day off.

Luca Proffit was the poster boy for pretty. He and one of Petal's other pretty boys, Matt Chase, had gone back and forth—every other dance or event Luca would be the king or the most this or that. He dated cheerleaders and girls who drove to school in shiny new cars. He'd always been like a dream to her. So very handsome and nice. Gentlemanly. His parents were not affluent, but they were respected and loved by most people in town.

He was one of those beautiful, golden blonds with brown eyes. Good natured. Laid back and affable. She'd wanted him for as long as she could remember. Having him had been sort of a dream.

Ava looked over to Angelo again. "So you, Mr. Big-Shot Entertainment Lawyer, how's tricks?"

"Tricks are very fine indeed." He put down his fork and looked her in the eye. "How long are you here for, Ava?"

That was abrupt.

"I don't know. I figured I'd go home after the memorial service."

"We only get two days of your time?" She knew she wasn't imagining the annoyance in his tone.

"My assistant is dog-sitting. Al will eat his entire house if I stay gone too long."

Angelo's scowl turned into a smile. "You have a dog named Al?"

"I do. He came with the name actually. I figured it'd be mean to just start calling him by a stranger's name."

"What kind of dog is this house-eater? Husky? Doberman? German shepherd? "

"He's a terrier, a Jack Russell. He thinks he's a wolf though, so don't tell him. Anyway, he'll be fine with Travis, that's my assistant, for a while. But he's very particular, my Al. He and Travis are friends and all, but he's my dog and he is quite assertive on this point." She grinned.

"You should stay until Sunday. Stay and spend time with us. Bicentennial Day is Saturday. We can see the fireworks from my dock." Luca took her hand, entwining his fingers with hers.

To be wanted that way left her feeling exposed and needy.

"I have to run home tomorrow. I have a hearing Wednesday morning. But I'll be back here by the memorial, I promise you."

Crap, the tears again. She blinked them back, and Angelo shook his head. "Why are you so afraid to cry in front of us? Hmm? It's just me and Luca. You all hard now?"

The smooth veneer he'd been wearing since he arrived slipped, and that rough-and-tumble kid surfaced. His country clicked into place, thickening his accent.

"Why are you mad at me?"

"Because you're holding back. You go away for ten years. Ten fucking years, Ava. Oh, you call me now and again and leave a voice mail. Or you send me an email. But that's not you. That's a piece of you."

"Oh, and flowers every five months is you?"

"No. It's not. I'm a hypocrite. Sue me."

She stabbed her steak, eating it with relish. "You're still an arrogant, pushy bastard."

"You're still the hottest fuck I've ever had."

She turned, her eyes narrowed. "That all I am?" She clicked her teeth, trying to recall the words.

Angelo paused, looking her over with the sort of concentration and scrutiny that made him so successful. "If you were, I wouldn't give a shit if you left on Wednesday. Good fucks aren't hard to find."

Oh. Well then.

"Especially when you live in a mansion and drive a BMW." Luca snorted.

"Very true. There's a reason why I busted my ass to finish law school after my knee went out."

The two of them laughed together and she relaxed, feeling utterly at home.

"I'll stay until Sunday."

Four

Luca woke as the sun was rising. He got up to check his email and call his secretary to leave a message that he'd be out until Monday. He turned on the coffeemaker and headed back to his bed.

Though his curtains were closed tight against the morning sun, the light from the bathroom cut a swath across them. Ava was backed up against Angelo, tucked underneath his chin, his arms wrapped around her.

Angelo's hair was unbound, an inky pool against the pillows, over his skin. Ava's mouth was pulled into a little bow, her brow unfurrowed. After two more rounds of enthusiastic, sticky, sweaty sex and a midnight hot-tub soak, she'd curled up between them and gone to sleep with a quiet little snuffle.

Protectiveness surged inside him. He wanted to wipe away the lines on her forehead, wanted to kiss her and let her release the tears she held on to so tightly. Heaven knew her parents didn't deserve a single bit of her sadness.

Her eyes opened slowly, locking on him as he stood in the doorway.

"Go back to sleep," he said quietly. "It's early still."

She eased herself out of Angelo's arms and came to him, walking straight into his arms and pushing him into the hall, closing the door so Angelo could sleep.

"I was dreaming of you and I opened my eyes to see you right there. Real." She kissed his chest and he buried his nose in the tousled curls, breathing her in.

"Funny, I was just thinking something similar."

And suddenly the ache was back and he needed her so much it tore through him, leaving him ragged.

He kissed her neck, nibbling across her shoulder. "Seeing you in my bed made today the best morning I've had in a very long time."

"Mmm." She sighed happily, running her fingers through his hair. "I love your hair. I love how soft and curly it is. Sexy. It goes with the scruffy beard, which I heartily approve of. Much like I approve of that." She arched into his hand as he slid it up her belly and found her nipple hard already.

"You're probably sore," he managed to croak out as she grabbed his cock.

"I am just fine. Fine enough for another round. I want you in me."

How could he refuse? Even if he'd wanted to, which he didn't, the lure of a sleep-warm, sweet-smelling Ava, naked and open to him, was way more than a mere mortal could turn down.

Taking her hand, he led her downstairs and opened the doors to his back deck. In the early morning, the air was warm, but not inferno hot like it would be in a few hours. Up close to the house, the deck was sheltered by large bushes and hanging plants. No one could see the hot tub or the chaise he laid down upon, unless they were standing right there.

She rustled in the things they'd left out there the night before and came back to him with a smile and a condom.

"And here I thought I was the boy scout. Ride me, Ava. Sink that sweet, hot pussy down my cock."

"Mmmm, yes, I think that's a very good plan." Within moments she'd rolled the condom on and was perched above him, surrounding his cock with her cunt, leaving him writhing and senseless.

Up and down, she worked over him, her thighs rock hard as she lifted up and shimmied back down. There was no sound but the harshness of their breathing and the sound of the water lapping at the shore of the lake.

Luca knew just where to kiss her, how to twist her nipples just hard enough, how to thrust up as she pressed down. His hands on her skin made her want more, unleashed a craving she thought she'd killed a long time ago.

Inside her, his cock had a bend to the right, enough that each time she slid down over him, he stroked all the best parts deep inside.

"Harder, baby," he urged, his fingers finding her clit.

There was nothing but the two of them, skin to skin, the scent of clean sweat, sex, warm earth and bark from all the nearby trees. He saw right through her, unsettling her, even as it titillated to be seen so clearly.

Bracing her hands on the chair back, just above his head, she used the angle to thrust back on him harder and harder until her muscles began to tremble. With all the ways and times she'd climaxed over the last twenty-four hours, she didn't think she had it in her to go again, and yet, there it was, lightning fast and all consuming.

Luca made a sound, a sort of desperate snarl. "Goddamn, your pussy gets so hot and so tight when you come. You feel sooo good."

She smiled down at him, her breasts swaying as she continued to slam herself against him over and over, nearly frantic as she came, feeling the lurch and jump of his cock as he followed her into climax.

"Nice way to wake a man up," he mumbled against her as she moved to pull off his cock.

She kissed him as they managed to stand shakily.

"What's on tap today?" he asked as they went back inside.

"Nothing really. All the details for the memorial service are handled. I should stop in and see your parents of course. Otherwise, I'm free."

"Ava! Damn it, if you've run off again, I swear I will hunt you down and drag you back here kicking and screaming." Angelo stomped out onto the second-floor landing shortly after his bellowed call.

His narrowed gaze took her in as she stood below. She waved at him. "Good thing I haven't run off then."

"Don't crack wise." He'd put undershorts on and she grabbed a T-shirt from a nearby chair. It smelled like Luca as she pulled it over her head. In a way it felt like armor because what she saw on Angelo's face was more than anger, it was hurt, and she put it there.

She had a thing. A promise to herself to own her shit. And this was hers to deal with.

"I'm not cracking wise. I'm attempting to diffuse a potential fight. Because I don't want to fight with either one of you. I said it yesterday and I'll say it again. I'm sorry I left the way I did. It was wrong. Not the leaving part, that was totally necessary. But the way I did it was cowardly and unfair."

"Oh. Well. I accept your apology for that then." He appeared to be reasonably appeased. "I woke up and you were gone. It just . . . touched an old memory I guess." He kissed her, hugging her tight. "I see you and Luca had some fucky-times, eh?"

Luca laughed. "That's what you get for sleeping in."

Angelo stretched, catching her staring at the wonder of his body. "Now that's a nice compliment there. What's the plan for today? I need to run back home later this afternoon. I've got a hearing in the morning, but I have today free. Or we can all go back to my place. I have a pool. We can be away from here for a while. We'll come back for the service, and then we can decide from there where to go. My hearing will be over by ten at the latest. You two can grab me after and we'll head back here."

She liked that idea a lot. And she knew he wanted to show the house off to her. "I think that's a great idea."

Which is how she found herself slathered with sunscreen and swimming laps in Angelo's pool.

He dived in, swimming powerfully, gracefully, pacing her until she finally gave up. "You win! Cripes, you'd think you were an athlete or something." Laughing, she pulled herself out and thanked Luca for the towel he handed her.

He smirked and went back to swimming, so she settled in under the big umbrella with Luca, and they watched, contented by the sight of that caramel skin, the slide and flow of his muscles as he sliced through the water.

"He's so beautiful."

She smiled at Luca. "He is."

"You seeing anyone?" This he asked her in a forcefully casual way.

"I was for a while. I've been single about a year now." She shrugged. "What about you?"

"I broke off an engagement last year."

She growled and then blushed. How she'd hated that news when Maryellen had told her Luca and Melanie Deeds had been engaged. The nerve of that bitch to think she deserved a man like Luca!

He chuckled. "I take it you didn't like Melanie?"

"Not as your wife, no. And, well, not at all really. The Melanie I remember was a stuck-up bitch who liked to cause trouble."

"That's her."

"But she did it with double Ds and very short skirts. Man can forgive a lot with all that showing." Angelo, water sluicing off his muscles, left the pool and joined them, straddling the chair Ava sat on.

"Sure, all but that part where she tries to show those double Ds to a man's best friend."

Ava sat back, surprised. "You're joking! That *bitch* came on to Angelo when she was engaged to you?"

Luca grinned. "My bruised ego is all better. Thank you for your indignation, baby."

"Showed up at the front door, halfway naked and offered herself up to me, easy as you please. She sure didn't like me slamming the door in her face and calling Luca right away."

"So you didn't, you know, share her or anything?" She missed the nonchalance she'd been going for by a solid mile or three.

"You are the only woman Luca and I have ever shared." Angelo drew his fingertips up her spine languidly. "I've been in other three-somes," he said, leaning down to kiss her shoulder. "But none of them were this."

She allowed herself to admit it, allowed the bonelessness of relief to slip into her system. She wanted to be indelible to them. Even if they never spoke again once she went back to LA, she wanted them to never forget her. Silly, maybe, selfish even, but these men meant more to her than anyone on the entire planet and always would.

"How can you not know that?" Angelo asked as he untied the back of her bikini top.

"Never hurts to remind a girl," she murmured, leaning back into him as he kneaded her breasts, pulling and twisting her nipples.

Without warning, he picked her up, standing in one easy movement. "I'm so impressed." Laughing, she squeezed his biceps.

"Inside. I need to be inside."

He stalked through the open doors and into the cool, dark of
the house. Instead of his bedroom, where they'd napped for a while
earlier that day, he took her into what appeared to be a game room,
depositing her on the edge of his pool table.

"Just as I thought." He looked to Luca. "I knew she'd look good
enough to eat perched up there."

"I'm going to get the felt wet," she whispered. The sun had
dried her hair, but her bottom was still damp.

"You'd better. Here, let me get the rest of your bathing suit."
Luca grunted as he pulled her bikini bottoms off.

Luca needed her. Stupid as he'd had her just a few hours before
and then a few hours before that. And so on. Five minutes after
having her, he wanted her again.

"Luca," Angelo whispered in his ear, his hands on Ava around
Luca's body, "you made a promise to me last night. Remember that?"

One of those big, sure hands that had been on Ava now slid
down Luca's back, pausing to cradle his ass before moving into
the front of his shorts and fisting his cock. He'd made a comment
about taking Angelo on, mostly as a joke. Mostly.

A shiver ran through him as he met Ava's eyes. "I remember it,"
he said quietly.

"After." Angelo stepped around Luca then, turning his face and
catching Luca's chin. When Angelo kissed him like this, he lost his
ability to think. The strength of his arms as he held Luca in place,
the slight scrape of their jaw stubble, the surety of his tongue and
lips. He'd never wanted another man with this kind of intensity.
Had kissed a few here and there, wondering if he was gay. He'd
resisted any tags, but he'd accepted bisexual. How could he not
as his cock hardened in Angelo's grip? He never sought out other

men after the short period of time in the aftermath of Ava's leaving town. None of them had been anything to make his pulse speed and his senses spiral away the way Angelo did.

And none of it had ever been as good as it was when Ava was there as the key, as a bridge between their different worlds and personalities.

"So beautiful," she sighed softly.

"He tastes even better when you're on his lips," Angelo said as he broke the kiss. "You had her last time, Luca. It's my turn."

He moved lightning quick, easing her back onto the pool table, her legs hanging down, ass on the edge of the wood. Greedy for her, he licked down her belly, pausing at her pussy, driving her to the edge of climax with his mouth. Licking and sucking, drawing all the soft sighs and moaning cries he could, greedy for each reaction. Greedy for her taste, the feel of her against him and, he thought as he surged up, Luca's hands busily rolling a condom on his cock, he was greedy to be in her.

He pressed in slowly, knowing she had to be sore, though she hadn't complained or been anything but eager for their attentions. Being wanted that way did something to that no-longer-hungry kid deep inside. Her desire was safe because he knew it was real, knew it was for all of him, dark corners and all.

Each bit he pushed in was one step closer to falling head over ass in love with her. Something he'd tried to avoid for most of the time he'd known her. And when she opened her eyes, her gaze catching on his, he felt it to his toes.

"More."

"I don't want to hurt you," he managed to gasp out.

"Please."

He wasn't sure if she was asking him to hurt her or to fuck her harder, but it was the raw edge to the request that had him thrusting hard and deep, had him luxuriating in the ragged groan she gave up. He wanted to lean down and bite that sweet, pale skin, wanted to flip her over and fuck her so hard she couldn't speak. The ferocity of his need for her made his hands shake as he ruthlessly reined it in.

"Just . . ." She broke off, shaking her head.

"Tell me." He paused, midthrust, trying to ignore the drumbeat of need his pulse took to in her presence.

"Mark me. Use me. I'm here and I'm yours. Don't hold back."

Luca's guttural moan slid over his skin as he stared down at Ava. Looked down at the woman, the only woman who'd ever gotten inside him this way.

He gave in to that need for her, bending as he fucked her, bending close enough to lave over the side of her breast, and then he bit.

She gasped and then cried out. Her cunt squeezed him so tight he thought he'd come right on the spot. He jerked back, worried he'd hurt her, though her body told him a different story.

Instead of telling him to stop, she arched up closer to where he'd jerked back, grabbed his hair and pulled him in.

"Christ, you're going to kill me," he rasped out, licking along the underside of her left breast and kissing across to the right one.

"Only because you're afraid to give in and fuck her like you want to," Luca whispered like the naughty angel on his shoulder. "Does she look hesitant to you?"

They both turned their attention back to Ava where she lay, spread out like the most delicious dessert tray he'd ever seen. Just waiting to be eaten. Her nipples stood dark and hard. She'd replaced the rings with bars similar to the one he wore in his piercing. Her pussy gripped his cock in slick heat, her hips rocking to meet each one of his thrusts.

Quickly, before he could think about it anymore, he pulled out, rolled her over and found her again within moments, pushing inside.

"Luca, get on the other side of the table and hold her hands."

He did, body language mimicking hers as Luca leaned forward, taking the hands she'd stretched out above her head.

Angelo bent to speak in her ear. "I'm going to fuck the hell out of you, Ava. And then I'm going to fuck you some more. If I go too far, tell me to stop and I will."

She whimpered, not in pain or fear, but with a need that matched his own. So he filled it. Speeding his thrusts and adjusting the force.

"I'm watching my cock come out of your cunt all shiny with your juices, pretty bird. All red and hard."

Luca held her hands, locked gazes with her and smiled. So fucking beautiful he didn't have words.

"You're next, Luca. Don't forget I aim to have you bent over this pool table, too."

Her eyes closed a moment before her gaze returned to Luca. His heart sped at Angelo's words and her reaction to them.

Angelo's features were a hard mask of aggressive sexuality. His teeth bared, hair free, sliding over his shoulders and arms, tickling Ava's skin when he'd lean close to whisper something filthy or to lick or bite her back.

Sweet, fiery Ava was not. No, she was the picture of a sexually submissive woman, her body open to Angelo, her eyes glossy. Somehow it was that juxtaposition of her normal in-charge, bossy self with this . . . vision of raw sex, of letting Angelo lead and of her clearly loving it that got to Luca so much.

Angelo let it all go, Luca saw it come over him, saw him give in to just exactly what he wanted to do to her. He walked his fingers up her back, dragging his nails down to her ass. She arched her back with a gasped cry, pulling Luca as she wormed to get closer to Angelo.

Luca watched, nearly dream-like, as Angelo ran his fingers through her hair. Gently. The look on his face reverent. And then his lids dropped a bit as he tightened his fingers, pulling her back as he leaned his upper body against her, pinning her to the table as he continued to fuck her.

He yanked, turning her to receive his kiss and the sweetly punishing nips of her bottom lip. She whimpered and then groaned, breathing her entreaties into Angelo's mouth.

Luca froze there, struck utterly senseless at the sight before him. Carnal and beautiful, hard edged and yet loving. This was stripped down, wide open. This was making love every bit as much as sweet and gentle was. Angelo gave her everything, and she took it, offering herself to him in return.

He saw the exact moment when Angelo fell in love with Ava, written all over his face as he realized it and then the shake of his head as he shoved it aside.

Ava gave up trying to stay afloat in the maelstrom of Angelo's sexuality. Stopped fighting it and let him take her where she needed to go. He growled, low in his throat, so feral and masculine it stole her breath.

Each time he nipped at her flesh, each time he circled her clit with his fingertip as he fucked into her cunt so hard her nipples abraded the felt on the table. Each time he whispered that he loved the curve of her ass, or her shoulder, she surrendered a little more to him, lost herself in his touch, the edge of pleasure/pain blurred just so very right it was narcotic.

He manipulated every part of her as he built her orgasm. He played her body, drawing out her pleasure with exquisite skill so she walked a knife's edge.

Luca's hands held hers still, and when Angelo broke from a kiss, he angled her head back to lick his way up her neck. When she focused, it was on Luca's face. Beautiful Luca who gazed at her as if she were everything. And she felt it to her toes, loving the way he made her feel just by looking at her.

She should not be there. Should not have come back. Should have left her past in her past and kept on with her life on the West Coast. But she *was* there, she was utterly unable to deny that these men were inextricably part of her, and she had lost her will to keep them out, lost her will to keep lying to herself that this was just some fun fling she could use to keep her mind off her mother.

It was more and they all knew it.

And with that thought, Angelo pushed her over, increasing his touch against her clit as he fucked into her with ferocious, short digs and then one as deep as he could go, coming with a snarled curse, his mouth against her skin.

Angelo rumbled a very satisfied groan, kissing her shoulder before pulling out gently. Luca made his way over, petting over her as he helped her stand. He ground his cock into her belly as he bent to kiss her.

She melted into his arms as Angelo came back to them, pressing himself to her backside. Luca feasted on her lips, leaving her light-headed as he broke the kiss.

She pressed her fingers there, to hold that feeling against her skin.

"Do you know how it feels to be looked at the way you do me sometimes, Ava?" Luca asked. "I look back and I see so many things in your eyes. It's flattering and humbling and so sexy."

She swallowed, hard, totally beyond words. She tipped her chin in silent thanks.

Angelo kissed down her spine. "Ava, I want you on that pool table. I want to look at you when I'm fucking Luca." He picked her up, placing her carefully on the table, and she moved quickly, not wanting to miss a thing.

Her gaze had gone to Luca as he'd moved into Angelo's arms. Their kisses were so different from how they kissed her. Now there was scant evidence of the gentleness and the finesse. This was

Angelo about to do to Luca what he'd done to her, owning them, marking them as his in some indefinable and yet totally undeniable way.

Before too long, that familiar throb had begun. Angelo's hands were all over Luca, caressing, kneading, his nails scoring over Luca's nipples and down his belly. The rope of his braid slid forward.

"I need the lube, pretty bird."

She rolled to grab it along with a condom and hand them back. Luca's gaze locked on Ava's as Angelo reached around and began to jerk his cock. The other hand worked the condom on and prepped Luca. Moments later Luca's gaze blurred as he nearly shouted, "Oh God, right there."

"Shhh." Angelo brushed a kiss against Luca's shoulder. "Relax. We haven't done this in a long time. Let's take it slow."

"Fuck, fuck, fuck, yes." Luca arched back onto Angelo's fingers.

God, her face was on fire from blushing, but she could not turn away from them. Testosterone rolled off them in waves, dizzying her, setting her skin on fire, her nipples hardened nearly to the point of pain. Each time she shifted, her labia slid against her clit, sending ripples of pleasure out from her core.

"Make yourself come, Ava. I can see how much you want to," Luca gasped and Angelo growled his agreement.

She drew it out as Angelo moved over Luca. As Luca submitted to him. Luca's skin gleamed with sweat, his eyes halfway closed, one hand was wrapped around his cock, his fingers tangled with Angelo's.

Angelo fierce and badass as he took what he wanted. As he loved Luca as surely as he had her only minutes before.

"Give it to me, Luca." Angelo's voice was nearly a snarl.

"Make me," Luca gasped back.

Her finger rested above her clit as she watched, not wanting to go over just yet.

"Fine by me, blondie."

Luca's laughter choked into a curse as he threw his head back and groaned his climax.

Angelo's head fell back, his hair nearly touching the floor, his fingers dug into Luca's hips and he came.

"Shower. Snack and nap. In that order," Angelo said, kissing Luca soundly.

Luca held a hand to her as he straightened. "Come on, baby."

"I really need a shower, cause, boy oh boy, do I feel dirty after watching that."

Five

The hum of the moderately well attended memorial service covered Angelo when he leaned in to speak to Luca. "I'm glad there's a group of folks here." Angelo and Luca watched her as she spoke with Polly Chase and the various and assorted Chase daughters-in-law across the room. He'd worried that few would take a few minutes to remember a woman most folks avoided. Worried that it would hurt Ava and he'd see shadows in her pretty blue eyes again.

"Between your mom, Mrs. Chase and Ramona, Ava just might realize being The Rand Girl isn't always a bad thing."

She was beautiful in a navy blue dress with a little white sweater over it. Solemn and serious, but also soft and sweet. Her hair was back, exposing her throat, but not the back where he'd given her a love bite just hours before.

He couldn't explain why he liked it, why it sent satisfaction roaring through him to see her naked with the marks he'd made on her skin. The caveman part of his brain approved mightily.

He forgot himself in her skin. Something he found at turns invigorating and scarier than all hell.

Luca took care of her in his way. Made sure she ate a little. Her color had brightened as the memorial went on. Angelo hoped it was because she realized she had a place in town. Even if she'd written Petal off, Petal still had a place for her.

Her smile, when she dealt with the people who came by, was shy and sweet. Tentative at times. His heart had ached for her in those flashes of the old Ava. And yet her back remained straight and she didn't look at the ground.

At the end, when it was just his parents left, Luca gave Angelo a look and they both moved to collect her.

"Dinner tonight before you go to Atlanta and breakfast on Saturday then?" Maryellen said to Ava before glancing back to her son. "Don't forget fireworks on Saturday for the Bicentennial Day picnic. Ava was just telling me you were going to stay with Angelo in Atlanta until Sunday."

"But hello, fireworks and a barbecue with your dad's baked beans. I'm defenseless against that." Ava's smile was genuine and Angelo responded in kind. "We can come back Saturday morning just as easily."

"Good. Yes, I think that's a good idea. Rest up and get rid of those dark circles." Maryellen brushed a thumb against Ava's cheek.

"We'll feed her well, I promise, Mrs. Proffit." Angelo kissed Maryellen's cheek and she hugged him. She'd long since stopped trying to get him to call her anything else. It was his way of showing his love and respect for a woman who was very much like his own mother.

"We know you three have plans, but we like to spend time with Ava, too." Maryellen squeezed Ava's hands.

A man Angelo and Ava recognized came into the room. Ava

excused herself and Angelo moved to follow, but she held her hand out to stay them. "I'll be right back."

"Who is that?" Luca watched the interchange at Angelo's side.

Angelo never took his gaze from her as he answered, "He owns most of the houses on Riverbend. He's likely here asking for money for Marlene."

"Here at a funeral? Why are we not punching this piece of shit?" Luca fisted his hands just thinking about it.

"If we get involved when she told us to back off, we're weakening her in front of him. Look at her face, Luca."

"What? She's upset."

"Is she? Look at her, really look at her."

Luca focused and saw that instead of pain or anger, her face was utterly impassive.

"She's not giving him anything. Let her do this on her own."

"She doesn't have to though, Angelo. She's not some helpless girl. She's"—he glanced at his mother, who hiked her brows—"she's ours, that's what she is. She's our family and we're hers."

But she turned around as the man left, no upset on her face, so he let it slide. "I believe your mother has invited us to their house for dinner. She promised me smothered pork chops, and you know my general adoration and love of the smothered-type foods."

He put an arm around her waist and she put her head on his shoulder. His mother's eagle eye missed nothing, and Luca knew she'd be on him about this when they were alone.

As he helped her into the car, he smelled her skin and roses. Without meaning to, he bent to brush his lips across hers.

"Thank you," she murmured, kissing him again before settling back into her seat.

He paused as his heart pounded so loud he was sure everyone could hear it. *Oh hell*, he wanted her to stay. Or agree to spend part of her year there, or something. Anything to keep her in his life.

Six

She was supposed to go home that evening. Go back to Los Angeles and to her life. She tried not to disturb either man as she crept from bed, but Angelo's arm banded her belly and pulled her back to his body.

Her eyes closed, she drew a deep breath as he entered her. His heart beat steadily against her back as he took his time, one hand at her hip and another entwined with hers, their fingers clasped above her head.

It was as if he simply could not get enough sex with her and Luca. His appetite was stunning and marvelously inventive. Never with anyone else had she been so satisfied. Never had she been so well matched, and well, at times it felt as if they adored her. It was a heady thing, filled with possibility.

It scared her to death.

On her other side, Luca woke, sliding toward them, his mouth at her shoulder and up her neck. And then sandwiched between them as they kissed.

"What does it feel like with him inside you?" Luca asked.

"I can feel his heart beating inside my pussy," she gasped.

He closed his eyes a moment. "Yes, it feels like that to be inside you, too."

"Turn over, Luca. Back up to Ava, yes, like that."

"Pretty bird, help me here," Angelo rumbled as her fingers tangled with his again, this time around Luca's cock. The scent of cinnamon drifted from the lube Luca had poured on his cock.

Angelo worked them both with effortless precision. His rhythm was relentless, but there was absolutely no doubt in her mind that he was totally in control. It was dizzying how much it worked for him. The other day on his pool table something had changed and deepened between them, not just as Ava and Angelo, but as their group, as Ava, Angelo and Luca.

She didn't want to let this go, and yet she was terrified to ask if they wanted her to stay. Terrified this meant way more to her than to them.

Luca moved his hips, nearing climax she knew. He moved with powerful grace, and she leaned forward to lick and kiss across his shoulder, loving his taste. "You're close, Luca. Mmm, your cock gets so hard right before. I swear I can feel your energy building. When you're in me, I can feel this." She squeezed him, and Angelo's cock jerked inside her in response.

Luca's muscles began a fine tremble, and he muttered a curse.

"Just having you right here makes me ache." At this whispered confession, both men groaned.

A stuttered movement and Luca came then, even as Angelo's cock hit deep once, twice and three more times before he dug his slick fingers into the flesh at her hip and came.

And she was lost again as two mouths were on her, everywhere, until there were two tongues on her pussy, Angelo's hands holding her wide as he ate her.

Luca kissed up her belly, back to her nipples. It went on as she rode the waves of pleasure until finally Angelo took pity and let her come.

The three of them lay there, muscles jumping, sweat cooling, entwined in some way with legs and arms. Angelo absently pet her hip as Luca rested his head on her shoulder. She didn't want to get used to this calm, to this sort of connection, because she sure as hell didn't have it back in LA.

"I'm going to need to start going to Pilates again." Ava rolled from bed. "You two underline the need for me to be flexible."

Angelo laughed. "You're very bendy. I like that in a woman."

"I'm showering. You two need to decide what to do about breakfast," she called out as she headed into Luca's master bath.

"We just going to let her go back to Los Angeles today?" Luca shoved his hair back from his face. Her scent was on his skin, where he wanted it. Where it may not be for very long if she got on that plane and went back to her life.

"If that's what she wants, I guess."

Luca, pissed off, sprung from bed and began to pace. The scent of cinnamon hung in the air, his cock still tingled from it. "You guess? So this is what to you?"

"What is it to you?" Angelo countered, sitting and looking so delicious Luca had to turn his back.

"Apparently more than it is to you."

"Really?" That slow drawl was back, and Luca took a chance and looked over his shoulder. "You'll have to excuse me when I call bullshit on that. I'm the one who decides who and what means something to me. I've done nothing to make you feel as if I don't care. Doesn't mean I plan on throwing a fucking tantrum over it."

They locked gazes, and to Luca's dismay and yet delight, his cock began to revive. "Tantrum?"

Angelo's grin told Luca he'd meant to needle.

"You're a cock."

Angelo barked a laugh. "Yeah? Good thing you like cock then, huh?"

Before he could lob back a crack about how *he* wasn't the one embarrassed to admit that fact, Ava's voice rang out.

"What on earth are you two fighting about?" she called out from the other side of the door.

"The usual, pretty bird." Angelo got out of bed. "We'll talk about this later," he said to Luca before tapping on the bathroom door. "You done with the shower?"

She came out looking freshly scrubbed, her skin dewy with lotion. Luca's heart stuttered for a moment, as it always had when he caught sight of her face.

Angelo paused, caught by her as well. Luca wanted to shout, *see!* at him, but Angelo's hands were already on her, her eyes already losing focus. "Shall we get some breakfast at The Honey Bear?" he asked, pausing the rain of kisses he'd been laying across her shoulder as he held her hair in his grip.

"Mmmm, yes, that's very—*ouch!*" She lazily swatted at him, laughing as she did it.

"You taste so good, I had to take a little bite."

Luca laughed then, taking in all the love bites Angelo had given her on her torso, easily hidden with clothes, but a reminder of who gave them to her. Luca wanted this, damn it. He wanted her laugh in his hallways, wanted her scent on his sheets, wanted Angelo's voice in his ear as his hands were all over him.

"Breakfast at The Honey Bear is a very good idea." She paused and Luca saw the lines of strain around her eyes. He moved to her, not knowing what was wrong, but wanting very much to fix it.

"What is it, baby?" Luca asked, kissing the side of her mouth, loving the way she relaxed into him for a moment.

"I need to go to her house," she said in a flat voice, the Ava he'd first met. The warmth and languid relaxation he'd been feeling dropped away when he realized she was speaking about her mother.

"You sure you need to?"

"I doubt there's anything to salvage, even if I wanted some piece of her. But the landlord came to the memorial service on Wednesday. He told me he was going to send in cleaners tomorrow so if I wanted in there, today would be the last day." He'd also told her her mother had owed two months' rent. She'd pay that when she went to the house.

"Want some company?" Luca on one side, Angelo on the other, she was surrounded by a wall of delicious man-flesh and yet, the subject matter had sucked all the joy from that. Luca cupped her cheek. "It won't be easy."

Did she want company? Yes, probably. But she didn't want him to see the place her mother had lived. It had been a dump when Ava lived here, and she couldn't imagine how it was now.

"I'm sure you have work to do. I've kept you away from your jobs for a week now."

Luca's gaze narrowed as he looked her over closely. "I'm the boss. I took the week off. I've been checking in. Anyway, Sundays are dead."

"It's okay. I need to do this alone."

"Haven't you figured out yet that you don't? You don't need to do anything alone. I'm here for you, Ava. Angelo is here for you. Why do you push us away?"

She turned to look out the windows, turning her back on them both, wishing she wasn't so very naked just then.

"I'm not pushing anyone anywhere." She turned around to prove that and realized she was a total liar.

"Great. We'll have breakfast and then we can all go to your mom's house to help you go through things." Luca leaned back against the highboy dresser, totally naked and apparently totally at ease with that. Not that she was complaining or anything. He was gorgeous.

"How about we all have breakfast and then you two can go about your business while I deal with Marlene's house? That makes more sense. I'm not cleaning it out or anything. I don't give a rat's ass about whether she'll get the deposit back." That and she vowed a long time ago she was done cleaning up after her mother's mess.

Tossing his hands up in the air, clearly pissed off, Luca huffed and stormed from the room. She sighed. Most likely it was for the best. If she left while he was mad, the break would be easier. Right?

Angelo pushed from where he'd been leaning against the door-jamb. "I'm not that easy to push around, so let's just cut the crap, shall we? What's going on with you?"

"I just . . . I need to do it alone. I'm not trying to hurt anyone, but this is mine. It's not something I want to share. I just want it to be over."

He nodded, getting it.

"I get that. But you also need to get that we're not going to judge you by whatever it is she's got going on in that house. You're not her."

"I do. And I don't want to deal with anyone else's feelings but mine." He began to argue and she put her finger over his lips. "No. Really. I appreciate that you'd both want to support me and help. Your not being there will help."

"You know, Ava, you might try remembering that sometimes things are bigger than how you feel about them." He said nothing more as he moved around her and into the bathroom, leaving her naked in more than one way.

* * *

Maryellen Proffit knew what it was to grow up down here in these rattrap houses. She pulled her car around the corner to Riverbend Avenue. Her grandparents had lived here. Just three blocks from the house Marlene and Rick Rand once lived in.

Luca had brought her in that morning for breakfast, looking sullen and pouty. Angelo couldn't take his eyes from Ava and Ava, well, at least she had more color than she had at the memorial service. Clearly there had been a disagreement of some kind, and Maryellen aimed to get to the bottom of it before that girl left town again.

After cornering Luca when he'd come back to grab some coffee, Maryellen had managed to get him to tell her what was wrong. Her boy, her sweet, pretty son had absolutely no idea why Ava wouldn't let him see what that house must look like.

"This isn't about you, Luca," she'd told him. "She's embarrassed most likely."

"Why? Why would she think I cared about what her mother did or didn't do? What kind of man does she think I am that I can't take some dirty dishes in the sink?"

"Awful soon for that, isn't it?" Jasper asked as he flipped pancakes.

Maryellen had wisely hidden her smile. "Jasper Proffit, you told me you loved me two days after you took me on our first date."

Luca's eyes widened. "Love? Well, I don't . . . of course I care about her. It's no secret we dated before she left Petal. She and Angelo are my closest friends, even if I don't talk to her very often. And it's a lot more than two days after a first date anyway. I've known her since she was sixteen years old."

"Let her grieve in her own way." Jasper kept flipping pancakes. "Be there to pick up the pieces when she falls apart."

When Luca had gone back to the table, Ava had watched him

approach with eyes only for him. Maryellen thought of the way
the girl had looked at her son, with love and concern, and that's
what had made her get into the car and head over there after giving Ava some alone time to tackle the demons waiting for her in
that house.

The girl had become a daughter to her and if anyone needed
some mothering, it was Ava Rand.

The shiny rental car looked wildly out of place parked at the
curb. She pulled in behind it and grabbed her things before purposely striding toward the front door.

Ava wore her headphones and tried to ignore the heat and the
smell. She'd tied a bandana over her hair, a wise choice considering
the amount of dust in the house.

It hadn't changed much since she'd lived there. The same garage-
sale couch with the pullout bed sat in the living room in front of a
now busted television. An ancient VCR the size of a condo sat on
the table next to it.

No pictures on the walls. The bedroom her parents had shared
was uninhabitable. Truly she had no idea how her mother managed
to get in there to the bed, much less the will to step over all the dirty
plates, piles of clothes and boxes of crap.

What of this had formed her? Had twisted up inside her, coiled
like a snake. She shook it off. She had made better for herself,
damn it.

The place had branded her insides. Nothing good was there for
her. Not now and sure as heck not then. The broken swing set her
father had put up for her back when she was six still stood, rusting
in the tiny space of patchy grass behind the house. She looked out
the dingy window and remembered, even though she didn't want to.

"Luca told me you were coming over here today."

Startled, Ava pulled the headphones off and spun to face Maryellen Proffit.

"I sure do know you didn't want anyone to see this." She waved a hand at the place. "But I'm not anyone else, Ava Rose Rand."

She marched over and gave Ava a hug. "Now then. What are you still doing here? Hm? Do you need something? A little piece of this? Because between you and me, sweetie, it's okay to let yourself love them. Even though they didn't deserve it, or even if they did." She shrugged. "This is for you."

Ava opened her mouth and then closed it when tears loomed so close if she'd uttered a single sound, her control would crumble and she'd lose her shit.

So she nodded and Maryellen took her hand, squeezing it.

In the end, it had been a stack of pictures she'd found out in the sleeping porch Ava had claimed as a small space of her own growing up. She'd forgotten the hidey-hole until she'd stood in the doorway.

"I think we need some ice cream. What do you think, Ava?"

Maryellen had simply taken over. Part of her wanted to rebel against it, against that fierce sort of motherhood she'd put on and dared anyone to get in her way. But the rest of her, most of her, had relished simply being taken care of.

"You ready to go?" Maryellen had guided her out of the memories of that cramped little porch she'd tried to dress up with magazine pages and whatever else she could find to spruce it up. She'd taken her books with her to Los Angeles.

"I guess I took it all with me when I left."

"Who you are surely is a lot about this house, Ava." Maryellen drew her from the house. The statement panicked her.

"Lord above, I hope not." She shuddered, looking around the neighborhood.

"Of course that's so. You're the kind of person who handles her own business. Who doesn't waste time on blaming your messed-up childhood for her mistakes so she can keep on making them.

You're strong and this"—Maryellen indicated the house and the surroundings—"is why."

Maryellen smiled in that way she had, seeing right to the heart of a person. She brushed a smudge from Ava's chin. "You're exceptional, Ava. Don't let anyone tell you otherwise because I know the truth."

Afraid of the rest of the truth, she stepped back, trying to push it all from her mind. "I have to drop a check at her landlord's."

"Why don't you let me do that? Hm?"

"Stop being so nice to me for a minute or you're gonna make me cry. I promised myself when the Greyhound bus got to the state line that I'd never let them make me cry again. *I will not cry.*"

Maryellen's eyes filled with tears and Ava scurried past her. "He just lives two doors down. I'll be right back."

His house was kept up better than the others. His car nicer, lawn mowed. But he'd always kept three big, scary dogs. She hated those dogs, hated seeing how mean he'd been to them, how mean he'd made them.

The one currently growling at her from the other side of a flimsy looking fence was probably the grandchild of some of the dogs who'd growled at her each time she brought the rent here.

He opened shortly after she knocked, looking her up and down. "Lookie here, it's The Rand Girl, all grown up. Yer momma used to be pretty like you." He laughed in his wheezy way, and she itched to be gone.

"I brought you the back rent for Marlene Rand's place. Do whatever you want with the contents." She thrust the envelope his way and stepped back.

"I'm sorry for your loss. Marlene wasn't no mother-of-the-year material, I know that. But she did love you. She talked about you sometimes. Show pictures of your place out in Los Angeles."

If she pressed the heel of her hand against her chest hard enough, maybe she'd make it through without losing her shit.

"I . . ." She nodded briskly and turned, nearly stumbling in her rush to get away.

"Come on, sweetheart." Maryellen guided her to her rental car. "Let's go get us some ice cream and a big box of tissues."

Seven

"Let it go." Angelo tossed the paper he'd been pretending to read down onto the table on Luca's back deck. "She needs to be alone. Your momma's gonna run over there at some point, you know she will."

"Why not us, Angelo? Huh? Why after all we've shared does she still hide shit from us?"

He sighed. "Luca, you have no idea what it's like. Growing up poor is one thing, but the way she did? She's ashamed of it."

"But how can we show her it's not something for her to be ashamed of, especially with us, if we let her hide it?"

"You think you're going to fix her? Is that it? Luca riding in on his white steed to steal her away from her past? Help her pretend her mother wasn't a pill-popping, alcoholic whore who turned tricks for OxyContin? Hmm? Your love gonna save her from the fact that her father used to beat the shit out of her when he got back from one of his benders down in Riverton, where he gambled away his entire paycheck and left them unable to buy food? You don't know shit about it. She's trying to shield you from that. Let her, for fuck's sake."

If Luca hadn't known all of Angelo's little side steps, he'd have been riled by the tone. Instead, he waved it away. "She's better than that. Why shouldn't she be able to forget it? Not that it didn't shape her, I get that, I'm not an idiot. She's clearly not that girl anymore. Is it so bad I want to help her get around something that tries to draw her back to that place? Why shouldn't I want to give her a normal life?"

"She's not without flaws, Luca. She's fucked up like everyone else in the world. You can't put her on a pedestal like this."

"Fuck you. Why do you treat me like I'm stupid and lovesick?"

"Because you *are* lovesick!"

"I love her. I'm not lovesick." Luca shook his head and walked back into the house.

Angelo followed. "It's been a week, Luca. You're in love after not quite seven days?"

"I am really sick and tired of people treating me like I'm naïve or stupid. I fell in love with Ava a long time ago. Probably a few weeks after the first time I kissed her. She was gone a few months later and I moved on. But I never just turned my love for her off."

"We need to have a long conversation about how you envision this going from here."

"Aren't we doing that right now? You don't want her? Really? Because I'm too old to lie to myself especially when hey, *I want her*. I've been with her and then without her for a really long time. Now she's here and I sure as hell don't want to go back to being without her again."

Angelo took a breath and weighed his words carefully. "It's not that I don't want her. It's just not simple, and you know it."

"Fuck simple. What has simple got you, huh?" Luca raised a

brow in question. "Your longest relationships are less than six months. You live in a great big house with a lot of empty rooms. What's filling your life right now?"

"Where the hell do you see me fitting into this fairy tale you're building? Hm?"

"What do you mean? You think I'd try to push you out or something? Are you so blind you don't know how I feel about you, too?"

In three steps Angelo was nose to nose with him, breathing hard.

"Don't be a tease, Luca."

"I'm not teasing. You're the one who never takes a male date to your black-tie events."

"I don't date men. I've fucked a few. You included."

"Always trying to be so casual. Sure, you fuck around a lot, but they don't stay over and your life, like your house, is a big, empty space you can't seem to fill. What is it? You like being alone so much? Does it feed your guilt appropriately for getting away from that shithole you grew up in?"

Angelo's mouth twisted, but he didn't deny it. Couldn't, Luca knew. His life was just as empty, only at least he could fucking admit it.

"My big giant house is just fine, fuck you very much. I do just fine, and the last thing I need is complicated stuff like a girlfriend *and* a boyfriend." Angelo's words were meant to be cutting.

"You trying to piss me off so I'll back off? Hm? Too late, I'm already pissed, and it has nothing to do with that total bullshit you just spewed."

"Bullshit? Do you know how much money I'm able to sock away for college for my nieces and nephews because of the television work I do? You see many guys with boyfriends getting that sort of work? Oh, I know, let's complicate it even further with a woman. I can tell *Us Weekly* that I'm *just like us* because I have one of each."

"You think we need to take out a billboard for that? I'm not asking you to wear an 'I Love Luca When He Sucks My Cock' T-shirt, you know. It's not like Petal is New York City or anything. I'm not taking out ads in the paper to announce our threesome. Clearly we'll all have to be circumspect in our behavior."

"You're fooling yourself, Luca. Gunning for getting your heart broken. This can't work."

Angelo looked miserable. Luca understood it, felt it often enough. But he knew one thing more than anything else—if he didn't at least try, he'd be miserable anyway.

"You do what you need to, but I am standing here in the open telling you I am in love with Ava and I'm going to ask her to work things out, try to have a relationship of some kind. I'm telling *you* I love you and I want you to be part of this discussion with her."

Angelo was on him without warning, his mouth sealed over Luca's, stealing his breath. "I shouldn't want either of you, damn it."

Luca grabbed Angelo's cock through the front of his jeans. "But you do. You drag yourself over here every six months or so and drink too much before you'll allow yourself to want me. Three times in ten years you've given yourself permission to touch me. This last week has been, well fuck you, it's been really good with both of you, with the three of us. I won't pretend I don't want that. How will it be with you if she stays with me? Will you pretend you don't want her, too? Hm? Because I *will* love her. I *will* touch her and fuck her and we will have a life, and if you think you can deny yourself that except for a taste every few years, you're lying to us both."

Angelo wanted to shove him back almost as much as he wanted to haul him closer. He settled for half of both, shoving Luca back against the nearby wall so hard the picture hanging there swayed a little. He followed with his body, pressing himself against Luca, arching and rolling his hips.

The sweet agony of cock against cock, even with denim in the way, shocked its way up his spine.

The want, the craving for not just Luca, but for Ava and what they all had together, pooled in his gut. His hands ably ripped the front of Luca's jeans open, grabbing his cock. Luca groaned, jutting lean hips forward.

"That's right, you wanted this and you're going to get it." Angelo's words seeped from his clenched jaw.

"So give it to me and stop talking about it already."

With a strangled laugh, Angelo hauled Luca over toward a nearby couch where they fell, still laughing as clothes were ripped off enough so that skin finally met skin.

That's when Ava came in, and the beauty of it slapped at her, along with the sinking sensation that she wasn't necessary here at all. That she'd been fooling herself to think it was about the three of them. She'd simply been a way for the two of them to be together.

Angelo looked up then, catching sight of her. His smile stayed until he must have noted her expression.

"Ava?" He stood, the fly of his jeans giving her a V-shaped flash of hard, flat belly and the shock of his well-trimmed pubic hair at the very bottom.

"Sorry. I . . ." She took a step back, thinking about the best way to get the fuck up out of there and get to the airport.

"Sorry for what?" Angelo moved to her with purpose, even as she eyed the back door she'd just come through. He was so strong there, so big and masculine, concern on his handsome face. She couldn't bear to look at him.

She wanted to touch him, would have just hours before. But now it felt as if everything had changed. "Interrupting. I didn't knock. Or ring the bell. Or anything."

Luca approached, disheveled and so beautiful she paused to just look at him for a moment. It had to last her after all, last her until, well, forever, she guessed.

"Why would you? Is something wrong?" Angelo pulled her into a hug and growled until she relaxed.

"It's just been a day I guess. I need to get packed." She tried to pull away from Angelo, but he held on tight.

Luca got in her face, standing at Angelo's shoulder. "Just like that? You come back here wearing a stranger's expression and you're going to pack and leave? What. The. Fuck. Happened?"

"Nothing!" She couldn't look at them without crying, so she focused on her feet, realizing the toes of her sneakers were dirty. "It's just time for me to go back home."

"You're looking at the floor. I don't think I've seen you do that the entire time you've been back. Did someone hurt you, Ava?" Angelo shook her to get her attention. "Did someone do or say something when you went to Marlene's?"

"Your eyes are red, baby, I can see you've been crying. Why would you be ashamed of that? You don't have to be so tough, you know." Luca's concern tore at her.

"You're scaring me, Ava." Angelo let go of one of her arms to tip her chin. When her gaze met his, she nearly lost it again. "Tell me what it is so I can fix it." There was so much emotion in his voice it scared her.

"Just let me go. I'll get out of the way and you two can . . . get back to everything. You've been great and all, entertaining me this last week." She felt stupid. Humiliated that she'd entertained the idea of trying to make this work out in some sense. She should have known better.

"Entertaining you?" Luca's fear now took a back seat to his anger. "Is that what this has been for you? You drop in and fuck me for a few days and now you're leaving? Again?"

"You started it! I was staying in a hotel. I was going to leave on

Wednesday night. You touched me first, you fucked me first." She hadn't meant to scream it, hadn't intended that thread of pain to sound so, so loudly, but it was there nonetheless.

Angelo angled himself between the two of them. "Stop this. Ava, clearly something is wrong. You were not like this earlier today, and I get that seeing the house was probably a shock and all, but you're not making any sense. What is this bullshit about letting us get back to everything? About us entertaining you for a week?"

She couldn't think straight with them so close. "Damn it, let me go!"

He did, but his gaze remained locked on her. "Don't even think about leaving this room before we get this all straightened out."

"You're not the boss of me, for fuck's sake!"

"You clearly need a boss, Ava. Don't think I didn't feel your cunt ripple around my cock each time I was exactly the boss of you. You're acting like a stranger. Now, before I get in my car and go out looking for someone's ass to beat in retaliation for whatever was done to you, why don't you tell us yourself."

"I *am* a stranger. Don't you get that? You two have always had each other. But I haven't been here. I've been just fine for the last decade. I can manage my own life. I have a good life. A good job. I don't have to worry about whether or not I can afford milk or bread. I don't need anyone or anything. I told you, it's just been a long day. No one hurt me. I need to leave now." She moved toward the stairs, and Angelo didn't stop her. Her heart broke a little more, but she managed to hold it together as she jogged up to the master bedroom as fast as she could.

Angelo stopped Luca as he rushed past. "No. Wait a second."

"Why? She's clearly upset at what happened today and is afraid to share. Didn't you just hear me tell you, not even thirty minutes ago, that I wanted to make a go of things with her? I love her, Angelo. I don't want to be without her ever again."

"She's not upset about something that happened at the house. She wouldn't look at us, Luca. We're the ones who've upset her."

"What? Why would you think that? Things were just fine earlier today. Yes, I was pissed and hurt that she wanted to hare off on her own, but when she left to go to her mother's place, things were better between us. The hugs, the kisses and the promises to be back by supper, those were real."

"I know. If I didn't know how all right she was about you and me being together, I'd think it was that. She seemed so stricken when I looked up at her."

Luca eyed him suspiciously. "She gets off on watching us together. I know she does. When you fucked me, after her, on your pool table, she's the one who brought the lube. She's the one who laid out right in front of us and fingered herself while she watched. She's not jealous. She knows how we feel about her. Anyway, I thought you weren't interested in trying to work anything out."

Angelo scrubbed his face with his hands. He didn't want to be interested. It would be a public relations nightmare if word got out he not only had two partners, but that one of them was male. He could lose those extremely lucrative television jobs. Most likely his clients at the firm wouldn't care as long as he kept making them money.

He wanted to get in his car and go home.

Luca watched him without speaking.

"I shouldn't." But he couldn't imagine how it would feel to lose her again. Even if he and Luca tried to have a relationship on their own, there'd be a space where she was supposed to be. And, he admitted to himself, he loved her. She was integral to him.

"But?"

How had it come to this? He and Ava were the hard ones. The ones who tried to protect Luca. And yet it was Luca who stood so straight and tall, so sure of his path ahead. Luca who was the only one not running and hiding from something.

"Let's go up there and get it out of her."

Luca's anger dropped away, replaced by his smile, and Angelo's heart turned over in his chest.

Eight

Ava's hands shook as she shoved her clothes into her case.
She'd worry about wrinkles once she got back home.

"Just hold it together," she whispered to herself, trying to ignore
the masculine rumble downstairs. She'd just say good-bye, thank
them for the last week and go. There was no reason to come back
to Petal again, so there'd be no reason to promise anything of the
sort.

A clean, easy break was what they all needed. She could be
an adult about it. It had been great sex, and they'd kept her from
thinking too much about her mother and everything. It was silly to
be upset, after all, no one ever made any promises to her.

"You're such a fucking liar," she sneered as she pushed to stand,
heading for the bathroom to grab her toiletries.

Her things had sort of taken residence in his bathroom, she
thought with a melancholy air as she grabbed bottles and tubes,
sliding them into the bag and zipping up. Just that morning she'd

thought how nice that looked, her brush next to his on the counter, Angelo's hair-product tube snuggled with hers.

Stupid. That's what she was.

When she turned to go back into the bedroom, Luca popped his head around the corner. "There you are. Time to drop it and just tell us what the fuck is going on with you." He crossed his arms, making him look even more sexy, and she narrowed her eyes at him for looking so good.

Angelo was on the bed, stretched out like a big predator, his hair loose, like he knew she liked, *bastard*, his gaze on her like he had a right to get her all stirred up right before she rode off into the sunset so he and Luca could be alone.

"I hope you're not going to propose one for the road. I'm a little sore."

She dumped the toiletries bag on top of the clothes.

"Why are you being such a bitch, pretty bird?" Angelo's stillness sent a shiver up her spine. She'd never make it through the day without masturbating, damn it.

"I'm not. I'm trying to go, and you two are acting as if you're trying to stop me, which is silly, isn't it?"

He whipped his head a bit. "Come again?"

"I get it! God!" Frustrated, she knew the tears would come no matter what, so she may as well just get it said.

"You get what? Baby, who are you? You left earlier today and you were our Ava. Beautiful and sad, but this"—he motioned, meaning the three of them—"was working just fine. You can't deny that. And you come back and you won't look at us. You're mad or we hurt you, is that it?"

"I am not mad. I just, well, anyway, I've overstayed my welcome and now I'm in the way. Just let me leave without any more drama." She heard the entreaty in her own voice, but couldn't stop it.

"What are you talking about? In the way of what?" Angelo was up and standing before her in a flash. The heat of his body blanketed hers. "I feel like we're speaking two different languages. But you're not leaving here until we've resolved this."

She tried to move her head, to look anywhere but up into those knowing brown eyes, but he wouldn't let go of her chin.

The sting of tears burned her eyes, her throat closed and a sob broke from her lips. His eyes widened and then two sets of arms embraced her.

She had nothing left. She'd thought she'd rebuilt herself in the last decade, but having to walk away from these two men, these people she loved more than anything or anyone in the universe would kill her. Maybe she'd take one of those six-month cruises and lick her wounds. Take a lover or five.

She nearly snorted at that.

"You gonna tell us, or do we have to beat it out of you?"

"Baby, we want you to stay here, don't you get it? You're running out of here like a scalded cat, and I don't know why until you tell me," Luca spoke, his lips against her ear.

"Why are you doing this to me?" she demanded, trying to push away.

"What? Tell me and I can explain. But at this point neither of us knows what you're talking about." Angelo loosened his embrace enough for her to look up at him, or over at Luca, but she kept her gaze fastened on the floor.

"And look me in the damned eyes when you talk to me, Ava. For fuck's sake, you're not that girl anymore and I was never that guy." Angelo's voice was angry, enough to have her head up, chin out.

"Why are you both acting like you want me here when it's totally obvious you are just fine without me? It offends me to be lied to."

Tears had begun to run down her cheek, so she wiped her face on Angelo's loose shirttail when he wouldn't let her free. Served him right.

Luca finally spoke, "*Fine without you?* Is that what you think? I've spent the last week thinking on ways to ask you to stay here, thinking on a plan that could get us together somehow. All of us. I want you to stay here, Ava. I want you to be with me every single day."

She stared at him. "Stop! Oh my God, this hurts way more than you think it helps. My heart is broken. I can't take it. Please just let me leave before I embarrass myself any further."

Angelo stared at her, stunned. He struggled to put together what she'd said, mainly because her crying had gotten to that stuttery, hiccupy stage and it was hard to understand her. He'd never tell her so, but seeing her this way got to him. Seeing this strong, nearly unbreakable woman break had burrowed under his skin, spiked his adrenaline to just fix her and make her happy again.

Fuckety-fuck, he was in love with her in the grand, I'd-slay-dragons way.

"Embarrass yourself how? What haven't we done in front of one another? *With* one another? What do you have to be embarrassed about, and why do you keep saying you want to leave? Who broke your heart so I can pummel him?"

"I l-l-love you both so much." She wiped her face on his shirt again, and he tried not to laugh. "Bu-uu-t I can't be your beard. I just c-c-can't. I can't watch you love him and not me. It's shallow and p-petty and tot-tally unworthy of you both, but I can't."

Luca met Angelo's gaze as he shook his head.

"Beard? You think that's what we want?" Luca's heart hurt for her as each sob wracked her body, but at the same time, it soared because she confessed she loved them both.

"I already have a beard. So does Luca. It makes kissing him scratchy, and he gets my thighs red when he sucks my cock. He was about to, actually, when you came in. Like he has before, with you right there in the room and a few times over the years, when you weren't."

"Three times, not that I was counting." Luca kissed her temple. "Of all the things I want from you, you posing as my woman so I could have a relationship with my man is not even on the list. I don't want you to pose as anything. I want you to be my woman for real."

"When I came in and you two were together, laughing, touching, it was beautiful, as beautiful as it always is. But you were better without me here. I saw it for what it was and realized I'd been a fool."

Luca let go long enough to grab a handkerchief and hand it to her.

"I agree." Luca shrugged and Angelo snorted. "You're being a fool right now. I love you, Ava. Before you got here, Angelo and I were talking about how to work things out so we could all be together. I can't tell you I don't want him. Hell"—Luca looked up to Angelo, who looked steadily back—"I love him, always have. I told him that, too."

That frown line of hers appeared between her eyebrows, and Angelo, laughing, smoothed it away with his thumb. "We both decided you were worth the risks. As improbable as this all is, it feels too good to walk away from, doesn't it?" He kissed her cheeks, tasting her tears. "I love you, Ava. I sent you flowers every five months because I couldn't let go of you. I don't want to now, either."

She blinked up at them, nose running, breath hiccupping. "You do? You both do?" She looked to Luca.

"Yes. Baby, yes. We want you with us. However we can make it work. If you're bothered by Angelo and I being together when you're not around, we'll work that out."

"No!" she blurted out. "No. That's not what . . . I wasn't bothered that you were together without me. I just . . . I just thought there wasn't room for me."

"Plenty of cocks and plenty of places for us to use them." Angelo's lips curved up. "There's room for you. An Ava-spaced spot in our lives that's been empty for ten years. You can't come back here, make us fall for you even harder and then run back to LA."

"I didn't expect this." She licked her lips. "But I'm glad for it anyway. I'm sort of like a pit bull, you know. Just warning you, once I get hold of you two, I'm not letting go. My job is pretty portable." She smiled hopefully.

"I may have noticed your tenacious streak. Does this mean you want to try?"

She cupped Luca's cheek. "How do *you two* see this working anyway?"

"Carefully, with liberal amounts of sex to keep everyone calm and happy." Luca winked. "I love you. He loves you. You love us and that's the foundation for a strong future. We'll have to step carefully, but if we all talk about things openly, I think we can make it work."

"Your mother knows. She came to the house today. And helped me through it. She said enough that I know she understands this thing is more than just you and me. She asked me if I loved you. Over ice cream and around your dad, who was totally trying to eavesdrop."

"And you told her?"

"I told her I did. That I've loved you since I was a girl and you two played football and broke all sorts of hearts in town. And I said I loved you now. I told her it was complicated and she said, 'Angelo,' and I said, 'Yes, I love him, too.'"

Angelo watched her carefully, the mask of the hardened youth firmly in place. She wanted to wash that look away forever.

"She told me she knew and that things wouldn't be easy, but that usually easy was boring anyway. And then she changed the subject."

He allowed himself to smile, leaning down to brush his lips over her forehead.

Angelo hugged her tight and looked over to Luca. "It would seem we've got some issues between us. You sure you want all this baggage, Luca?"

"Hell yes. You'll have to deal with mine, too. That's love right there, baby, baggage and all."

"This won't be easy, you know. This is complicated and pretty freaking alternative-lifestyle. Angelo, people know your face. You're a celebrity. What if folks find out?"

"I can't lie. If and when this comes out, some will react very negatively. I've made a pledge to help my nieces and nephews pay for college. My media money is all for that. Naturally, I'd prefer to keep this quiet and private. Not to hide it because I'm ashamed," he added quickly and she nodded. "But if people find out, they'll find out. I can't *not* touch you, Ava, any more than I can't *not* be with you. We'll take it one step at a time."

Luca pressed in again. "So? What do you say? Come back to Petal and you'll always have a front-row seat for fireworks on our dock. You can always escape to Angelo's to swim in the pool."

"Or get fucked on my pool table." Angelo's eyes lit. "Both of you. Perfect height to take you from behind, Luca. Perfect height to lay you out, eat your pussy until you scream and then flip you over to fuck you until you scream again."

They left her momentarily speechless as each ground his erection against her.

"Anyone want to take a road trip from LA in a moving truck with me, my stuff and my dog?"

She was still laughing as they took her to the mattress. But not for long.

JUST FOR ONE NIGHT

MEGAN HART

One

"Gorgeous." Jeremy looked over Kerry's shoulder at their mutual reflection as his hands came to rest on her hips. The smooth fabric of her dress bunched a little under his fingertips.

At the heat of him against her back she shivered, studying herself with a jaded eye. She turned her face from side to side, checking out the dangling bead-and-chain earrings that brushed her neck, which was bared by her upswept hair. Then her makeup, applied a little more thickly tonight than was her norm. And finally, again at the dress that Jeremy had picked out for her. There was a lot of cleavage. She leaned back against him a little, meeting his gaze in the mirror.

"You think so, huh?"

He kissed the side of her neck. The swift, hot flick of his tongue created an answering pull in her cunt. Jeremy's fingers slipped higher, over the dress's sleek material. He cupped her breasts, pushing them together so they almost spilled out altogether. "Definitely. He'll fucking love it."

Kerry laughed even as her stomach took a slow, rolling tumble. "I hope so."

"He will."

"He wasn't into me so much back then. What's to say his tastes have changed?"

Jeremy tweaked her braless nipples so they stood out against the material. His breath gusted over her neck, and Kerry's clit pulsed, just once. She shifted, the silk of her panties rubbing her bare pussy. Jeremy had shaved her nearly bare, leaving only a landing strip. She never shaved that close, just trimmed her bikini area and kept her curls close-cropped. This bare flesh against the silk was new. Exciting. Distracting.

"He could be gay," Kerry added. "That would explain a lot."

"Baby, a gay man would pop a rod at the sight of you in this dress. Brian Jordan doesn't have a chance."

She turned then to face him. Her arms slid up around his neck. In her three-inch heels she could look him in the eye. "Are you sure about this?"

Jeremy's gaze flickered, but he smiled. He cupped her ass and pulled her close to him. He ground his crotch against her, his cock thick and hard beneath his jeans. "It's what you want, isn't it?"

Kerry nodded and kissed him. "Well . . . sure. But . . ."

Jeremy had dragged the admission out of her late one night in the summer heat, windows open and even sheets too heavy for sleeping. He'd been kneeling between her legs, lapping slowly at her clit. Teasing her toward orgasm, then pulling back just enough to keep her from surging over. He'd made her tell him secrets. The fact that she'd once dreamed of giving up her virginity to Brian Jordan had only been one of them.

"But nothing. You wanted him back then. You told me you did. And now's your chance to get him. What's wrong with that?"

"Nothing's wrong with it. Just that . . . Are you sure you're okay with this?" She studied his face, looking for any hint or inkling of a lie.

Jeremy laughed and rubbed her ass in slow circles, then stepped back. "You're still coming home to me, right?"

"Of course."

"And you're going to tell me every dirty, nasty detail. Right?"

Kerry drew in a breath at the thought of it. Not just of doing it—seducing and fucking Brian Jordan. Living out an adolescent dream. But of coming home and telling her boyfriend of eighteen months about it. "Most men wouldn't be okay with their girlfriends fucking another guy. Much less want to know all about it."

"What can I say? I'm not most men."

She knew that already. Eighteen months in this relationship and Jeremy managed to surprise her almost every day. She wondered if she'd ever learn him the way he seemed to know her. "No. You certainly aren't."

He spun her around to face the mirror again. One hand anchored her hip. The other inched her skirt up over her thigh. His fingers traced patterns on her skin, then over her panties. Kerry watched, mesmerized, as his forefinger circled the silk over her clit with such a light touch she could barely feel it.

"Relax," Jeremy said into her ear. "He's gonna fucking love you. I told you that already."

"I don't need him to love me. Just want me." Kerry shivered again at Jeremy's brushing touch. She wanted to tip her hips, push her cunt into his hand. Get more. She didn't. Every muscle in her body felt taut, tense. "Just for one night."

Brian had spent a good fifteen minutes in the parking lot behind the wheel of his car, checking his hair, his breath, the front of his suit for wrinkles. Reunions were supposed to be all about showing up and showing off, seeing what your classmates had done—or hadn't done—with their lives. Sure, he was glad to see old high school pals he hadn't seen or heard from in years. It was always cool to catch up with people he'd once spent more time with than his own family. On the other hand, he'd kept in touch with anyone who was really important to him, even if it was only through the vagueness of Connex updates. So this reunion was maybe just an excuse to compare the size of one another's bank accounts . . . or balls.

Brian had a lot to brag about. He had a great job, a sweet apartment, a nice car. Time had been kind to him, too. Fifteen years and a conscientious workout program had put some muscle, not fat, on him. Only one or two strands of silver streaked his dark hair, and only a line or two around the eyes spoke of laughter, not age. In his regular life he was damned happy with what he saw in the mirror, so why did the reflection of his eyes in the rearview make him want to burn rubber and peel out of the lot without even going inside?

Two words: Kerry Grayson. He'd seen her name in the RSVP list on the website the reunion committee had set up and couldn't decide whether to fist-punch the air or groan. She was definitely not one of the people he'd kept in touch with, though he had seen her once at a party the summer after their freshman year of college. And he'd never admit it, but he'd stalked her Connex profile more than once, checking out her photos and musing over her relationship status—"It's complicated."

What did that mean, anyway? That she had a boyfriend or a husband and it wasn't working out? That she was single but didn't want the world to know?

Finally, he forced himself to get out of the car. He shook each pant leg to get the creases out. Twisted his watch on his wrist and tugged at his cuffs. Slid his tie a little tighter against his throat. He was as ready as he was ever going to be, which was to say not very.

He could hear the music already as he walked through the Hotel Hershey's lobby toward the ballroom. A blend of late eighties and early nineties pop hits, stuff with a heavy bass beat and lyrics he didn't know. The table in front of the ballroom had a lot of folded white cards with names written on them in fancy black script. Brian found his right away but tried to make it look like he hadn't so he'd have time to scope out the others. Kerry's was still there. Damn.

"Brian Jordan. Hey, handsome."

Brian turned to face the feminine voice behind him and got tugged into an impromptu and not entirely welcome hug by a mass of blonde hair and a cloud of perfume. "Hey . . . uh . . ."

"It's me. Gina? Gina Barton!" She nudged him. "Wow, long time no see, huh?"

Gina Barton. Of course. He'd taken her to homecoming their senior year. Felt her up in the backseat of his parents' car. She'd dumped him after that but had continued to flirt with him mercilessly for the rest of the year. He'd never figured out why. Back then he'd never been able to get a handle on why girls did what they did. Not that he'd gotten much better at it over the years.

"Gina, sure, hey. You look . . ." She looked older, for one thing. Harder. She looked like she spent a lot of time exercising and tanning, and it hadn't been good to her. "Good. It's good to see you."

She hugged him again, her boozy breath wafting over him. "C'mon inside. Open bar only lasts another half an hour, and the hors d'oeuvres, too."

Brian allowed himself to be led through the double doors into the ballroom, which had been set up with a DJ and dance floor at one end, tables covered with white cloths and balloons in the middle and the bar at the other end. He spotted a couple of guys he'd played soccer with and waved, but Gina wasn't about to let go of his arm. She tugged him toward the bar, keeping up the conversation about who was here, who wasn't coming, what they were having for dinner and a thousand other things Brian didn't really care about.

He did his best to look interested though, sipping at a glass of Jameson and soda while Gina tossed back a shot of tequila. He was saved by the entrance of a couple that he didn't recognize but she did. Then, just as she'd done fifteen years ago, she dumped him and ran off.

Brian spent the next few minutes hanging at the bar, nodding across the room at people whose names he thought he should know but wasn't sure he remembered. He'd just taken another sip of his drink, relishing the burn of liquor in his throat, when he saw her. Kerry. She paused in the double doors and several flashing red-and-blue lights crisscrossed over her.

His guts hit his shoes, and he choked a little on his drink. She looked . . . perfect. There was no other way to describe her. Everything about her, from the fancy twisted hairdo to the clingy dress that swung just above her knees and dipped low in front, was enough to make him a praying man. Brian had met very few women who could leave him speechless, but he couldn't have said a word just then if someone had poked him with a sharp stick.

She scanned the crowd. Looking for someone, maybe? Found them, he saw, when she waved, grinning, and crossed the room to hug a couple of women. Just like high school dances, he thought. Boys on one side, girls on the other, with a few brave souls mingling on the dance floor. That would change as the night wore on, helped by booze. But for now a wave of nostalgia swept over him so fiercely he had to give himself a surreptitious sniff to make sure he didn't smell like Drakkar Noir.

Kerry had been in all of Brian's classes since kindergarten. In tenth grade they were lab partners for biology. Senior year they'd had trigonometry together. He'd sat just behind her. Brian had never been able to figure out what perfume she wore, something light and flowery, but even now remembering the scent made his cock twitch. It was a wonder he hadn't flunked the class completely, since he'd spent so much time thinking of baseball, not math. He could remember watching the way her earrings swung. Every time she shifted in her seat, bumping his desk, he'd felt it in his dick. They'd been partners in class when the teacher gave them free time to prepare for tests and in the third period study hall they shared in the library, where they'd spent more time laughing than studying. They'd spent hours on the phone with the excuse of higher math connecting them, though he could remember a hundred conversations they'd had and none had involved numbers.

But he'd been a lame-ass punk, he'd never asked her out no matter how much he'd wanted to. Then he'd found out she was going out with some guy from another school when she showed up for class one day wearing a huge class ring wrapped with yarn to keep it on her finger. That's when he'd asked out Gina, and Kerry had stopped asking him to help her during study periods.

He'd never asked her out, but he had kissed her at that party during the summer between freshman and sophomore years of college. She'd smelled the same as she always had and tasted better than he'd imagined. They'd both been drunk, the music pumping a lot like it was now. He could remember how she'd breathed his name when he put his hand under her skirt, how she hadn't pushed him away when his fingers found her heat. Unfortunately, he couldn't remember much past that except the next day's hangover.

"Brian. Hi."

Shit. She was right in front of him, and he was just standing there looking like an asshole. How had he crossed the entire room to her without paying attention? His feet had known what his dick wanted, he guessed, and Brian cursed himself for looking like a dumbass.

"K-Kerry. Right?" Ah, shit again. Like he didn't know her name.

She tilted her head the tiniest bit to the side to look at him. "Yeah. It's me."

"Long time . . ."

"No see, right," she finished for him with a low, throaty laugh that tightened his balls. "But hey, that's what reunions are for, right?"

"Is it?"

She stepped a little closer to say into his ear, "Sure. Well, that and catching up with old . . . friends."

She'd leaned a little too close for casual conversation. Brian's crotch was getting tighter by the second, especially when he caught a glimpse of the glitter she'd dusted on her cleavage. At this angle he had quite a view.

"Let's get a drink," Kerry said. "Catch up."

She was off to the bar before he could reply, tempting him with the swing of her hips to follow. And he did, just like a dog, trotting after her though his drink wasn't even half finished. He caught up to her at the bar, where she'd ordered some sort of fruity, girlie drink the bartender served up with a slice of orange in it. She sipped, eyeing him over the glass.

"So. Brian. I guess now's the time when we brag about our jobs and our amazing love lives and compare notes on how many toys we've managed to acquire, right?"

He glanced around the room at the groups of twos and fours, then at her. "That seems to be the standard. Yeah."

Kerry sipped at her drink again, then set it down along with her place card at the table closest to the bar. She shook her head, setting her earrings dancing so Brian could only stare, mesmerized at the glitter of light reflecting off the beads. "Fuck that. Let's dance, instead."

He was already putting down his drink and letting her take

his hand. Following her again, this time to the nearly empty dance floor, where Kerry turned and faced him with a smile that lit up her eyes. She looked mischievous. She looked blazing hot.

Brian didn't know the song, but at least it had a good beat. Too bad he was a lousy dancer. Kerry laughed as she twirled and shook her hips and he did the frat-boy shuffle, one-step, two-step, side to side. He wasn't even going to try and get any hand action in there. They had the whole dance floor to themselves, at least, and probably the attention of a lot of people in the room, but Brian didn't care.

"You're a great dancer," he said over the music.

Kerry only laughed and spun, moving her feet in some complicated pattern he couldn't keep up with. Her skirt belled around her thighs, and when she turned back to him, she reached for his hand. "You're not."

Brian laughed, too. "I know. I suck."

She lifted a brow at that but said nothing. She moved closer to him. She smiled.

And they danced.

At least until the DJ broke in to tell everyone it was time to take their seats for dinner. Kerry winked at him. In an inspired bit of choreography, Brian spun her out at the end of his arm, then back in, right up against him.

"I guess we need to sit down." Brian licked his mouth and tasted sweat. The hollow of her throat gleamed with it, and he had a sudden vision of himself leaning down to lick it. That didn't help the pressure in his pants at all.

"Tell you what," Kerry said with another smile. "I have a better idea."

Two

Maybe it *was* the dress.

Maybe it was just the night. The music, the booze. Nostalgia. It didn't matter. All that mattered was that Brian had followed Kerry upstairs to the room she'd rented for just one night.

Kerry twirled just inside the door, so her dress flared around her thighs. She'd passed up sexy stockings and garters for the freedom of bare flesh, though despite Jeremy's wicked suggestion, she hadn't gone without panties. Her dress fell against her legs as she held out her hand to Brian, who'd hesitated just inside the doorway.

"Com'ere," Kerry said.

He took a few steps forward to take her hand. "You're beautiful, you know that?"

She linked her fingers with his, tipping her face toward him. God, he was so freaking tall. Even in her heels she barely reached his chin. "You think so, huh?"

Brian eased her closer. "Yeah."

He smelled good. Something faintly soapy and fresh, not like cologne. The thought of him in the shower, washing, those big hands moving over his chest and under his armpits, between his legs . . . Kerry shivered a little. She put her hand on his shoulder, the other still caught tight in his.

"You wanna dance again?" Brian asked in a low voice.

"No." She pushed up on her toes to offer her mouth to him, though she didn't kiss him. Not yet. Strong, tall, broad male pressed all along the front of her, and she balanced herself against him. She looked him straight in the eye. No point in being coy. "Do you remember the night of Jackson's party?"

He drew in a breath and his fingers tightened in hers. "Yeah. Well . . . most of it, anyway."

"You were pretty drunk."

He winced. "I know. I remember that."

"Do you remember kissing me?"

"Yeah." He grinned, suddenly not seeming so shy.

Brilliant. He'd always had a great smile. It was even better now that his face had some time on it.

"Do you know how long I'd wanted to kiss you before that?" Kerry asked, answering before he could reply. "A long time, Brian. A really long time. I wanted you so much, Brian. It was like . . . burning."

She thought he might laugh at that and wouldn't have blamed him if he had. He didn't even grin. Just blinked, that lovely, perfect mouth glistening as he ran his tongue along it.

"But you never said anything."

"I was in high school," Kerry said. "I was stupid and shy."

"But you had that boyfriend . . ."

"Because you didn't ask me out." They were dancing now, though there was no music. Slowly circling, the hotel room's smooth carpet snagging only slightly now and then on her heels.

"And he did. So that night at the party, I was determined not to let the opportunity pass me up."

"And I blew it." Brian stopped moving. He shook his head and that gorgeous dark hair fell over his forehead. "I guess I passed out or something."

"Or something like that, yeah. Do you know how many times I've wondered what it might've been like if you hadn't?"

"A lot?" he said, sounding hopeful. "I did, anyway."

"A lot," she agreed in a low voice, thick with desire.

This time she did kiss him.

He kissed her, too, mouth already open, tongue stroking along hers. She pressed herself against him, feeling the heat of his crotch on her belly through the thin material of her dress. The thought he might already be hard sent a shiver of anticipation rippling through her, and her clit throbbed. When his hands slid down her back to cup her ass, Kerry sighed into his mouth and pulled away.

"You used to sit behind me in that stupid trig class. Every so often you'd stretch out your legs and bump my chair or the backs of my calves. All I could think about was the fact you were touching me. I almost failed that class, thanks to you," she said.

Brian looked down at her. "I'm such a jerk. I never knew."

Kerry laughed and kissed him again, softer this time. "I know. It wasn't something I could exactly just blurt out, you know? 'Hey, Brian, by the way, I totally make myself come every night thinking about you and also, I'd really like to lose my virginity to you.'"

She knew she could be surprisingly blunt, but she still didn't expect Brian's reaction to her lightly said words. He blinked rapidly, his hands tightening on her butt, and his jaw dropped. She thought he might be trying to speak, but could only stutter, instead.

"Too much information?" she asked with another laugh.

Heat flared in his gaze, and it was Brian's turn to surprise her. He kissed her, hard, then bent his knees just enough to scoop an arm beneath her thighs and lift her. Kerry cried out, giggling into his kiss, and clung to him as he cradled her against his very broad chest. Four or so steps took them to the giant bed with its thick comforter and half a dozen pillows. When he laid her on it and crawled up over her, Kerry lost the breath for giggles.

"I used to jerk off in the shower every morning," Brian murmured against her throat as he kissed her, "hoping it would be enough to get me through first period trig without popping a boner right there. Every morning, Kerry. It never worked. All you had to do was give me that sideways smile over your shoulder, like you knew just what I was thinking, and I'd nearly tear a hole in my jeans."

"We were stupid," Kerry said.

Brian pushed up on his hands, denting the mattress beneath her as he moved between her legs to press his thigh against her. He stripped her bare with his gaze, and Kerry arched beneath that look as though he'd actually taken off her clothes. Everything about this had become a little hazy, a little blurred. Like some kind of dream. She wasn't sure if she wanted to slow down and savor every moment or simply take it for the roller-coaster ride it was. She wasn't sure she *could* slow down.

"I'm still stupid," Brian said. "Just warning you."

A sense of humor on a dude was so fucking sexy she wanted to eat him up right then and there. "Com'ere."

She pulled him by the tie down to kiss her again. Brian settled his weight carefully on her, one hand cradling the back of her head. He rolled them just enough to tangle her skirt around her thighs, but that was all right because in the next moment his hand was sliding up her bare flesh to cup her silk-covered ass. His belt buckle was cold on her suddenly exposed belly.

She already knew he was a good kisser, but now unlike that long-ago summer night when alcohol had both fueled and derailed them, Kerry could really appreciate Brian's talent. That, or like everything else about him, he'd simply gotten better with time. He skimmed her mouth before turning the kiss deep. Never too much tongue, never sloppy.

Without taking her mouth from his, Kerry tugged on Brian's tie to loosen it. Next came the buttons of his shirt, one by one, until she could run her hands over his chest. He had more muscles than she remembered. More chest hair, too. Brian Jordan had grown up . . . and deliciously. She skimmed her hands over his nipples, feeling the heat of his skin and the beat of his heart under her palms. At last she had to break the kiss long enough to look down and figure out how to wrestle him out of his suit jacket.

"I want you naked," she murmured and looked up at the sound of Brian's indrawn breath. "What?"

"Just . . . you're so . . ."

She paused to lick her lips, studying him. "I'm so what?"

Brian shook his head and ran his fingers through his hair, pushing it out of his eyes as he sat up a little. "This is all like something out of my teenage stroke fantasies. That's all. Women don't . . . I mean, I haven't been with any who . . ."

A little alarmed, Kerry sat up, too. "Any who what?"

"Any who just go for what they want like this." His hand slid over her hip, pushing her dress up higher. "It's always such a dance. What do I do for a living, what kind of car do I drive, where am I taking them on a date . . . They have to fuck with the lights off so I don't have to see the size of their thighs."

"Sounds like you've been dating the wrong kinds of women," Kerry said against his mouth as she kissed him again.

It was Brian's turn to laugh, albeit sheepishly. "I guess so."

She rolled him onto his back and straddled him, pinning his wrists next to his ears and giving him a grin. Under her, Brian's cock felt thick and hard, shielded by the fabric of his pants. Kerry rubbed against him, watching every twitch of his expression. Brian licked his lips, pupils dilating. His hips bumped up a fraction of an inch when she slid back and forth, but he didn't try to pull his wrists from her grip.

Kerry drew in a long, slow breath. "Tell the truth and shame the devil," her grandma had always said. "Brian Jordan, I've wanted to fuck you since I was in tenth grade. I'm not going to miss a second chance at it. Okay?"

He nodded. "Okay."

She leaned to kiss him, taking her time. Grinding her cunt down on his bulge. Already her heartbeat was picking up, her pussy hot and slick with wanting. The muscles of her belly jumped as he sucked gently on her tongue.

Kerry sat up and gathered her dress in her fists. She pulled it up over her hips and belly, then her breasts. Finally over her head, leaving her in nothing but her tiny silk panties. Her skin pebbled and her nipples peaked at once, though the room wasn't cold. She put her hands on his chest, watching his face. Everything she'd ever wanted was right there in front of her. The only question was, where to start first?

She glanced between them, thinking of the nights she'd spent imagining Brian's cock. How long? How thick? How would he feel on her tongue, how would he taste when he came in her mouth? In the beginning her fantasies had been formless and vague, but sexual experience had given her something more distinct to imagine. She licked her lips thinking about it, then slid over his thighs and undid the button and zip on his pants before he could even move.

With another grin, Kerry tugged his pants and briefs down over his nicely muscled thighs and calves, over his ankles and feet. Fuck, he had pretty toes. She tossed his pants on the floor and looked up at him, gauging his reaction. He looked a little stunned, but his prick didn't seem to mind . . . and oh, it was as long and thick and beautiful as she'd always imagined it would be. Her heart stuttered as she shifted on the bed.

Something about how he was still half dressed, tie askew over his open shirt and jacket, made his other nakedness so much sexier. The way he'd propped himself on one elbow to watch her helped, too. He looked like a cover model, especially with the hair falling over his eye, and Kerry, determined to savor and memorize every single second of this night, leaned back to look him over.

"Perfect," she murmured. Brian sat up to shrug out of his jacket, but she shook her head. "Leave it on. I like it. It looks like I'm seducing you so fast you can't keep up."

"You are seducing me so fast I can't keep up," Brian said, but his hands stilled in their efforts to remove the rest of his clothes.

She slid her hands up his calves, then his thighs, noticing every ripple of muscle, every crisp, curling hair. She felt the heat of his crotch before she touched him, and she made her caress gentle, feathery, drifting fingertips across the sweet, heavy sac of his balls to finally curl around the base of his cock. His heart beat there, keeping good time. He groaned, and she drew in another breath, quicker than the last.

She stroked him, up and down, palming the head of his cock even as she leaned to nuzzle against his belly. Her lips traced a pattern over his abs. She closed her eyes, drinking this in, for the first time feeling a little nervous.

In her fantasies he'd pulled her hair, shouted her name. In her fantasies she gave him the best blow job he'd ever had . . . but what if she couldn't deliver? Sure, she had a lot more experience than she'd had back then, but so did he. What if she didn't live up not just to his expectations . . . but her own?

Brian touched her hair. His fingers tangled. Not pulling, not that, but a soft tug that nevertheless shot electric fire through all her nerves. That was it. One small, tender tug.

She could do this.

Kerry opened her eyes. She drew her tongue along his belly. She took Brian's cock into her mouth inch by delicious inch. Her hand came up to meet her mouth as it came down. She left his cock slick with her spit. When she pulled back, she sucked a little hard at the tip and found the tender divot beneath the head with her tongue. A scratch of teeth, just the tiniest bit, and her lips closed tight around him again.

When Brian touched her, one big hand slipping between her legs to settle his thumb on the front of her panties, Kerry didn't even pause. She just opened her legs enough to give him full access. In the next minute, Brian's fingers slid beneath the leg band of her panties and found her heat. He sank so easily into her with one finger he added another right away, even as his thumb kept up the steady pressure on her clit. It was nothing like her fantasies had ever been.

It was better.

Her cunt was molten from the attention he'd been paying her clit, and it wasn't going to take much longer for her to come. Keeping a hand on his cock, Kerry moved up Brian's body to kiss him. He slipped his hand from between her legs and surprised her by rolling them both so she was under him. Tables turned, Kerry lay back with a laugh and put her arms over her head, arching as Brian's mouth moved from hers to her throat, over her breasts.

When he tongued one nipple and then the other, adding a gentle suck, she murmured his name. Brian paused, one hand on her belly, where it had once again been on its way down. When he bent back to her skin, wet from his mouth, he blew hot breath across it. His fingers slid beneath her panties, finding her clit as unerringly as he'd done before, but only for a second or two. Next he was up to slide her panties down, leaving her entirely bare before him.

She'd imagined this, too. Somehow even without the lit candles and flowing curtains, it was still pretty damn good. It got better when Brian kissed his way down her body and centered his mouth, finally, on her clit.

Kerry tensed at the touch of his tongue against her. Too much, too little . . . she was already so close to orgasm he didn't have to do too much to send her over, and she really didn't want it to end. Not so fast. Not before they'd spent hours naked and sweaty, living out every single dream either one of them had ever had.

"Shhh," Brian murmured against her.

Kerry hadn't realized she'd muttered a small protest until he spoke. She wanted to tell him she didn't mean for him to stop—she wasn't one of those other women worried about her thighs or anything else. She found no words, though. Not when his lips tugged softly on her clit just before his tongue lapped at her in a steady pressure that hit her just right. Nor when his fingers returned to their place inside her. Then she managed a low moan, but couldn't make herself speak. Even if her lips and teeth and tongue had complied, her brain had become saturated with sensation. No words to find.

It was too late to tell him to slow down, go back, ease off. Even if Kerry could've found the voice to tell him, she was too close. Pleasure had built and built, coiled like a spring. She shifted her hips, pressing herself against him. She heard Brian groan as one hand slid beneath her ass to hold her closer to his mouth. His fingers slid in and out of her as his mouth kept up its magic on her clit.

She was the one pulling his hair now. Shouting his name in a hoarse, lust-roughened voice she barely recognized. Kerry gave herself up to ecstasy, riding the waves of orgasm that left her shaking and spent. Just when she thought she couldn't take any more, Brian eased off, staying close but no longer licking and sucking at her. His fingers inside her stilled as her cunt clenched around them. He rested his cheek on her thigh, and the thick darkness of his hair tickled her there, but Kerry didn't laugh. She couldn't manage the breath for anything other than a sigh.

Maybe half a second passed as she blinked rapidly and breathed in and out, finding her way back to earth. She looked down at Brian between her legs and marveled at how right it seemed to see him there. She loosed her grip in his hair but stroked it back from his face. She found her voice.

"That was a great start," Kerry said. "Let's keep going."

Three

"Can I take the rest of my clothes off now?"

Kerry laughed, tipping her head back, and God, she looked so beautiful it made Brian want to . . . well, to do more of what he'd just done. She cocked her head to give him an up-and-down look that might've made him feel a little ridiculous, what with his dick hanging out the way it was below the hem of his shirt. Brian didn't feel stupid, though. She had this way about her that he'd always admired and that had gotten better as she got older. Kerry was honest, but she was also more than that.

Forthright. That's what Kerry was. Forthright and unafraid. Brian liked that a lot. It made him feel like he could be unafraid, too, even half naked and sporting a dick that could drill concrete.

"Sure, Brian. Take off your clothes."

"The seduction's not over, is it?" he asked, tugging on his tie to pull it completely free.

Kerry snuck her naked toes up his belly to press the end of the tie against his chest. "Not even half. Leave the tie on. Take the rest off, but the tie is just too hot to lose."

He laughed and did as she said, stripping out of his rumpled jacket and flapping shirt. Kneeling on the bed wearing only a tie, he again waited half a second to feel stupid but didn't.

Kerry sat up to tug at the tie, bringing his mouth close to hers. "I came so hard I saw stars."

"Good." Making a woman come had always seemed like some mystical, magical talent Brian was happy to possess even if he couldn't be at all sure he ever knew what he was doing. He kissed her, wondering if she'd be squeamish. He hated it when a woman didn't kiss him after he went down on her.

Kerry had no problem with it, and he shouldn't even have doubted. She really was like no other woman he'd ever been with. She captured his lower lip with hers and tugged playfully before releasing him. He jumped a little when she took his cock in her hand.

"I have condoms in my bag," she told him. "Which I think is someplace on the floor."

Brian tried to crane his neck to see if he could glimpse it without moving too far from her exquisitely stroking fingers. Kerry's laugh turned his face back to her, and he sank again into her kiss as she moved her hand up and down on his prick. Right then it was all he could think about. Sinking into her, pushing inside her, filling her—that would have to wait just a couple minutes. Yeah. Just a few more.

Somehow they ended up facing each other on the bed. Kisses became more urgent. His erection pressed just right on the softness of her belly as her nipples scraped his chest. It was just like he'd always thought it would be back in high school with one major difference. This time, he was pretty sure they were going to go all the way.

"Condoms," Kerry said as Brian kissed her jaw and found a sensitive spot just below the curve of her jaw. She gasped when he sucked her skin.

"Yeah," he said, and kept kissing.

At last she rolled on top of him, which was great, and then off him, which left him blinking, owl-eyed, trying to catch his breath. Kerry padded across the hotel room's thick, plush carpet and bent to grab her purse, giving him a full-on view of her very sweet ass. She turned with a triumphant grin, a familiar-looking box in one hand. In the next moment she'd taken three leaping steps to jump onto the bed, bouncing them both so hard the headboard hit the wall.

She bounced again before dropping to her knees beside him. She leaned to kiss him. "Condoms."

Of all the ways he'd ever thought this might go, one thing stood out as different. Brian had always thought making love to Kerry would feel good, would be hot, and it was. He'd just never thought it would be so much fun.

She looked perplexed when he said this and paused with the condom half opened. A small crinkle he wanted to kiss away appeared between her eyebrows. "You didn't?"

"I didn't think . . . I mean there's fun. And then there's *fun*," Brian tried to explain.

Kerry nodded, one brow lifted. "Like I said. You've been with the wrong kinds of women."

That was certainly true, and he'd guessed it before but knew it even more so now. Brian watched her tear open the package and pull out the rubber. Then she was sheathing him with it, and even that felt so good he had to count backward from ten and think of baseball, just the way he had back in those trigonometry days.

Brian had been with women for whom sex was a ballet. Carefully choreographed, sometimes with pretty costumes, often with delicately performed maneuvers. There was nothing like that now.

Kerry slid herself onto his cock without fanfare, her brow still furrowed, her eyes half lidded with pleasure. When she settled fully on him, they both groaned, and she smiled, though her head was already tipping back as she moved.

"Oh," was all she said. Then a second later, "Oh, Brian."

Sometimes when the woman was on top he had trouble hitting just the right rhythm. Pushing up was harder than pushing in, and anticipating this, Brian braced his feet on the bed and slid his hands to Kerry's waist. He shouldn't have worried about it—she took over the way she had right from the start. Putting her hands on his chest, she rocked against him, up and down, adding the same twist with her hips she'd used with her hand. Drove him freaking crazy, that little twist. For the first time in his life, Brian was actually grateful for the condom slightly dulling the sensation. Without it, he was sure he'd have shot off already, less than two minutes into this.

He'd already given her one orgasm, which was something of his style, since making a woman come during sex was always harder. But in this position, it was easy enough for Kerry to take one of his hands from her hip and slip it between them, centering his knuckles against the pressure point of her clit. That she was so comfortable and easy about showing him what she wanted sent another rush and hustle of desire arcing through him like electricity.

When she came the second time, he actually felt it in the clutch and pulse of her clit and cunt against him, and even though he was rocketing toward orgasm himself, there was no missing the shake and shimmy of her body or her low cry. He was too stunned to be proud or smug—all Brian could do was watch Kerry's gorgeous face as it twisted in her climax.

She opened her eyes at the height of it, biting her bottom lip, her gaze slightly dreamy and unfocused before something in her eyes shifted and she pinned him with a look. "Fuck . . . Brian . . ."

Her fingers curled, sharp nails digging into his chest just enough to pinch and not to hurt. A second later she flattened her palms against him, slid them over his nipples and then tweaked. The unexpected sensation sent his hips bucking, balls getting tight, cock as hard as iron. Pretty much all thoughts escaped him in that moment, a heartbeat away from coming.

He saw stars, too.

Orgasm swept him up, then flattened him. Brian heard himself mutter Kerry's name, then something wordless and low. Everything got bright and he blinked against the flare of light as the entire world centered itself in his dick . . . and then, it was over and he was left shuddering and gasping.

"Mmm," Kerry murmured, leaning down to press her mouth against his neck, nuzzling. "Wow."

Brian put his arms around her, breathing in the scent of her hair and concentrating on the soft skin of her back. He let his fingers tiptoe down the knobs of her spine to end at the dimples at the base of her back. He breathed, in and out, trying to get back to reality and hating that he had to.

Kerry pushed up to look at him with mischief glinting in her eyes. "Not too shabby, Mr. Jordan."

"Gosh, thanks," Brian said, totally fine with being teased since the state he was in prevented him from being anything but fine with everything.

"I mean it." She sounded more serious that time. She kissed his mouth, then cupped his face with her hands. "It was totally worth waiting almost twenty years for."

A smile twitched his mouth. "Yeah. I thought so, too."

Kerry giggled and rolled off him, careful to disengage without dislodging the condom, and Brian took care of it, as discreetly as he could, tossing it into a handful of tissues and the garbage pail. She was watching him when he turned back to the bed. He half expected her to jump up and run to the bathroom, but Kerry only reached behind her to tug down the comforter and toss it on the floor, then sprawled out on the sheets with the pillows stacked comfortably behind her.

"So tell me, Brian, everything you've been up to for the past fifteen years."

Brian crawled into bed beside her and took his share of the pillows. "Everything?"

"Oh yes," Kerry said. "I want to hear it all."

So he told her, and even though he didn't think there was much to tell, they talked for hours until they both grew heavy eyed and the conversation slurred and Kerry reached up to turn off the lights next to the bed.

When he woke up in the morning, sprawled out across half the bed with the scent of her still all over him and a morning erection just begging for a second round . . . Kerry was gone.

Four

"**P**ancakes for breakfast? Sausage? Wheat toast . . . ? Oh, Jeremy. Fresh-squeezed orange juice?" Kerry, rubbing at her eyes and stifling a yawn, padded across the kitchen floor in her bare feet and paused at the table. "What is all this?"

"You got in so late last night—well this morning, really—that I figured I'd let you sleep in. And make you breakfast." Jeremy turned from the stove, flipper in hand to take care of the last set of golden-brown pancakes to match the others still steaming on the plate.

He did things like that. Treated her like a princess. Sure, he could be moody and uncommunicative, secretive even . . . sometimes a little bossy. But times like this with breakfast staring her in the face, served by a very handsome man wearing nothing but a grin and an apron, Kerry counted her blessings. She crossed the tile floor and turned him from the stove to kiss him.

"It looks good," she said and squeezed his ass. "This looks better."

"They're gonna burn," Jeremy said into her mouth, eyes sliding to the side to watch the stove top. "Let me just turn off the burner."

He did with a snap of his wrist, put down the flipper and took her in his arms. "Morning. Or afternoon, whatever."

She laughed and kissed him again. It lingered this time. Jeremy was a very good kisser . . . but she found herself thinking of Brian, how every stroke of his tongue had echoed in her cunt. Kerry shivered.

"You should've woken me," Jeremy told her. "I wanted to hear all about the big night. I assume it worked."

"Oh, it worked, that's for sure. It was the dress. You were right."

Jeremy shook his head. "It was you, babe. I told you, no man could pass you up."

"I didn't want to wake you," Kerry told him.

That was only part of it. When at last she stumbled into their bedroom, she'd been so exhausted she could barely see straight. Jeremy had been snoring, ears plugged tight with the foam earbuds he used to block out the noise of the fan she liked to have whirring on her at night. She'd planned to wake him and tell him every detail the way he wanted, but faced with reliving what had been one of the best fucks of her life, Kerry had been unable to do anything but shower and slip between the sheets, still thinking of Brian. She'd just wanted to hold on to it for herself a while longer, that was all.

It didn't mean anything.

"So? How was it?" Jeremy's hands slipped over her silk robe to settle on her butt.

"Good."

His smile thinned a bit. "Just good? That's it?"

"No . . . no." Kerry shook her head, putting on a smile that felt a little forced. Heat flushed her cheeks and she realized with a start that she was embarrassed. Even felt a little guilty, which was just stupid since Jeremy'd encouraged her to go after just one night with Brian. Live the fantasy, he'd said. "It was good. I mean, it was really good."

"Yeah?" His hands moved over her ass, then under the robe to find her bare skin. "How good?"

"Twenty years of waiting good," Kerry told him honestly, because he'd asked and she'd never lied to him before so wasn't going to start now.

"Fuck, baby," Jeremy muttered at that. "Tell me. I want to know about it."

She'd have known he was getting turned on even if his cock hadn't started nudging her through the apron. She saw it in the gleam of his eyes, the throaty tone of his voice. It turned her on, too, knowing that whatever it was she'd done or would say was getting him hard.

"He looked good," she said. "Nice suit. Tie. Hair combed back but long so it could get messed up."

She and Jeremy were moving in an infinitesimally slow dance, their feet inching along the tiles in a minuscule circle. His gaze flared at her words. His smile twitched.

"Mr. Businessman."

"Something like that. He owns a car dealership."

"Oh . . . Mr. Salesman." His lip curled only the tiniest bit, but it made Kerry feel defensive.

"It was his dad's. Anyway, he worked there in high school and college and stuff. Now he owns it. Does that really matter?"

"No. I guess not." Jeremy bent to nibble at her throat.

The hot press of his teeth and tongue sent a shiver through her. "We danced. Hardly anyone was dancing, but it was fun. And then I asked him to go upstairs with me."

Against her neck, Jeremy paused. When he spoke, his lips tickled against her skin. "Just like that?"

"It's what I wanted," Kerry reminded him, not moving, though with her head tilted this way to give him access to her throat, she felt off balance.

Jeremy slid his mouth over her throat and jaw to finish at her mouth. "You brazen hussy."

"Hey, in that dress how could I have been anything else? Besides, when you only have one night, you want to start it as soon as possible. There wasn't anything else going on at the reunion I was interested in, really," she told him. "Sure, I could've won the raffle for the new HDTV, but I really just wanted to fuck Brian Jordan."

"I remember you telling me that once or twice." Jeremy tugged the tie of her robe so the silk fell apart and bared her breasts to him. He bent to suck her nipples until they stood up hard and tight. Just the way she liked it. "So . . . did he do this?"

Her voice had gone a little guttural. "Yes."

"He sucked your nipples?"

"Yes," she breathed as Jeremy bent back to suck and nibble at her tender flesh.

His hand shifted between her legs. "Fuck, babe. You're so wet already. Were you wet for him?"

"Yes."

Jeremy made a low sound and pinched her clit between his thumb and forefinger, tweaking it so she had to hold tight to his shoulder when her knees buckled. "Tell me what he did. All of it."

Kerry drew a breath, trying to find the words. Not sure she could speak them aloud, not with Jeremy's fingers working magic between her legs. Not sure she could find words to describe how it had been last night with Brian.

"I wanted to suck his cock, you know. I used to think about it. Imagine it. I used to look at my friend's mom's *Playgirl* magazines. We'd pore over these pictures of naked men, and I'd wonder if that's what Brian's dick looked like. And it was . . . just . . . oh, God." She had to stop, catch her breath. Jeremy had backed her up against the countertop, far from the hot stove top, and lifted her on top of it. Cool granite caressed her ass, distracting her.

He pushed her legs apart. "Tell me what it was like."

"It was just right. Not too long. Not too thick. I was worried he might have some sort of monster cock. He's a big guy, and . . ." Kerry shuddered and closed her eyes.

Jeremy laughed, low, his fingers still working on her clit. "Look at me."

She did.

"So he had the perfect prick. Nice. Was it pretty?"

She blinked, shifting her weight to tilt her hips against the pleasure his fingers were providing. "Pretty?"

Jeremy's smile quirked on one side. "Yeah. Did he have a pretty cock?"

"Yeah. Fucking gorgeous," Kerry said and waited to see if this would offend him. "I wanted to suck it. I used to think about it all the time. So I did."

Jeremy twitched a little. His gaze got hotter. "Did he eat your pussy, Kerry?"

A small noise escaped her at that question. She nodded, unable to answer. When he bent to take a long, slow lick of her cunt, she gripped the edges of the countertop so hard, her knuckles cracked.

"Like this?" Jeremy breathed on her wet flesh, then used his tongue to delicately drill her clit. Again, just how she liked it. He knew just how to please her. Turn her on. Get her off. When he used his lips to tug on her clit, Kerry tipped her head back to touch the cabinets behind her. "Did he eat this sweet cunt just like this? Lick your clit, huh?"

"Yes," she said on a moan.

Jeremy's tongue made smooth, steady strokes on her clit. He shifted her toward the edge of the counter and slid two fingers inside her at the same time. The pressure felt so good her hips gave an involuntary jerk, but Jeremy's other hand kept her anchored on the counter.

"Your pussy tastes so sweet, I bet he ate it right up. I bet he thought he was the luckiest fucking man on the earth, didn't he?" Jeremy's voice was muffled against her, every word another press and caress against her. "Did you come when he ate your pussy?"

She shuddered at the memory. "Yes, I did."

Jeremy pulled back and licked his lips. He leaned to kiss her, and Kerry tipped forward to give him her mouth, but he held back at the last second. He pulled her forward, off the counter, balancing her so she didn't fall. "Turn around."

She did, looking over her shoulder. "What . . ."

"Did he fuck you?"

"Yes," she said. "You know he did."

Jeremy pushed his hand between her legs from behind. His erection pressed her ass; automatically, Kerry leaned forward, hands on the counter, legs spread. Offering herself.

"Like this?" Jeremy whispered as he pushed inside her.

Filling her. Stretching her. Kerry let out a slow gust of breath and closed her eyes, taking him all the way in, even though this position was a little awkward. "No. I was on top."

"You like it on top," Jeremy said with a small laugh that sent another twinge of some strange emotion through her. Something like guilt. Something like excitement. Both so tangled up she couldn't separate them now, even if she could think straight. "But I like to fuck you from behind, Kerry. I bet he'd have liked it, too."

"He liked it just fine the way we did it," Kerry said with a small laugh that cut off as she drew in a breath when Jeremy moved inside her.

"No doubt. I bet you had him coming so hard the top of his head came off, didn't you, babe?" His hands smoothed over her back, over her ass. A wet finger slipped into her crack and pressed against her asshole, so she jumped—Jeremy knew she wasn't much for backdoor action, though he liked it. "I bet you looked so hot, didn't you. Riding him? Did you come when you were fucking him, too?"

"I did," Kerry managed to say as her orgasm rippled closer.

It wasn't what Jeremy was doing, fucking into her. It was what he was saying. What it made her think about. It was everything she'd done the night before, and oh, fuck, even though she'd taken a shower she hadn't washed him entirely away. She could still smell Brian on her, maybe just her imagination but there just the same. Taste him. It was the years of her fantasies all over again, but this time, based on reality.

Last night she'd fucked Brian Jordan, and he'd made her come not just once but twice, and now she was fucking another man in the kitchen they shared and she was going to come again. Her body didn't think this was a bad idea, why should her head? Or her heart, for that matter, which had begun pounding solidly as Jeremy's talented fingers and cock worked her closer and closer to coming.

Her fingertips skidded on the granite, which felt cool under her cheek when she pressed it there. Just for a second—Jeremy was fucking into her harder now, moving her whole body, and her skin skidded on the granite before she lifted her head again. Kerry couldn't think, couldn't move, could only let the waves of pleasure build and build until they spun her, tipping and tossing and shaking with all of it. She felt the press of Jeremy's fingertips harder against her ass and tensed, but he wasn't pressing inside. Even so, she was so turned on this added sensation pushed her over the edge. She gasped when she came and bit down on the two hard syllables of a name that did not belong to the man coming inside her.

He cried out, grinding his pelvis against her before slowing. One more thrust, then another, slower. Breathing hard, Jeremy leaned to press his face against her back. His cock softened, slipping out of her, followed by the thin, hot stream of fluid that reminded her they hadn't used a condom. Another difference between last night and this. Kerry grabbed a handful of paper towels and did a hasty cleanup before Jeremy turned her for a kiss.

A very smug, satisfied kiss, she thought when he pulled away with a grin. Not that she wanted him to be jealous—that would've been like she'd done something wrong. Cheated on him or something. And it wasn't cheating if he knew about it. Hell, had encouraged it. So no, she didn't want him to be jealous—but did she want him to be smug?

"What's that look?" she asked him as she tied her robe around her again and headed for the table to fill her belly with pancakes that would need to be reheated.

"No look. What look?" Jeremy took the last couple pancakes from the plate on the stove where he'd left them to make love to her. He gave her an innocent stare.

"Are you familiar with the phrase 'cat's got the cream'?"

He laughed. "Babe, you got the cream. All of it."

Normally Kerry would've laughed at this off-color humor, but today it sounded a little cruder than usual. She didn't laugh. She poured herself a mug of coffee, still hot, and sipped. Studying him.

"It really did turn you on, didn't it?" she said.

"Well . . . yeah. Of course. Why wouldn't it?"

She and Jeremy lived together. Shared bills, drove each other's cars without thinking twice about it. They didn't say they loved each other the way other couples did, a statement he'd told her in the beginning made him uneasy because it usually meant the other person was getting ready to leave, and though Kerry had always thought that was silly, she respected his wishes. Besides, as Jeremy always said, love wasn't in the words but in what you do.

Jeremy adored, worshipped, admired and cherished her. He

thought she was the bee's knees, the cat's pajamas, the best thing since sliced bread. He treasured and prized her, held her in high esteem.

But he hardly ever said he loved her.

"Well," Kerry said, "it's over now. It was just for one night, anyway."

Jeremy nodded and slid the plate of wheat toast toward her like this was any other Sunday morning, just the two of them, content in their relationship even if it wasn't quite like most other people's. "Right. Just one night."

Five

"Your game is way off, bro." Dennis clapped Brian on the back hard enough to send him stumbling—if Brian hadn't been expecting it, that is.

As it was, he managed to stay steady on his feet. "Yeah. Sorry."

"No prob. I'll gladly kick your ass." Dennis took the basketball from Brian's palm before Brian could stop him. He dribbled. He set up a shot and took it. Then he turned. "Seriously, though. What the hell?"

Brian hadn't even gone after the ball. Part of it was that every muscle ached. He'd been working himself hard lately. Really hard. Up early every morning for a run, an hour in the gym, these pickup one-on-ones. Anything to get his mind off Kerry and the night of the reunion. Of the morning after when she'd just up and disappeared. Part of it was that he just didn't give a rat's ass about basketball the way Dennis did. Dennis had played in high school when Brian had been spending time on the soccer field. It was something

Dennis never let him forget, and most days Brian rose to the challenge good-naturedly. Just not today.

"Distracted, I guess," Brian said. "I'm going to hit the showers."

"What? What the . . . ? No, bro. No." Dennis bounced the ball toward Brian so he had to catch it or let it fly away off to the side of the court. "Spill it."

"Spill what? Nothing to spill." Brian caught the ball easily in one long reach Dennis could never have mastered and passed it back.

"You've had your head up your ass for the past two weeks. Seriously. What's going on?" For once Dennis wasn't cracking jokes. He held on to the ball, too. He actually looked concerned. "You can tell me."

Brian wanted to tell someone. He'd been holding in the memory of that night until he felt he might explode from it. It wasn't like he could walk into the showroom and announce, "Hey, everyone, I not only got laid at my high school reunion, but it was by the girl of my dreams who's been in every stroke fantasy I've had for the past twenty years." Yeah, that would go over really well.

But . . . Dennis? Dennis had been Brian's best friend by default. Neighbors as kids, their moms best friends, they'd gone to preschool together and had never quite managed to piss each other off hard enough to break apart. Dennis had been a player in high school, dating girls and dumping them without mercy. While Brian had been trying to shrink his hard-on for Kerry Grayson in trig, Dennis had been banging any girl who'd let him get in her pants and taking blow jobs from the ones who wouldn't. Dennis had married his college sweetheart, settled down, had two cute daughters and a house with a dog.

What the hell would Dennis know about it?

" 'Fess up, pally."

"You know I hate it when you call me pally," Brian said as he swiped the back of his hand across his forehead. "Look, I really need to hit the shower. I have stuff to do at home."

Dennis scoffed. "What? Heat up a leftover pizza? Watch some Internet porn?"

"Whatever. Yeah." It didn't sound any better when Dennis said it than when Brian had been thinking about it.

"That's bullshit. Come home with me. Becky's probably making something really good."

Brian had spent his share of dinners with Dennis's family. Nights on their couch, too, once in a while, though not for a long time. Hell, he'd been the best man at Dennis's wedding.

"I slept with Kerry Grayson."

Dennis's jaw dropped. "No shit."

Brian didn't feel as triumphant as he'd tried to sound. "Yeah. At the class reunion—"

"Damn, I knew I should've gone to that, but we couldn't find a sitter. You punk! That was two weeks ago!"

Brian dodged the punch Dennis tried to land on his shoulder. "Yeah. I know. It wasn't something I wanted to brag about."

"Why the hell not? After all this time, you boned Kerry Grayson. Finally." Dennis paused, frowning. "What happened? You didn't pass out on her this time, did you? Shit, man. Tell me you didn't."

"I didn't."

"She got fat? Grew a mustache? Became a lesbian? No, wait. That would probably be hot."

Brian had to laugh, finally. "Nothing like that. She looked hot. She came on to me, actually."

Dennis was silent for a second. "Fuck my life."

"Fuck *your* life?" Brian flipped Dennis the middle finger. "You have a great life. Becky's great. The kids are great."

"It's not getting laid at my high school reunion by the piece of ass that got away," Dennis said. "But, yeah, I guess it's okay. Dude, you've had a boner for Kerry Grayson since senior year. And now . . . you banged her."

Brian gave him a pained look. "Please. We didn't . . . bang."

"Fucked," Dennis amended. "Screwed. Did the horizontal tango, knocked boots. Did she call you Mr. Flintstone 'cuz you made her bed rock?"

Something about Dennis's commentary always put a new spin on things. Brian laughed and tossed the ball back and forth between his hands. "It was good. She was good. It was all good."

"So? What's the problem? You got to put something to bed— literally," Dennis said seriously, "that's been hanging you up for years. What's the problem?"

"I can't stop thinking about her."

Dennis sighed and shook his head, then clapped Brian on the shoulder. "Dude. Dude, dude, dude."

Brian shrugged him off. "Yeah. I know. I looked her up on Connex and everything. But I haven't emailed her or anything."

"You request a connection?"

"No."

Dennis made chicken noises.

Brian shrugged. Maybe that had worked in elementary school, but not now. "Like I'm going to just randomly request a connection on Connex? Lame. We spent the night together, and in the morning she was just up and gone."

"And you're complaining?"

"Kerry and I were friends, man."

Dennis snorted. "A long time ago, you were friends. And let's face it, you were friends because you wanted to fuck her. That's all. Now you have. What's the deal, man? Was it that great?"

It had been the best sex he'd had in a long time. "It was good."

"You keep saying that. I think what you mean is that you came hard enough to leak brains out your ears, maybe, and you want some more of that. Am I right?"

"Something like that." But not everything like that.

Brian and Kerry had been friends. Good friends. Sex had come between them back then, he knew that now. Maybe not literal, actual sex, but lust. Romance. Whatever it had been. Stupidity. He didn't want that to happen again.

"Well . . . just request a connection from her. Then you can send her a message through Connex. Give her a call."

Brian had already looked her up online. Found her address and phone number. Knew where she worked. It made him feel like a stalker.

"You already know her number, don't you? Rat bastard, I see it in your face," Dennis crowed. "So what are you waiting for? Call her. Ask her out. If the pussy was that fine . . ."

"It's more than that," Brian said.

Dennis's eyes got bigger. He sighed. "Oh. Dude. You are fucked."

Brian shrugged. "I'm going home."

"No. You're going to call her. Right now." Before Brian could stop him, Dennis had sprinted to Brian's gym bag and pulled out his phone. "You have her in your contacts! I knew it!"

"Give me that!" Brian got there in a few strides, but not fast enough. Dennis was already thumbing in the numbers, engaging the call and thrusting the phone toward Brian.

Shit. Even if he hung up, her caller ID would probably show his name. That would look even . . .

"Kerry?" Brian said, his voice only a little raspy. "Hi. It's me. Umm . . . It's Brian. Brian Jordan."

Jeremy walked in on her as she was saying goodbye. Kerry pressed her thumb to her phone's touch screen and disconnected. Her breath felt hot. Her cheeks, too. Her heart was still pounding, though not as hard as it had done when she looked at her phone and saw Brian's name and number show up.

"Who was that?" Jeremy asked like he didn't really care, and he probably didn't. He tossed the mail onto the table and kicked off his shoes, lining them up on the mat by the door, then going to the fridge to peer inside.

"It was . . . Brian Jordan." God, just saying his name made her feel giddy. Kerry curled her fingers around her phone and pressed it between her breasts like that would stop her heart from beating right out of her chest.

Jeremy's head appeared around the fridge door, his eyes goggled. "Get the fuck out!"

"He wanted to meet me for coffee."

Jeremy stood, carton of milk in one hand, and closed the fridge door. Kerry searched his face, trying to gauge his reaction, but all she saw was the same old Jeremy. He cracked open the carton and poured himself a glass, then grabbed the package of Oreos from the bread box. She waited while he dunked one just long enough to make it soft, but not so long it would disintegrate.

"You going?" Jeremy pushed the cookie into his mouth, and droplets of milk clustered in the corners of his lips.

"I said I'd have to let him know."

"So you didn't say no." Jeremy swallowed the cookie and used his thumb to wipe the corners of his mouth.

Kerry put her phone on the table and went to him, though with the milk and cookies in his hands it was hard to get close enough to kiss him. She settled for holding on to his hips. "I'll tell him no."

Jeremy shook his head. "Why? Don't you want to have coffee with him?"

The truth was, the invitation had sent a thrill right through her. Before she could answer, Jeremy put down the glass and the cookies and took her in his arms. He looked at her with slightly narrowed eyes, a look she knew meant he was thinking about something. Hard.

"You should go," he said.

"No. I mean, why?" Kerry shifted closer to slide her hands up his chest and link behind his neck. "That would be awkward."

"Why? Because you fucked?"

"Well . . . yeah."

Jeremy laughed and kissed her, but briefly. "I thought you told me you and the fabulous Brian Jordan had been, like, best friends."

"That was a long time ago."

"So? Friends have coffee together, right? You could meet him for coffee. Why should it be awkward just because you had sex?"

"Theoretically you're right," Kerry said dryly. "However, the fact is that while we used to be friends, there was always that underlying sexual-tension thing going on, and now . . ."

"Now there's no tension. You should be even better buddies." Jeremy kissed her forehead and pushed past her, leaving the cookies and milk on the counter in his typical haphazard manner. "Grabbing a shower before I watch *Runner*. You coming?"

Kerry didn't move until he was almost through the doorway, then turned on her heel to follow him. "Jeremy. Wait."

"Babe, I feel gross. Talk to me while I shower. Or better yet," Jeremy said with a wicked smile that arrowed straight to her cunt, "you can come help wash me."

She laughed at that—also typical. "Yes, master."

"Ooh, I love it when you call me master." Jeremy walked backward down the hall for a few steps, reaching out to grab at her.

Kerry danced out of his reach but kept following him. "It would just be weird, that's all. Meeting him for coffee all casual-like. Yes, because we fucked. But also because . . . well, because I have you."

In the bathroom Jeremy didn't even pause in unbuttoning his

shirt as he answered. The shirt hit the hamper with unerring precision. He might be a little sloppy in the kitchen, but Jeremy was fastidious with anything that belonged to him. "It's not like I don't know you slept with him. And it's not like I wouldn't know about you having coffee. So what's the deal?"

Kerry leaned in the doorway to watch him stripping down. Jeremy might not be big and broad and tall, but damn, he was fit. Lean and sculpted. And lucky, she thought with a bit of envy. He hardly even had to work at it.

"The deal is that I'm with you, that's all. That thing with Brian was supposed to just be a one-time thing. I mean, I'm glad you were okay with it and all, and I had a good time. But it's not meant to get stirred up again."

Jeremy, naked now, faced her. "You think it would?"

"No." She shook her head so her hair swung. "Of course not. My feelings for Brian are just memories, that's all."

He tilted his head a bit to look at her. "So, like I said. What's the deal? It's just coffee. You're not gonna get on your knees to give him head right there in the coffee shop." He leaned into the shower to turn on the hot water, which squealed as it came on, the way it always did. "Although that would be totally fucking hot."

"Jeremy," Kerry said, annoyed.

He didn't look chastened, just stepped into the water and gave her another grin. "What? It would. Fuck, babe, I would love to watch that."

She frowned. "You would?"

"Sure. You give great head. And I love the way you touch yourself when you do it. How you get yourself off when you're sucking me. Tell you the truth, it's what I think about when I jerk off." His cock was rising even as he spoke, and Jeremy slid an un-self-conscious hand down to stroke himself further erect. "Damn, it makes me want to do it right now."

She wanted to tell him to close the shower door so water didn't spray all over the floor, but that would block her very nice view. Kerry didn't move from her place in the doorway, but everything inside her tightened as Jeremy's fist closed over the head of his prick and moved downward. Watching him fuck his hand fascinated her. Taught her a lot, too. And turned her on.

"You'd really want to watch me sucking another man's dick? Really?"

"Oh. Fuck, yes." Jeremy tipped his face into the spray so the water sluiced down his chest, over his cock. He looked at her again, water beading on his skin. "I told you, babe. Totally fucking hot."

An image of herself on her knees in front of Brian sent waves of heat over her that had nothing to do with the steam coming from the shower. Her nipples got hard, and she was glad her arms were crossed over her chest to hide this sudden, visible proof of how much the idea aroused her. She didn't move, but instead became hyperaware of her clit and the pressure of the seam of her jeans against it.

"Yeah," Jeremy said as though she'd said something. "Right there on your knees in front of him, your skirt hiked up. Showing that sweet ass, maybe a hint of your pussy from behind. No stockings and garters, none of that clichéd lingerie shit. Just your bare skin. Shirt open so I can see your nipples . . ."

He groaned and thrust his hips forward into his hand as he took a step back to lean against the tiled wall. He let go for a second, his cock bobbing and tapping his taut belly, then used a handful of body wash to lather himself. The water washed most of the suds off right away, but his hand kept moving. Stroking. Kerry watched, her gaze going back and forth between the delicious sight of his hard cock and his face. She loved watching him come.

"Yeah," he said, almost to himself, but looking at her. "And you'd take him all the way in, wouldn't you? All the way down your throat, Mr. Pretty Cock himself. Mr. Salesman."

"Don't call him that," she whispered, unable to talk any louder with her throat gone so dry.

Jeremy smirked, his eyes heavy lidded. "Maybe he'd put his hand on the back of your head, huh? Pushing you a little. Making you take it, right? But you totally could, babe, because you're just that fucking good. And you like it. You love it. Don't you?"

She did love it. That was the truth. Brian wouldn't do that though, she realized through the slow-syrup haze of arousal covering everything as she watched her lover stroke himself. Jeremy was the one who liked to put his hand on the back of her head, both of them pretending he had to coax her when the fact was she willingly took him as deep as she could. That she reveled in making him groan and moan.

Games. That was what Jeremy liked. Like this one, right now.

How long could she keep from touching herself? Or going to him, getting on her knees for him in the shower? Water pounding down, covering them, wreathed in steam. Kerry shivered. Jeremy saw it. He always did.

"Yeah, so he'd fuck your mouth just right. Is that what he did that night? Fucked that pretty mouth of yours? And you touched yourself, didn't you? Slid your fingers into your pussy, got them so wet, right? That's how it was. That's what you'd do, if you were sucking him right now. In front of me."

But that wasn't how it had been, Kerry sucking Brian's cock while she took care of herself. Brian had touched her, instead. He'd been the one to slide his fingers inside her, then up and over her clit, rubbing. Making her come. Not herself, but him.

"Damn, babe, I'd get so hot watching you I'd fucking bust my briefs right off." Jeremy's hand moved a little faster. He spread his legs, letting the shower hit his crotch. "And he'd be coming in your mouth, I'd be coming all over my fist and you . . . Oh, fuck, babe. You'd be coming, too. Wouldn't you?"

"Yes," Kerry told him, still in a whisper. She uncrossed her arms as her hands cupped her breasts, her thumbs passing over her nipples. One hand moved to cup herself through the denim. It wasn't enough pressure, but it still felt good.

"Take your clothes off," Jeremy told her.

She stripped out of her T-shirt and jeans, bra and panties, too, leaving everything balled up on the wet bathroom floor before stepping into the shower with him. The water was too hot. It stung. She gasped. When Jeremy kissed her, the water sealed their mouths and she had to break the kiss too soon because she didn't want to get water up her nose.

Jeremy took her hand and put it on his dick, then put his over it. He stroked slowly, so slowly she knew he was lingering deliberately. She thought he would push her shoulder, urging her to her knees. She was ready to do it, too, her mind full of the picture he'd painted. Her mind full of Brian.

Jeremy surprised her. That was typical, too. He was the one who got to his knees and pushed her back against the shower wall. He spread her with his thumbs, finding her clit with his tongue with unmistakable aim. He laved her flesh, and all Kerry could do was arch herself into the caress. She looked down at him, indescribably aroused by the sight of his right shoulder dipping as he stroked himself while he worked her cunt with his tongue and lips.

She blinked water from her eyes, wanting to see him, but then gave up and closed them. She gave up to sensation, too, letting it wash over her the way the water did. Incredibly, Jeremy kept talking even as he ate her pussy—the words were mumbled now, a little incoherent, but the added hum of his voice on her clit was what ended up sending her over. She didn't quite know what he was saying, but it didn't matter. She was coming in rippling undulations of ecstasy.

This orgasm, maybe because it had taken so little time to reach, was sharp. Bright. Kerry's muscles jerked with it, pumping her cunt harder against Jeremy's tongue. Until at last, blinking away the water, she looked down to see him staring up at her with a grin. So taken over by her own pleasure, she hadn't even heard him give the telltale grunting groan that usually signaled his orgasm, but that grin told her he'd come. Jeremy got to his feet and held his hands out to the water, washing them, then turned his face to the water to do the same.

"You should totally meet him for coffee," he said over his shoulder, casually.

Kerry didn't answer.

Six

"Chai latte." Brian set the cup on the table, followed by his own mug of black coffee he'd poured himself from the urn on the counter. He made his hands busy so he didn't have to look right at her.

"Thanks." Kerry's chair scraped as she moved.

Brian sat. He warmed his hands on the mug though they weren't cold. He just wanted something to do with them so he didn't do something stupid. Like, oh, reach across to take hers. He wanted to touch her, but other than the perfunctory half hug she'd offered when they greeted each other, Kerry had stayed far enough out of reach to make even a fake accidental brush of his hand on her sleeve impossible. Not that he could blame her. He should never have asked her out for coffee.

"Great day, huh?" Kerry gestured at the large front window through which sunshine poured in a strangely delineated square, leaving the rest of the coffee shop in cool shadow. "I know everyone's going to be complaining that it's too hot, but I like it this way. Beats all the rain we've had the past few weeks."

Great. They were talking about the weather. Brian hadn't bought coffee, he'd just paid for a one-way ticket to Lametown. He nodded, though, and sipped coffee so he could pretend his mouth was too full to speak.

"I'm glad you called me," Kerry said in a lower voice.

Hot coffee scalded his tongue. Brian winced. "You are? I mean, good. I mean, I'm glad."

She smiled, and he got the feeling she knew exactly what he was thinking. Which would've been some trick, since Brian wasn't exactly sure what he was thinking himself. Images of naked, writhing bodies mingled shamelessly with footage of them walking hand in hand along a beach with their shoes off, kicking at waves. He was such a freaking sap.

"I mean it," Kerry said.

Brian swallowed the taste of coffee that really needed some cream and sugar. "Me too."

Her smile got wider, bright as the square of sunshine surrounding them and just as hot. Brian tugged his tie a little, wishing he'd bought an iced drink. She'd be able to tell he was blushing.

But then something happened. Kerry started talking about her job—she worked as a registered nurse in labor and delivery at Harrisburg Hospital. It was clear she enjoyed her work, but more than that, her stories made Brian laugh. She was the same old Kerry, talking with her hands, adding accents and facial expressions to her jokes to make them funnier—and not in a contrived way or anything. Just being herself.

Maybe this hadn't been a mistake.

Brian sat back and watched her, his bitter coffee forgotten as she managed to pull information out of him he'd never have thought to tell her if she hadn't asked. It seemed that after their marathon conversation the night of the reunion there wouldn't be much ground to cover, but Kerry had a way of making Brian feel like she was interested in everything he did, not just the "important" stuff. Forty minutes later, they were laughing so loud they turned heads, and he did it.

He reached across the table and took her hand.

Kerry's laughter didn't cut off abruptly. More like it slid away into silence, though she was still smiling. She looked down at their hands, his much bigger and covering hers. He'd messed up, Brian thought. She was going to give him a sympathetic look and pull away.

Instead, Kerry turned her hand so she could link her fingers through his. "This is nice, Brian. Really nice."

He squeezed her fingers lightly. "Yeah. It's like—"

"Third-period study hall," she finished with him at the same time. "Yeah. I thought so, too."

"Aside from this," Brian said, barely lifting their hands.

"And the . . . other," Kerry said.

The night of the reunion, she meant. At least that's what he hoped she meant. Brian smiled. "Yeah. That, too."

They sat and stared at each other like a pair of idiots for a minute. Then Kerry's eyes flicked over his shoulder, and her smile disappeared. She looked apologetic.

"Brian, I have to go."

He nodded, acting like he wasn't disappointed even though his gut sank. "Oh. Sure. Right, of course. I guess I should go, too."

Kerry extricated her fingers from his and stood. "Thanks for the tea. And the talk. It was really great catching up with you. We should get together again some time."

Brian stood, too, wondering where it had gone wrong. She was looking at him with wary eyes, her smile definitely fake. Even after all these years, Brian could tell the difference.

"Sure. That would be great. I'll call you."

"You do that." She sounded like she meant it, but she didn't quite meet his eyes. "Thanks for the . . . I already said that."

"It's okay." He forced a laugh and stood awkwardly as she moved around the table.

He thought she might hug him, but she didn't even give him the one-armed social embrace she'd given him earlier. She patted his shoulder almost like an afterthought. She made a phone of her thumb and pinky and held it to her ear, then pointed at him. He nodded.

Then she left.

Brian didn't turn to watch her go. That wouldn't be a ticket to Lametown; that would be a first-class pass to Loserville. For one. He gathered the trash, threw it away and then took his mug back to the counter. All of that business took maybe five minutes, long enough for her to hightail it down the street and make the escape she'd seemed set on, so when he stepped out of the front of the coffee shop and saw her standing there, ready to come back in, he said the first thing that came to mind.

"What are you still doing here?"

Someone was behind him, trying to get out. Someone was behind her, waiting to get in. They were making a logjamb in the doorway, and both Brian and Kerry moved away at the same time. They ended up on the sidewalk a few feet from the door.

"Brian, I—"

"Kerry—"

Both stopped. Laughed. Brian wiggled his fingers, telling her to go first. Kerry took a deep breath and looked into his eyes.

"About that night," she started and said nothing else.

It wasn't right to talk about this in the middle of the sidewalk, right out in public, but they had no other place to go. Brian took her upper arm gently and led her to under the awning of the natural foods market next to the coffee shop. Nobody was going in or out of there. The bright sun didn't reach beneath the awning. Shadows painted her face. He wished he could take a picture, just then, but settled for trying to memorize it.

"I'm not sorry about it," she said.

"Me neither." That was an understatement.

"And it really was good to see you again, Brian. I mean it. This was so much like old times . . . but better, somehow. Maybe because we're grown-ups. I thought maybe that what happened would get rid of some of that old tension."

"Did it?"

She shook her head and gave him a more genuine smile. "No. Not at all. If anything, it made it worse."

He'd been holding his breath and now let it out in a rush. "Yeah. Yeah, it's all . . . Kerry, it's all I've been thinking about. You. You and me. And—"

She shook her head, and Brian shut up. "Just one night, remember?"

"Why does it have to be?"

She blinked rapidly and drew in a breath. "Brian, I have a boyfriend."

The earth moved, and not in the good way. In a very, very bad way. Acid lurched from his guts into his throat, burning. Making it impossible to speak, though his mouth opened. Brian took a step back.

Boyfriend?

Of course Kerry Grayson had a boyfriend. Of course she did. Why wouldn't she? Why would a woman as amazing as her be single? Just because Brian hadn't been able to commit to any woman for longer than a few months made him a screwup, not Kerry.

"Brian. Wait."

He hadn't really been paying attention to his feet taking him away until her voice stopped him. He didn't turn. Her hand touched his sleeve, and he wanted to pull away but didn't.

"I'm sorry, Brian. It's not what you think."

He shrugged. Started walking. "I don't think anything. I'll see you around."

Or not.

"Brian!"

He'd made it all the way to his car before she caught up to him. "He knows."

He stopped, not looking at her. "He knows what?"

"My boyfriend," Kerry said in a low, sad voice. "He knew that I'd had this . . . thing . . . for you forever, and so he just told me to go for it."

He turned. "Just go for it? Your boyfriend told you to sleep with me?"

"He was okay with it."

Brian swallowed bitterness. "Good for him."

"Hey," she said softly. "I'm sorry. I just thought, you know. One night. That it wouldn't matter. I didn't think you'd call me."

"Why wouldn't I, Kerry? I mean . . . God." Brian scraped a hand through his hair, hating the way it fell over his eyes. "I thought . . . never mind."

"Brian. I'm sorry. I really am. But this doesn't mean we can't be friends, does it?" She tugged his sleeve, and for one moment he thought she was going to take his hand. At the last minute, she let hers fall. "I mean . . . we used to be friends."

"That was a long time ago." It came out sounding harsher than he meant it. No, scratch that. It sounded exactly as harsh as he meant it to.

She got a look he remembered. A tiny crease between her eyebrows, a slight downward tilt of the corners of her mouth. He'd pissed her off, hurt her feelings. Well, too bad.

Kerry lifted her chin. "So . . . in other words, it was just a sex thing? If you can't fuck me, you don't want to have anything to do with me, is that it?"

That wasn't it. Not even close. Brian shrugged in reply rather than say so out loud.

She moved closer. She wasn't wearing heels as high as the night of the reunion, but she managed to get up in his face, just the same. "That's really shitty, you know that?"

"Worse than cheating on your boyfriend?" Brian shot back, stung because what she'd said would've been true if that was his reason.

"I didn't cheat on him." She paused. "I didn't cheat on *you*, either."

Her words punched him in the gut. He couldn't look her in the eye, afraid to be what Kerry was. Honest. Forthright. If he looked at her, she'd make him say what he was thinking, which was that was exactly how it had felt. Like she'd cheated on him.

"So . . . that's it? We fucked, now we can't be friends? Did you ask me to meet you for coffee just because you thought you'd get in my pants?"

"It wasn't like that," Brian said in a low voice.

She laughed without humor. "Right. That's why you can't even look me in the face."

The day was too bright for this sort of conversation. Too many people were around, walking back and forth. He really should get in his car and drive away, forget this whole mess.

"Look at me," Kerry said.

He did, reluctantly but helpless not to. She was frowning, her arms crossed. Then, surprising him, she took him by the tie and tugged him down to her level.

"If that's all that matters to you, Brian, then here it is. Take it."

And she kissed him.

Seven

She hadn't expected to kiss him, had expected even less for Brian to respond, but right there on the sidewalk in front of the coffee shop, their mouths met. Hard. She was standing on her tiptoes and pulling his tie to get his mouth to hers, and the kiss should've been swift. A statement more than an embrace. Except then Brian's hands found her waist, and he pulled her closer to him, and their mouths opened, tongues seeking each others' heat, and the kiss became something so much more than she'd intended.

Brian broke the kiss. From a distance his eyes looked solid brown, but this close, she could see the pale flecks of gold circling the black depths of his pupils. He blinked a few times, mouth open and wet. Then his hand came up and tugged her fingers away from his tie. He stepped back.

"Don't," Brian said. "Just . . . don't."

He turned and pulled his keys from his pocket, aiming a keyless remote at the door of the gray Volvo two cars away from them. He was a big man who looked suddenly smaller, and guilt swept over her. She'd done that to him.

"Brian," she said in a low voice, not shouting.

He didn't turn.

She shouldn't have kissed him. She knew that. It was selfish. She had no real excuse—she might've pretended it was to prove a point, but the real reason was that ever since the night of the reunion, she'd been unable to stop thinking about him. Kissing him. Fucking him.

Why then had it hurt her feelings so much to know that was the only reason he'd invited her out?

"Girls," Jeremy said fondly but with a roll of his eyes that irritated her. "What did you think he wanted you for, babe? Cawfee tawk? Really? Of course he was hoping he'd get laid."

"So then why did he walk away when I kissed him?" Kerry demanded, forgetting she'd left out that part of the story up until now.

"Wait a minute, what? Back it up. You kissed him?"

She bent over the sink to splash her face with water, closing her eyes. "Yes. I kissed him. I was mad."

Jeremy laughed and handed her a towel when she came up for air. "That's not really a good reason. You should've kissed him because you wanted to take him someplace and jump his bones."

Kerry snapped the towel out of his hands and dried her face, then hung it on the rack. Irritated, she turned away to smooth cream into her skin. "Maybe I did."

Jeremy was silent at that, for so long Kerry finally had to finish her nighttime preparations and look at him. He was ready for bed. Bare chest, low-hanging pajama bottoms that showed the treasure-trail line of hair leading from his belly button down to his pubic hair.

"Does that bother you?" she asked quietly.

"That you wanted to?"

She nodded. Jeremy pulled her close. She thought he might kiss her, but he only looked at her, eyes moving over every inch of her face before settling on hers.

"No. It doesn't bother me. Because you told me, right? Then it's not a lie."

This should've made her feel better and didn't. "I just told you I kissed another guy. That I wanted to have sex with him. You're not bothered at all?"

"Babe," Jeremy said, sounding so reasonable she knew the tone was meant to point out how irrational she sounded. "It's not like I didn't know."

"What's that supposed to mean?" Annoyed, Kerry pushed away from him to finish getting ready for bed. This meant pulling her hair on top of her head with an old faded scrunchie she'd worn . . . yes, in high school. Probably in that damn trig class.

Kerry didn't give him time to answer. Jeremy followed her to the bedroom, where she tossed back the comforter, sat on the bed, feet still on the floor, and began covering her arms with lotion. The bed shook when Jeremy crawled across it from the other side to stretch out behind her. His fingers traced along her spine where her tank top had ridden up to expose her back. The touch sent a not-unwelcome chill through her. Then another when he replaced his fingers with the heat of his tongue.

"Answer me, Jeremy."

"It means that I knew you still wanted to fuck him, that's all."

Kerry twisted to look down at him. He gave her an unapologetic grin. She didn't return it. This was complicated now, more than she'd ever thought it would get.

"You wouldn't have gone to meet him for coffee if you hadn't," Jeremy continued matter-of-factly. "Just like he wouldn't have asked you. Dudes don't generally have crazy, random, mind-blowing sex with a woman and then call her up for coffee just so they can talk about the weather. Women don't, either. Not really."

"You think men and women can't be friends?"

"Nope. Not once they've fucked, anyway."

He sounded so glib, so smug, she wanted to poke the smile right off his handsome face. She settled for turning her attention back to the lotion she was vigorously applying to every inch of exposed skin. Behind her, Jeremy laughed softly.

"You're not pissed he wants to sleep with you, Kerry."

"No?" She gifted him with a glance over her shoulder.

Jeremy sat and rested his chin on her shoulder as he put his arms around her. His back pressed hers, and Kerry softened into his embrace. She turned her head the smallest bit to rest it on his.

"You're pissed because you offered it, and he walked away."

A frown slashed her face, but she couldn't deny the truth. Jeremy kissed her bare shoulder. His hands slid over her belly, then up to cup her breasts. His mouth moved to her neck, and Kerry tilted it to give him free access.

"He was upset when I told him about you," she admitted.

Jeremy paused in kissing her. "Why'd you tell him?"

Again she twisted to look at him. "Because it's the truth. I have a boyfriend. I have you."

"It might've gotten you laid if you hadn't." He said it like he was joking, but the smile didn't quite reach his eyes.

"And it would've been a lie!"

"Hey, hey," he soothed. "I didn't mean to make you mad, too."

Kerry forced away her irritation. "It was a mistake to sleep with him, even if I did want it so much. I have a boyfriend. We have a relationship, Jeremy—"

"I told you, I wanted you to do it. I wanted you to have something you wanted so much. What, that makes me a bad guy now? Wanting you to be happy?"

To her surprise, he pulled away from her with a scowl and pushed over to his own side of the bed. He punched the pillow a few times before tossing himself down on it, facing away from her. Kerry blinked.

"No. I didn't mean that you were a bad guy. But I shouldn't have done it. It hurt Brian, and I can't blame him for being hurt. And I don't want it to hurt us."

"It won't. I told you that. It was just—"

"Yeah, just one night. I know. We said that." She paused. "But just now I told you I wanted to do it with him again, and you seemed to think that was still okay. You encouraged me to have coffee with him, as a matter-of-fact. And now I find out you thought all along I wanted to sleep with Brian again, and you don't seem bothered by it at all, which I should be happy about—"

"Yeah," Jeremy cut in. He sat. "You should be happy about it, Kerry. Because most guys wouldn't be. They'd be pissed off you even thought about fucking another guy, but I didn't get mad. I told you to go for it. To get what you want, what would make you happy. Where's the crime in that?"

"No crime." But it felt like there should be one. "I'm just trying to understand."

Something flickered in Jeremy's gaze. He drew his knees to his chest, linking his fingers over them to hold them in place. He rested his chin on them and looked at her with an expression she couldn't read.

"I like the idea of you with other men. It turns me on. It always has."

Kerry chewed the inside of her cheek, mirroring his position. Sitting this way made a barrier between them, and she hated that it felt like they needed one. "Okay."

He didn't laugh. Didn't smile. Just gave her that flat, unreadable stare. "You didn't seem to have a problem with that a few weeks ago."

That sounded too close to an accusation for her tastes. "The idea of me with other men is different than the reality of it, Jeremy."

"Oh, like the difference between fantasizing forever about fucking Brian Jordan versus actually doing it?"

"Yes, exactly like that!"

Jeremy's expression didn't change. "I thought you'd enjoy it. And I wanted to know about it. I liked hearing about it. It gets my dick hard, what can I say? It's getting hard right now, thinking about you with him. I'm not asking you to go out and fuck random guys without telling me, Kerry. But you wanted him. Bad. Brian Jordan. Fuck, he's like some sort of . . . Mecca for you, or something. When you talked about him, you just transformed. Your eyes lit up. You always pretended like it was no big thing, but I could tell it was more than that. So, hey, I encouraged you to fuck him. You got what you wanted and so did I. So did he, for fuck's sake. What's the big deal?"

"No big deal. It happened. It's over now. It won't happen again."

Jeremy snorted. "You think because he walked away that he doesn't want you? You really think knowing you have a boyfriend could possibly keep him from fucking you again? He's a guy."

"You . . . you want me to sleep with him again?" She tried to sound confident and unconcerned, like this was the no big deal she'd previously claimed. Truthfully, her heart had started pounding and her throat went tight, her cheeks heating.

At last, he gave her a smile. "When you're on a diet, what do you want more than anything?"

"Milk and cookies," she said at once.

"And what do you think about the entire time you're telling yourself you can't have them?"

"Eating milk and cookies," Kerry admitted. "And then I drink an entire half gallon and eat the whole package."

"And then you moan about how your pants don't fit."

"Infidelity isn't milk and cookies, Jeremy."

"It's not infidelity if it's not a lie, Kerry. You spent a fuck-long time wanting him. Maybe you just need to get him out of your system. And him you, it sounds like. Maybe you just need to fuck yourself raw, you know? Get past it." Then, softer, "It doesn't have to change what we have, babe. Right?"

"No. No, it doesn't."

But somehow, Kerry thought it already had.

Eight

Brian couldn't sleep, which sucked, because he was exhausted. Ever since the day in the coffee shop he'd been unable to go longer than a few hours without waking up, tossing and turning. Never an early riser, now he was up before the sun, heading for a run just to get the thoughts of her out of his head.

Dennis had told him he was a loser for walking away, and Brian hadn't bothered to explain his reasons. Yeah, he wanted to get laid. Yes, he still had the volcanic hots for Kerry Grayson. And no, he wasn't so much of a pussy that he thought it had to "mean something."

Except it did. Or he wanted it to. Or it felt like it should. Not the being friends part—sure, they'd been buddies back then but time had passed. People changed. Just because they seemed to still have a lot in common and enjoyed talking to each other didn't mean they had to become besties. He didn't really think they'd be able to fall back in time to when they'd been close enough to know just what the other meant with nothing but a raised brow and a smile.

Brian had to face it. He was hurt she'd used him to cheat on her boyfriend. Or not cheat, as she put it, even though he didn't see how any guy who was lucky enough to have Kerry as his girlfriend could possibly be stupid enough to know she was off with another guy and not lose his mind about it. She hadn't lied to him. He hadn't asked if she had a boyfriend, after all.

Now at least he understood what the "complicated" meant on her Connex profile.

It didn't help that the pictures from the reunion were starting to show up. He and Kerry were both tagged in a bunch of them. Apparently their little tête-à-tête on the dance floor had been quite a show.

He groaned, looking over the various photo albums. Kerry, her head tipped back in laughter. Kerry, that gorgeous body outlined in the dress that had made his head spin. Him, looking down at her with a look on his face that was so clearly, stupidly infatuation his cheeks heated looking at it.

There were shots of them dancing, too. Kerry swirling, her hem lifted to show off her shapely legs. Brian, looking like an ass but laughing as she spun out at the end of his arm, their fingers linked. And then another, blurred, of the moment she'd spun back in and ended up pressed against him so tight he thought he could feel her panties through her skirt. That one was out-of-focus, Brian and Kerry not the subject of the photo. Just a moment, caught in the background of something else.

He remembered it, though. How it had felt to have her pressed up against him like that. It had felt more like a reunion than any of the silly place cards or name tags had made him feel.

Shit. There was video, too. For a moment he hesitated before clicking on it, but desire won out over common sense. He moved the cursor over the "play" button on the embedded video.

The music and voices were too loud, the colors too bright, but this was some footage shot from someone's digital camera, not Oscar-worthy cinematography. Not that it mattered. A wide shot of the ballroom. Then a close-up on Gina, talking excitedly about something, her words slurring.

In the background, Brian and Kerry dancing.

His dick filled at the sight, more from memory than what they were actually doing. They hadn't been grinding or anything. They looked like they were having fun. Hell, they had been having fun.

He spun her out. Then back in. There it was, the moment, caught on video. Kerry pressed against him, one of her feet on the floor and the other up behind her in a clichéd, black-and-white-movie pose. They were laughing, but he held her close, his hands now on her hips.

And then, there it was. The DJ, voice muffled in the video but clear as crystal in Brian's memory, announced dinner. In the tiny window, Kerry leaned forward and said something to Brian, who was happy to see he didn't look as stunned as he'd actually been. They both smiled, nodding. And then . . . exit, stage right. They disappeared from the edge of the video.

That was when she'd taken him upstairs. Now his dick fully tented his sweatpants. Brian clicked off the video and logged out of his Connex account. He sat in front of his computer with a prick so hard it hurt and balls the color of Superman's tights.

It wouldn't have been the first time he'd wanked in front of his computer, helped along by porn clips of women with monstrously huge tits and platform shoes. The idea of it didn't appeal now. The only woman in his head was Kerry, and he wasn't yet so much a loser that he was going to jerk off sitting here and thinking about her.

No, he was going to go upstairs to bed and do it.

Brian took the stairs two at a time, trying to think down his cock, which wouldn't be eased by anything but a good old-fashioned stroke session. Okay, so it made him a pathetic, lonely loser. That wasn't news. Halfway to the bed, he stripped out of his sweatpants and T-shirt. On the bed he settled himself against the pillows and pulled out a bottle of lube he kept in his nightstand. Everything a guy needed for a little solo action.

At least he hadn't sent away for one of those silicone tubes that Dennis had sent him the link to. The kind with a mouth, pussy or asshole at the end of it. Something for every taste. Dennis had said he didn't order one, but Brian thought he probably had.

Actually, thinking about Dennis's sex toys was making Brian's cock shrink a little bit. But not enough. Because then he was back to thinking about Kerry again. He squirted a palm full of lube and cupped his balls with one hand, then took his dick in his fist.

It always felt so good, that first stroke. All the way down, then all the way up. His fingers curved, closed over the head, and he lay back to spread his legs even wider. Kerry's mouth had been tighter and hotter than his hand. Her pussy, too. Sweet, hot, tight and wet.

He wasn't going to draw this out. This wasn't lovemaking or even fucking. It was self-maintenance, that was all. Clear out the balls so he could maybe get some sleep and face tomorrow with a fresh head. Maybe just get her out of his mind once and for all.

He was getting close when his cell phone rang. He was going to ignore it, but unfortunately, Brian had forgotten that he'd left it under his pillow. The ringtone was distracting him, so he fumbled for it with his free hand and was just about to send the call to voice mail. When he saw who was calling, his thumb slipped and connected the call instead.

"Brian? It's Kerry."

Kerry. And there he was with his dick in his hand. An inferno flooded him. This was worse than getting caught reading girlie mags by his mother back in the day. Worse, somehow, because the sound of Kerry's voice did nothing to shrink his dick and only made the feeling of his still-moving hand all the better. Worse because she had no idea, and he was like some sort of crazy stalker perv, jerking off without her knowing.

"Brian?"

"I'm . . . here," he managed to say. He gripped his cock tight, no longer stroking. It didn't make the pleasure die down. If anything, he felt even closer to spilling.

"I just wanted to say I was sorry for what happened. I should've told you right up front, but I didn't. So . . . I'm sorry."

"It's okay." It wasn't, really, but he wasn't exactly able to say much more.

His hand drifted slowly, slowly up his erection.

"It's not okay. But . . . Brian . . . listen. Here's the thing. I shouldn't have gotten mad that you asked me out for coffee because you were interested in more than friendship. Because . . . well, that's the reason why I said yes."

He closed his eyes. Licked his mouth. Imagined the taste of her. His brain was fuzzy. "*Why* did you say yes?"

"Because I was interested in something other than friendship. I mean other than *just* friendship. Of course friendship is important. And good. And I'd like us to be friends, Brian."

Slowly, slowly. Up. Then down. His cock felt huge, gigantic. Balls heavy. His toes had started to curl.

"Uh-huh."

"And . . . I really want to fuck you again."

His hand clamped down, effectively cutting off the orgasm ready to boil out. "What?"

"I haven't been able to stop thinking about it. About you. I think the only way to get it out of my head—"

"Wait. Wait," Brian said in a thick voice. "What about your boyfriend?"

"He's okay with it. I told you. But I want you to be okay with it, too."

"With what?"

"Brian," Kerry said after the briefest pause, "do you want to fuck me again?"

"Yes," he said without a second thought. "I can't stop thinking about it, either."

Then, he tried to be like Kerry. Honest and forthright. "I'm lying here with my dick in my hand right now, thinking about you."

Silence. Shit. He'd fucked up.

Then, "Oh . . . Brian. Oh God."

"I'm sorry," he said hastily, but she cut him off.

"No, no, don't be sorry. That's so . . . it's so sexy," Kerry whispered. "Oh God, Brian. Right now? You're jerking off right now?"

"Yes," he whispered, too, though he had nobody to overhear him. "I was looking at all the pictures people have been putting up online and I started thinking about you, and that night, and . . ."

She sighed into the phone. "That's beautiful."

He found a laugh. "I don't know how beautiful it is."

"You," Kerry said, "are fucking gorgeous, and your cock is delicious. And beautiful. And the thought of you making yourself come is making me want to touch myself, too."

He admired her ability to say what she was thinking. Intimidated by it a little, but at the same time, hellaciously turned on. He made a low noise in the back of his throat. He wanted to stop, or at least tell her to stop, but . . . hell, he was too close now.

"You're close, aren't you? I can tell by the sound of your voice."

He muttered a sound of agreement. His hand moved faster as his hips pumped. The phone gripped in his other hand pressed his ear hard enough to hurt, but Brian couldn't focus on that now. It was enough to hear Kerry's whisper urging him on.

"I wish I was there right now," she said. "I wish I could be there to see you."

This all felt so wrong and so right at the same time. "Kerry . . ."

It was all he could get out before his throat tightened on a groan and he gave himself up to the pleasure that wrung him dry. He came in hard, short bursts. The smell of sex covered him. His cock throbbed, balls tingling. His strokes stopped. He drew in a breath and opened his eyes, blinking to clear the haze of arousal.

"You okay?" She sounded like she was smiling.

"Umm . . ." Brian looked down at his bare stomach, glistening in the aftermath. "Yeah. I'm okay."

"That was pretty amazing. Talk about good timing."

She was making light of this, and Brian wished he could let her. He sat up and grabbed a handful of tissues to wipe his skin and took care of cleanup while juggling the cell phone. "Yeah. About that."

"Before you say anything, please. Just think about what I said."

"About wanting to have sex with you, even though you have a boyfriend?"

She paused. He hoped that meant she was at least thinking about the importance of her words. "Yes."

Brian tossed the crumpled tissues into the garbage can and settled back onto the pillows, crunching them to prop himself up. "I don't know, Kerry. It just seems wrong."

"It's his kink," she said. "He likes to think about me with other men."

His stomach tumbled. "So this isn't just me? Because—"

"No," she cut in. "God, no, Brian. It's just you. I promise you, this isn't our normal thing. I mean, Jeremy has this thing about seeing me with another guy, I guess. It's not that uncommon. But no, it's not anyone else. I wouldn't. I mean . . . I don't want to. It's just you. It's been you for a long time."

"We both keep saying that. But you said only one night, too. What happened to that?"

"It wasn't enough," Kerry said in a low voice.

"No," Brian answered after a second, meaning every word he said. "No, it wasn't. Not at all."

Nine

It wasn't a date. Kerry reminded herself of that. Not a date in the traditional sense, anyway. They'd gone to dinner, sure, but that had seemed appropriate, and besides, Jeremy'd had plans tonight, so she'd have been eating alone anyway. And they'd walked along the riverfront, not holding hands or anything romantic like that. And when they got in his car to go back to his place, Brian had held the door open for her, a courtesy she'd forgotten could be so damned sexy.

Now she stood in his living room while he poured them both glasses of wine she wasn't sure she could drink. "Great place."

He looked up from the bar separating the kitchen from the living room. "Thanks."

His place was in one of the buildings that had been trendy a number of years ago, apartments carved from an old shoe factory. Brian's flat was a nice, big three-bedroom that easily matched the size of her entire house. Too big for one guy, even though it was really nice.

"How long have you lived here?" She took the glass of wine he handed her and sipped it, letting the mouthful rest on her tongue before she swallowed.

"Five years." Brian looked around the room and set the glass on the coffee table without drinking from it. She noticed that. "They had some sort of financial trouble and were selling apartments for less than what I could've spent for a town house, and the maintenance and stuff's included in the tenant-association fees. So I bought it. Want a tour?"

"Sure." Kerry put her glass down, too.

Brian showed her the living room and kitchen, both furnished tastefully but sparsely. A separate dining room had only a card table and four folding chairs, and Brian laughed as he showed her. "I don't have many dinner parties."

"I can see that. What's through here?" A short hall led to the first bedroom that had been set up as an exercise room. "Wow. Nice setup."

The entire far wall had been mirrored. As Kerry stepped forward and Brian followed her, she glanced up to catch him staring at her with a look she wasn't sure she could interpret. They both stopped, her gaze snaring his in the reflection.

When he moved closer behind her, Kerry was already tilting her head to expose the line of her neck. When he kissed her there, she closed her eyes with a sigh. Brian's hands fit naturally on her hips, his thumbs settling into the dimples on either side of the base of her spine. His heat covered her. She was glad they hadn't carried their glasses. It would've been tough to find a place to put them down in here.

"Kerry."

She opened her eyes and watched him mouth her neck and the slope of her shoulder, exposed by the neckline of her sweater. "Hmmm?"

Brian looked up. "You smell good."

She smiled. "Thanks."

He turned her to face him. They kissed slow and leisurely, without the frantic pace of the last time. Brian cradled the back of her head, another courtesy Kerry wouldn't have expected to be so sweet. The height difference meant she had to tip her head back pretty far even though he bent to reach her. That hand on the back of her head, his fingers sinking into her hair, made a huge difference.

Even so, to ease the distance between them, Kerry pushed up onto her toes and slid her arms around Brian's neck. The kiss ended naturally, both of them taking a breath at the same time. She smiled, looking deep into his eyes.

"Hey," Kerry said softly.

"Hey."

"You have other rooms, huh?"

Brian laughed and kissed her again. This time when he scooped her into his arms, Kerry wasn't as surprised. It was different, feeling so small, and she laughed and kicked her feet as she clung to him. Brian had to turn sideways to get them both through the doorway, but once in the hall he kissed her as he walked, not seeming to mind her weight one bit. Kerry let out a little squeak against his lips, though, as he stopped in a second doorway but didn't go through.

"Guest room," he said, tilting her so she could see inside to another sparsely furnished room. Another few steps down the hall, Brian said, "bathroom."

At the end of the hall he stepped with her through a double doorway, both doors open, and into a large bedroom.

"My room." He moved easily to the bed, though Kerry could feel his arms beginning to shake, just a little bit.

"I'm impressed," she said as Brian laid her on the bed. "I thought for sure you were going to drop me."

"Never." He made it sound like a promise.

His kiss felt like a promise, too, but one Kerry thought was meant to be broken. Brian kissed her differently than he had the night of the reunion. More confidently. Or maybe the change wasn't in him, but her. That first night she'd set about getting what she wanted. Tonight, Kerry felt somehow more shy.

They kissed for a long time, longer than she'd have expected. She couldn't remember the last time she'd just made out with a guy without it leading automatically and swiftly into sex. Every time his hands moved over her, skating along her shoulder or over her belly, Kerry tensed, waiting for him to cup her breast or slide between her legs.

"Tease," she murmured finally, when Brian had yet again moved his hand over her thigh without even pushing up the hem of her skirt.

He gave her an unapologetic grin. "I thought tonight we could take our time."

"Here I thought you might be trying to re-create all those horny and unfulfilled days of high school." Kerry could tease, too.

"Maybe that, too." Brian moved in to kiss her, but paused a breath away from her mouth. "Back then I'd have been too afraid to touch you. You'd have said no."

"I wouldn't have. I won't now." She arched a bit, though their mouths still didn't meet.

His fingers circled lightly on the outside of her skirt. When he kissed her this time, damn if she didn't feel like they were back in high school, playing "will you, won't you?" Brian's fingers curled the hem of her skirt, then brushed the inside of her thigh. Kerry shivered.

"Yes?" he whispered.

"Yes."

Brian pressed closer. His fingers moved higher. His tongue

stroked hers. His knuckles brushed the outside of her panties. "Yes?"

"God, yes."

It was hard to kiss a smile, but she managed. It was a little harder to keep kissing him when she gasped, which she did when Brian pushed his fingers beneath the waistband of her panties. He found her clit at once, not circling it, just applying steady and gentle pressure.

"Yes," Kerry whispered as his mouth left hers and found the tender and sensitive spots of her neck and throat. "Fuck. Yes, Brian. Just like that."

He made a low noise at her words, and Kerry noted the reaction. He liked dirty talk? Good. She liked talking dirty. Jeremy—but she wasn't thinking of him right now. Everything was here, not there. This man, not that one. Everything now was Brian Jordan, the real thing, not a dream.

He rubbed her clit just the way she did when she was pleasuring herself. Few men had ever touched her that way, with the same amount of pressure, the same pace. He even dipped down inside her to coat his fingertips with her wetness the same way she did.

Pleasure vibrated through her. She rocked her hips in time with his strokes. Brian kissed her harder, deeper, mimicking the thrust of his fingers inside her with that of his tongue. She wanted to tell him to stop, to get naked, or at least to take his cock out and fill her with it, but desire had made her dumb. Within minutes she was so close to coming it was too hard to think straight, much less verbalize. The best she could do was a low, throaty hum of encouragement.

Brian had stopped kissing her, but Kerry, back arched and eyes closed, couldn't bring herself to reach for him. Everything centered between her legs. The slow stroke-stroke of his fingers inside her, thumb on her clit. She fisted her hand in the front of his shirt, twisted the fabric, while the other reached over her head and found the comfort of the headboard spindles. She gripped it tight, tensing with her impending orgasm.

Calling it waves of pleasure was such a fucking cliché, but that's exactly what it was. The first wave lifted her and she rode it, cresting and crashing. Tumbling. Head over heels, Kerry plummeted into ecstasy. Then up again, not as high, but the downward plunge was twice as hard. The headboard creaked under her grip. She cried his name, plus some other things she couldn't have made sense of had she tried. Fuck talk.

Kerry opened her eyes. Brian watched her, his gaze dark, mouth set, brow furrowed. He looked like he was concentrating, hard, but when he saw her looking, he gave her a brilliant smile that forced another last set of ripples through her.

Kerry fell back against the pillows and let go of his shirt and the headboard. Her fingers ached a little from holding so tight. Brian slid his fingers out of her cunt but rested them over her panties.

"Wow," she said.

"I love to watch you come."

Kerry swallowed, catching her breath. "A man who likes to watch women come is a good, good man, Brian."

His smile quirked. "Not women. You."

The breath she thought she'd caught stuck in her throat. "Brian—"

He shook his head. "Never mind."

She didn't want to go there. She did, however, want to go someplace lower. Kerry rolled to face him and cupped his delightfully hard cock through his jeans. "What's this?"

"Golly, I'm not sure. Maybe you could find out?" The "aw-shucks" tone suited him perfectly. So did the choir-boy expression—wide eyes, hair falling just so over his forehead.

"If I didn't know better, I'd think you were totally innocent. Fortunately, I do know better." Kerry unzipped his fly and slipped a hand inside to find him through the soft fabric of his boxers. "Brian, baby, you have got such a pretty cock. Let me see it."

There was already heat between them, but at her words Kerry felt a rise in the temperature. She looked at his face. Blushing? Oh God. Too fucking precious.

Brian tugged open the button on his jeans, opening them wider, and pushed them down his hips. Kerry moved back to watch him as he wriggled free of the layers of denim and cotton, then as he reached over his shoulder to pull his shirt up and over his head. Naked, he stretched out next to her, his cock pointing upward.

She didn't move. She drank her fill of the sight of him. All lean, strong male. Muscles defined but not overexaggerated. Belly flat and taut, hinting at a six-pack but not flaunting one. He used that workout room just right.

"You're making me nervous," Brian said.

His cock showed no sign of fear. Kerry leaned to take him in her hand. She stroked him just twice before she tugged her sweater off over her head, leaving her in a pale blue lacy bra. That didn't last much longer. Nor did her skirt and panties. Naked, she pressed herself against him, offering her mouth. Between them, his cock twitched on her belly.

Brian kissed her. His hands roamed her back, then over her ass. She wasn't surprised when he rolled her. Brian pushed up on his arms. A shift of his hips just an inch or so lower, and he'd be inside her. First, though, he reached to pull open the nightstand drawer and take out a condom. He held it up.

"Ribbed for her pleasure? Very nice," Kerry said.

"I'm a nice guy."

"You"—she cupped his balls before sliding her fist up and over his cock—"are an extremely nice guy."

Brian knelt, and Kerry helped him roll the rubber down. They both stared at his erection, fully sheathed. Then at each other.

Brian surprised her with the swiftness of his kiss, with how fast he covered her with his body, how quickly he guided himself inside her. Kerry gasped when he pushed into her cunt. Brian pulled away the barest bit, his lips brushing hers with each word.

"Too fast?"

It wasn't. She answered him with a kiss. She moved her hands down his sides to grip his hips, urging him forward. "Fuck me, Brian. Hard. Right now."

But he didn't. He eased in and out of her as carefully as he'd kissed her for that long hour he'd taken before touching her. Brian held his weight on his hands, looking down into her face, adding a roll of his hips that brought his pubic bone directly against her clit. Over and over again he pushed inside her.

Kerry had never come this way—oh, she could push a hand between them and use her fingers to bring herself off at the same time, but this . . . this was different. This was incredible. Every time she thought certainly he would have to give in to his own desire, fuck faster, finish, Brian only took that extra moment to rub himself exactly where she needed it.

"Brian . . ." It was all she could manage. She rolled her hips, pulling him in deeper. She needed him, all of him, inside her as far as he'd go.

At last, maybe driven by the sound of his name, Brian fucked faster. Deeper, almost but not quite hard enough to hurt. Kerry hooked her heels over his calves, and they moved together in perfect time.

She came hard, pleasure like a slap. An explosion. Brian shuddered against her. They came together, something so startlingly wonderful Kerry couldn't breathe.

After, curled in his arms, she felt herself drifting into contented sleep and had to force herself to blink herself awake. Carefully, she sat, thinking he'd fallen asleep. Not wanting to wake him, she crept from the bed to find her clothes.

Brian's voice stopped her as she stepped into her panties. "I want to see you again."

Kerry paused. She turned. She calculated schedules, the practicality of juggling this "one night" with the rest of her life. None of that mattered when she went back to the bed to kiss him again. When she whispered against his mouth the only answer she could give.

"Tomorrow. I'll see you again tomorrow."

Ten

Three weeks.

For three weeks, Brian had been sleeping with Kerry, knowing that every time she left him to go home, she was going back to the other guy. She didn't pretend otherwise, though Brian did. When he called her and that other guy answered with a casual, "Oh, hey, Brian. Hold on, I'll get her," or worse, "She's in the shower, can she call you back?" something inside Brian tightened like a fist.

"Hey, Brian." Dennis punched Brian's shoulder. "We ready to rock and roll, or what?"

Brian shook himself. "Yeah. Right, rock and roll."

He passed Dennis a key marked with a paper tag and stepped aside to let his friend ogle the sweet little red Volvo convertible he was taking for a test drive. The top was already down, and Dennis was practically rubbing his hands with glee. They both knew it was sort of a joke. Dennis would trade his currently filthy station wagon in for a newer, cleaner model basically just like it. His days of convertible driving were long past, what with the wife and kids and dog and everything Brian envied. Even so, it never hurt to let Dennis take the car for a spin, get people to check it out.

"So," Dennis said as soon as they'd left the parking lot and had passed across the highway onto some twisty-turny back roads that would take them through the best of Pennsylvania farm country. "What's up with you? Haven't seen you at the gym for basketball, nothing. You don't even answer my Connex posts, you douche."

"Yeah, not sending you seeds for *Farmtown*, that really makes me the douche, huh?" Brian rolled his eyes and focused on the ribbon of road ahead of them.

Dennis turned off the music. This was a move so unprecedented that Brian turned to him in shock. The look on Dennis's face was worse. Something bad was up.

"I'm worried about you, man," Dennis said.

For a moment Brian wasn't sure he'd heard right. "What?"

Dennis slowed the car, then pulled into a gravel drive leading about a mile back to a big white farmhouse. He put the convertible in park and twisted in the seat to face Brian. "I'm worried about you."

The day was perfect for riding with the top down, but sitting here in the baking sun wasn't as good. The heat in Brian's cheeks didn't help. He shrugged, not sure where Dennis was going with this but knowing it couldn't be good.

"I'm fine."

"You are so not fine. You look like shit." Dennis reached to flip the end of Brian's tie. "Doesn't match. And dude, you always match."

"I couldn't care less about my tie, okay?" Brian tucked it back against his shirt, checking it out surreptitiously. Dennis was right. Damn it.

"It's her, isn't it? Kerry Grayson. What happened? She dump you?"

"You can't dump someone you're not going out with."

"So . . . you're pining for her? She hasn't called you back? Hey, she won't send you seeds for *Farmtown*?" Dennis laughed.

Brian didn't. "Oh, she calls me back."

Dennis sobered but looked confused. "Huh?"

"Kerry and I have been, as you say, fucking like crazed weasels for the past three weeks." Saying it that way tasted bad, and Brian swallowed, wishing for a piece of gum or bottle of water.

"The hell you say!" Dennis looked first shocked, then gleeful. "She dump the boyfriend? What, he's coming after your ass?"

"No. And no. She didn't dump the boyfriend, and no, he's not after my ass. Apparently, he's got some kink about her being with other guys." Brian grimaced, then looked at his hands, balled into fists on his thighs. He forced them to relax. "He knows everything."

"Wait a minute. She fucks you, then goes home and tells him every detail? Like, every little thing?"

"Yeah."

"Hot," Dennis said so low under his breath it was clear he didn't mean Brian to hear it.

"Fuck you, Dennis."

Dennis looked contrite. "Sorry. I mean, what a bitch."

Brian glared. Dennis held up his hands. Brian twisted the air-conditioning knob onto high, a futile attempt at cooling off.

"Sorry," Dennis repeated. "But . . . you're doing it with her. The sex must be pretty fucking good."

"It's stellar," Brian said sourly. He didn't mention all the times he and Kerry spent together not fucking. Watching a movie, taking a walk along the riverfront. Talking on the phone. Texting silly catchphrases from high school they both remembered and nobody else did.

"And?"

"And she goes home to her boyfriend when it's done. She lives with him. I'm just the side piece." Brian's lip curled. So did his fingers. This time, he didn't force them to open.

"And?" Dennis said again, then held up his hands when Brian glared at him harder. "Sorry, man. Sorry. It's just . . . what do you want? You're getting great sex from the girl of your dreams without any of the hang-ups, right? I mean, you don't have to deal with the shitty parts. Am I right?"

"Maybe I want to," Brian said.

"Oh, dude. Dude." Dennis shook his head and looked sorrowful. "Seriously?"

"I like her. I—"

"Don't even say it." It was Dennis's turn to grimace and hold up his hands. "That way lies madness, my friend. And lemme tell you, I mean madness. Not fucking Sparta or some shit. You will lose your damn mind if you keep up that line of thinking."

"Too late." Brian shook his head. "She's . . . She's Kerry Grayson, man."

Dennis looked sad, and this disturbed Brian more than anything else had. So did the hand Dennis clapped onto his shoulder and the sympathetic squeeze of his fingers. "You, my friend, have got yourself into a crock of shit. You should get out of it as fast as you can."

"I can't."

Dennis sighed. "You mean you don't want to."

"I don't want to."

"Then at least stop tearing yourself up about being the side piece. Take it for what it's worth. Or something." Dennis frowned. "I know she's your dream girl and all that . . ."

"It's more than that. She used to be my dream girl. Now she's my dream woman. Forget it. You don't understand." Brian looked out to the green fields beyond. They stank strongly of cow manure, which is why his throat closed and eyes stung. Right.

"And you're sure her guy doesn't mind?"

"I told you, he's into it."

"Well . . . have you met him?"

Brian turned. "Hell no."

Dennis raised both brows. "You haven't even met him?"

"I just said no!"

"Huh." Dennis put the car back into drive, but looked over at Brian before pulling out of the driveway and back onto the road. "Don't you think you should?"

Eleven

"Wow. Candles." Jeremy pulled an impressed face, then sniffed the air. "And you made lasagna?"

Kerry's laugh sounded forced as she kissed him. "It's your favorite."

Jeremy pulled her closer to look into her eyes. "You sure about this? You seem really nervous."

"I'm fine." She kissed him again and pulled away. "I have to check the garlic bread."

"Babe, relax. It's just dinner, right?" Jeremy followed her into the kitchen to watch as she pulled the loaf of garlic bread from the oven and set it on top of the stove to cool.

She turned, taking off the oven mitts, and then went to the sink to wash her hands. She needed to occupy herself to keep herself from thinking too much about this. Brian and Jeremy in the same room. With her. Kerry's skin crawled for a second, though whether it was with loathing or excitement, she couldn't be sure.

It had been Brian's idea. They'd made love, and it had been as good as it always was, but afterward in the dark he'd asked her about Jeremy. Before that he'd never even said Jeremy's name. Never asked one word about him. Kerry had never hidden anything from Brian, but it was very clear that Brian wasn't interested in knowing anything about Jeremy. At least, not until two nights ago when Brian pulled her close and asked if he could meet him.

"It's just weird," she said finally, unable to look away from Jeremy's knowing gaze. "You and him. Together."

"I feel like I know him already."

What Jeremy didn't know was that Kerry hadn't told him everything. Oh, sure, when he pushed inside her asking if this was how Brian did it, if this was how Brian made her come, she always said yes, because that got Jeremy off. But it wasn't true. Not exactly. She didn't tell him how it really was with her and Brian, and hadn't since the first few times. It felt wrong, somehow, to mix what she felt with one man into what she felt for the other. It was different with each of them, and that's how it should stay.

"I don't know why he's so suddenly interested," she said.

"Maybe he's scoping me out."

She studied him. "And you don't care."

The words came out flat. She'd stopped asking Jeremy if he were jealous about the time she spent with Brian, because the answer was always the same. And he proved it, too, that he really did get turned on by hearing her talk about what she did with another man. She sought his face for any sign, any hint or glimmer of jealousy anyway, though she knew by now there'd be none.

"He sounds like a cool guy. Hey, you're not asking him to move in with us, are you?" Jeremy laughed as though that were the funniest thing he'd ever heard.

"No." Kerry didn't laugh.

The front doorbell rang. Jeremy looked toward it but didn't

move. Kerry stood, frozen. She didn't want to open it. She didn't want these two pieces of her life to join. The bell rang again. Before she could move, Jeremy moved easily across the kitchen, out the door. Kerry couldn't make her feet move but forced herself to follow. She got into the living room just in time to see Jeremy open the door.

Brian was on the other side. Oh God. He'd combed his hair, slicked it back with water or gel, she couldn't tell. He'd shaved. He wore a pair of nice black trousers, shiny shoes, a white dress shirt. No tie or jacket, but he looked polished and put together just the same. Jeremy on the other hand, wore faded jeans with ragged hems and an old T-shirt. Scruffy beard, rumpled hair.

The men stared at each other for a second too long before Brian held out his hand. "Brian Jordan."

"Jeremy Kent. C'mon in." Jeremy shook Brian's hand and stepped aside to let Brian pass.

Brian smiled when he saw her. That was a good sign. He held up a bottle of red wine, the kind she'd told him she liked best. "I brought this. I hope it's okay."

"It'll be perfect. I made lasagna." What did she do now? Move forward? Kiss him? Shake his hand? Kerry froze again.

This was never how she'd imagined her life would end up. In all the years she'd thought about what it would be like to end up with Brian, nowhere had there ever been another guy in the picture. In the times when she'd imagined herself settling down with Jeremy, maybe getting married, maybe just living in sin for a while, she'd never pictured another guy, either.

It had been a long time since she'd imagined herself marrying Jeremy.

"C'mon in." Jeremy held out his hand for the bottle. "Nice. I'll get some glasses. Make yourself comfortable. Babe, maybe Brian wants some of that cheese spread you put out."

It disturbed her, somehow, to see Jeremy acting the part of gracious host with the man Kerry had spent so many hours fucking. Jeremy never played host when anyone else came over. She was the one fussing over cheese platters and veggie trays. To look at him now, you'd think he'd been the one to invite Brian instead of her.

Kerry drew a deep breath and made a choice. She crossed the room with false confidence and offered her cheek. Not her mouth. That would've been too weird. "Hi, Brian."

"Hey." He squeezed her hip, just for a second, but long enough for her to feel it all the way to her toes. Then he looked at Jeremy. "Cheese sounds great."

"Let's go in the kitchen. Kerry'll make you feel like we're fancy folks, but that's just not right." Jeremy lifted the bottle. "Let's get this cracked open."

Dinner went better than she thought. Almost too well, as a matter of fact. Jeremy proved to be just as charming to Brian as he'd always been to Kerry. To everyone, really. Jeremy was just that way. He put Brian at ease with jokes, asking exactly the right sorts of questions to keep the conversation rolling. Brian answered, not quite as spontaneously funny as Jeremy but holding his own.

If Brian minded the way Jeremy casually linked his fingers through Kerry's to kiss her hand when he praised the meal, he didn't show it. Or when Jeremy squeezed her ass as she passed, or when he slung an arm around her shoulder and bragged, saying, "She's an amazing woman, isn't she?"

All Brian said was, "Yes. Absolutely."

Kerry, for her part, was quieter than usual. Jeremy didn't seem to notice, but she felt the weight of Brian's gaze on her. Jeremy for all his touchy-feelyness barely looked at all.

Maybe he never really had, she thought suddenly as Jeremy started in on another one of his stories. At least, he never had the way Brian did. The way Brian was now.

After dinner, in the living room where they'd all gone at Jeremy's suggestion, Kerry sat on the couch next to Brian while Jeremy took a seat at the chair across from them. His eyes were bright, his jokes a little more frenetic. Brian, in contrast, had gone slow and low. He still answered Jeremy's questions and laughed at the jokes, but his focus remained on Kerry.

It was coming. Kerry knew it was. If it wasn't what Brian had intended when he asked if he could come over and meet Jeremy, it surely was what Jeremy'd planned when he said he thought that would be a great idea. And then . . .

"So, Brian." Jeremy's voice, finally, dipped lower than usual. He leaned forward. "This is kinda awkward, right?"

"Yeah. A little." Beside her, Brian didn't shift closer to her.

He might as well have, though, for how sensitized she'd become to him. Her nipples peaked, but Kerry couldn't tell if it were from arousal or the chill skittering up and down her spine as she watched the two men in her life face off. Only it wasn't like that. Jeremy wasn't threatening. Brian didn't seem threatened.

The only one in the room who seemed to feel uncomfortable was her.

"But I'm glad you came over. I'm glad we had a chance to meet. It's not every day a guy gets to meet his girlfriend's boyfriend, right?"

Kerry's muscles twitched. She and Brian had been very careful to never call each other boyfriend or girlfriend, reserving that title for her and Jeremy. Brian cleared his throat. Jeremy's eyes gleamed.

"I figured it was time," Brian said. "Since I've been fucking her for almost a month."

The bottom of her stomach fell out, exactly the way it did on the first downhill rush of a roller-coaster ride. Brian, unlike Jeremy, even unlike herself, hardly ever swore. She'd heard him say fuck a few times, but always while they were . . . well, fucking. Hearing him say it now was unbearably sexy and disturbing at the same time.

Jeremy leaned forward a little bit more. "Yeah. She's amazing, isn't she?"

Brian nodded without looking at her. "She is."

"Believe me, man, I've been hearing about you since I first met her. Brian Jordan this, Brian Jordan that. Brian Jordan was the one I wanted and never had." For the first time, Jeremy's voice had an edge to it. Kerry's cheeks burned in mortification at the way he tossed out the words. They were true, she'd said them to Brian himself, but it was different hearing them come from Jeremy. "I'm glad she finally had a chance with you."

"Yeah?" Brian's voice sounded a little tight.

Kerry tensed. Her palms were sweating. The easy casualness of dinner had been replaced by something else. She looked back and forth from Brian to Jeremy.

"Jeremy," she said quietly.

"It's okay," Brian said. "I'm glad you had a chance with me, too."

Kerry swallowed. "Maybe this wasn't such a good idea."

Brian looked at her, his usually open expression unreadable. "I thought it's what you'd want."

"How could—?" She broke off, catching herself. She looked at Jeremy, still leaning forward, his eyes gleaming with interest. He rubbed his palms on the thighs of his jeans. His lower lip was wet. He'd licked it.

Brian looked at her, then. "I thought it would be better this way, you know? So it wasn't between us like some secret. I mean, it's not a secret, is it? Any of this? You tell him all about us, right? That's what you like, man, right?"

Jeremy looked at Brian. Then he nodded, slowly. No more jokes. "Yeah. I like it."

"You like hearing about what we do?"

"I fucking love it." Jeremy's voice hitched. "You know when she comes home from being with you, I can smell you on her. She smells like sex. And she's so fucking hot, coming in with her hair all messy, that mouth all rubbed raw from where you kissed her. And her pussy's still so wet. You can't even imagine how fucking hot it is, man. And it's like all I have to do is touch her, just a little, and she's off like a fucking rocket. Because she's still thinking about you."

Kerry shuddered and closed her eyes for a moment. She swallowed, her throat tight with emotion she couldn't put a name to. Electric, sparking heat twisted inside her, but what that meant, she couldn't say.

"She never talks about you," Brian said.

Kerry opened her eyes. Jeremy blinked, for too brief a moment looking taken aback before the gleam returned to his gaze. He smiled and shrugged, held out his hands with the palms up.

"It's my thing," he said. "I take it it's not yours."

Brian shook his head in silence.

Jeremy nodded. Something passed between them. Jeremy looked at Kerry.

"You want to fuck him right now, don't you?"

Actually, she did not. She did not want to fuck Brian here, in this house she shared with Jeremy. In front of Jeremy. Yet Brian was turning toward her, and she tipped her face to kiss him because it was Brian, and she couldn't resist taking just a taste, no matter what else was going on.

Brian didn't kiss her. He paused just before he reached her mouth, but unlike the times he'd so teased her, she didn't feel like this was part of some game. Brian searched her eyes. His hand came up to cup her cheek, then to brush her hair off her shoulder. His smile didn't reach his eyes.

He said into her ear, "I can't do this anymore."

Then he stood. Jeremy stood, too, looking perplexed. Kerry couldn't move.

"I have to go," Brian said. "Jeremy, nice meeting you."

"But . . . wait a minute." Jeremy never stuttered, but now he did. "I thought you'd . . . But don't you want to . . ."

"Oh, I want to," Brian said easily enough without even a glance at her. "I want to so bad it hurts. I just can't. Not like this."

"I could leave," Jeremy said hastily. "I mean, I get it. You don't want to do it in front of me. That's cool. I don't want to harsh your scene, Brian, that's not my thing."

"No. Don't leave." Brian shook his head. "This is your house. That's your girlfriend."

Jeremy blew out an irritated breath and looked at Kerry. "Yeah . . . and you're the guy who's been fucking her for almost a month, remember?"

"Oh yeah, I remember. The problem is, I can't forget."

With that, Brian left.

Jeremy waited until the front door closed behind him, then turned to her. "The fuck's his problem?"

Trembling, Kerry fought the sting at the backs of her eyes. "Forget him."

The problem was, just like Brian, Kerry was pretty sure she couldn't forget.

Twelve

He almost didn't answer the phone when she called, but in the end Brian could no more let a call from Kerry go unanswered than he could forget her. "Hi."

"Brian. I'm sorry. I never should have had you over."

"No. It was important I see." He sighed into the phone, thinking of the nights they'd talked in the dark this way. Sometimes he'd had a hand on his dick while he listened to her make herself come. Now he couldn't stop wondering if Jeremy had been beside her, watching. Listening. Hell, maybe helping. The thought sent a shudder of distaste through him.

"See what? Jeremy?"

"You," Brian said. "You with him."

Silence, broken only by the harsh hitch of a breath.

"He's a decent guy," Brian said. "I wanted to hate him."

"Do . . . do you hate me, instead?" she asked in a tiny voice that made him hate himself.

"No. I could never. But I can't do this anymore, Kerry. I thought maybe I could, but I can't."

Another hitch of breath and the soft sniffle that meant she was crying. His gut clenched, but her tears couldn't change anything. Brian closed his eyes in the dark, the phone to his ear, and hoped she'd hang up.

"I'm sorry, Brian."

"Hey." He tried to sound jovial and only sounded slightly manic. "Don't worry about it. We both got what we wanted, right? Finished up all those years of wishful thinking."

"That's not it," Kerry said. "That's not what it was. Not all of it, anyway. I miss you, Brian."

"It's only been a couple days."

"I can't miss you even if it's only been a couple days?" She sounded a little more like her normal self, and he had no trouble imagining her small grin.

"I don't want you to miss me at all."

"But I do." Her whisper burned him even through the phone.

"You're his," Brian said, the weeks of frustration coming out at last. "Not mine. And I can't fucking stand it."

Kerry gasped; the sound was so different from the noise she sometimes made when he entered her that he wanted to curl up and die from it. "I'm not . . . his. I'm not something to own, Brian. You can't buy and sell me like a damn car."

"No, I can't buy you. I guess I just leased you for a while."

She gasped again. "What a shitty thing to say!"

"Tell me it's different," Brian said, ashamed of taking such a cheap shot and helpless to stop. "I'll tell you you're a liar."

"You knew . . . maybe not from the start, but you knew about him," she said in a low, hoarse voice. "And you were okay with it. So don't act like it matters now."

"But it does, Kerry. I don't care if Jeremy doesn't mind sharing you. I do. I can't." His voice cracked, and he cleared his throat, determined not to let her hear him sound so upset. "I want you all to myself. I love you."

There. It was out. It had been like ripping off a bandage, but having said it, the pain was fading quickly. It would leave a scar, though. Brian was sure of that.

"Brian—"

"Don't," he cut in. "I don't want to hear any more, Kerry. Okay? I can't."

She hung up before he could.

"What did he say?" Jeremy looked up from the book he was reading in their bed.

Kerry had made sure to splash her face with ice water to remove any sign of her tears, but she couldn't disguise the pain in her voice. "He doesn't want to see me anymore. He said . . . he doesn't want to share me."

Jeremy snorted, rolling his eyes. "Lame."

Maybe it was the blur of tears, but Kerry looked at him with a fresh vision. "Why is it lame?"

"Babe, c'mon. He knew all along what he was getting into. Some guys just can't handle it. I mean, sure, he wants you all to himself, who wouldn't?"

"You," she said.

Jeremy looked guilty. Caught. The expression passed, replaced by one of concern. "Don't be like that."

"But it's true, isn't it?" She made it a question, not a demand. She already knew the answer.

Jeremy put the book aside. "I told you. I like the idea—"

"You'd have watched me fuck him right in front of you."

"Yeah. I would've. But he couldn't handle it."

"I couldn't handle it, either," Kerry said. "I didn't want to."

Jeremy shrugged. "Okay, fine. His loss."

But it wasn't Brian's loss. It was hers.

"Let me ask you something," Kerry said carefully, knowing already this was the end of everything, hoping at least it wasn't too late for the beginning of something new. "Do you love me?"

Jeremy's gaze flickered. "Babe. You know I do."

"You don't say you do."

"You know how I feel about that sort of thing . . . It's not what you say, it's what you do."

She lifted her chin, expecting more tears and feeling only emptiness. "And what you do is let me go off with another guy. And you don't get jealous. Or even care."

"It's not that I don't care," Jeremy said, then paused, brow furrowing. "Ah, fuck. He said he loves you. Didn't he?"

She didn't say anything.

"You think that just because Mr. Salesman in his sharp suit and expensive ride says he loves you that he means it? He was okay with fucking another man's girlfriend, Kerry. What sort of guy does that tell you he is?"

"And you were okay with me fucking him," she said evenly. "What kind of guy does that make you?"

"You love him." Jeremy's lip curled. "Why? Because he's a great lay? Because a hundred years ago he got your panties damp? None of that's real, Kerry, don't you get it?"

But it was real. And she'd been a fool not to see it. Kerry went to the closet to begin throwing some clothes in a bag.

Jeremy followed. "Wait a minute. Just wait. I love you, Kerry. Okay? Is that what you want to hear?"

It had never much bothered her that Jeremy didn't say it, and that made her sadder than anything else that had happened. She turned to face him. "I'm leaving you, Jeremy."

"Why? Because he doesn't want to share you?"

"No," Kerry said quietly, knowing it was unlikely he'd ever understand. "Because you do."

Thirteen

She stood so long on the doorstep she was certain he wouldn't answer, but finally Brian, tousle haired and sleepy eyed, opened the door. Kerry didn't wait for him to invite her inside. She kissed him, hoping against all reason he wouldn't push her away.

He didn't.

Brian's kiss was like coming home. All those years she'd spent thinking about what it would be like, and now she knew. She didn't want to give this up, not ever. Not for anything.

"I love you," she said into his kiss, the words too muffled so she pulled away to say it again. "I love you, Brian Jordan."

He didn't ask her about Jeremy. Didn't question the bag she tossed onto the living room floor. Brian just kicked the door closed behind her, picked her up, and walked with her to the bedroom without stopping her kiss. Not even to breathe, so by the time they got to the bedroom, both of them were gasping a little for air. Halfway to the bed, he tripped.

For one eternal moment, Kerry was sure they were both going to end up on the floor, possibly with a trip to the emergency room on top of it. But Brian caught his balance, holding her tight. He grinned.

"Not going to drop you," he said.

Kerry, her arms tight around his neck, kissed him. "Promise?"

"Always," Brian said.

And then they were stretched out on his big, soft bed with nothing and nobody between them anymore.

FLIPPING FOR CHELSEA

EMMA HOLLY

Shay: 1997

"This sucks," growled eighteen-year-old Seamus Cudahy, better known as Shay to his friends.

He bounced the back of his head on the sagging plaid couch cushion. He and his brother, Liam, had been lying on their stomachs on the carpet in Liam's above-the-garage apartment, playing *Street Fighter II* on the PlayStation. Ten minutes into trying to massacre each other, they'd given up, sitting back with matching who-are-we-kidding looks. They did that sometimes—moved as if they had one body—though they didn't share actual genes. This had been happening so long they didn't notice it anymore.

Well, Shay noticed, but he kept that to himself mostly.

"Screw it," Liam said, pushing up with a groan. Dressed in black jeans and a loose white T-shirt, he padded barefoot to his vintage dresser. The thing had cost him two bucks at a junk shop and two weekends fixing it up enough for the drawers to slide in and out, a project Shay had helped him with. Now his brother dug a half-smoked blunt from his clean-sock stash. Their mom didn't snoop, or not too much, and Liam and Shay were careful not to shove her nose in things she didn't want to know anyway. Plus, Liam was twenty-one. Even living under her roof, for which he insisted on paying rent, there wasn't all that much she could say. The worst she could complain about was him corrupting his younger brother. Considering Liam was better at keeping Shay out of trouble than anyone, that wouldn't hold water. There was no one in the world Shay looked up to more.

With a shrug that said he had his own thoughts running through his head, Liam turned his boom box on. Hardly to Shay's surprise, U2's *Achtung Baby* began to play.

It wasn't chance that Chelsea's favorite CD was in the drive.

Liam dropped back to the floor in front of the couch and gave Shay the hand-rolled to light. It was neat and perfect, like everything Liam made. For a guy who worked in construction—full-time now, and not just summers—who had more scars on his knuckles than Shay had hairs on his chest, he sure could work delicate. Shay wasn't as good with his hands yet, though he liked making things. Taking his time and seeing them come out right satisfied him in a way he couldn't explain.

Once Shay had the blunt going, he took a cautious draw and passed it to Liam. Shay liked hanging with his brother but didn't really like being stoned. Letting go of his self-control made him uneasy. More comfortable with relaxing, Liam took a deeper pull, the tip flaring bright in the gathering dusk. His chest swelled to hold the smoke, then fell when he let it out. His hulking shoulder settled against Shay's as he rested the hand that held the blunt on his knee.

Shay was no shrimp, but Liam was bigger than him all over—more muscles, more height, everything. Unless Shay had another growth spurt, he'd probably stay that way. Hell, Shay was probably lucky he'd made six feet.

Over on the boom box, Bono was swearing some girl was "the real thing," no doubt bringing Liam back to the topic Shay had brought up.

"This sucks big time," he belatedly agreed. "But it's not like we can tell her not to go. A full ride to Dartmouth, man. That's huge."

Shay grunted, his legs stretched out and his ankles crossed in a leaner mirror image of Liam's. Chelsea going all Ivy League *was* huge. Their best friend since childhood was such a smart-ass they sometimes forgot how plain old smart she was. Her gran was over the moon about her scholarship. Shay was proud of her, too, enough that his chest got hot when he thought about it. He couldn't help it if he wasn't looking forward to her being so far away. Though she was a year ahead of him, they often hung out together. Maybe it was laziness—friends in the 'hood, friends at school—or maybe it was because they'd both lost their parents and then found new ones. Whatever the reason, they'd always been easy with each other.

"Senior year is going to blow without her."

Liam punched Shay's arm, the gesture gruffly reassuring. "You'll do okay. And I'll still be around."

"I know you've saved enough to move out."

Rather than answer right off, Liam drew another toke. The fading twilight silhouetted his sharp profile. Shay had once listened to a girl go on for ten minutes about his aquiline nose. She'd have melted into a puddle if she'd seen Liam's sensual lips purse to blow out a stream of smoke.

"I told you," he said, his voice slightly fuzzed. "If you decide not to do the college thing, we'll get a place together."

"You don't have to do that. I can take care of myself."

Liam turned his soft green gaze Shay's way. His wavy brown bangs, which their mother had been bugging him to cut, cast a shadow over his eyes. "You're mine to look out for as much as you are Mom and Dad's."

He stated this calm and firm, like saying the earth was round. Shay was his; not open to debate. Shay's gut tightened down low, in a way he tried to ignore. He liked girls—man, did he like them. This twisty feeling, whatever it was, no matter how often he felt it, was nothing to worry about.

"I'm not fresh off the plane anymore."

Liam broke into an unexpected grin. "You were so green," he snickered. "Like, shamrock green."

"I was six."

"You'd never seen a stoplight before. You thought every black guy we met wanted to play hoops with you."

"I was *six*."

More than youth had been behind Shay's greenness. He'd been born in a tiny fishing village in Connemara, on the west coast of Ireland. When he was five and a half, his parents had taken a second honeymoon in Dublin, where they'd been the incidental victims of an IRA bombing. Liam's father had been Shay's dad's best friend growing up. Though Patrick O'Brien had emigrated, he was Shay's godfather. Despite the tie, six months of red tape had required cutting before Shay could come to the States. He'd been cared for, of course, by his parents' other friends in the village, but that hadn't been the same as having a family to belong to. Liam's folks had given him that the moment Mrs. O swept him into her arms at the gate at LaGuardia.

Poor little tyke, she'd said, squeezing him to her breast. *Don't you worry. We've got you now.*

She'd meant that *we*, too, never letting then nine-year-old Liam treat him as anything but a brother he was lucky to have, an edict made easier by the fact that the O'Briens had so much love to give both their boys. Aside from the occasional outbreak of competition, he and Liam hardly ever fought. The only reason he wasn't Shay O'Brien was that Mr. O hadn't wanted his old friend's surname to disappear. *Your ours,* he'd said when Shay asked about it, *but you'll always be a Cudahy.*

"Sap," Liam teased, seeing the sheen rising in his eyes at the memories.

"Ef you," Shay returned, pulling the blunt from his lax fingers.

Liam didn't protest, only dropped his head back and sighed. "Don't let me smoke anymore. I've got to be up at five to drive Chelsea to New Hampshire."

"Not a problem," Shay assured him. He debated pinching out the smoke. He was buzzed enough, his muscles relaxing as the weed kicked in. It was almost possible to let his depression go, to believe this was a night like any other in the Bronx's "Little Ireland." The windows above the garage were open, and the sound of lawn mowers trimming stingy squares of grass drifted in on the warm end-of-summer air. Being house-proud was the rule in Woodlawn. Shay had always liked that. He thought people should care about where they lived, no matter how big or small it was.

"So this is how it's going to be," said a voice from the shadows at the head of the narrow stairs. "I go to college, and you two sit in the dark missing me."

Shay's temperature spiked at Chelsea's appearance, his johnson punching out in a hard-on so full it stung. The instant boner made him glad his camouflage pants were baggy, though he still had to pull his knees up to hide the hump.

"Hey," he said, grabbing his shins for good measure. "We thought you were spending tonight with your gran."

"Gran kicked me out. Said if I was going to pace, I ought to wear out your carpet."

Chelsea and her gran loved each other, so this was said fondly. She crossed to the hand-me-down floor lamp next to the old plaid couch, switching it on with a briskness that was as familiar as the rest of her. The three of them had been inseparable since

the day she'd showed up next door at the age of ten. Seeing her
in that pool of light, nearly all grown up, was a punch Shay's
eighteen-year-old hormones hadn't asked for. Chelsea wore a pair
of farmer-style knee-length shortalls, with bright-white slouch
socks and orange Keds. The combination would have been tom-
boyish but for the skintight cartoon logo T-shirt that hugged her
underneath.

Shay doubted Bart Simpson had ever done so much for a pair
of breasts.

He swallowed, his mouth gone dry, as she grinned at him. Chelsea's body had really turned into something these past few years.
Rounded but tight, with sexy little muscles she'd earned helping
her gran fix things around their old house. Her dirty-blonde curls
exploded from the messy ponytail she'd scraped together behind
her neck. Her eyes were a dreamy blue under faint, straight brows,
her lips full and rosy in her soft oval face. Only her chin told the
tale of how stubborn she could be.

The boys at Dartmouth had no idea what they were in for.

"Hey, Chelsea," Liam slurred. The back of his head was still on
the couch as he turned it toward her. He was smiling a bit goofily.
Shay knew his brother had the hots for Chelsea—and had been
turned on by her for a while. He also knew he'd held back from
asking her out because she was younger. Tonight, though, he didn't
seem to be hiding his attraction. When Shay glanced at Chelsea, she
was smiling goofily, too.

Just once Shay wished she'd look at him that way.

A second later it struck him that Chelsea wasn't as surprised by
Liam's expression as she should have been. She'd been starry-eyed
over him forever, though her chosen prince tended to treat her like
a well-loved pest. With a pang he couldn't control, Shay saw he
must have missed some developments in their relationship.

Unaware of Shay's constricted chest, Liam made a purring noise and rolled sideways onto his hip. His gaze traveled warmly up and down their friend. "You look good, college girl."

"And you sound stoned." Chelsea flushed with pleasure even as she planted her fists on her curvy hips. "I could smell it from the garage. If your mother catches a whiff, she's going to be praying for both of you at St. Barnabas's tomorrow."

"Shit," Shay said, stabbing out the stub on a dented metal beer coaster. Knowing that wouldn't be enough, he jumped up to set the whirring box fan facing out on the windowsill. The metal rattled on the uneven wood, but it would clear the air.

"Turn up the music," Liam said sleepily, clearly too mellow to share Shay's fit of guilt. "Then come sit down with me."

Chelsea humphed at him, but she went. The twangy guitars that gave "Mysterious Ways" its groove swelled louder. She returned to Liam but, rather than sit in the spot Shay had left, she stood over him and looked down. Maybe she guessed why Liam picked the album. Her little smile was knowing, her confidence something Shay hadn't seen before—at least not in regard to Liam. Blood throbbed like a mariachi band in his groin, this situation doing something *extra* to the lust she'd been the first girl to stir in him.

"Dance with me," she said to Liam, her hand held out like a dare.

Liam snorted, but his lips had fallen open, his gaze locked helplessly on hers. His cheeks were flushed, maybe from the weed but probably just from her.

"Come on," she coaxed, her voice gone husky enough to have sweat prickling in Shay's armpits. "Last chance before those Dartmouth boys get ahold of me."

Shay only realized he'd stopped breathing when Liam rose. His movements were stiff, and Shay saw what Chelsea wasn't bold enough to look for: Liam was as hard as he was. The front of his black jeans looked like a fist had been shoved in there.

For a moment, Liam seemed afraid to touch her. Whatever new flirtation they'd been sharing lately, Shay suspected they must not have slow danced before.

"Here," Chelsea said, placing both his hands lightly on her hips. "I'm pretty sure this is how it goes."

Liam looked down at her and wet his lips. "Chelsea . . ."

"Coward," she taunted, her voice verging on a laugh.

"Squirt," Liam returned. Then, like a saint surrendering to temptation, he pulled her slowly against him. His eyes closed as her body met his, as her head settled on his chest. He murmured her name again, nearly groaning it. Chelsea wound her arms more snugly around his waist.

Throat tight, Shay watched them sway to the music from his post by the dark window. They acted like they'd forgotten him, their shuffling circle growing ever smaller, their hands smoothing up and down each other's backs. Chelsea turned her face from side to side on Liam's white T-shirt, a move so tender and carnal it hurt to see. Liam looked like he hurt, too. His big hands drifted lower on Chelsea's body, finally palming her butt to lift her to what had to be an agonizing erection.

As he squeezed her to it, Chelsea and Shay made the same soft sound.

Liam's eyes opened like they'd had weights on them. He was facing Shay, and Chelsea wasn't tall enough to block his view. He must have seen Shay's unguarded yearning, because something that could have been regret flicked like a whip through his expression. He let Chelsea go and stepped back from her. When she gaped at him in confusion, he let out a nervous laugh.

"I think you'd better give Shay a good-bye dance, too."

"*Shay,*" she repeated in a tone that said she thought Liam was being dense.

"I'll start the CD again," Liam said, moving to do it.

He knows, Shay thought. *He's figured out how I feel about her.* Was *this* why Liam had never made a move on Chelsea, and not just the age difference?

His cheeks flamed with a confusing combination of embarrassment and lust. He felt suspended, unable to decide precisely what he wanted or how he should respond. Chelsea turned her head to him, her expression unsure as well.

You want her, Shay told himself. *That much there's no doubt about.*

College changed people. This might be his last chance to hold her.

"Come on," he said, arms out in invitation, his voice as light as he could make it with his heart thumping in his throat. "You've danced with me before."

It was true. They'd been each other's back-up partners for school dances when, for whatever reason, one of them couldn't get a date. Shay had never told her he always made sure he couldn't get one if she was in that boat. Even before his crush had gotten this ferocious, she'd been more fun to take.

"Fine," she surrendered. "You can have a good-bye dance, too."

He knew she sensed the difference in him the second he wrapped her close. He'd always been careful not to betray himself around her. Now he really held her, not tightly but not like a friend, either. She tensed when she felt the hardness between his legs, the ache he couldn't keep from nudging her with. Though her hands came up to his chest, they didn't push him away.

"Easy," he whispered next to her ear. "You know I won't hurt you."

She tipped her head back to look at him. "Are you stoned, too?"

"No. I'm just doing what I've wanted for a long time."

Her breath caught inside her throat. "Shay . . ."

"Don't be sorry for me," he said.

Her soft, rosy lips were parted, and it seemed the most inevitable thing in the world that he should kiss her. Again she stiffened, but just a little. He couldn't let her be scared off. His hand came up to cup the back of her curly head. He was so gentle his tongue barely brushed hers inside her mouth.

And then the most amazing thing happened.

She kissed him back. The stiffness in her muscles melted, just gave way like maybe Shay wasn't the only one who was tired of trying to want only what he should. With a hum that set fire to his bloodstream, she stretched onto her toes and curled her hands behind his shoulders. Shay's whole body sang with desire. She was showing no hesitation. Her tongue was pushing back at his, stroking his, her breasts crushed against his chest. He turned his head and dove deeper, groaning at how good she tasted. He wanted to say her name, but he'd have to stop kissing her for that.

She made the same hungry noise she'd uttered for Liam.

It killed everything inside him that could have reined him in. He turned his head and sucked her sweetness savagely into him. His hand fumbled with the metal that held her right overall strap in place. The denim fell and he cupped her fullness, her nipple a hard, hot pebble against his palm. She wasn't wearing a bra. She'd come here bare beneath that tight T-shirt.

"Chel." He groaned, and dropped his mouth to lick and suck the pulsing peak through the thin cotton.

Her head fell back, her hands fisted near his spine to urge him closer. Her body was shuddering, like maybe she was going to come or just wanted to a whole lot. He unhooked the other strap and changed breasts, using his teeth to catch the part of her no sane man could have resisted. She must have been really sensitive. The gentle bite caused her to suck a breath as well as shudder. Maybe she wanted to have the same effect on him. Her palms cruised down his back to mold around his butt, her slender fingers actually pushing between his thighs from behind. The caress was so bold he had to grind his hips against her. Chelsea didn't seem to mind. She was shoving just as eagerly back at him.

They must have made a picture, the way they were wrestling to get closer. Springs creaked from what seemed like a long distance.

"You two are something," Liam said from the couch. "I could watch you go at that all night."

He was buzzed for sure, and maybe Shay was, too, if he could forget himself this much in front of Liam.

The spell was broken, though Shay doubted this was what Liam meant to do. Chelsea pushed back from him awkwardly. Her cheeks were scarlet, her hair a crazy halo around her head, at least half of it escaped from her ponytail. Her kiss-bruised lips were the most delicious vision he'd ever seen, even if she was biting them. Shay touched her face to soothe her. She stepped farther away even as he did.

"I think I need a beer," she said, trying to make a joke of it.

"Nuh-uh," Liam contradicted. "You don't want our mom praying for you, too."

She'd been looking at Shay, but now she turned to Liam. "You know it's you I want to be kissing."

Liam's face darkened, his jaw muscles clenching beneath the flush. Shay recognized his best stubborn look. "You liked Shay's kisses fine a minute ago."

"Damn it, Liam."

She actually stamped her foot, which—under any other circumstances—both guys would have thought was hilarious. Under this circumstance, it caused Liam's eyes to narrow and the back of Shay's neck to tense.

"I'll make you a deal, squirt. One kiss for me and one kiss for him. Shay deserves as good a chance as you've given me."

"You're crazy." She didn't sound completely sure of this.

Liam shrugged at her. "Most girls would love the idea of having two big strong Irishmen after them."

It was Chelsea's turn to slit her eyes, a smoky darkness entering them. "You think I won't do it."

"Maybe I hope you will." Liam's grin was smug: the experienced older man who always knew better than she did. Shay's heart abruptly tripped faster. Chelsea found few things more infuriating than that superior attitude. He just *knew* she would say yes.

When she tossed her head, the rest of her curls sprang free. She used her fingers to massage her scalp. The way this stretched her body was incredibly sexy—maybe more than Liam was prepared for. With her own smug smile, Chelsea wriggled her half-undone shortalls down her hips. They'd seen her legs in swimsuits—modest one-pieces, usually. Her taut, long muscles were still a treat. While Liam's jaw dropped, she toed off her orange Keds. Her tiny panties were light blue satin with lace trimming.

Bart looked totally X-rated with her nipples poking out behind him.

"Lose the shirt," Shay said, the words grating from him harsh and unplanned.

Chelsea's eyes came to his. What they held, he couldn't have said, only that it excited him. Something had changed when she kissed him, or maybe just came out of hiding. Sweat began to trickle to the small of his back. She crossed her arms to grip the hem and peel it over her head. She tossed the top at Liam, who was almost too stunned to catch it. Shay wasn't sure he'd ever swallow again.

Her rack was totally prime, full and perky, like something out of a magazine. It made his cock hurt to look at it.

"Remember, you asked for this," she said.

Then she was striding to Liam in socks and panties, the strut drawing their gaze away from her bouncing breasts for a few seconds. Shay hadn't known she'd had this in her; she wasn't exactly a femme fatale. Obviously, that wasn't holding her back tonight. She straddled Liam, one knee to either side of his thighs. His hands found her hips as if they couldn't decide where it was safe to settle. Shay saw his battered fingers squeeze convulsively on her flesh. She looked so little being held in those paws that the contrast tugged a shiver straight up his spine.

"Do you *really* want this?" she asked.

Her voice was breathy, but Liam's was just plain gone. He nodded, wide-eyed, and then—almost without transition—their lips were fused in the deepest, most desperate kiss Shay had ever seen.

He had to move closer. Watching what they were doing was like being teased with the meaning of life itself—too good to miss out on. With a grunt of hunger, Liam tugged Chelsea's hips down, plastering her groin to his. Immediately, they started writhing like they'd screw each other straight through their clothes. Liam's hands kept shifting between her breasts and the scraps of blue satin on her butt—an understandable conflict. When Shay reached the couch—having been drawn there like a sleepwalker—he sank to the cushion next to Liam, one leg folded beneath his weight.

Chelsea's hand stopped groping Liam to grab Shay's knee.

Shay must have gone a little crazy. Liam was kissing Chelsea like he'd hoover out her tonsils, and she wasn't much better. He should have been hurt or jealous or—hell—just polite enough to leave them alone. Instead, he took her hand from his knee to wrap it as tightly as he could around his insane hard-on. His prick was so long her grip barely covered it.

A second later, he didn't care. Her thumb began to rub a fiery course along the side of the straining ridge, the firmness of the pressure causing his eyes to cross. The intense sensations nearly took his head off. Desperate for that not to happen, Shay made a sound like a throttled cat. Caught in his own struggle, Liam tore his mouth free at the same time.

"I'm sorry," he gasped. "I want to take you so bad. I'm sorry, but I can't help it."

His big tanned hands were covering her breasts again, massaging her rhythmically. The way she wriggled said how much she liked that.

"Why should you help it?" she gasped back.

Liam cursed, understanding the full permission she was implying. He shifted underneath her, wincing as his stretched-out zipper strafed the crotch of her blue panties. Shay stared at the wet spot where the cloth clung between her folds, then at how huge Liam was. Given how mesmerizing these things were, the added weight that settled on his dick took a moment to register.

"This is why," Liam said.

He'd put his hand over Chelsea's, his long, broad hold neatly swallowing hers. If Shay thought he'd been in danger of losing it before, that was nothing to the warnings that streaked through his nerves now. His two favorite people were cupping him, and he was panting like a dog for air. He had to have grown an inch in two seconds.

Chelsea's grip tightened under Liam's. It felt so good he wanted to cry.

"You think you can't want me because he does?"

Shay almost didn't recognize her voice, it was that husky. She was breathing harder. Liam was, too, if it came to that.

"He's Shay," he said simply.

"What if—?" Chelsea cleared her throat and started over. "What if I let you both have me?"

"Yes," Shay said before Liam could do more than goggle. "That's okay with me if it is with you."

"Yes," Chelsea seconded, her gaze focused like a laser on Liam's. "Say yes, Liam. This is what I want as my good-bye present."

Liam's eyes cut to Shay. "This won't hurt your feelings?"

How could Shay explain how much he wanted exactly this, how it was a fantasy he hadn't dared to admit he had? He shook his head, then ran his fingertips across Chelsea's bare shoulders. Her skin was silk, and she closed her eyes at the soft caress. Watching, Liam's throat bobbed as he swallowed. "We can both help her enjoy it."

"You're sure?"

"Positive." Shay rose, drawing a light grip down Chelsea's arm until he caught her wrist. She let him tug her off Liam and onto her feet. Her wide-eyed gaze made him suddenly feel assured. "I'm going to finish taking your clothes off now."

He peeled off her socks and panties, the soaked state of the latter a thrill he kept to himself. Girls could be weird about those things. He was on his knees, and Chelsea tentatively stroked his black hair. That one touch was enough to give him chills. He knew without question what he wanted to do next.

"Hold her for me," he said to Liam.

Shay turned Chelsea by the hips until her back was to Liam's chest. As soon as Liam's arms were there to catch her, he urged her gently onto his lap.

"Don't be shy," he said, his hands exerting a soft but insistent pressure on her reluctant knees. Though she made a little noise of protest, he soon had her legs sprawled wide around Liam's thighs. The chance to stare at her pussy tempted, but instead he gazed more directly into her eyes than he'd ever gazed into anyone's. "I like doing this," he said to her doubting face. "I want to go down on you."

"You sure you know what you're doing?" Liam asked dubiously.

Shay ran his thumbs up the wet channels of her folds, delighted to find her twitching under the stroke. Chelsea was hot in more ways than one. "I might have a crush on her, but I haven't been living like a monk."

He grinned at how her eyes rounded at him, then put his mouth where his money was.

She'd been squirming already, but at the first tug of oral suction, she jerked her hips toward his mouth and moaned. Liam wrapped his arms around her, his strength letting her thrash as much as she liked. Loving that they could make her do this, Shay held her knees wide and went to town.

Her clit was a little berry he could suckle against his tongue. He flicked the point all around it until he discovered her hottest spot. Apparently, it was a good one. She went wilder than any girl he'd done this to before.

"Wow," Liam said as he struggled to hold her. "Remind me not to underestimate your skills."

It wasn't just Shay's skills; it was Chelsea's natural responsiveness. Thirty seconds later, she bowed hard and groaned in orgasm. Shay felt as happy as if she'd given him a gift, joy bubbling up in him.

"Do it again," he whispered against her quivering thigh.

The next time took at least two minutes, but her climax was way stronger and her hands knotted in his hair enough to cause pain. When he looked up her body, Liam's fingertips were pinching her very red nipples out. Shay was pretty sure he'd timed the pressure to match her shooting over the edge. It was weirdly satisfying to know they'd both paid attention to what she liked.

"Geez," Chelsea breathed, her eyelids fluttering open. Still riding the glow, her gaze took a moment to focus on Shay's face. He had both thumbs curled into the first inch of her pussy, stretching the passage just a little to keep her aware of what she was feeling there. She was wet enough to trickle creamy heat over him.

He didn't think he could have described how incredible she smelled.

"I'd give you another climax," he said, his voice as growly as a rock singer's, "but I think you'd rather have Liam inside you now."

Her lips fell open. For a second, he thought she might deny it. The idea that she'd consider letting Shay have her first meant more to him than she'd ever know. She blinked and craned her head back at Liam.

"Is that what you want?" Liam asked. "For me to make love to you?"

"If you wouldn't mind," she said shyly.

"Babe." Liam shook his head and laughed, his disbelief a reaction Shay understood. "You're killing me here."

"You need to take your clothes off. You, too," she added when Shay laughed.

Both men pulled their shirts off in unison. Chelsea looked at Shay, quickly scoping him down and up, like she wasn't certain it was allowed. Then she turned back to Liam, who was shucking his jeans as well. His chest was pretty massive, but it was his tight white briefs that had her pressing palms to her gasping mouth. Liam's erection stretched out their front like a steel flashlight.

Liam rescued a condom from the back pocket of his jeans and let out a shaky laugh. "Don't you worry about the size thing. The last thing I'd ever do is to hurt you."

She didn't deny it was an issue. It would have been to any girl with sense. Knowing this, Liam pushed his underwear slowly down his legs, like she was a deer he was afraid to startle. His dick popped up, thick and long and veiny, bouncing with his pulse now that it was free. He took a little time rolling down the latex. Shay didn't think he was trying to tease, just that the fit was close. Teased or not, both Shay and Chelsea wet their lips while they watched. Liam's cock stood even higher when he finished. The head was shiny, the color deep pink with blood. Chelsea stared at it, swallowed, then lowered her hands as far as her heart, which was thudding in her hard-tipped breasts. She cleared her throat when Liam's eyes lifted from his task.

"I know you won't hurt me," she said, straightening her shoulders determinedly. "Even when you treat me like a pest, you're always sweet to me."

Liam's eyes went as bright as stars.

"Babe," he said, and took her face in his hands. He looked at her before he kissed her. The moment his tongue went in she cried out into his mouth.

They love each other, Shay thought as he watched them, his ribs tightening strangely. What he felt wasn't envy. If he were honest, what he felt was more like a desire to be part of them.

"Now," Chelsea tore free to plead. She was squirming under Liam's caressing hands, the flush that stained her all over beautiful to see. "Shay got me too excited to wait longer."

The confession startled Shay, and maybe Liam, too. Liam searched Chelsea's gaze, drawing one big hand around her hip to slip it between her thighs. When he took a grip on her little mound, his fingers kneaded into the folds. She rocked her pelvis to him as if it were impossible not to. Her wetness made a deliciously sexy sound.

"Please," she whispered. "You can feel how ready I am."

"You've been wanting this for a while," Liam said.

"Since before I knew what the feeling was."

Did "this" mean the same thing to Liam that it did to her? All Shay could tell for certain was that Chelsea's answer struck Liam dumb. Then he smiled, heavy-lidded but broad, like sunrise breaking over his handsome face. Shay knew some long-held cravings were about to be satisfied.

With a laugh, Liam boosted her into his arms by her bottom,

her curvy legs swinging up to hug him around his waist. He laid her on the couch still clinging to him, his knees and one hand holding their weight as he maneuvered.

"College girl," he said, "I hope you're ready for a *long* lesson."

Chelsea ran her knuckles around his face, then stretched out her arm for Shay. "Come," she said, smiling as she beckoned. "You're too far away over there."

He was only a step away, but he came and took her hand and held it. He realized he was naked, though he only vaguely remembered throwing off the last of his clothes. He was skinnier than Liam, but Chelsea didn't seem to notice, and he knew lots of girls liked the way he looked. She squeezed his fingers, her hand damp and hot on his. Struck as speechless as Liam had been, he sank to his knees and rubbed his face against her shoulder.

"Shay," she murmured. "Believe me, I love you, too."

When she turned back, Liam caught her mouth and kissed her so deeply Shay heard their tongues moving. He shuddered, his cock kicking hard with lust. He couldn't help it. This was a ringside seat to a fantasy.

It was more than that for Liam. He moaned, muscles clenching in his ass as he rocked his hips greedily closer. He backed off, came back, then rubbed his hardness lingeringly up her belly from head to balls. It must have felt pretty nice. His eyes opened dazedly afterward.

"You sure you're ready, Chel?"

"I have done this before," she said.

"When?" Liam and Shay burst out. "With who?"

Chelsea rolled her eyes. "Last year. And it doesn't matter who. Let's just say this person didn't live up to his reputation. It was all over very fast."

The dill-weed captain of the chess team popped into Shay's head. Hadn't Shay seen him and Chelsea talking a few times between classes?

"Chelsea?" he said. "For future reference, when a guy in a bow tie tells you he's good in bed, he's lying."

Chelsea's brows shot up at his bull's-eye.

"He's right," Liam said. "A guy who works with his hands is a better bet."

Clearly amused, Chelsea traced Liam's full-lipped mouth with her other hand. "Never mind all that. My point is you can go straight ahead and take me. No screaming will ensue."

Liam dropped his forehead to hers. "Don't be so sure of that, college girl."

She laughed, then gasped, because he'd worked his hand down between them to shift his cock into position. Shay could see the big broad head disappearing between her curls.

"Boy," Liam said roughly, after which he gave a firm, careful shove. He went in and in until Chelsea's slender neck arched up off the couch. He moaned the whole time he went, starting to tremble as her pussy engulfed him. Chelsea was simply gasping, her hot grip on Shay's hand a vise. When Liam finally took a break from pushing, she immediately hitched both legs higher and kissed his chin.

"You like that?" he asked.

Chelsea bit her smile and nodded.

"I'm not in too deep for you?"

"Nuh-uh," she said. "You can go all the way."

Heat seared Shay's cheeks at the idea that there was more. Liam closed his eyes, filled his lungs with air, and ground in until he was done.

"Oh God," he cried, his big body undulating at the feel of her. "Chel." His face twisted with pleasure. "I can't stand this. I've got to move."

She urged him with little murmurs, and a heartbeat later he was thrusting. He didn't pummel her like some guys that excited would have. He kept himself to long, smooth rolls of his powerful hips—deep in, almost out—his muscles bunching and releasing like some machine. Chelsea wasn't as practiced, but she sure pushed back good at him. Both were making throaty, drawn-out noises like this was the best thing either of them had felt.

Shay was willing to be forgotten, considering the charge he got as their audience. Chelsea didn't forget him, though. She just waited until Liam was fully caught up in fucking to tug her hand loose of Shay's. He was on his knees beside them, close enough to the couch that she could reach right down for his cock. The fingers she wrapped around it were hot as fire.

Shay didn't want to make a noise, but he couldn't help it. Her grasp felt too good running up and down his hardness.

Liam glanced over but seemed too preoccupied to be offended. He grunted as Chelsea performed some pleasurable action Shay couldn't see.

"You keep tugging him like that," Liam warned her breathlessly, "he's not going to last long enough for you."

Chelsea's gaze only came to Shay's for a second. "I think he will. I think Shay's really good at waiting."

Liam's thrusts wavered at her sureness, but he recovered. "Yeah?" he said, smiling down at her. "Maybe I'm the one who's had enough waiting."

"Show me," she said, her breath coming faster. "I'm ready to go, too."

He pushed up on his arms, his big broad chest coming off hers. Chelsea's gaze slipped down the rippling slabs of muscle, which caused Liam's face to darken. He had to know she was watching his cock go in.

"Hold on tight," he warned.

He'd never stopped thrusting, but now he put his all into it. Chelsea's hand lost its rhythm on Shay's cock. It looked like Liam was approaching blastoff faster than she was. His teeth were gritted, his grunts rising. Happy to help the odds, Shay palmed Chelsea's nearest breast, firmly scissoring her reddened nipple in his fingers. Chelsea gasped loudly in reaction.

"Oh yeah," Liam growled, his next drive really jolting her. "You're . . . making her even wetter. Keep . . . doing her good like that."

His encouragement tripped some switch in her. Chelsea arched and groaned as the climax slammed into her. Shay knew her pussy had to be tightening. A wordless cry broke in Liam's throat. He was coming, too; his eyes screwed shut with pleasure, his hips shuddering tight against her.

Shay couldn't help imagining the big spurts of come jetting into that snug condom.

"God," Liam gasped when it finally finished. He pulled out, wincing, and sank to the side of her. His weight partially pinned her. The couch wasn't big enough for it not to. Seeming fine with that, Chelsea caressed the arm he'd dropped across her stomach. Her chest went in and out with her hard breathing. Though she'd released Shay's cock near the end, Shay's hand still covered her heaving breast. Unable to resist, he circled her swollen areola with two fingers.

Her head turned to him on the cushion. Her hair was a wild nest of golden curls, a perfect picture of sexual disarray. "*Shay.*"

His pulse began to trip faster, especially in his groin, where his arousal was now vicious. The dark way she said his name wasn't pitying. Her eyes seemed to glow as they locked with his, as she wriggled out from under Liam to sit up. Her flame-blue stare dipped down to Shay's penis, which was more than hard as stone right then. Shay wasn't huge like Liam, but he was big enough. Her stare wound him up so good a drop of fluid rolled down the tip.

"Stand up for me," she said.

He needed the couch to steady his weight, but he stood. Chelsea drew her fingers lightly up his shaft, one set to either side of him. Her thumbs found the bead of wetness, and Shay sucked in a breath. More pre-ejaculate welled as her thumb pads rubbed gentle circles into that screaming skin. The sound that ripped from him was tortured. Clearly liking it, Chelsea pressed her soft pink lips to the slippery spot.

The wet tip of her tongue came out to tease him.

"You're very excited," she murmured against his slit.

"Chelsea . . ."

Liam was sitting up groggily behind her. He peeled off the condom, and that tightened Shay's lust, too. His seed was shining on his soft penis.

"Don't argue," Chelsea said, licking Shay's knob with the flat of her tongue this time. "I know what I want to do."

Shay could guess what that was easily enough, but he wasn't sure how to handle the logistics. Should he move her away from Liam? Or let Liam watch like he had? While Chelsea didn't seem to feel a need to shield him, Shay sincerely doubted Liam fantasized about seeing other guys get off.

"I think you need to move your feet wider," she said.

She tapped his knees and even that juiced him up. *Hell,* he thought, spreading his feet apart the way she wanted. Liam could look away if this freaked him out. Chelsea's hands smoothed up the back of Shay's calves, shifted around to knead the front of his thighs. Then she moved them to cup his balls. The gentle pressure had his breath hitching. His cock stretched toward vertical.

"Tell me if I do anything you don't like," she said.

He didn't know how that could happen, especially when she rubbed her cheek in catlike enjoyment along his shaft. His hair stood up as he felt her inhale, and then her mouth sank over the bulbous head. A moan rose up from his belly, the sweetness of her warm, wet sucking overwhelming him.

She'd done this before. It bothered him for a second, but he couldn't complain about the results. She knew how to be careful with her teeth, how to use her hands to stroke and rub where he was too long for her to swallow. Her head was moving up and down him, her caressing fingers spreading pure delight everywhere they went. He closed his eyes and let the blissful waves of sensation roll over him, trying not to let them push him to the brink too fast. God, it was good. His hands slid from her shoulders up to her ears. When she sucked again, his hips rocked forward.

"Careful, bro," Liam said. "You look like you're far enough."

Shay shuddered at the reminder that Liam was there. Chelsea must have felt the reaction. Her lips tightened on him, the suction strengthening for her next pull.

"Jeez," Shay swore, torn between needing her to ease up and desperately wanting more of what she was doing.

Chelsea pulled off him with a small pop. "You don't have to hold back, Shay. You can come as soon as you want."

"What you're doing feels too good to rush."

"You've been waiting. And this doesn't have to be the last time."

He looked down, groaning, into her soft blue eyes. Her mouth was still close to him, lush and reddened and wet. Her lips matched his dick in color, while her throat matched his heart in the rapid beat of her pulse. She slid her hands to his ass and squeezed.

"Let me finish you," she coaxed.

How could he refuse when she asked like that?

"Okay," he said, his excitement surging dramatically in anticipation. "Suck me hard then, and don't let up."

She grinned at his order but she did it, her commitment to her goal obvious. She wasn't going to let up, not until he exploded. His thighs took almost no time to knot like stone. God, she was good:

fast and tight, with an amazing knack for using her tongue to rub
bolts of fire into his best nerves. Not wanting to choke her, he had
to shift his hands back onto her shoulders, clutching her there hard
enough to bruise.

He had about ninety seconds to enjoy his headlong gallop.

"God." He gasped, the climax boiling up in his balls. "Chelsea.
Chel."

She knew it was coming, but she didn't back off. The circle of
her lips tightened on him, her tongue flicking fast and hard on the
ultrasensitive tip. The trick pulled a harsh cry from him. Her hand
surrounded his up-drawn scrotum and contracted.

He let go, soundless now except for a gasp. The spunk foun-
tained from him like he'd had it damned up for years. She took
it until she couldn't, her hand pumping him instead. His shooting seed slicked her palm like oil. This final increase in sensation
was so strong, so unbelievably erotic, that the blaze blotted out his
thoughts.

He was dizzy when it ended, half surprised to find himself on
his feet. It took a few more seconds for his eyelids to lift.

He was looking straight at Liam, as he hadn't had the nerve
to before. Liam was staring slack-jawed at his relaxing cock. That
was natural enough, Shay supposed. Chelsea's mouth had just been
there, and most guys would have been curious enough to watch
a blow job that awesome. What startled Shay was that Liam was
steel-hard again, all eight throbbing, bottle-thick inches, or whatever the hell he was. Even more worth noting, he was wanking
his erection. It wasn't a casual I'll-just-keep-myself-warmed-up
motion. His fist was exerting sufficient pressure to stretch the ten-
dons around his base, suggesting the state of his hard-on was pretty
bad.

Evidently, watching Shay get sucked had gotten him seriously
horny.

Something Shay could only call euphoria possessed him. He reached out to Liam, to curl his hand under his. Liam's gaze jerked to his as they touched.

"Shay," he said in surprise.

And then his erection dropped.

Shay let go like he'd been burned, though the case was more the reverse. "I'm sorry, man. You didn't want me to do that." He spun away, searching the cluttered floor for his clothes. "Crap. Where are my trousers?"

He found them and yanked them on, nearly tripping in his eagerness to be dressed. The mortification that gripped him was as strong as the joy had been. He grabbed his shirt and pulled it over his head.

"Stop that," Liam berated. "I was just . . . You took me by surprise is all."

"I was stupid," Shay said. "Beyond stupid. I was the dictionary definition of idiocy."

He was saying too much. He was giving himself away even worse. He knew that the instant Liam caught his upper arm. Shay looked desperately at Chelsea, but she was blushing as bad as him. Shay dragged a hand through his hair.

"Just forget I did it," he said. "I'll get out of both your ways now."

Liam's fingers tightened to keep him there. When he spoke, it was as if Shay were still a child. "Shay, are you attracted to me?"

"No." He tried and failed to laugh. "That'd be crazy."

Liam's green eyes were worried, not buying it. Seeing how concerned he was, how he'd care about his adopted brother no matter what, Shay had to face the truth. He loved Liam as much as he loved Chelsea, and in very much the same way. He was never going to be able to put his romantic feelings in neat boxes.

He put his hand over Liam's, giving it a reassuring squeeze, just like he would have before this happened. Pretending nothing was different was the hardest thing he had ever done.

"I'm fine," he said. "Just chalk it up to the pot. Chelsea, if I don't see you before you go, have a blast at Dartmouth."

He pulled free of Liam successfully this time. Down the stairs he went, out of the garage. The sound of Chelsea and Liam calling after him barely slowed his steps. They'd be better off without him. They knew how to be normal. He reached the street and ran down it until the dark swallowed him. He only stopped when he lost his breath. He wasn't crying, but he might as well have been. With all his heart, he wished he didn't know what he did.

His life would never be as simple as it had been just an hour ago.

Chelsea: 2011

Playing it cool wasn't Chelsea's strong suit. Try though she might, she couldn't stop staring at Liam as he drove them past the swanky brownstones of Brooklyn Heights. The day was gorgeous, with dappled sunshine gleaming off the hood of his black work truck. Chelsea had plenty to think of besides old flames: her upcoming project, the lunch she'd skipped because she was too nervous to eat it. As to that, her latest meeting with her accountant could have kept her thoughts occupied. And still her eyes kept drifting to Liam O'Brien.

He looked good. He'd always looked good, of course, even as the gawky thirteen-year-old she'd fallen in love with when she was ten. Then, he'd been all shoulders and legs and elbows, with a voice as likely to be tenor as baritone. Now, his thirtysomething face seemed mature, its greater decisiveness suiting him. His wavy brown hair was short, showing off how cleanly handsome his features were. His mouth was as sinfully sweet as ever, pure temptation to weak females. The hands that gripped the Silverado's wheel displayed the battering she remembered from his days in construction work. By her surreptitious count, no less than three of his nails were black from various bashings.

Liam had never gotten in the habit of sitting on a job's sidelines, though he was a highly respected restoration contractor now. O'Brien, McMead and Purefoy was *the* firm to hire for anyone who bought an old house around the city. They were her first choice, certainly, which almost explained why she was next to him in this truck, struggling not to squirm like a schoolgirl on the nice leather.

That got harder when a red light pointed out the awkwardness between them.

Liam cleared his throat like he also might be uncomfortable and slid a quick glance at her. The bright May day turned his eyes spring green.

"You look good, Chel. You did something to your hair."

She touched its now smooth ripples self-consciously. "That's the magic of modern styling products. Looking like a crazy Muppet wasn't impressing loan officers."

"Well, it's good." He cleared his throat again, his knuckles whitening beneath their scars. "All of you looks good."

The driver of the Audi behind them leaned on his horn.

"Light," she said, noticing only then that it had turned green.

"Right," he said, and pulled through the intersection with his cheeks gone a shade pinker. "How long has it been anyway?"

Chelsea was grateful for the chance to let her own flush ebb. "Since we saw each other? Seven years, I think. Not since Gran's funeral."

Liam's hand came over to rub her arm. "I was really sorry about that, Chel."

"I know you were." His kind green gaze brought the aching

feelings of friendship back, but she didn't look away. "I really appreciated seeing you at the service. And after, too."

He nodded, his attention taken up by maneuvering through the flow of traffic. His hands spun the wheel so smoothly she felt herself grow wet. "I wish—"

He cut himself off, and she wondered what he'd been going to say. They'd dated, or tried to, twice after crossing paths at the funeral. To say that hadn't gone well was an understatement. Her head had been too wrecked over losing Gran, her sole caretaker after her parents died. She hadn't been able to let herself connect to anyone back then. Later, when she'd decided to stay in Brooklyn rather than return to New Hampshire, she'd have been happy to hear from him. Unfortunately, he'd been living in Manhattan, and she hadn't quite brought herself to pick up the phone and call him.

There'd been too much baggage to get over, too much heartbreak to risk by starting up again. Shay had seemed the smart one. If you had to let go, better to let go clean.

Liam had been following his own thoughts while she was quiet. "Your gran's house was your first flip, wasn't it?"

"Yes." She smiled at the memory. She'd been a trader at a financial firm, hating every minute she spent at work. Desperate to quit, desperate not to *think*, the exhausting, frustrating, exhilarating work of fixing up that old house for resale had saved her sanity. She'd realized what money meant when her own bottom line was at stake. She'd learned how to hire a crew, how to goose them to do their best, how to work beside them without driving them crazy. A few of those early crew guys were still with her. Her pride in that made her sit straighter and shoot a grin at Liam.

"I sold Gran's place a week after listing it. And made enough profit to fund my next project. I remember thinking Gran was looking out for me from beyond."

"And now you're the big boss lady."

"Just like you're the big boss man."

He laughed at her banter, the tension she hadn't realized was in his shoulders easing as he rolled them against the seat. "I'm glad you came to me for this."

She was glad, too. She'd been nervous before she called him. After seven years without speaking, and fourteen since they'd been close, thinking he'd even remember her had seemed silly. He had, though, greeting her in his office with a warmth that was obvious. He'd been curious, and wary, and finally interested as she explained what she had in mind. What he hadn't been was standoffish.

It had seemed a miracle at the time.

"I'm glad, too," she said, the admission a trifle husky as it came out.

Since he was turning onto Peach Place, she hoped he wouldn't notice.

"It's the second house on the right," she said. "With the crab-apple tree in front."

Liam grunted, squeezing the pickup into the first space he found. Peach Place was a narrow lane connecting Montague and Remsen. Like many of the streets in the area, a stretch of lovely 1860s brownstones lined it on either side. The block was New York history in a bubble, the shining towers across the river in Manhattan all that anchored it in their time. Most of the Italianate row houses were rehabbed already, the one she'd bought being the exception, though it looked nice enough from the outside.

She swiped damp palms down her jeans as she stepped out of the truck and onto the sidewalk. If Liam turned out to hate her baby, he was going to break her heart. Her accountant's, too, probably.

His expression didn't give anything away. Professional now, he planted himself at the foot of the entry steps to give the narrow five-story structure a once-over.

"Brownstone's good," he said at last. "Whoever quarried and

installed it did a good job. There's no spalling that I can see. Windows are original. Not the glass, though."

The windows were long and graceful, like princesses standing tall. The moment she'd seen them, her soul had let out a sigh.

"All right," he said, finished with his survey. "Lead the way inside."

Though it looked far worse in there, once they were past the trashed vestibule, he rewarded her with a low whistle. He moved straight past her to the front parlor.

"Look at the freaking plasterwork on that molding. And the carving on that fireplace surround." He craned his neck to check out the ceiling medallion. "Chelsea, that's an original chandelier under those cobwebs!"

"I know." She was absurdly delighted by his amazement. "This place has been in one family since it was built. It still would be if the latest heirs weren't cash-strapped."

He turned to her with passion flaring in his green eyes. "I can't tell you how rare it is to find a house of this vintage that's been untouched."

"Oh, it's been touched," she warned. "You haven't seen the nineteen-seventies kitchen."

"Still." Obviously seduced, he wandered out to the slim stairway. His hand caressed the rickety banister. "It'd be a crime to cut this place into condos."

"I have to," she said, completely understanding the pang he felt. "It's the best way to recoup my investment. If I try to keep the whole thing together, it'll be so pricey it could take years to sell."

"*If* you sell."

"I'm a businesswoman. I can't tie up my capital that way."

He said nothing, just proceeded slowly through the rest of the home. As she'd expected, the seventies kitchen inspired some choice curses, but—like her—Liam saw the underlying potential. The lovely bedroom floor left him speechless, as did the tangled ghost of the brick-walled garden down the back stairs. When he turned to her there, his face was stoic.

"It's gonna cost a fortune," he said. "New plumbing, new electrical, new roof. I'm willing to bet the beams in your basement need jacking up, because your filth-encrusted parquet floors are slanting like the deck of the *Titanic*. Basically, we're gonna have to take the place apart with kid gloves and reassemble it the same way. Even if you got a bargain, even if nothing too big goes wrong, you are not gonna make a fortune flipping this house around."

Chelsea released a gusty sigh. "That's what I figured. I just couldn't resist it."

He stared at her for a second before snorting out a laugh. "You know you're not supposed to fall in love with your investments."

"I *know*. Why do you think I always flip ranchers?"

"Jesus." He touched the side of her face like he might caress it. A moment later, before she could decide what she hoped he'd do, he dropped his hand and squinted up the row house's plain brick posterior. "Repointing," he said, thrusting one finger at the crumbly mortar. "Another bill to add to the mix."

"Don't rub it in," she moaned.

Laughing, he dropped his arm around her shoulders. To her probably stupid pleasure, he left it there. "It is gorgeous. And you *did* get a damned good deal."

"Deals I'm good at. Now and then, I forget to be sensible."

"I assume you'd want your own crew to be involved."

Chelsea's heart sped up. This sounded like he was going to take the job. "Yes," she said, striving to maintain a calm demeanor. "They're not experts in this work like your guys, but I promise they're quick learners."

The arm he'd draped around her gave her a little squeeze. "Chelsea, the last thing you need to worry about is me not knowing how good you and your people are."

The pleasure of him being aware of her reputation brought a quick burn into her eyes. She blinked it away before lifting her face to him. "Are you saying you'll let me hire you?"

He smiled at her with his eyes. The crinkles that appeared around them did distracting things to her train of thought. "You'd see a lot of me. Probably every day for the next six months."

"I'm hardly afraid of that, Liam." She blushed when she heard herself. She'd said his name like they were lovers.

"Good." His tone was soft as well. His gaze held hers, the moment drawing into something not businesslike at all. She told herself she was glad he broke it by stepping back. "Why don't I feed you, and we can talk about this some more."

"You don't have to do that."

"Oh, I'm pretty sure I do. A, I heard your stomach growling, and, b, the last time I took you to a restaurant, you ran out before the hors d'oeuvres."

"Liam—"

"Let me," he said, his hands framing her face. "Let me enjoy my old friend being here now."

She couldn't resist him. Maybe she didn't want to in the first place.

"All right," she said, butterflies gone wild in her stomach. "Dinner sounds great to me."

"So . . ." Liam lifted a pot lid to assess its merrily boiling contents. "You buy the ugliest house on the block and turn it into the best."

"Yes, but only the best for *that* block. If you turn a flip into the best house for some upscale block five streets up, you won't get your money back."

Liam knew this, Chelsea was certain, but was attempting to put her at ease. He hadn't taken her to a restaurant, but to his gasp-inducing twenty-fourth-floor apartment in Midtown. The place was spacious by city standards—three beds, three baths, the open concept living/dining/kitchen as sleek as a spread in a magazine. Its modernity revealed a side of Liam she hadn't known existed, along with letting her know how well his firm must be doing.

Chelsea admitted she was a teensy bit intimidated, and also weak in the knees from the wide floor-to-ceiling view. Preferring to look at him for reasons both complicated and dangerous, she rested her spine and elbows on his gleaming white quartz island.

"It's just a house," Liam said, reading her wry expression. "*My* house. Note the mail tossed on the dining table. And the napping blankie on the sectional."

"The white leather sectional," Chelsea corrected. "Which you probably imported from Italy."

"Eh." He waved his hand in dismissal. "Leather's easier to clean if you spill something. I should—" He looked around as if he'd lost something, and she realized he was nervous, too. "Would you like me to pour you a glass of wine?"

"Stomach's empty," she said, her lips curving just a bit. "Doesn't seem like a good idea."

"Breadstick then? Or I could throw the salads together now."

The sleeves of his pale yellow oxford shirt were rolled above his elbows, baring his strong forearms. Unable to resist, Chelsea brushed the dark gold hair on those corded muscles with the back of her hand. "You don't have to fuss over me. I'd be happy grabbing a sandwich in a café."

"No, no." His laugh seemed more directed at him than her. "I'm fussing for my own sake. This way, if you run out, there'll be no pack of waiters to pity me."

Chelsea turned her palm to lay it across his forearm. Liam looked at it, then at her. His eyes gave away that this wasn't really a joke to him.

"I didn't mean to run out on you that night. I just couldn't handle, well, hardly anything then."

"I know." Visibly coming to a decision, Liam snapped off the burner and exhaled. His attention was all hers then, the intensity of his focus making her a little too warm inside. When his hands came up to chafe her shoulders, tingles swept to the need coiled between her thighs. Never mind drinking a glass of wine on an empty stomach, seeing Liam after such a long stretch of datelessness probably wasn't her best idea. Though they'd only been together the once, she remembered very well how good and *right* he'd felt making love to her. Maybe he was remembering, too. His gaze slid down to her nipples—which weren't cooperating with her desire to get her toes wet one at a time. He blinked as if she'd distracted him, then dragged his eyes up to hers again.

"You running out that evening hurt because it was what *he* did. All I wanted was to make things better for both of you."

"No one could have done that. Not really."

"I wanted to try," he said stubbornly.

But how much did you want to? she thought. *Enough to love Shay the same way that he loved you? Enough to forgive me for not being able to choose only one of you?*

She bit her lip, her feelings too raw to expose right then. She'd never explained that last part to Liam. She'd let him think embarrassment alone was behind them drifting apart. She turned her gaze to the distant door of his apartment, her heart clenched tight for what she'd lost. All the old problems still lay between them, the tangle of loyalties she couldn't figure how to unknot. Liam was a traditional man. Chelsea could pretend she was, if it was important enough, but her nature was always going to be more complex.

Liam drew her from her thoughts by giving her shoulders an exasperated squeeze. "*Chel.*"

"Do you hear from Shay?" she asked in a tiny voice.

Emotions flickered across his features. With more patience than she deserved, he tucked an errant curl back behind her ear. "We see him at Christmas. And for Mom's birthday. Even Shay wouldn't break her heart and miss that."

"I hear his carpentry shop in Boston is doing well."

A smile tugged at Liam's mouth. "I guess you've been keeping track."

"Googling," she admitted, then forced herself to go on. "He was important to me, Liam. He was the first friend I made after I lost my parents—my best friend, really. I wouldn't forget either one of you."

"He was my best friend, too."

Chelsea guessed Shay had been more than his brother. When he'd decided to leave home at eighteen and support himself, it couldn't have been easy for Liam. Feeling for him, she stroked the warm skin of his temple, beside the sweet green eyes that were welling up with sincerity. Falling for this man again would be as easy as falling off a log.

She didn't expect the frustration that twisted across his face.

"I can't," he said, his grip suddenly capturing her wrist like iron.

"You can't what?" The question was breathy for more reasons than surprise. His body crowded hers against the island, so much taller, so much *maler*, that she didn't want to break free. Something long and hot was nudging at her belly, something thick and insistent. All her pent-up longings melted like butter.

"I miss you, too," he said, as if it were an accusation. "When I heard your voice on the phone, I swear my heart turned over. I miss you loving me, and I miss being in love with you. My life is good now. I have friends and a job I love. Every day, I get to accomplish things I'm proud of. Part of me, though, never came back to life after you left. I can't still be worrying about Shay's feelings if there's even a chance of making this work with you."

Chelsea's hormones were short-circuiting her brain. And maybe her heart was, too. *Don't hurt him,* she ordered sternly. *Be sure of what you're doing.* "We . . . I . . . I can't deny it touches me to hear you say that, but—"

"Look, I get why you're nervous. We haven't been together in a long while. I know you're probably thinking we need to get to know each other as we are now."

She *was* thinking that, but it wasn't the whole story.

"We could wait until the job is done," she offered tentatively. "It'd be awkward if we started dating and then broke up."

Liam wagged his head. "I'd go crazy seeing you every day. You don't know what you do to me. I'll swear on anything you want that, no matter what, I'll help you turn that house into a palace, but please don't make me wait six months to do this."

She thought he was going to kiss her, but instead he pulled her gently against him, decimating her defenses by the simple act of enveloping her in his arms. He was warm and big and his hold seemed like the only real home she might have left. He bent his neck until his lips were against her hair. "I missed you, Chelsea, so fucking much you wouldn't believe it."

His roughly uttered words were almost too sweet to trust. Because she wanted to, she wrapped her arms around him with more strength than probably was wise.

"I'd believe it," she said into his hard chest. "I felt so stupid, not being able to forget you in all this time."

He groaned, not only for what she'd said, but because their aroused bodies were pressed so closely together. His sweat smelled good, as did his faint aftershave. His hands roamed her back, almost ventured onto her ass, and—after an instant's hesitation—slid up to massage her shoulder blades again.

That he wanted to be bolder was obvious.

"Chelsea," he said, his face nuzzling her neck. His heart was pounding as his lungs moved shallowly in and out.

When he did no more, she realized it was up to her. He wasn't going to push her. She let her own hands roam and turned her mouth toward his.

Their lips found each other on a mutual gasp. The kiss started sweet, but soon it grew deep and hard, their tongues relearning each other to the music of hungry moans. As Chelsea wriggled to press her itches to the right spots, Liam apparently decided he was permitted to hold her butt.

"Chel," he panted, his fingers kneading forcefully through her jeans. "Is this just a kiss we're having? Do you want me to stop?"

He'd leaned his forehead on hers to ask. Her body trembled from wanting him, her hands knotting in the front of his yellow shirt as if secretly planning to rip it off. Did she have to solve *every-thing* before she did this? Couldn't she just enjoy the moment?

"I don't want you to stop," she said. "Not for anything."

He'd been holding back before when they kissed. Now he devoured her, hauling her up and using his weight to pin her against the front of his fancy European refrigerator. He ground his hard-on into her, groaning at the give of her pussy beneath her jeans.

Chelsea tore the tails of his shirt out of his trousers. His back was sweating as she drove her hands under it. Taking this as permission to do the same, Liam shoved up her top, hitched her higher, and sucked half her breast into his mouth through her bra.

Chelsea choked out a strangled cry. Her nipples had always been a hot zone for her, and Liam wasn't shy about suckling them.

"Get undressed," she pleaded as he switched sides to nip the other. The pressure of his teeth was perfect. Her hips bucked tighter against him. "God, Liam, don't waste time."

His eyes were burning as he pulled back. "I remember this," he said thickly. "I remember how fucking hot to go you were."

She didn't know how to be insulted, especially since *he* seemed so exultant. He let her slide down him, let her measure the rock-hard ridge thrusting out the front of his pants. To her relief, once she was on her feet, he started tearing off his clothes.

They both wrestled themselves down to their underwear: she in scraps of pink push-up lace, he in gray boxer briefs. Chelsea's underwear wasn't always so fancy. Considering how she felt about Liam, her "just in case" choice seemed justified. Once she saw how good he looked, she was grateful. In truth, she was having some trouble breathing. Liam was a big guy, and his abs were Greek-statue good, his long muscular legs fuzzed with the same dark gold hair that graced his forearms. Between lay Chelsea's idea of porn. Liam's briefs stretched over his erection, the shape of it stark and clear. The blood-flushed head poked above his waistband, pre-come glistening in the slit. He looked up from disrobing to gawk at her. Though Chelsea knew her job kept her in good shape, she wasn't prepared for his reaction.

"Jesus," he cursed. "You're even sexier than I remember."

She didn't have time to thank him. He was on her in a second, scooping her up to carry her down a hall.

"I have a bed," he said as she clung to him. "A big, soft bed with a sturdy frame."

She laughed and hugged him, nothing in her in that moment but lust and joy.

He wasn't laughing, but she didn't mind that, either. With a look of intense sexual purpose, he tossed her onto his mattress, pushed his dampened underwear down his legs, and crawled over her like a wolf in man form.

The blistering French kiss he gave her nearly burned her lips off.

"Liam," she groaned when he broke long enough for air. His weight was on her, and she had to struggle to kick free of her panties.

Liam rose to his elbows and snapped her out of her bra. His cock throbbed along her thigh as if it were drumming her. His callused hands smoothed over her now-bare breasts, shaping them lovingly. Chelsea's body stretched like a cat.

To her surprise, he didn't move to take her.

"I gave up," he stopped to admit, though she was so ready she was melting. "The night you ran out on me in that restaurant, I finally gave up. Up till then, I'd assumed we'd be together again someday. For seven years, I kept myself together by believing it would happen."

"I'm here now," Chelsea said, covering the hands that caressed her breasts.

He shook his head, unconvinced. "I went home that night and got very drunk. Missed my first day on a site in years. You didn't know you were doing it, but—by God—you devastated me."

"I didn't mean to."

"I know." He smiled, just a little. "And it's not like I told you what I was hoping for." His thumbs circled her nipples, drawing them painfully tight. His expression was still haunted. "I need so much from you now it scares me."

Liam being afraid was no small event. He was one of the least dramatic people she knew. She rubbed her leg reassuringly along his. "Tell me what you need. If I can, I'll give it to you."

She could see him wondering if he dared open himself that way. The question he ended up asking wasn't what she expected. "Are you using contraception?"

"Yes," she said, "but—"

"I'm healthy," he said. "I swear I'd never lie to you about that."

She trailed one fingertip around the smile line framing his serious mouth. "I know you wouldn't."

Her trust caused his eyes to darken. He let his chest sink to hers, the meeting of hard to soft, of smooth to hairy delicious. Then, with his gaze locked on hers, he dragged his big body over hers—inches up, inches down—his naked skin to hers.

"I want to be bare inside you," he said gruffly.

It seemed important. "Yes," she said. "Take me any way you want."

He didn't waste time making sure she meant it. He rolled them deftly onto their sides. Even as her breath caught, his hand smoothed down the back of her thigh. When he reached her knee, he curved his fingers behind the bend, pulling up until her leg bracketed his thigh. The combined heat of their groins was incredible.

"Feel me go in," he growled.

She couldn't help but feel him. His big rounded tip was heated silk parting her wet folds. He probed, then pushed, and then a groan ripped out of her throat.

"Oh God," she gasped, fingers clutching him as her eyelids closed.

No one else filled her like he did. No one trembled with awe as he slid inside. She moaned in protest when he backed his hips off before reaching the end of her. She knew she was tight, but she wanted them joined so badly she thought she'd cry.

"Chel," he said, stroking her side to soothe her. "Give yourself a minute to get used to me."

"I feel like I don't have a minute."

He laughed as if he didn't have enough air. "Then give *me* a minute. You feel so good; if I'm not careful, I'm going to go before you."

That brought her eyes open. His face *was* strained, his cock extremely full and hard inside her, though he wasn't penetrating her completely. She slid her hands up his back, then took him by surprise by pulling his body on top of hers. He gasped, the shift in weight doing what he'd been too cautious to. As her pussy took all of him, all either of them could do for a couple seconds was squirm with intense pleasure.

"Don't worry," she panted, once she was able. "I'm not going to take long."

He swallowed, moved his hips so that they pressed hers harder, and reached up to brace one hand on his platform bed's wide head-board. Chelsea took her own grip on his hard, muscled waist. They needed no words then. His eyes told her what hers probably told him: that it had been a long wait for this. With one last pause for air, he drew back and started plunging in so strongly she knew she hadn't exaggerated her readiness.

Her neck arched back as very welcome sensations rocketed through her nerves. Oh, she remembered this: being so excited that she didn't have to be coaxed, knowing her partner was utterly there for her. Freed from any worry that she'd respond, she raced for the finish, loving the harsh cries her abandon called from him.

His hand clamped over her bottom, his teeth clenching. Wanting him even deeper, Chelsea tried to stretch her thighs wider.

"Come," she urged, feeling the giant climax well up in her.

"After . . . you," he said between grunts.

"*With* me." She was so close she was panting, her inner muscles wanting desperately to clutch down on him. If they did, she knew the friction would be too good not to fly over.

Liam's hips pumped faster. He tried to say something and couldn't. He was going deeper, harder, his balls beginning to slap her despite how tight they were.

"Do it," she said, fists clenched at the small of his back. "Shoot your seed into me."

She'd hit on the right demand. This was the secret thing he'd wanted when he'd asked to take her bare: to mark her in the most primitive way men could. His thrusts turned uneven as she pressed the button, then sped up even more. He growled from trying to restrain his climax, his expression twisted like the pleasure was killing him.

"Feel me," she goaded. "Feel how wet my pussy is twitching on your cock."

He shouted and she went over at the same time—hard, bright spears of bliss that had her sheath tightly fisting him. He must have liked it. He was flooding her, or maybe it was the other way around. She spilled over with heat and pleasure, but he didn't stop driving in and out, making muffled noises like he was still hungry. Only when she came a second time, even harder, did he let his weight relax over her.

Adoring the feel of his big, hot body, she dug both hands deep into his hair.

"Don't," she murmured when he tried to move.

"I'll crush you."

"Mmm. Don't want to breathe anyway."

He laughed almost silently.

Since he'd stayed where he was, she massaged his shoulders, reveling in how broad they were. He had so much power—and so much consideration in the way he controlled it. She found a knot on the left that begged for more pressure. To her surprise, as she worked to ease it, his hips shifted restlessly against her.

"You're still a little hard," she said in amazement.

"Been wanting you too long," he mumbled. "We might have to do that again."

"*Noo*," she teased in mock horror.

"Yes," he retorted, and stuck his tongue in her ear.

She giggled, which made him tickle her, which had them rolling around like kids on his king-size bed. His half-hard cock slipped out of her too soon for her taste, though this did allow her to get her hands on more parts of him.

"God," he sighed, finally settling with her sprawled breathlessly over him. "I am still completely in love with you."

She pushed up on her forearms to look at him.

"You don't have to say it back," he said.

"I can say it." His eyes had been worried, but her touch of defensiveness amused him.

"I can!" she repeated. "I'm still in love with you."

He took her face in his hands, thumbs caressing her cheekbones, smile so tender and understanding she knew he'd heard the "but" she was trying to leave unsaid.

"Don't make me explain everything," she pleaded. "I want to enjoy tonight."

"So do I," he said, and pulled her up to kiss him.

After they made love again, she really had to shower. Liam followed her into the large tiled space. They probably would have gone another round among the two zillion jets if her stomach hadn't resumed grumbling. Chelsea was embarrassed, but Liam simply laughed, bundling her in a too-big bathrobe and tugging her to his kitchen to eat lukewarm pasta and meat sauce.

Despite the temperature, Chelsea thought it might have been the best spaghetti she'd ever had.

When their plates sat empty on his island, they leaned back with matching sighs. Liam had pulled on some old gray sweatpants. He probably didn't mind the way her eyes kept admiring his bare torso. People who worked out in gyms only hoped to end up like him.

"I am sated," Chelsea announced, hands folded happily over her stomach.

Liam smiled at her, his expression warm enough to draw a hint of heat back into her sex. He made her heart beat faster even as a wonderful sense of security spread through her. He still wanted her. He still loved her. How in the world had she gotten so lucky?

"Time to spill," he said, battered fingers turning his wineglass in a circle. "Tell me what you didn't want to before."

Chelsea gnawed on her lip. Liam covered her hand with his, reassuring her with his eyes. She couldn't deny he deserved answers.

"Okay," she said, fighting back a sigh. "I expect you realize I got my crush on you the day I moved in next door."

One corner of his kissable mouth twitched. "You were a very romantic ten-year-old."

"Well, I know my feelings were childish. What's important is that they never went away. You really had the qualities I fell in love with. You were kind and funny and the best-looking older boy I had ever met. Basically, even at that age, I had excellent taste in men."

"But?" he prompted when she paused to gather herself.

"But there was Shay." She watched Liam as she told him, praying she could keep this from hurting him. "Loving Shay snuck up on me. One day, he looked at me and everything he felt about me was in his eyes."

"And you felt it back."

"I felt . . . I didn't want him to be sad. I wanted him to be happy, and I wanted to be the one who made him that way. So I knew. I knew I cared as much for him as I did for you. Believe me, I didn't want to admit it. You were everything I wanted. You had a right to someone who could give her whole heart to you. So I pretended I didn't feel it. I tried to commit myself to only wanting you."

"Until that day up in the garage."

Chelsea turned her palm to his. "Until that day."

He didn't pull back, and he didn't seem surprised, though his eyes were cautious. "Did you know he had feelings for me?"

"I had inklings. I'd have had to be stupid not to. We hung out a lot, and considering my crush on you, I certainly recognized the signs. I think—" She stopped and squeezed his hand a little tighter. "I think what bothered me was that him having a thing for both of us never bothered me. The fantasies I had once I figured it out . . . I had no idea the mere possibility would flip my switch so hard." She shook her head ruefully. "I'm lucky you two didn't make me flunk senior year."

Liam didn't respond to her attempt at humor. "And now?" he asked quietly.

That was the question, wasn't it? The one she couldn't weasel out of even in the privacy of her mind. "Now I still feel a lot of what I did then. I just can't promise you every single piece of my heart."

Liam's hands pulled slowly back to the edge of the countertop. He gripped it so carefully he seemed worried he'd break the stone.

"Okay," he said. "That's honest."

"Don't say it's honest," Chelsea objected, part of her wanting to curse his decency. "You ought to be kicking me to the curb. You're such a wonderful man. You shouldn't have to deal with a woman who can't give all of herself to you."

"*I'm* wonderful." Liam let out a shaky laugh. "Don't you think I have flaws? I let you down. I let Shay down. If I'd found a way to get through to him, he wouldn't have exiled himself. He'd be here, with his family, where he belongs."

"You are what you are, Liam."

"Maybe I'm not as sure of who that is as I used to be."

Chelsea couldn't read what was in his eyes. "What are you saying?"

He stood, turning her on the swiveling stool to face him. He ran his hands down the sleeves of her borrowed robe. "I'm saying don't give up on this yet."

"I wouldn't give up. Not on you. Not unless you made me."

It might have been her most shameful confession: that she was too selfish to walk away. He should have been angry, but: "I'll never make you," he swore.

Chelsea's fingertips rested on his stomach to either side of the line of hair that dove down from his navel. His sweatpants hung low on his solid hip bones, their front rising alluringly. When Chelsea turned one hand to slide it inside the garment, Liam inhaled sharply.

"I want to fuck you again," he rasped.

She didn't mind how he put it. What she wanted wasn't soft, either. She was glad he hadn't dragged his underwear back on. He jerked when her hand found his hot thickness. She remained on the stool, knees spread to let him close. Exposed by the position, wet cream ran from her as she drew her hand luxuriantly up his cock. With someone else, she might have been self-conscious about her own reaction. With him, tonight, everything seemed all right. The shudder that shook his body was a true thrill.

"Chel," he said, like she was making him impatient.

"I love touching you," she murmured. "Let me tease you a little first."

"Only if I can tease you."

The gaping robe made her sex fair game. He tucked his hand underneath and around her pussy, one thumb easing inside her heat. Chelsea lost her breath at the slow rotation he made with it. He didn't kiss her, but his cheek came down to rub against hers. Though he'd shaved in the shower, he still had some male roughness. She shivered as his thumb went around again.

He'd never lied about being good with his hands.

"You like having me inside you," he said throatily. "As I recall, you like being rubbed outside, too." His other hand pulled the robe's tie free, taking her clitoris between his thumb and two fingers. Delicious feelings spread through her at the multiple pressures. "Babe, you have no idea how I love hearing your breath speed up."

He was breathing pretty fast himself, especially when she remembered to stroke what her hand had wrapped. Their heads were close together, both angled downward to watch the other's reactions. Liam's cock had grown thick enough to prevent her fingertips from meeting.

"How long are we going to keep this up?" she asked breathlessly.

"Just until one of us cries uncle." His eyes rose long enough to sparkle humorously at her. "Boy, oh, boy," he laughed softly. "I hope I can keep you."

He dropped the lightest of kisses onto her waiting mouth. The contact was too sweet for her present mood. Her tongue came out, then his, and then he was probing her hungrily.

"Well," said the visitor whose entry they'd been too busy to register. "I guess my timing could be better."

Liam

Liam snatched his hand back from Chelsea's pussy out of reflex. "Shay," he said, his heart thumping even harder. "What the hell?"

Shay stood at the perimeter of the kitchen, the keys to Liam's apartment flashing on the ring he was swinging from one finger. Liam had mailed those keys to him almost as soon as he'd bought this place, though Shay had never seen fit to use them. When he came to town for Christmas visits, he stayed in a hotel. The sardonic half smile that quirked Shay's mouth told Liam he knew exactly what he'd walked in on. "You did say your door was always open to me."

"It is." Liam was aware that Chelsea had hopped to the floor and was hastily tying her terry robe. "It's good to see you, man."

Lean as a whip in his faded jeans and baby blue polo shirt, Shay rolled dark eyes. Liam could see why women went for his adopted brother, with his straight black hair and his jaw as sharp as a trowel. His hip-shot stance lent him the glamour of a world-weary movie star. Ignoring Shay's disbelief at his welcome, or maybe because of it, Liam pulled him into a back-slapping hug. After a second, Shay returned it.

"Jesus," Liam said, feeling his boniness. "Don't you remember to eat up there in Boston?"

Shay pushed back with Liam's hands still gripping his upper arms. Liam suspected the eyes that met his were purposely hard to read. "My cooking isn't as good as Mom's."

"Well, have a burger now and then. You're gonna blow away if you're not careful."

"Hey, Shay," Chelsea greeted from behind Liam. She'd retreated to the six-burner stove, and her cheeks were probably pinker than she wanted them to be. When Shay shifted his gaze to her, his chest lurched briefly up and down.

"Hey, Chel," he said in return.

It would have come off more casual if his voice hadn't gone rough in the middle.

Chelsea dropped her eyes and turned redder.

"Let me get you a beer," Liam said, taking pity on all of them.

He pulled a bottle from the fridge, cracked it and handed it to Shay. Shay thanked him, then took a long swallow.

"Not that I'm not happy to see you," Liam said, "but what's the occasion?"

Shay set the beer on the island, one thumbnail picking at the label. He shot a glance at Chelsea before he spoke. "I broke up with—well, I'm not sure I'd call her my girlfriend—let's say, the woman I was dating. Some of the things she accused me of got me wondering what I'd been doing with my life lately."

"If she left you, she was an idiot," Chelsea said.

Shay rewarded her defense with an amused smile. "She might not have been the best match for me, but an idiot she was not. As you might remember, I like smart girls."

"Maybe not as smart as you think."

Her tartness startled him, which Liam enjoyed.

Clearly trying to regain his balance, Shay gestured with the beer toward her. "You look good, Chel. The hair is just like I remembered."

"Shit," Chelsea exclaimed, hands flying to the wild mass of curls. "I meant to put something on it after . . . my shower."

That it had been Liam's shower as well was obvious.

"So." Shay took another pull on the beer, his self-deprecating humor now back in place. "You two, huh? That's nice. Mom said you bought a house up in Brooklyn Heights. Made a point of telling me you'd be around. I guess she didn't realize different developments were brewing."

Chelsea's eyes widened at his sarcasm. She hadn't met this new, bitter Shay before. To her credit, it took her about two seconds to see through it.

"Shay," she said, mildly scolding. "Put down that beer and say 'hello' like a real person."

She ended up having to take it from him, but when she hugged him, he returned the embrace. His head came down next to hers, both their arms tightening.

"Chel," he groaned, his face buried in her hair.

"I missed you," she responded, no readier to let go than he was. "You're such a bastard for not keeping in touch with me."

Liam knew the moment holding her began to kick Shay's gonads. His eyes closed and he inhaled, his cheek rubbing her curls like he was memorizing the feel of them. Chelsea's hands slid up his arms and settled on his shoulders. Liam was pretty sure this was in preparation for putting space between them.

"I had a fling," Liam said.

Both of them turned to him. Shay's expression was definitely the more annoyed one.

"I'm not trying to ruin your moment. I had a fling. With a guy."
Chelsea's head jerked back in surprise.

"When was this?" Shay asked with both eyebrows raised.

Now that he'd said it, Liam's hands were shaking. He clenched them beside his hips. "About a year back. I thought I should . . . try it out."

"Because of me." Shay had stepped away from Chelsea and had a grip on his beer again, though he wasn't actually drinking it.

"I did it because of me. Because the idea was—had been—in my head for a while. I thought I might like it."

"And did you?"

Chelsea was leaving this interrogation to her old buddy. When Liam glanced at her, she was smiling faintly at the mirror finish on the dark hardwood floor.

"It was fine," Liam said. "At least the sex part. I wasn't so comfortable with the guy. I don't think I liked him enough."

"You don't think you liked him enough." Shay was staring at Liam with his mouth open. Liam's shoulders hitched in a shrug.

"It was awkward. I'm not good at casual hookups."

Chelsea made a soft sound.

"Are you *laughing* at me?" Liam asked.

"Yes?" Her voice rose like there might be a doubt. Biting her smile, she closed the small distance between them to wrap him in a tight hug. Liam didn't mind that, though he'd rather have understood why she was doing it.

"My God," she murmured against his chest. "Sometimes you are too much for words."

"Well, how could I know what I liked if I didn't try?"

"You couldn't." Amused, Chelsea leaned back in the circle his arms had automatically cinched around her waist. "And of course you couldn't do your test run with Shay, because what if it didn't work?"

"Exactly," he agreed. "That would have hurt his feelings."

Behind her, by the island, Shay rubbed one thumb up the furrow between his brows. "Liam, that day over the garage—no offense, bro—but when I touched you, your dick went limp."

"You freaked me. I hadn't been thinking of you that way—at least, I don't think I had. The thing is, what happened that day stuck in my mind all this time. Sometimes pictures of it flash back when I'm, you know, getting myself off."

Liam felt stupid beyond belief spelling this out. When Shay looked at him, though, and Liam saw the signs of arousal darkening his face, the wave of heat that rolled through him was astounding. Chelsea must have felt it. She went very still in his arms. Liam wondered if she knew his cock was stirring.

"Do you ever—" Shay cleared his throat and continued. "Do you ever think about that day on purpose?"

"Sure," Liam said, trying not to sound too uncomfortable. "I mean, it makes jacking off better. It gets me excited."

"Which parts of it get you excited?"

Liam guessed Shay wanted to be certain Liam wasn't mistaken. He forced himself to be honest. "You going down on Chel did it for me. Me holding her while you made her come. Sometimes I think about how you looked naked. How hard you were when you watched me and her."

Liam couldn't help how gravelly his voice had gotten. He was picturing all the good stuff right then. Shay fell silent to think about what he'd said.

Liam's back was sweating when Chelsea rubbed her hands soothingly up it. "Are you saying you want us to try being together now?"

She was flushed, her blue eyes bright within their thick lashes.

"Yeah," he said. "That's exactly what I'm saying."

"This is a risk," Shay warned. "We could make things worse than they are."

Liam's smile came without effort. "What have we got without it? What have the three of us got that's so good we can't afford to give this a shot?"

He was pleased that neither of them argued.

"All right," Chelsea said. "I'm in."

Shay let out a snicker.

"What?" she asked, twisting in Liam's arms to face him.

"Of course you're in," Shay said. "Little Miss I-Love-Threesomes."

He'd stepped close enough that Chel could swat him.

"Let me at her," Shay said laughingly to Liam. He stopped laughing a second later, realizing what he'd said. *Let me at her. Let me finally have her.*

Liam let go. Watching Shay tug Chelsea to him spurred a thick rush of excitement. Chelsea's lips were parted, her eyes gone round. Liam could see she was aroused but unsure how to handle this. His skin buzzed from the flood of adrenaline, his cock shoving out the soft cotton of his sweatpants. The pair's gazes locked with a heat Liam registered from a foot away. As Shay regarded Chelsea, his face broke into a smile that wasn't the least bit bitter.

"You and me, babe," he said softly, a promise meant just for her. "We're going to do this before anything else goes down. No matter what happens later, you're going to have me inside of you."

Her eyes searched his and then she stretched up to kiss him. Coolness forgotten, Shay moaned like she'd gut-punched him. In half a second, they were plastered to each other, kissing like maniacs. Shay's hands dove beneath her robe, then helped her wrench out of it.

Liam had an excellent view of Shay's hands squeezing her taut buttocks.

The sudden choked sound Shay made was in response to the cupping, rubbing grip Chelsea had taken on his zipper. She might be the one who was naked, but she'd certainly gotten the upper hand. With no hesitation whatsoever, she massaged a course down his monster bulge, all the way from the metal button to deep between his legs on the seam.

"God." Shay gasped, writhing under the hard and apparently skilled caress. *Fuck.*

He grabbed the back of his collar to yank his shirt over his head, baring new territory for her hands to explore. Skinny or not, Shay's torso was really cut. Chelsea's fingertips turned his nipples to tight red points. "The couch," he rasped, starting to shuffle back toward the living room.

"Yes," she panted in agreement, leaving Liam to decide if he should follow.

It was Shay who caught his eyes and nodded. "We know you like this part," he said.

He liked this part, and it was easier, and he couldn't deny Shay and Chelsea deserved to enjoy themselves after all this time. His throat closed on his excitement as Chelsea gingerly opened Shay's faded jeans. The downward rasp of the zipper sent an answering zing through him. Shay's jeans fit loose, and she had no trouble dropping them down his legs. Nothing spoiled Liam's view of those, or of the hard red jut of his erect penis. Shay's pubic hair was inky against skin the sun hadn't touched.

Chelsea seemed to admire the contrast. She trailed one finger down his torso's midline, then curled it under his shaft.

"Commando," she purred as she pulled the hook of her finger up his shuddering hard-on. "That is extremely bold."

Smugness fought with shy pleasure in Shay's expression. He handed her the wrapped condom he'd tucked in his wallet. "Why don't you dress me?"

Chelsea opened the package and smoothed it over him, the motions of her fingers gentle and lingering. Liam guessed all men had their fixations, because Chelsea doing this seemed to be Shay's. With a look like he'd gone to heaven, Shay's hands came up to surround her breasts, his technique for teasing her nipples shaken by the drag of her thumb around his now latex-covered glans. His distraction didn't keep him from looking down her body.

"Chel," he gasped, "you're even prettier than I remembered."

Chelsea's grin let Liam know she was about to be a smartass. "What about him?" she asked, jerking her head to the side. "Is Liam prettier, too?"

Shay slid a glance at Liam, then *down* Liam, his face too red to get any duskier. "He's not prettier, he's harder, but harder looks good on him."

The pair laughed in harmony at the joke, which truly turned the crank on Liam's arousal. Apparently, being admired by both of them was another turn-on for him. Shay made Chelsea gasp by boosting her up his body, her legs winding around his waist with a lovely tightening of muscles. Shay's cock stood nearly straight between them, its swollen tip just resting on her belly. The hand that held her bottom copped a good feel of it.

"Need more time?" Shay asked huskily.

Chelsea shook her head, her soft pink lips rolled between her teeth.

"Good," Shay said, "'cause I think I'm about to die if I don't have you."

He lowered them both to Liam's white sectional, then maneuvered them sideways. Shay ended up kneeling on the leather with Chelsea, who knelt higher, straddling him. Shay's hands massaged Chelsea's hips, his thumbs reaching into her prettily trimmed thatch to tug the glistening edges of her folds apart. Her labia grew even wetter as he pulled them apart far enough to bare her swollen clitoris. Chelsea squirmed at the tease, her impatience obvious. Luckily, Liam's body didn't know how to be jealous. Everything inside him loved how eager she seemed for Shay to drive his hardness up into her. Seeing this, in person, was more potent than fantasies. A sound he couldn't contain rumbled in his chest.

Shay hadn't been looking at him, and he didn't turn now. "Drop your pants, bro," he said. "Chelsea will want to watch what this does to you."

Liam dropped them with fumbling fingers, cool air hitting the blazing skin of his erection. He remembered how Chelsea had reached for Shay's cock that night fourteen years ago. He didn't see her glance over, but she must have.

"Just a kiss," she pleaded with Shay softly.

Shay smiled and dropped one to the tip of her nose. "Come closer," he said to Liam. "Chelsea wants to kiss you."

They all knew Chelsea didn't mean on the mouth.

She steadied Liam's cock so gently she must have thought he would break. Her lips molded to his penis, and then the flat of her tongue swept wetly over the pulsing head. Liam's cock twitched, miniature lightning bolts setting his nerves twanging. He sucked in his breath to warn her it was too much, but she backed off with a smile so knowing he nearly came from that.

Shay was panting like her tongue had been stroking him. The evidence of his excitement was another whip crack to Liam's cock.

"Don't go anywhere," Chelsea said.

"No worries," Liam assured her hoarsely.

Shay's grip tightened on her hips, effectively drawing all eyes to him. His cock had an upward curve, the strut underneath like steel. The thing was too stiff to need an assist. Using only his hips, he ran his knob up her furrow, then down it, and then—just as she uttered a pleading cry—he shoved all the way into her. The thrust was rough and had both of them making pleasure-pain noises. Given his size, Liam wouldn't have been able to pull it off. Watching Shay do it was a weirdly compelling, vicarious thrill.

"God," Chelsea breathed, sounding like having him inside her felt very good. "Is it okay if I move now?"

Shay was holding her in his arms as tightly as she was holding him. Possibly he wasn't able to speak. He nudged her up in his lap, a rolling motion of his pelvis that caused Chelsea's head to fall back limply. He did it again, this time lifting her by the hips as well.

She seemed to pull herself together, shaking her crazy curls and shifting her hands to grip his lean but very broad shoulders. Her thrusts met his then, roll surging smoothly into roll until Shay simply lost control of his vocal cords.

"Ah," he cried, tight and tenor, each time her pubis slapped as close as it could. "Ah, ah, ah."

They went faster, the force of each collision increasing, their skin gleaming bright with sweat. Chelsea's flesh would have jiggled more if Shay hadn't been covering her breasts. She moaned as the angle he was driving into her changed subtly. Liam remembered how her insides felt like hot, wet velvet, how her sheath clung so snugly to an intruding shaft that it needed to be oiled by her excitement. Her pussy must have contracted, because Shay's face twisted and his breathing suddenly turned harsh. He caught each of her nipples between a thumb and forefinger.

"Me," he ordered, the word not easy to make out. He had to be close to coming, but he swallowed determinedly. "Chelsea, look at me."

She looked—half blind but gorgeous—riding him like a Valkyrie. "*Shay.*"

He used the grip he had on her nipples to shimmy them in and out. Chelsea went over, and a moment later Shay joined her violently. One twisting vein stood out on his forehead as his narrow hips convulsed into her. Both their orgasms continued for a while.

At last, they sagged against each other with Shay's cheek resting on her near shoulder. They petted each other, tender and lazy. Chelsea kissed Shay's ear, then murmured into it. *I love you,* Liam thought he saw her lips say.

"Me too," Shay mumbled back to her.

He pulled back to smile into her eyes. In that moment, Liam knew he didn't exist for them. How little he minded surprised him.

Then again, maybe he was wrong about not existing.

"We haven't forgotten you," Shay said.

Shay hadn't looked around. Chelsea pressed her lips to his perspiring forehead. "I'm pulling off you," she warned.

Shay made the noise Liam would expect from losing her warmth on him. The protest became a sigh as she removed and discarded the wet condom. Though he was soft, he shifted restlessly on his haunches when her fingers stroked over him. Liam was pretty certain Shay wasn't done wanting her.

"I love penises," Chelsea said. "They are just the silkiest things."

Shay snorted in amusement, after which his head turned sleepily toward Liam. "Got any more jackets stashed?"

For a second, Liam's brain wouldn't work. Shay's face had been transformed by release. It was utterly relaxed and open, utterly beautiful. Finally having sex with Chelsea had brought out a side of him Liam hadn't seen before.

"Bathroom," he said, working not to stammer. "I'll grab the box."

His legs felt funny as he strode down the hall, as if he'd locked his knees too hard while he played voyeur. His erection hadn't flagged when the show ended. It pounded harder as he opened the mirrored cabinet where he kept his condoms. He was heavy, itchy, the aching weight of his prick telling him things he wasn't as prepared to know as he'd thought. He wanted Shay. His body wasn't the least freaked by the idea. Only his head needed to catch up.

He dropped his hand to the almost alien thickness that stood out from his groin. He didn't pull, just tightened his fingers around the girth. Even so, delicious signals rode up his nerves, fluid squeezing suddenly from his tip.

Was Shay going to want to take him? Or was Liam supposed to fuck him? Would Chelsea maybe touch herself while she watched?

That idea had his balls knotting with fullness.

Liam cursed and released his cock.

He was going to do this. It was going to be all right. He might come in the first two seconds, but—hell—as horny as he was feeling, he'd just start up again. Grabbing the box of condoms, he strode back to the living room.

There he found the contents of his fantasy come to life.

Chel was splayed on the couch fingering herself. Shay knelt between her legs, rapt as she masturbated, his hands gripping his own clenched thighs like he very much wanted to take hold of something else. His cock was already harder than half mast.

"Don't make yourself come," Shay said in a harsh whisper. "You have to hold back for Liam."

Lust spiked inside Liam with frightening force. Right then, if he could have fallen on both of them, he would have. The need he felt was savage. Fucking wouldn't satisfy it. He wanted to despoil.

Chelsea spotted Liam and flushed the color of sunset.

He couldn't let her be embarrassed, not when he felt so unbelievably alive. "Don't stop on my account," he said huskily. "Shay isn't the only one who likes watching you do that."

"He talked me into it," she said, her hands drawn guiltily to her breasts.

Liam stood over her, looking down. "It's a special Irish gift," he agreed gravely.

She stared at him, then broke into a laugh. "Got your own 'Irish gift,' I see."

She gestured toward his massive, pounding erection.

"Oh boy," Shay chuckled, getting a load of it.

Liam had no chance to grow nervous. Shay touched his hard-on, and then Chel did, and then four warm hands were surrounding and stroking him. Liam nearly bit his tongue at how good their combined caresses felt. Fingers fondled his tip, his balls, the quivering muscles of his stomach. Overwhelmed, he dropped his hands to their hair as each pressed nipping kisses to either side of his ribs.

He'd lost these two when Chel went to college, none of them able to bridge the awkwardness of discovering they were a triangle and not a trio. For too many years to count, he'd wished he'd known how to make things easier for them. Now, tonight, they were doing it for him. The sensations that powered through him were extraordinary. Nothing but kindness lay behind their touches, nothing but a desire to bring him pleasure.

He coiled with anticipation as both their mouths approached the end of his penis, hard exhalations washing over its nerve-rich skin. His breath rushed out as two pairs of lips molded over and licked his glans, one tongue sweeping out and receding only to be followed by the other. The rhythm nearly hypnotized him, but then the tongues began to parry. Shay and Chelsea were kissing each other even as they kissed him. Liam's body, or maybe his erotic psyche, tried to turn inside out.

This was a turn-on to beat them all.

"Please," he hissed, reluctantly, half a minute later. "You're gonna make me explode."

They released him, but it took a couple blinks for his eyes to open again.

"You are too fucking gorgeous when you're this hot and bothered," Shay said to him. "I've got to have you while you're like this."

Liam more than understood the urge. "Okay," he said. "But can I take her while you do it?"

Fortunately, this request wasn't a faux pas. Shay's grin of answer was saturnine.

"Oh yeah. Watching you fuck her would put the cherry on top for me."

Chelsea had no protests, either.

"Should I lube him?" she offered.

An overnight bag Liam hadn't noticed before was sitting open on the brushed steel cube of his end table. A tube of lubricant, and not a small one, lay on top of the clothes inside. Shay caught sight of what had snagged his attention.

"I wasn't assuming," he hurried to explain. "Just thinking positive, maybe. Girls like lube, too, anyway."

"I don't think I'm in a position to object," Liam said breathlessly.

"Good," Chelsea said, hopping up to grab it. "This is going to be fun."

Her enthusiasm was infectious. Liam found himself smiling as she briskly instructed him to bend forward and spread his legs.

"Bossy," Shay observed as Liam braced both hands on the back of the sectional. "I find that oddly sexy in a female."

Chelsea kissed Liam's backside, then slid two lubricated fingers slowly inside his ass. Liam definitely hadn't anticipated how this would feel. The pressure was interesting, then pleasant, and then it twisted into something so excruciatingly erotic that he couldn't help letting out a groan.

"You've done this before," Shay said admiringly to Chelsea.

"No comment," she laughingly responded.

She removed her fingers, then returned them with more lube yet. Liam's spine arched strongly as her fingertips crossed the sweet spot they'd massaged before. This time, he didn't have enough breath to groan.

"*He* hasn't done this before," Shay murmured, one palm rubbing Liam's back. "I guess your 'fling' didn't include taking it in the ass."

Liam couldn't answer. All he could do was shake.

"It'll feel even better when this is Shay," she promised. "He'll be warmer. And supersmooth. And he'll pulse like crazy inside of you."

He believed her. He simply wasn't sure he was ready.

"All yours," Chelsea said, easing her fingers out again. She wiped them on Liam's discarded sweatpants, then ducked under his arms to kneel in front of him on the white leather. She was on her heels and perky as hell, the sight of her tight little aroused body causing his hormones to react with brand-new spurts of interest. Chelsea didn't seem aware of this. With the caring that was very much a part of her, she touched the side of his face. "You okay, Liam?"

He nodded, his skin giving little jumps in strange places as Shay moved into position behind him. Shay's warm, hard hands slid up to his shoulders like he was planing a piece of wood.

"We can stop," he said, as concerned as Chelsea. "You don't have to do anything you're not comfortable with."

With an effort, Liam dredged up his voice again. "The only thing I'm not comfortable with is how fucking much I want you to do me."

"Ah." Shay laughed breathily. "Well, I'm sorry then, but I find that problem totally impossible to resist."

There was a bit of logistical jockeying as Shay aligned their heights and instructed him to relax. His hands parted Liam's butt cheeks, and then the moment of truth arrived.

They'd prepared him—physically anyway. There was wetness and pressure but very little discomfort. All the same, Liam bit his lip at the penetration. The long inward glide felt like what Chel had done, only more, because Shay's prick was a good bit bigger—not to mention more rigid—than a pair of fingers. Shay must have liked the sensation of going in. He sighed out a moan of pleasure, relief and arousal mingling as his pelvis rocked forward. When he was in as tightly as he could go, it was like a second heart throbbed in Liam's ass. Shay's slightly bristly cheek settled on his spine. Both of them were trembling.

"It's okay." Liam rubbed the arm Shay had wrapped around his chest. "You feel good inside me."

Shay turned his face back and forth between Liam's shoulder blades. He pulled back and thrust slowly in again. Liam's body liked the penetration even better the second time. The sensation of being stretched was a killer. The nerves Shay was pushing over seemed to connect and tug the ones humming in his cock. When Chelsea cupped his balls, very gently, the pressure that swelled beneath told him he was too damn close to coming.

"You don't have to take me," she whispered. "You can just concentrate on him."

"I want to," he said, even as his teeth gritted with pleasure. "I want us . . . all connected."

More wriggling around culminated in Liam dropping to his knees on the floor and Shay coming near to it. Throw pillows found new uses, and Chelsea's hips were pulled to the edge of the sectional. Her legs wrapped both their bodies as Liam's hand tipped his cock down to her entry. They'd all been laughing breathlessly up till then, but the moment Liam's broad head notched her, the moment he let his weight shift forward to press inside, their laughter turned into matching groans.

Shay's hips joined his in the motion of taking her, adding his strength to Liam's. That done, he stretched one hand past Liam to take a death grip on the back of the couch. Shay's cock was noticeably harder inside of him, a change that wound Liam up almost more than he could handle. Chelsea was just plain juicy, her muscles clutching him so wetly Liam suspected he could have gone at her as vigorously as Shay had. The thought of that had exhilaration arrowing through his groin.

"I can't move," he gasped to Chelsea. "I am too effing ready to go."

"You don't have to," she said, her palms smoothing up his chest. "All I want now is to feel you."

He wanted more for her, wanted everything his brimming heart had to give. His eyes stung as Shay's mouth curved on his vertebra.

"Touch her," he said, as soft as if he were purring. "Bring her over, and I'll bring you."

Shay was all confidence now, steady and focused as he withdrew and then rolled forward. He laughed when Liam and Chelsea let out low cries. Again he rolled, harder, joggling Liam into her. Shay's muscularity made it seem easy, though he'd begun to grunt with enjoyment as he slung himself in and out. His driving, even rhythm didn't need long to take a toll. Knowing he'd better hurry, Liam jammed his thumb over Chelsea's clit. Rough or not, he hit the right spot to rub.

"God," she growled, her neck arching.

Shay didn't have to be told to let his thrusts off the leash. Liam gasped at his increase in power and speed. Sensation slammed through him, tingling from deep inside him to the tip of his cock. He was in Shay's hands then, unable to slow his body's reactions, or even to want to. Liam felt so good, so safe in every atom of his being, that pleasure rose up like a rocket.

Happily, he wasn't the only one in that state.

"Je-*sus*," Shay said, going jerky as he lost his grip on himself. "*Fuck*."

Liam arched to let him in deeper, which had the added effect of making the hot spot over his prostate Shay's direct target. His vision blurred at the intense pummeling ecstasy. Instinct drove him deeper into Chelsea, who cried out at the passionate thrust.

Propelled by so much stimulation, his ejaculation truly seemed to explode. He was speechless, thoughtless, and when Chelsea's pussy clamped in climax around his spasming cock, he nearly went body-less as well. Shay was coming with them, snarling against Liam's shoulder as every one of his muscles went hard as stone.

Shay's climax went on and on, longer even than the first time. He'd been wanting them both for so many years that finally getting them must have been epic. Liam rather liked coming like a freight train himself. Secret kinks weren't so bad, if this was the result.

Golden after-waves were lapping through him when he noticed Shay had locked the fingers of his left hand to Chelsea's right, like they'd been drowning and needed someone to hold on to. The sight brought the burn of tears back into his eyes. He loved that they loved each other—as much as he loved them loving him. The world could think what it liked. This was how they were supposed to be. This made bigger people of all of them.

"Wow," Shay said at last from behind him. "I think Chelsea might be on to something with this threesome idea."

He was teasing, but Chelsea swatted him anyway. "Just for that, I *am* taking the credit."

Groaning, Shay pushed off Liam, whose knees were more than a bit grateful. Happy but exhausted, his head fell to the pillow by Chelsea's curls.

"You too," she said, shoving at Liam's chest. "I need to be stretched out in a bed."

Liam could have slept where he was, but he guessed girls needed more comfort.

He rose, wobbling a little but pleasantly. He held out his hand to her.

"All right, princess," he said. "We'll let you rest for now."

Chelsea

Shay disappeared into the master bathroom, muttering about long drives and stinking like a pig. His absence left Liam and Chelsea to collapse on the big firm bed by themselves. Chelsea lay on her back, her body singing with the myriad of pleasures that her two favorite men had just pounded into it. If this was what it meant to be a princess, she was signing up for more. Her number one prince was facedown on the duvet—possibly unconscious, though his big warm hand was still linked with hers. That simple sweetness tugged her lips up into a smile. Then the shower came on, and her number two prince started belting out an old U2 song, more or less on key. Liam surprised her by squirming onto his side and humming along with Shay. His soft green eyes were sleepy but very fond.

"'Mysterious Ways,' huh?" she said.

"Used to be your favorite."

Liam wasn't the biggest talker, but he sure could express himself when he wanted to. Happier than she could remember being before, Chelsea wriggled close enough to trace the line of his pretty mouth. The words she chose deliberately echoed his of earlier.

"Boy, I hope I can keep you," she said.

His eyes filled, which she wasn't expecting. He caught her fingertips and kissed them. "You mean, you hope you can keep us both."

He hadn't phrased it as a complaint.

"Yes," she said. "And please don't think that means I love either one of you with anything less than everything I have."

He smiled like she had, joy too big to contain rising up in him. "I know, Chel. You love me more because you love him, too."

She'd never been able to put it this clearly to herself. Her throat closed tight, and she felt like *his* tear was spilling hot from her eye.

"Don't you run away again, though," he said. "If we have troubles, we face them together."

"Right," she managed to get out, and he pulled her against his chest.

They were lying like that, arms around each other, when Shay strolled out, naked but for the towel he was drying his dark hair with. Chelsea had to admire the hint of a strut that was in his walk. She'd forgotten how cute he was when he was pleased with himself. He'd seduced—and impressed—both of them tonight.

"And the lovebirds leave room for me," he said as he crawled up next to Chelsea. His sigh as he relaxed was a sound any one of them could have made. Liam reached across her to squeeze Shay's arm. The gesture was old and new. It drew another small, happy noise from Shay.

"I have something I want to say," he announced. "No one I've slept with—chick or dude—ever meant anything to me compared to you two."

Chelsea rolled over to look at him. He was smiling faintly at the ceiling, hands folded lightly atop his ribs.

"How many have there been?" Liam asked warily.

"One less than however many partners Chelsea admits to."

"Shay!" She was laughing even as she shoved him. "I am not some floozy."

Shay turned his head to her, his smiling eyes filled with more acceptance than his words might imply. His brows wagged suggestively. "Had to pick up those tricks of yours somewhere."

"A *few* places," she said. "Not a damned regiment."

"Wouldn't care if it were," Shay said complacently.

"Fine," Chelsea surrendered, seeing what he was getting at. "No one I slept with meant anything to me compared to the pair of you."

"Really?" Liam said with endearing hopefulness. "You're not just saying that?"

She couldn't help laughing. In their different ways, Liam and Shay both boosted her ego. "Really. Together and apart, you ruined me for other men."

"And you hadn't had sex with me when you left," Shay observed. "I really am awesome."

"Give him another pillow," Liam advised. "I think his head is swelling."

"Which head?" Shay teased, and drew Liam's hand to cover the lower one.

Liam didn't resist. He cradled Shay's cock instead, his back spooning Chelsea's as his thumb rubbed gentle circles along the relaxed shaft. His touch was curious and light, but apparently arousing. Shay's penis began to lengthen within his work-hardened palm, the flare and head getting darker as his blood took a U-turn back into them. Liam shifted behind her, an unmistakable stirring occurring behind her butt. An ache of longing gathered between her legs, surprising her by coming again so soon. Liam's mouth brushed the tingling skin between her neck and shoulder, his breathing a bit ragged.

She was going to have fun watching him discover the ins and outs of playing with his new toy. Heck, the fact that they all were lying here naked, and comfortable with it, was a delight in and of itself.

"Man." Liam sighed. "If I weren't so tired . . . You two are like some feast where I want to eat everything at once."

"Mmm," Shay said, his eyes drifting shut even as his spine stretched in enjoyment. Chelsea's arm felt very natural crooked over his chest. "You know, if we keep this little adventure going, we might have to tell the folks."

"Ugh." Liam's hand paused for a moment and then resumed petting. "What happened to deniability is a virtue?"

"Gonna be hard to hide. Plus Dad might be cooler than you think. He visited me in Boston a couple times after I cut out. Told me no matter what I did, now matter how long I stayed away, he and Mom would welcome me back."

"I did not know that," Liam said. "He never mentioned it."

Shay patted Chelsea's arm. "Dad has deep waters."

Their mom was a different matter. She was conservative. On the other hand, she adored her boys, and Mr. O'Brien did have a knack for talking her around. Liam and Shay's Irish charm hadn't come to them from nowhere.

Liam heaved a big sigh. "I'm not ready to think about them yet."

"All right. How about deciding which one of you is going to give me a job."

Chelsea's head lifted from its cozy spot on his shoulder. "Why would you need a job?"

"Because I sold my carpentry shop. The ex-sort-of-girlfriend made such a big deal about me being 'emotionally unavailable,' I figured why not be totally that way?"

"So you sold out?"

"Lock, stock and band saw."

"Boy." Chelsea went breathless at the news. "When you make up your mind, you don't make it up halfway."

Shay looked at her, at both of them, all flippancy erased from his manner. "I was tired of being unhappy. Tired of disappointing perfectly nice people. I *had* to take the chance that I'd find a piece of what I used to feel with you two. Even if it was stupid, I had to try."

"Me too," she said softly.

She put her head back down when he smiled at her, adoring the way both men gave her a little hug. Greed felt good when it earned a reward like this.

"I'll tell you one thing," Shay said. "I'd totally love to take a crack at helping you restore that brownstone."

Liam grunted in agreement. "Condos, though . . ."

"Oh yeah," Shay said. "Condos are evil. We should fix it up and then live in it ourselves. I mean, if you guys think that's a good idea. I have money stashed. Chelsea wouldn't have to go broke."

This was a dream Chelsea had entertained more than once: the three of them, joining forces on a job. How could she not when they'd chosen such complementary work fields? Her heart beat faster, and—on either side of her—Shay's and Liam's did the same. "Living together . . ."

"Yup," Shay said cheerfully. "Totally terrifying."

"Totally impossible," Liam put in. "The plumbing and the electric in that brownstone are shot to hell." He hesitated, and his pulse took another jump behind her. "We could live here together until it's done."

"I don't know," Shay drawled. "This place of yours might be too chichi for Chel and me."

"Ass," Liam said.

"We could try, though," Shay said softly, serious again. "See how it goes."

"Trying's good," Liam said.

She sensed them sharing a look. It made her feel warm all over, safe in ways she couldn't explain. She snuggled closer into Shay's side, her leg sliding over his even as Liam's heavy arm draped them both in a loose embrace. Shay was clean and soapy, while she and Liam still smelled of sex. If she could have bottled the combination as a perfume, she'd have worn it every day of her life.

Come to think of it, maybe she'd get the chance.

"What do you say, Chelsea?" Liam asked. "Do you mind us taking custody of your flip?"

She closed her eyes. All their heart rates were calming, their bodies relaxing into the new tangle. This was home: the three of them together. Whatever challenges they faced, she couldn't doubt this was the prize they'd all been hoping for.

"Nah," she said, smiling from her soul. "I never could let go of what I fell in love with."

ON THE JOB

BETHANY KANE

*My heartfelt thanks to my husband
for giving me so many wonderful Lake Tahoe memories*

One

Madeline was boiling with emotion, and Walker Gray was about to pay for it.

She stretched, arching her back and displaying her breasts more prominently for her audience of one. Her naked skin felt sun-warmed and smooth as she glided a hand through tanning oil from just below her breast, down over her ribs and across her belly, allowing her fingers to trail flirtatiously just beneath the top portion of the tiny red bikini bottoms she wore. She couldn't see exactly where he stood behind her, but she sensed his focused attention nevertheless. He wore a pair of sunglasses, of course, standard equipment for a former secret service special agent and present-day head of security for Hallas Technologies.

Madeline could imagine his eyes behind the dark lenses. They'd perfectly match the alpine lake before her—crystalline blue shot through with shards of green. She'd had a lot of practice envisioning Walker's eyes during the eleven years of his absence from Carnelian Bay, California.

More's the pity.

A low-grade electrical sensation buzzed just beneath her oiled skin, and that wasn't the only place set to tingling by the knowledge of his keen observance. Sexual tension coiled in her lower belly, the result of her tumultuous emotional state and the gaze of the man she'd once loved with all her being pinned to her nearly naked body.

Her nipples pulled so tight against the flimsy fabric of her swimsuit that she reached up and pinched at one lightly, then soothed the aching flesh between her fingertips. A twinge of pleasure streaked through her clit. She considered touching herself there, as well, but no. . . .

There was plenty of time to dish out his torture. Madeline Sayer may be getting more and more turned on by the second as she lay on the white dock that stretched out onto the clear waters of Lake Tahoe, but she was also angry. Eleven years of fury and hurt at Walker Gray's abandonment fueled her performance. He may have left behind a naïve nineteen-year-old girl when he'd left for Glynco, Georgia, to begin his training, but Madeline was all grown up now.

The sun worshipped her senses like a lover, its warmth beating down on her relentlessly. She gave herself to it, beckoning it with gliding caresses across her skin, arching her back slightly, tempting a kiss on her aching nipples. She rubbed oil onto her chest and trailed her fingers over the upper swells of her breasts, appreciating the firm curves in a way she could only do with his hawk-like gaze trained on her.

He was back there, watching her. He was on the job, and Madeline knew better than most how important his job was to him. He wouldn't abandon *it*, even if he had abandoned her. She held him in a trap, and it was sweet . . . delicious to torment him for his sense of duty, to make him pay for his noble intentions.

The driving rays of the sun on her nipples weren't sufficient. She glanced up, squinting into brilliant sunlight that was amplified exponentially by the clear blue water. Tony had taken out his boat earlier along with a visiting couple from the Silicon Valley, the Margraves. Not only was Tony's boat not within her vision, but neither was any other craft.

Time to play.

She glided her fingers over her breasts and pushed back the fabric of her bikini top just past the crests, exposing her nipples to the heat. They poked out of her top, eager for the sensation of the sun's rays and plucking, oiled fingertips.

The knowledge of Walker's gaze was a potent aphrodisiac. Liquid heat pooled in her pussy. She drove her tailbone down slightly, getting indirect pressure on her anus and sex. A soft purr of satisfaction vibrated her throat as she continued to rub her distended nipples.

She'd thought rarely enough of Walker in the past several years. Seeing him again so unexpectedly this morning had brought it all back in a rush, the strength of her feelings shocking her a little.

He used to touch her like this once—no, better, *much* better with his big, male hands and blunt-tipped fingertips. He enjoyed watching as he played with her breasts. Even back then, his gaze had added an extra sizzle factor to Madeline's excitement. He used to say it would help him slow down, to watch, instead of consuming her fast and furious like he desired. He'd been so careful of her back then, so deliberate. They'd given each other pleasure often, even if they hadn't ever had intercourse. Walker's older brother, Zach, had gotten a girl pregnant when he was seventeen. Madeline knew Walker had thought it'd ruined Zach's life to be chained to the area of his childhood and forced to give up on his dreams.

He wasn't going to take the chance on his future. Walker had always treated her like she was something precious until the day he'd told her he was leaving Lake Tahoe for good. That was when Madeline first understood he'd been so careful for his own reasons, not out of any tenderness or concern for her. He'd been cautious not to get too close because he'd known all along he would leave.

She pinched both nipples at once. Her hips squirmed against the hard wood of the dock. She used to be insecure about her small breasts until she'd become involved with Walker. It was his avidness over her breasts that first taught Madeline she was beautiful.

She reminded him of what he'd sacrificed as she stroked her erect nipples beneath a hot Tahoe sun. So what if they'd just been kids at the time, fools suffering from the heatstroke of a wild infatuation? She'd needed him, and he'd failed her. First Madeline's father had died unexpectedly, then Walker had left. Madeline's hurt had changed to anger over the years. Eventually, the sting had faded.

It had, anyway, until she'd walked onto the terrace this morning and seen Walker Gray talking to Tony.

Her clit begged for attention, but Madeline refrained. With effort. She longed to punish him, not only for eleven years ago, but for having the temerity to suddenly appear again in her life. His brisk, professional manner made a mockery of the fact that she'd been floored by his unexpected presence. He'd barely said two dozen words to her since Tony had asked her if she recalled their old friend from their high school and college days, Walker Gray.

She recalled, all right.

She'd make sure the bastard remembered just as graphically.

She sat up and took a sip from her glass of iced hibiscus tea mixed with lemonade. Her fingers strayed to the tie at her back. She pulled slowly on the string. She tossed the flimsy top next to the sweating glass and stretched out again on the dock.

It wasn't a big deal. She sunbathed topless once in a while on

Tony's boat. True, she'd never gotten the impression that her bare
breasts had received any of the focused interest from Tony as they
once had from the man who stood behind her in the yard. Sure,
she'd never have done it if it were another one of Tony's employees
standing guard. The point was, Madeline was perfectly comfortable sunbathing topless in this situation.

Perfectly aroused.

She doubted very seriously she would have ever cupped her
breasts in her slick hands from below, making the nipples point
upward, like dark pink arrows, to the sky even in front of Tony,
but the heretofore unprotected parts of her skin needed SPF, didn't
they?

It felt good, so warm, so arousing . . . so powerful.

She let one hand trail across the sensitive skin at the sides of her
ribs and across her belly. Her clit beckoned. It burned in protest at
being ignored. She slipped two fingers beneath the top of her bikini
panties. Her labia were moist and swollen.

She slid a finger into the juicy cleft and moaned in pleasure.

Was he suffering? God, she hoped so.

Her eyes popped open a few seconds later when she felt a hand
wrap around her wrist. He'd moved so quietly, and she'd been so
involved in her little game, she'd never heard his tread on the dock.

"What—?"

"Surely you're not going to ask me what I'm doing, Madeline."
She saw his clamped jaw and her shocked reflection in the mirrored
lenses of his sunglasses. "Because I would have thought that was
obvious. I'm giving you what you've been asking for."

She gasped in surprise when he slid his forearm beneath her
thighs and lifted. The next thing she knew she was flying down the
dock in Walker Gray's arms.

She sputtered, furious at his audacity . . . and more than a little
thrilled by it. "Put me down, Walker."

His long stride never broke.

Walker had been lean and beautiful in his teens and early twenties, as tawny and sleek as a young lion. He'd only grown more powerful as he aged. His hips and waist were still narrow, but he'd added some serious muscle in his shoulders and chest. She wriggled in his arms, her breath coming choppy and fast, trying to get him to release her, but it was useless. Those muscles were granite-solid. Her left nipple rubbed against the soft cotton of his shirt. She saw the line of his jaw harden.

"Put me *down*," she fumed as he stalked toward the beach house changing room. "Believe me, I haven't been asking for anything from you. I was minding my own business, sunbathing like I always do. Do you want me to scream for help?"

He plunged inside the air-conditioned dim interior of the women's changing room and showers. Tony owned Hallas Technologies, the largest computer security company in the country. When he entertained in Lake Tahoe, he tended to do it on a big scale. The changing rooms in close proximity to the beach had been built to make guests comfortable. When he invited a large party there, he even staffed the luxurious rooms with maids, towel boys and masseuses.

Madeline squawked when Walker abruptly plunked her down on the tile floor in front of one of the steam showers. The next thing she knew, he was pulling her arms above her head. She felt cool metal around her wrists and heard a clicking sound. He twisted his hand and slid something into his pocket.

She stared up at him, her mouth gaping open.

"What the hell do you think you're doing?" she demanded, outraged and bewildered in equal measure. He'd just handcuffed her to the top of the metal structure of the shower surround. She stretched on her tiptoes, back arched, her long hair swishing just above her bikini panties, trying like mad to move the chain between the cuffs up one inch over the top of the metal.

Just. One. Inch.

She growled in pure frustration when she came up short.

"Let me *go*."

Her heart charged like an out of control locomotive in her ears. She couldn't believe this was happening to her. She was in the shadowed changing room alone with Walker. He'd handcuffed her wrists above her head and he was staring down at her. He'd removed his glasses, but his eyes were cast in shadow.

He spread a large, sun-warmed hand on her hip as if to remind her of her naked vulnerability. She went utterly still while her heart continued to race like it thought she was running for her life. She had to lean her head back to look into his face. He topped six feet by several inches, making him nearly a foot taller than her.

She shivered when he caressed the sensitive side of her body from the waist to just below her armpit. It had always excited her to feel how much of her body he could span with his hand, his stark masculinity making her feel exponentially more feminine by contrast.

"All you had to do was ask. I would have been more than happy to oblige you, Madeline."

She sensed the depth of his fury for the first time. Walker was typically so cool, so controlled. He didn't lose his temper often, but when he did, he could be fearsome. She licked her upper lip in nervous excitement. What sort of inferno had she started with her little game of tease and torture?

"I don't know what you mean," she replied, her voice sounding haughty and hushed in the cool, dim room. "I sunbathe topless all the time."

His eyebrows arched. "And you typically masturbate while Tony's employees watch?"

"What I do is none of your business. You're being paid to make sure I'm safe."

"I thought you said you didn't need any protection."

"I don't. This whole thing you've set up with Tony is ridiculous. That man who shot at me was a random lunatic. Why would someone want to hurt me?"

"Why indeed?"

She jumped when he moved his hand and touched the side of a breast. Her nipples pulled tight.

"Is this how they taught you to protect a client?" she seethed quietly.

"I'm keeping a good eye on you."

"You're ignoring the duties of your *job*, Walker," she taunted.

"I'm doing exactly what I came back to Lake Tahoe to do."

Her eyes widened in surprise at that.

"Let go of me now," she grated out between clenched teeth.

"When you've gotten what you were asking for," he said quietly. His hand moved. She panted as he shaped a breast to his palm. Arousal stabbed at her clit.

"You've grown larger," he murmured as he used his fingertips to pluck at a nipple. She opened her mouth to speak, but the sight of him watching himself play with her breast left her speechless. Wetness surged from her pussy. "Not much," he continued as he filled his hand with her other breast. "I'm glad. You're so firm." He lifted both breasts slightly in his hands and then released her, watching as the taut flesh sprung back into place. "Look at that. You always did have the prettiest breasts," he said distractedly. "Your nipples get just as stiff as they used to."

Madeline moaned, strung tight on a wire of anger and arousal.

"No, don't," she whispered when he placed both of his hands on her rib cage, holding her in place, and bent, lowering his head. She knew she'd be a goner if he put his mouth on her.

But it was too late.

"Oh *God*," she groaned in pleasure when he inserted an erect nipple between his lips. His mouth felt hot. His tongue agitated the aroused flesh like a tender lash. Arousal—so sharp it was almost painful—zipped down to her pussy like a lightning flash. She twisted in his hold, trying to get more friction on her aching nipples. His hand shifted. He pinched at her other nipple with gentle, calloused fingertips, coaxing the flesh into further pronouncement.

He growled, low and feral, and twisted his head, finding her other breast with his mouth. He pinched the moist crest with forefinger and thumb as if to make up for his abandonment. Her excitement mounted.

"Bite it," she demanded in a harsh whisper.

He gathered both breasts in his hands and pushed them together. He slid a distended nipple between his lips and suckled. When he gave her what she wanted, she shrieked with excitement. Her pleasure swelled, made even more imperative by the subtle spice of pain his teeth wrought. Madeline was transformed into a bundle of raw nerve and throbbing need. She writhed in her restraint, desperate to press against him.

She murmured in dazed protest when he lifted his dark blond head a moment later. He held her breasts in his hands and inspected his work.

"Walker," she moaned miserably when she glanced down and saw how erect her nipples were, how the center nubbin had elongated beneath his mouth and fingers, how rosy they'd become as he sucked and blood gathered just below the surface. She'd lied when she said she sunbathed topless all the time. Her breasts were paler than the surrounding skin, a stark contrast to her tan and dark pink nipples.

"You used to be able to come from nipple stimulation alone," he said in recollection, his breath whisking across her moist nipple. He pursed his lips and blew at her softly. Shivers rippled down her spine. "Do you know how rare that is?"

She didn't answer, but groaned in an agony of arousal, wriggling in his hold.

He moved his hands to her sides, stilling her. She saw the gleam of his blue-green eyes in the shadows.

"Do you?"

"Yes," she whispered.

"And can you still? Climax from nipple stimulation alone? Can Tony make you come that way, Madeline?"

She opened her mouth to tell the truth, but made a choked sound as she cut herself off at the last second. He sensed the truth anyway, despite her stinginess in saying it. She could tell, because his lips quirked into a small, satisfied smile. *Bastard.* He knew he'd been the only one who could ever evoke such a response from her.

He lowered his head, and Madeline cursed under her breath. She was handcuffed with her hands above her head, helpless, hot and so aroused her pussy was drenched. She didn't have any choice but to stand there while Walker proved to her he could still create a riot in her flesh. She hated him for exposing her vulnerability, but she couldn't stop the pleasure that tore through her flesh like a fire rampaging in a rain-thirsty forest.

He suckled her the way she liked it, firm and just a little rough. She mewled and twisted like a helpless fish on a hook. He bit the tender flesh while continuing his relentless suction. He pinched her other nipple rhythmically: hard, gentle, hard, soothing.

Madeline cried out as she came. It hurt a little to climax without stimulation on her sex, sending tight, cramp-like spasms through her. She writhed, desperate to get pressure on her pussy.

"Shhh," he soothed when he released her nipple from his mouth. He went to his knees before her. She craned toward him, her wrists pulling at the handcuffs. He glanced up. "Don't, Madeline. You'll hurt your wrists. Do you *hear* me?" he asked sharply when she continued to stretch in her restraints, mindless with lust. She blinked, unable to speak in the midst of her crisis. "That's right," he whispered when she eased the pressure on her wrists. "I'll come to you." He jerked her panties down to her ankles and pressed his face to her pussy with no further ado.

She let out a scream of delight when he laved at her clit with a stiffened tongue. It was like he threw a switch in her body. Her former orgasm ratcheted up exponentially, detonating like an explosion. He continued to tongue her while he applied a firm suction, and she shuddered in bliss. Thank goodness the fabrics in the changing rooms were rich and luxurious, absorbing her sharp cries of pleasure, because she couldn't control herself.

Her eyes blinked open heavily a moment later. His head moved between her thighs as he gathered her cream, his actions unapologetically greedy. Madeline panted and tried to bring the room into focus while her orgasm still echoed in her flesh, thanks to Walker's stroking, stabbing tongue.

He slowly lifted his head. For a moment, their gazes held. In the distance, Madeline heard a shout and male laughter. She started.

"They're back. It's Tony and the others."

He didn't respond with the haste she thought the moment warranted. Instead he rose until he once again towered over her. He began to unfasten his jeans.

She gaped, stunned by his boldness.

"No, Walker," she whispered.

"We're going to finish this even if your fiancé walks right through that door."

She swallowed thickly. Tony wasn't her fiancé. They'd seen each other on and off over the years. After her father had died, Tony and his family had consoled her, made her one of them . . . and helped her feel she belonged in a world that had suddenly grown alien and cold with her father gone.

And Walker.

She knew Tony felt safe with her, unlike most of the women who crowded around him for his good looks and monumental wealth. Sex hadn't been a factor in their relationship for over a year now. It'd been her choice, although Tony was known to test the waters every couple weeks or so, shark that he was. It didn't upset her much when he tried. She understood Tony and forgave him his weaknesses. Tony went through women like Kleenex. That hadn't changed when she'd agreed to sleep with him years back. The realization that his infidelity hadn't wounded her much at all had been her first true indication Tony wasn't the man for her.

Tony insisted he could wait while the idea of marriage grew on her. She knew he occasionally referred to her as his fiancée with his friends and his parents. Madeline had grown weary of denying it.

She certainly wasn't going to tell Walker Gray she wasn't engaged to Tony. He already held too many cards in this little game.

She watched as Walker shoved his jeans around his thighs. His boxer briefs looked snow-white in the shaded room next to his golden brown tan. A moan of longing leaked out of her throat when she saw the heavy package of his cock behind stretched cotton.

No protest could form in her brain as he stretched back the boxer briefs and exposed his naked length. Lust burned everything else away. His cock fell free, the weight of the head pulling it at a downward angle. He leaned down and lifted her off her feet, bringing her flush against him. He reached and unhooked the handcuffs from the metal post. Madeline sighed shakily at the feeling of being pressed against his body. She lowered her arms to his shoulders, bracketing his head. Her legs wrapped around him, seemingly of their own volition, as he staggered a few feet, his knees bound by his clothing.

She gasped when her back thudded against the wall.

"Help me, Madeline."

It was an order. It was a plea. Whatever it was, Madeline

couldn't stop herself from succumbing to it. She shifted her body to accommodate him. She held his stare, wincing at the sensation of his cock carving into her flesh.

"Jesus," he mumbled in a pressured hiss. Madeline knew what he meant. They both had to apply a firm pressure to force her narrow channel to part for him. He fired her flesh even as he stretched it. She hungered for his stark, hard presence at her core. Her pussy may seem to be resisting harboring something so large, but once he'd conquered new territory, she melted around him, welcoming him like a warm, sucking kiss.

Outside, Madeline heard something hit the dock, as if Tony or someone had tossed some gear from the boat. Within the cool depths of the boathouse, she sweated in a blaze of need. Walker began to pump even before he'd fully sheathed himself. He was greedy, and she liked it.

She liked it a lot.

"Let me in, you little tease," he said between clenched white teeth. Strangely, it sounded like an endearment instead of an insult.

She pressed with all her might against his driving cock. She bit her lower lip and gave a harsh moan when his balls pressed against her damp, sensitive tissues.

"That's right. Now show me how you fuck with that tight little pussy."

But she was already showing him, just like he was showing her what he could do. It was difficult to tell who put on a more enthusiastic demonstration. She drove down on his length just as he slammed into her. Madeline couldn't catch her breath. Just when she did, he'd pin her against the wall with his cock, and air would pop out of her lungs. He held her in an iron grip just above her waist, his hands stretching onto her back and encompassing a good portion of her torso. His muscles flexed tight beneath his cotton shirt as he jerked her back and forth on his cock, the relative ease of his mastery over their movements shocking and thrilling her.

They were both so lost in their greed, united in their goal for more friction, more pressure, more bliss, that they were hardly aware of anything else. They heard Tony's and Hal Margrave's casual banter in the distance and the sounds of feet hitting the dock, but they were knotted exclusively to each other in those frantic seconds.

He pumped into her to the hilt, and her breath exploded out of her. He paused. A drop of sweat trickled from the side of his forehead down to a whiskered jaw. He held her against the wall, her body skewered on his cock, and rotated his hips slightly. Her legs were parted wide. He ground his pelvis against her exposed clit.

"If I'd ever been here before, I wouldn't have been able to leave. I'm not going to be able to sleep or eat if I'm thinking about this pussy."

He watched her while she came, his face rigid, his body drawn as tight as a bowstring the moment before the arrow rips through the air. She shook in pleasure, all the while aware of his lancing gaze and feeling vulnerable for it.

Feeling beautiful.

He nursed her through her orgasm by moving his hips in tiny, subtle circles, giving her pressure on her clit. His cock throbbed high and hard inside her. She bit her lip to stop from keening. It felt decadent, so hot and forbidden.

"I'll just pop in and shower and meet you two up at the lodge," a woman's voice called from outside the entrance to the changing room.

Panic clutched at Madeline's throat. She gave Walker a wild glance. It was Kitty Margrave, Hal's friendly, middle-aged wife.

"Move. *Do something*," she whispered.

Her eyes went wide in shock. He did something, all right. He started to fuck her with long, thorough strokes, holding her stare the whole time.

"Walker," she mouthed helplessly. The thrusts of his cock in her pussy had sent her to shivering again with the aftershocks of her orgasm. She rested the back of her head against the wall and surrendered.

Anything else was impossible.

"Didn't you leave your clothes up at the lodge?" Hal's voice resounded in the distance. Madeline's heart seemed to want to explode out of her chest, but she just stared into Walker's blazing eyes as he fucked her, faster now, hunting down his own bliss.

"Oh, you're right, I did," Kitty said sheepishly.

"Maddie must have run up to the lodge for a book or something. I told her to bring one, but she said she wouldn't get bored," Tony said, the sound of his voice growing more distant as the three of them made their way through the sprawling lawn.

Walker saw the finish line, Madeline could tell. Not just from the feeling of his cock swelling huge inside her, but from the fact that he no longer tried to mute the sound of their flesh slapping together as he fucked her. She whimpered when he slammed into her one last time, his face contorted in an agony of pleasure.

He'd grown so erect, so swollen with need that it hurt a little to harbor him so deep while he exploded. She broke the skin on her lower lip with her own teeth when she heard his guttural, wild groan as he emptied himself inside her. She grasped his back with her handcuffed hands, absorbing his shudders, greedy to experience his surrender.

But it hadn't been him who had surrendered in those tension-filled moments, Madeline admitted as he panted, his head lowered next to hers, his forehead against the wall. It had been she who had sacrificed her pride by allowing a man she hadn't seen in eleven years—a man who had once rejected her—inside her mind . . . inside her flesh.

He lifted his head slowly. His short, wavy hair shone like dark, burnished gold in the shadowed room. He stared at her mouth. His face lowered over her.

"No," she whispered harshly. He'd been about to kiss her. Madeline couldn't take that.

"Your mouth is bleeding," he said quietly, his lips just an inch away from her own.

She slicked her tongue along her lip. "I bit it."

"I know," he murmured.

"Let me down, Walker." She hated that her voice shook.

He didn't move. Madeline felt his gaze on her, but she kept her eyes lowered.

"I came back for you, Madeline."

She did look him full in the face then.

"You fucking *liar*," she said incredulously. It was bad enough that he'd hauled her into this changing room, handcuffed her to a shower and screwed her until she didn't know her own name. Now he was telling her ridiculous lies. Those six words he'd uttered felt like the equivalent of a slap. Tears sprung to her eyes.

"Let me *down*. I need to shower. You came inside me!" Panic swelled in her breast. She cried out when he did precisely what she'd said, lifting her off his cock. He set her on her feet. Her teeth clenched in rising anger when she realized she was still attached to him with her arms looped around his neck.

"Hold on," he said sternly when she struggled against him like a wild animal that had just realized it was trapped. She held the spasm of emotion that wanted to leap out of her chest down with effort as he helped her unhook her arms from his head. He bent and pulled some keys out of his jeans. As soon as he'd unlocked the cuffs and her wrists were free, she staggered away from him. He caught her with a hand on her elbow.

"Leave me alone," she bit out, made even more angry at the realization that she was about to cry. Why had she just allowed that to happen? Now he held even more power over her, and he knew it. "Just get out of here. *Now.*"

She didn't turn around as she hurried into the room that contained a steam sauna and shelves filled with towels. He'd gone by the time she returned.

He'd done what she'd asked, for once.

Unfortunately, given what Tony had hired him for, Walker Gray wouldn't have gone far.

TWO

Walker glanced up from his computer screen when he heard the beep of a card being swept through the security entrance into Tony Hallas's large den.

"Has she come downstairs?" he asked, his fingers pausing on the keyboard.

Barry nodded and plunked down into a chair. Barry had obviously used his time off this morning to take advantage of the undercover assignment location and bask in the Tahoe sunshine. He wore hiking boots and canvas shorts, and his nose was sunburned to a shiny glow. "She's on the patio with Tony. She's an eyeful, I'll give her that, but about as friendly as a piranha on a diet. She sure doesn't try to hide the fact that she doesn't want our protection, does she?"

Commenting on Madeline's hostility seemed about as obvious as saying the Lake Tahoe view was spectacular, so Walker continued with his task of checking for attempts at breaching Tony's security system. There were only a handful of individuals on the planet as well trained at securing a compound from either a physical or technological threat as the Secret Service. Tony Hallas wasn't the president of the United States, but he'd hired Walker and his crew because he believed Walker could offer him similar protection in his Lake Tahoe vacation lodge. Even Tony, who owned the largest computer systems security company in the nation, had to admit he didn't know some of the stuff the Secret Service did.

"Do you know what Madeline just told me?" Barry asked.

Walker frowned as his fingers continued to fly over the keyboard. "I can just imagine," he murmured.

"She told me that I was infringing on her right to privacy by guarding her."

"Did you tell her that since she decided to have a relationship with Tony Hallas, she lost a few of her rights?" he asked evenly, his eyes fixed on the computer screen. "Anyone close to Tony is a potential security breach. Kidnap Madeline Sayer or threaten to kill her, and Tony is suddenly at risk for giving away software to China or Pakistan or who-the-fuck-ever who wants the opportunity to attack U.S. financial institutions."

"You mean beyond the stuff we think Tony hasn't already given to the Russian mob?" Walker gave Barry a wry glance before he continued his search. Barry had just mentioned the crux of the reason he, Barry and two other members of his team, Arthur Lange and Jim Stephano, were in Lake Tahoe undercover—because the Secret Service criminal investigations division believed that Tony Hallas had been selling software to the Russian mob, information that had been used for a recent hack into U.S. ATM accounts. Over 10 million dollars had been stolen before the breach could be sealed.

Tony hadn't questioned Walker's cover about moving back to Lake Tahoe in order to start his own corporate security operation. Tony had bought his cover because, in fact, that'd been precisely what Walker planned to do. He'd already handed in his resignation with the Secret Service and was counting the days until he returned to Lake Tahoe when they'd received some alarming intelligence in regard to Tony Hallas.

One of the Secret Services's missions was to investigate computer-based attacks on the nation's financial and banking infrastructure. Tony Hallas was suspected of breaching that security, and Walker was tailor-made to go undercover. Walker's boss had begged him to stay on the Secret Service payroll for a short period of time and lead the Hallas investigation.

Tony trusted Walker. They'd been friends since they were both seven years old. Walker's father used to be Tony's father's gardener, and the two boys had spent more than a dozen summers practically attached at the hip.

Until they'd met Madeline Sayer, anyway. Until they'd both vied for her attention. Walker had been the clear winner in their younger days. He'd left Tahoe, though, and the spoils went to Tony.

Barry rubbed his sunburned nose and continued. "I did explain things to Ms. Sayer about why she was a weak point in security, and do you know what she asked? How come we didn't have a person guarding all of Tony's friends?"

Walker stopped typing and glanced up. "He's not planning on marrying all of his friends," he said grimly.

"I told her that. How do you suppose she manages to pull off looking down her nose at you when she probably barely tops five foot four?" Barry mused.

Walker grinned. "Forces of nature can come in small packages."

He didn't waste time telling Barry that Madeline was actually one of the warmest people he'd ever met in his life. The fact that they were discussing her like she was a royal bitch was as good an indication as any of how off balance she was with him being there. It was something, he supposed, knowing he was having an effect on her. He couldn't be too choosy about her manner of reacting to him when the woman he wanted like his next breath was engaged to another man.

He'd hardly expected her to run into his arms. Not Madeline Sayer.

Walker stared out three floor-to-ceiling arched windows onto the shimmering blue lake cradled in the cup of the High Sierra Mountains. Tony's enormous, secluded lodge was made of river rock, pine and glass, but the glass dominated, giving a person the impression that the outdoors and indoors blended seamlessly. Even though Walker had grown up in a comfortable, modest apartment in Kings Beach with his father, mother and brother, he wasn't unused to being inside the realms of grand Tahoe estates. He'd often accompanied his father for jobs and had been a regular visitor at Tony's father's lush Tahoe City villa.

Walker wasn't really seeing the stunning Tahoe scenery on the other side of the windows, though. An equally riveting—and even more powerful—image crowded into his mind's eye: a naked Madeline staring up at him as defiance, fury and hurt warred behind her huge, dark eyes.

You fucking liar, she'd said.

Walker may be in Tony Hallas's house under false pretense, but he hadn't been lying when he told Madeline he had come back to Lake Tahoe for her. He could have started his security firm almost anywhere, but he'd chosen Tahoe at least in part because of his memories of her. The sharp pain of regret of having left her had grown into a dull ache over the years. When he'd seen the glossy surveillance photos of a Madeline all grown up, it'd been like a slug to the gut.

Tony had seemed so eager to change the subject when Walker asked him about a wedding date that Walker had wondered if one or both of them were dragging their feet about final commitment. If it was Madeline hesitating, she'd probably elope with Tony tonight just to spite Walker. Handcuffing her and having sex with her out in the changing rooms earlier hadn't exactly been the smoothest of moves on his part. When he'd volunteered to head up this assignment, he'd forgotten the full effect of Madeline.

The past eleven years had only made her more difficult to ignore.

Barry came over to the desk where he worked. "I'll take over here. You might as well watch out for Ms. Friendly. Tony told me to ask you to have dinner with them. They're waiting for you on the terrace."

Tony stood and shook his hand a few minutes later when Walker stepped outside to join the others. The particular terrace where they'd gathered was another example of architecture mimicking nature. The floor and surround consisted of the type of huge, smooth granite boulders found all over the Tahoe area. They'd been artfully arranged not to distract from the main attraction, the cerulean blue alpine lake. Natural pine outdoor furniture echoed the surrounding forest.

"What do you think, Walk? Can you make this place into a Camp David?" Tony asked.

"That might take a little more than twelve hours, but we'll get you in good shape quick enough. The perimeter of the lake is going to take some doing to seal, but I have the equipment I'll need arriving tonight. I was just running some diagnostics on your system."

Tony gave a mock frown. "I'm sorry I asked. Enough about work. I don't come to Tahoe to talk shop." Walker's gaze flickered to the right and landed on Madeline reclining in a lounge chair, looking like a vision in a white halter dress that set off her tan.

"It's what you asked me here for, Tony," Walker said wryly.

"Only partially. I asked you to Aspen Lodge because I wanted the company of a good friend."

"And to pick your good friend's brain about his government

security secrets," Hal Margrave added with a booming laugh and a wink. "Tony acts so nonchalant, but I bet he'll be looking for your opinion on how to convince the senate that U.S. banks are at high risk for hacking threats. Tony's looking for any morsel he can get to help convince those politicians the banks are as vulnerable as the country would be if we disbanded the military. That recent hack-job into American ATM accounts that was done from Moscow certainly has the politicians sitting up and taking notice."

Walker studied Tony's reaction to his friend's reference to the recent high-profile case of bank hacking. He suspected his old friend of creating the havoc in order to make his company's latest product all that much more appealing to the powers that be. Tony looked anything but guilty, however. He flashed a grin that hadn't changed much since he was a seven-year-old dreamer and troublemaker. Just like when he'd been a kid, Walker found himself grinning back. Tony was nothing if not charming. He would have been better off without that vast cache of charm. Having to work hard for something might have made him into a different person.

He really hated that Tony had gotten himself mixed up in this crap. If he didn't go to prison, he was going to end up with a Russian bullet in his skull.

"How about a mojito, Walk? Fresh mint from the garden. Not as good as your dad could grow it, but tasty." Tony walked behind the terrace bar and pulled down a glass. Walker glanced again at Madeline as Hal and Kitty murmured to each other. She was giving him a stare of blistering hatred, but it was hard to look away. Madeline had been beautiful as a girl—petite, dark-haired and dark-eyed with a face that could make a man do crazy things—but as a woman, she was nothing short of breathtaking.

Walker had almost sacrificed all of his dreams for her, but pride could go a long way in propelling a young man into his future.

Tony leaned across the bar as he was grinding up fresh mint with a pestle in a small marble bowl and spoke confidentially. "Sorry about Maddie. She's not too keen on you guys being here. Giving me the cold shoulder as well," Tony added, rolling his eyes. He'd only grown browner during his boat outing today, making him look like a sleek, Greek playboy frolicking in the Mediterranean. The image was both apt and completely off. Tony was Greek-American and Hollywood-handsome, but he was also a genius when it came to computers, a whiz with the fun-loving spirit of a perpetual ten-year-old imp and the libido of a seventeen-year-old boy.

Yeah, that was Tony in a nutshell. Why he'd decided to sell crucial software to the Russian mob had more to do with being adored and spoiled most of his life than any deep, dark thread of evil. Tony probably had figured it was an easy, harmless way to help convince U.S. financial institutions that they desperately needed him and his product. He knew the chances of getting caught were negligible.

He'd have been right if it hadn't been for a childhood friend. Tony had given Walker and his team full access to his private computers. It was just a matter of hours before they had the evidence they needed for an indictment. For his old friend's sake, Walker almost regretted how easy the operation was.

Madeline, Kitty and Hal were discussing restaurants in the Tahoe area when Tony and Walker joined them.

"I'll make a reservation for us at Spinner's Run for brunch tomorrow. You'll love it—terrific food and a wonderful champagne list," Madeline was telling Kitty and Hal warmly.

"I'd prefer you didn't go out in public until I can get a better understanding of what happened with the shooting," Walker said as he sat.

Madeline leveled him a glacial stare. Tony picked up her hand and shook it playfully, as if to tease her out of her mood, but Walker knew it would take more than a hand-squeezing to get through to her. He couldn't help but notice what a gorgeous couple they made with their sun-gilded skin, dark hair and white clothing, Madeline's delicate features and large, slightly tilted eyes making such a striking contrast to Tony's bold, masculine features.

The sight of them together made his blood boil.

"I refuse to be held in this house like a prisoner just because some idiot took a potshot at me while I was leaving my mom's house," she said defiantly.

Walker shrugged and sipped his mojito. "If you do go in public, it would be extremely selfish of you."

"What's that supposed to mean?"

"It means that we can protect you better within the bounds of the Aspen Lodge than we can out in public. If you return to your condo, or the real estate office where you work, or go to your mom's, or wander around wherever your headstrong-self desires, you put everyone in your vicinity at risk. How would you feel if someone else was shot because you went out to get your nails done? If I can contain you, I can contain the threat."

The fabric of her dress gaped slightly when she jerked forward, gifting him with the sight of the pale inner curves of her small breasts. Madeline's breasts had always driven him crazy.

"I'm not something to be contained, Walker," she seethed quietly.

"I think that's exactly what you are."

After an untold period of time, Tony gave a bark of laughter. Walker looked away from eyes so velvety dark brown, they looked black and depthless in the shade of shimmering aspens. Hal joined Tony in mirth.

"Tony said you three have known one another since you were kids. I can tell, only old friends feel so comfortable sniping at each other. So you attended Mount Caramel as well, Walker?" Hal asked amiably as he stroked his wife's shoulder.

"No. My father was a gardener. He was Tony's father's gardener, actually. He wasn't up for the tuition at Mount Caramel."

Madeline rolled her eyes and sat back in the recliner, obviously barely restraining a hiss of disgust. A becoming blush stained her cheeks. "Your father owned a reputable landscaping company. You make it sound like he was Tony's dad's servant."

"I thought that's what he was," Walker commented evenly before he took a sip of his mojito. Some things never changed, like the fact that Madeline refused to understand that Walker and his brother Zach came from a completely different world than the affluent lifestyle she and Tony shared. Walker got why she'd defended so much against his different background when they were younger. If she could have just convinced Walker that he had nothing to prove by taking the job with the Secret Service, he would never have left Tahoe and she wouldn't be hurling visual knives at him at this moment with her spectacular eyes.

"My point is, Mount Caramel was hardly a rich person's school. You always bring it up like it was, and it wasn't. It's your basic Catholic high school, not Eton," Madeline snapped.

"The only Eton the north shore possessed," Tony joked, oblivious to the tension in the air and Madeline's mood, which was about ten shades past annoyance. Tony didn't even seem to think much of it when Madeline snatched her hand from his and gazed out at the glistening lake, her face turned in profile.

"How's Billy doing, Walker?" Tony asked, referring to Walker's father. "Last I heard, he was living with Zach in Truckee."

"My dad died last year," Walker said quietly.

Madeline's head swung around. When he saw the expression on her face, regret swept through him for being so abrupt. Madeline had adored Billy when she'd been a teenager, and Billy had loved her back.

"No!" Tony exclaimed, and Walker's regret deepened.

His father had always been great with kids. He'd left his mark on Tony and Madeline. "What happened?" Tony asked.

"A stroke," Walker said. "It happened the day after Christmas last year. It was in his sleep . . . Quick."

"Zach was there?" Madeline asked throatily.

Walker nodded. "Yeah, and my nephew Kale."

"He . . . he didn't suffer? Billy, I mean?" she asked shakily.

He held her gaze and shook his head. Her lips—pink and full and naked of all makeup—parted. Walker suspected she thought of her own father's abrupt death eleven years ago. He saw her throat convulse as she swallowed.

"I'm sorry for your loss," she said softly. She cast her gaze back to the lake.

"I loved Billy. I'll miss him," Tony said, sounding a little lost. Tony's brain was hardwired with brilliant equipment, but he responded so frankly at times, so genuinely, it was like he was a simple child. The paradox of Tony wasn't lost on Walker. He guessed many women found that contrast between quirky genius and sweet boy-man endearing. Factor in a face and body worthy of a European playboy, and Walker supposed he could understand Tony's appeal for Madeline.

Sort of.

Not really, but that just might be jealousy talking, Walker admitted to himself as he covertly studied the clean lines of Madeline's profile set against the topaz jewel of the lake. Madeline had a mind like a steel trap. He just couldn't see her being wildly attracted to Tony—couldn't see it when they were kids, still couldn't see it now.

Madeline remained thoughtful and quiet as Hal and Kitty drew Walker into a conversation about what it had been like to be a Secret Service agent. Tony seemed relaxed and content as he listened, the prince in his castle, occasionally asking a few questions and joining in laughter. Madeline's gaze remained on the lake as it deepened in color with encroaching nightfall. She didn't participate in the conversation, but Walker sensed she listened with avid attention.

Or maybe he thought that because he was so hyperaware of her.

After a few minutes, Alessandro, Tony's engaging assistant who did everything from running errands to organizing parties and dinners, came onto the terrace and announced that he'd serve their meal indoors.

Late June days in Tahoe could sizzle, but the evenings cooled considerably. Dinner was served in a glass sanctuary on the west side of the house. Alessandro had set the table with a white tablecloth and several flickering pinecone candles. Tony took the seat at the end of the table and the Margraves sat side by side to the left of him. Madeline gave Walker a repressive glance when he pulled back her chair to seat her. Her sun-gilded back was bare in the halter dress she wore. She wore her long, dark hair in a sleek twist at the back of her head. He could tell by the stiffness of her spine she was miffed when he sat down next to her. He unobtrusively moved his chair nearer to her when he pushed himself toward the table.

He felt her start when he placed his hand on her dress-covered thigh beneath the table. For one second . . . two . . . three, he waited on edge. He barely had attention to focus when Alessandro approached, showing Madeline the label of the wine.

"This is the wine you requested, Ms. Sayer. Would you like to taste it?"

Walker waited, an expression of polite indifference plastered on his face. He'd made it clear to his director at the Secret Service, Mark Eldridge, that he wasn't impartial when it came to this investigation. He'd even warned Eldridge it wasn't a good idea to include him if Madeline was going to be involved. Walker had thought it only fair to tell the truth.

Eldridge had considered all the advantages Walker's inside position offered and sent him anyway.

Walker had convinced himself seducing Madeline could serve a dual purpose. He wasn't entirely being selfish by coming on to her with Tony sitting six feet away. Having an inside position with Madeline could only help matters—both personally and professionally.

Of course, all she had to do was react with insulted outrage at his bold move and Tony would kick him out for good.

Forget playing with fire. This was Madeline. This was tossing lit matches on a cache of dynamite.

Madeline's dark eyes remained fixed on her wineglass as Alessandro poured. She held herself unnaturally still. Walker shifted his hand higher on her thigh. The fabric of the dress she wore was thin. He felt the shape of her perfectly. His cock jerked in arousal.

She picked up the glass and tilted the amber liquid toward her lips.

"It's lovely, Alessandro. Thank you," she murmured.

Walker forced his mouth not to tilt into a small smile of triumph. Slowly, he began to gather fabric in his fist, lifting her dress, keeping his arm as immobile as possible. Hal bemoaned the fact that he and Kitty had to leave the following day. Hal and Tony began to discuss a future trout-fishing expedition on the Truckee River. Kitty asked Walker where he'd set up his offices in the North Lake Tahoe area, which started a casual conversation about the status of Lake Tahoe real estate. Since Madeline was a successful real-estate agent of luxury properties in the Tahoe area, her silence seemed a little strange. Walker hastened to talk more, covering her preoccupation.

Even though she didn't speak, Walker sensed her pitched focus. Her skin felt like warm satin against his fingertips. At first, her leg muscles remained rigid at his touch. His fingers slid against the sensitive skin of her inner thigh.

It was as if he'd activated a secret button.

She parted her legs. His fingertips moved like five heat-seeking devices.

Three

It was happening again, this hot, unstoppable rush of lust. Madeline couldn't seem to stop it, and she hated that. She despised being at the mercy of Walker.

Her pussy seemed to love it, though.

Taking part in polite dinner conversation while Walker's fingers inched stealthily toward the juncture of her thighs was like being told she needed to complete a complicated math problem while anticipating a delicious rush of pleasure. She felt his warm, large fingertips skim across the top of her thong panties. She realized she was sweating and reached for her glass of ice water.

"Look at that sunset, Walker. You can't tell me you had anything like that in Washington, DC," Tony said as Alessandro served their salads. He nodded toward the floor-to-ceiling panes of glass and the spectacular vision of the sun sinking behind the mountains, sending shards of gold-and-crimson light into the deep blue mirror of the lake.

Madeline barely heard him. Two long fingers had just dipped beneath her panties and slid between her labia. She shivered at the sensation of the hard ridge of his forefinger pressing firmly against her clit. She resisted an urge to press her chilled water glass against her cheek.

"No," Walker admitted gruffly. "It was always hard to surpass the memories of Tahoe. Everything I saw, everything I experienced, since then came up short."

Madeline gasped. Thankfully, the Margraves had turned, joining Tony and Walker in their appreciation of the sun sinking behind the distant mountains. They didn't notice her reaction as Walker began to subtly vibrate his finger against her clit, agitating the hungry flesh until it sizzled.

"Aren't you hungry, Maddie?" Tony asked a moment later when everyone started on their salads and Madeline just continued to stare blankly out the window.

"Of course. It looks delicious," she murmured as she picked up the heavy silver salad fork. Later, she wouldn't have been able to say what she'd put into her mouth. It might have been pickled fish heads, for all she knew. Every cell in her entire body seemed to have pitched into an alert focus of the weight of Walker's hand, the movements of his finger, the almost electrical pulse of energy that seemed to pass directly from his flesh into her own.

Tony patted her left hand. "I know having someone take a shot at you must have sent you into a tailspin. You haven't been yourself all day. Even though it happened on Tuesday, the shock of it doesn't seem to have fully settled until now."

Madeline blinked and pulled her hand out from under Tony's. It seemed wrong, somehow, like trying to breathe underwater, to have Tony touch her while Walker did.

"I'm not worried, Tony. Please don't *worry* about me being worried. It'll get us nowhere."

They launched into a topic Madeline had been avoiding for forty-eight hours now.

"I don't suppose the Carnelian Bay police have done much to uncover any leads about the shooting?" Hal asked.

"There isn't any Carnelian Bay police," Walker replied. She yanked her gaze off Walker's small, sexy smile with effort. He continued to stir her juices as he spoke; his movements tiny, but incendiary. Her breath had started to come jagged and shallow. At first she thought it was panic until she realized it was excitement. She'd never been sexually stimulated in public. The combination was bizarre and intimidating. "Carnelian Bay is unincorporated," Walker continued. "Some boys from the Truckee police department came to investigate the shooting. I drove to Truckee last night after Tony called me. The shot came from a Ramo M600 fifty-caliber rifle. Russian."

A puff of air flew past her lips when Walker's finger paused. She glanced over at him and saw he stared at Tony. Tony took a large gulp of his wine, his face unusually stiff and sober.

"Russian?" Hal exclaimed as he scraped his salad plate. "Do you suppose that means anything, Walker?"

"It means someone seriously has it out for Madeline. That's a professional sniper rifle."

"And the fact that it was Russian? Is that significant?" Kitty asked, looking concerned as she glanced at Madeline.

"Nonsense," Madeline blurted out. "There's nothing significant about any of this. The guy who took a potshot at me couldn't have been much of a *professional*. He missed by a mile." Despite Madeline's scathing tone—she was sick of the ridiculous topic of a conspiracy against her life—Madeline subtly pressed up with her hips against the weight of Walker's hand. If they weren't careful, the sounds of him moving in her wet pussy would soon become audible. That was how aroused she'd become.

"That is strange," Walker mused as he idly watched Alessandro start to clear the table. The scent of broiled salmon tickled at Madeline's nose, as if all the senses of her body had gone on hyperalert because of Walker's hand in her lap. He diddled at her clit, his actions striking her as tight and focused and casual at once, as if it were the most normal thing in the world for him to manually stimulate her during a small supper party.

"What do you mean?" Tony asked Walker. Madeline noticed Tony looked flushed and guiltily wondered if her own cheeks were pink as well.

"It seems unlikely, that's all," Walker said. "The shooter had purchased some high-tech equipment. He'd chosen his spot well. Everything about the incident screams of a professional hit if it weren't for the fact that he missed so drastically."

"A warning, perhaps?" Hal asked shrewdly. "You haven't sold any billionaires a money pit of a house lately, have you Maddie?" He picked up his fork and skewered a new potato covered in a delicate white wine and dill sauce.

"I should be the one seeking revenge on my clients given the steals they've been getting in this economy," Madeline murmured wryly. Thankfully, Kitty changed the subject. Madeline was highly conscious of Walker cutting into his seared salmon, of him sliding his fork between his lips, of the movement of his jaw. She thought the meal would taste like cardboard, but instead flavor burst on her tongue as she ate. It appeared that being sexually stimulated really did awaken all the senses of the body.

As the seconds ticked by and Walker continued relentlessly, anxiety mixed more acutely with her arousal. Her cheeks grew hot. The soles of her feet tingled in her high-heeled sandals. Her clit burned beneath Walker's finger. The friction was delicious.

She was going to come.

"Excuse me," she said breathlessly.

Walker's hand fell out of her lap when she moved her chair back. She stood jerkily. Alessandro, who had been in the process of clearing their meal, steadied her as she rose.

"You okay, Maddie?" Tony asked. He must have noticed her shaky voice and stance.

"I'm fine. Maybe a little too much wine. I'll . . . I'll join you all in a bit if I feel better," she said. She swept out of the room.

Before she reached the hallway, she heard Tony say in a low, confidential tone, "She's more upset about this shooting business than she's letting on."

Madeline hurried into a large powder room and shut the door. She was in the outer alcove of the bathroom, a grooming area where a lady could sit at the marble-topped vanity and comb her hair or freshen her makeup. Her breathing was coming erratic and choppy. Her clit throbbed. It was very damp between her thighs. She glanced at her reflection in the mirror. Her cheeks were bright pink and her eyes had the glassy sheen of sexual arousal.

How dare he humiliate her like that in public?

She placed one hand on her pussy and winced at the pressure. She was in the process of lifting the hem of her dress when the door opened and Walker stepped into the bathroom.

Madeline stared at him as he closed and locked the door. He looked shockingly real to her in that bizarre moment, all sleek brawn and tawny male glory. His skin had turned a darker shade of toasty brown, making his eyes look even more electrically blue-green in contrast. The whiskers on his lean jaw were brown with just a hint of gold. Even in her heels, he towered over her in the small room.

He glanced down significantly at her dress bunched in her fist. He stepped toward her. "I'll be finishing that."

Anger and arousal swept through her with a wave of heat. "You don't know how to finish anything you start."

"I'll apologize later if you like," he said through a stiff jaw. "I'll beg for your forgiveness for leaving, and for the fact that I wasn't here when your dad passed. I'll make it up to you. I don't care how long it takes. But the time for apologies isn't *now*, Madeline."

He grabbed a handful of her dress. Her pussy twanged in anticipation, but she jerked down on the fabric in protest.

"You're going to rip this dress," she said in accusation, staring up at him.

"Only if you make me," he muttered. He leaned down and covered her mouth. Her head swam. It was more of an attack than a kiss. Sensation—heat, pressure, his taste, pleasure, hunger—hit her like a slap to the face. After a disoriented moment, she kissed him back, her voraciousness nearly equaling his. Their tongues dueled angrily. She went up on her tiptoes. She placed a hand on the back of his neck and aggressively pulled him closer. He pulled up on her dress, but for some stupid reason, she resisted again, their silent battle of wills ramping up her desire instead of diminishing it.

After a moment of struggling while they ate each other like they were starving, Walker growled in frustration into her mouth. He lifted his head an inch from her face. She cried out in surprise when he grabbed her hands and pushed them to the small of her back. She'd been taken so off guard by his actions, she didn't have time to struggle. He bound her wrists with one hand and shucked her dress up to her hips with the other.

"Don't you dare ever walk away from me again when I'm touching you," he breathed out against her lips. She gasped when his fingers plunged beneath her thong and he stroked her again. This time his whole arm moved as he stimulated her hard and ruthlessly. It felt wickedly good. He tightened his hold on her wrists, forcing her to arch slightly. She stumbled a little, off balance. One of her breasts pressed against his ribs. She moaned and dipped her knees an inch before she straightened, getting friction on her nipple. "Do you hear me, Madeline?"

"I couldn't come in front of everyone," she mumbled. She ground her pussy against his hand. She felt so hot. She was going to light up like a crate of fireworks.

"You could have. You just refused," he muttered, his voice no longer edged with anger. "But you'll come for me now. Go on, beautiful," he ordered as he plucked at her upturned lips with his mouth and played her clit with forceful finesse. "You're juicier than a man's best wet dream. I'm going to fuck that juicy little pussy as soon as I watch you come."

His grim, sensual threat finished her. She winced as climax jolted through her, hot and electric. She gave in to it, thrusting her pelvis against his hand, grinding against him, greedy for each blast of bliss that shook her flesh. He watched her while she came. Before she was entirely finished, he placed his hands on her hips.

"Bend over," he demanded as he turned her, her back to his front.

"Walker . . . this is crazy," she mumbled. "We can't."

"We will."

They stood in front of an antique vanity and mirror. She saw his blazing eyes in the reflection. She slowly bent over, her gaze glued to his. He flung her dress up to her waist and jerked her thong down so that it fell around the ankle straps of her sandals. This was madness. Utter insanity. She realized she wasn't sure what the others thought the two of them were doing. Did they know they were both inside this bathroom together engaging in a sexual frenzy?

She watched Walker tearing at his button fly and realized she didn't care.

He reached into his back pocket before he yanked his jeans off his hips. It should have pleased her that he rolled on the condom, but instead it highlighted the fact that she'd been about to let him come fuck her naked once again. He spread one hand over a bare ass cheek and glanced up, meeting her gaze in the mirror.

"I came in you earlier. I left my mark. You make sure Tony stays away from my territory."

Her mouth dropped open. She couldn't believe he'd said that, let alone said it with such fury. There were depths to Walker's boldness she hadn't fully comprehended.

"Do you understand, Madeline?" he asked. In the reflection, she saw that his other hand was between his legs. He was holding his cock in readiness for penetration.

"Tell me you're not going to let him touch you," he grated out.

She grasped for the remnants of her self-respect—difficult to do when bent over a vanity with one's dress around their waist and ass in the air. She felt cornered, trapped between her pride and her desire.

"I'll promise you no such thing," she hissed.

For a few seconds he didn't move, and Madeline knew misery. Then he stepped closer, and she felt the tip of his hard erection pressing against her slit, stretching her delicate tissues. She gasped. Loudly. He placed both his hands on her buttocks. He lifted and parted her, forcing her to make room in her body for his presence. They stared at each other in the mirror as he applied a firm pressure and slid into her inch by inch. Her gaze remained defiant, but her body betrayed her in the way she melted around his teeming cock.

"Your pussy is mine. If you need to learn that the hard way, so be it," he muttered. He thrust, his jaw clamped tight. Madeline panted, her mouth hanging open, at the sensation of him encased and throbbing deep in her flesh. He flexed back and his length slid out of her. She bit her already cut lip to stop herself from screaming when he plunged his cock back into her and his pelvis smacked against her ass. She keened inside her tightly sealed mouth, but he was already withdrawing and hammering into her again. Walker was a strong man, and his cock was as big as the rest of him. It thrilled her somehow, the difference in their sizes. She couldn't help but be proud of her ability to take him so well when he took her so hard. Her position left her little protection. Her body was his to take, and take it he did. She tried to hold herself upright as he fucked her with powerful strokes, but it was like trying to remain motionless during a battering storm.

He thrust, popping her ass with his pelvis. His satisfied male grunts rang in her ears. He drove the full length of his cock into her repeatedly, holding her hips and buttocks in his hands, preventing her from moving.

It was possession, pure and simple.

She was so aroused at being the focused target of Walker's lust that she longed to touch herself. Her clit burned, well stimulated by the indirect pressure of Walker's thick, long, thrusting cock. She couldn't remove her hand, though, without crashing toward the vanity. He stormed behind her, and her position was made even more tenuous by the fact that she perched on four-inch heels.

The burn grew untenably sharp as he continued to fuck her, faster now. This was what Walker called "teaching her the hard way." Through a haze of lust, she distantly realized he was fucking her with the sole intent of personal satisfaction. He was punishing her for not giving him the promise he sought. She watched him in the mirror as he observed himself fucking her. A slight snarl shaped his firm mouth as he stared at his cock pistoning in and out of her pussy.

Suddenly he glanced up and caught her staring.

"Do you want to watch, too, Madeline?" he rasped as he continued to pump.

She didn't speak, but maybe he saw her answer in her eyes and her vividly red cheeks. He sheathed himself until his balls pressed tight against her. He placed both hands on her ribs and lifted her torso. His feet shifted behind her and Madeline followed suit. He pushed her down again until her hands braced against the door that led to the bathroom. They both panted as they examined the vision of themselves in the mirror. Walker was behind her, impaled in her flesh. She was bent at the waist, her hands bracing her against the door.

He began to pump again. She moaned in arousal at the sight of his cock sliding out of her body. He looked too large for her, but nevertheless, she took him.

And she loved every minute of it.

"Do you see that?" Walker asked quietly behind her as he fucked her nice and hard. The door she leaned against rattled in its frame. "That's my pussy. Your pussy was made for this cock."

"No," she whimpered, even as she watched, spellbound, at the sight of herself being taken so thoroughly.

Walker responded to her defiance by lifting his hand and smacking her bottom. He paused, just the first few inches of his cock embedded in her. A high-pitched whining sound vibrated her throat when he spanked her again. Not softly. It smarted. She stared at the long stalk of his cock protruding from her pussy and resisted an urge to beg. He spanked her bottom several more times. His face looked fierce and even a little fearsome in the reflection. She felt his cock pop up in the tight hold of her vagina every time he smacked her.

"This" . . . *smack* . . . "pussy" . . . *smack* . . . "is" . . . *smack* . . . "mine."

He thrust rapidly, swatting her every time their skin whapped together. It was too much. Her pale bottom grew pink. Madeline drowned in sharp, slamming waves of pleasure.

Her eyes sprung wide when he spanked her even harder than he had previously. She felt his cock swell high and hard in her, making her wince.

"Say it," he seethed.

"This pussy is yours," she gasped.

As if to reward her for her submission, he reached around and rubbed her clit vigorously. A cry leapt out of her throat as orgasm crashed into her. He gave a satisfied growl and began fucking her fast and forcefully, nearly knocking her off her heels in his fury of need.

He held her tight against him as he came. She felt him leap at her core. The harsh grunts and groans of release that tore from his throat hurt her for some reason. She knew he wasn't in pain, but it sounded as if he was.

Slowly, the tension drained out of his taut muscles. He stared down at their joined bodies while he panted, trying to regain his breath. Madeline became acutely aware of where they were—in a small, seven-by-seven-foot powder room.

In Tony's lodge.

They hadn't even bothered to quiet themselves. There at the end, they'd been going at it like two animals in heat. Chances were they'd been overheard, if not by Tony or the Margraves, then by someone on Tony's or Walker's staffs.

The fact that she'd been so involved in the moment, so overwhelmed by Walker, made her whimper in distress. She took a step toward the door and straightened on shaky legs, moaning at the sensation of Walker's still-formidable erection sliding from her body.

She tossed her dress down over her legs and bent to retrieve her thong, which was twisted around her ankles. He just stared at her with slow-burning, blue-green eyes when she turned to face him.

"Why are you trying to humiliate me?" she asked in a choked voice.

His rapid breathing paused. He looked so beautiful standing there with his jeans shucked down around his knees, exposing his long, muscular thighs, his sated cock still stretching the latex of the condom.

His chest moved again as he inhaled slowly.

"It's not humiliating to admit the obvious, Madeline."

Anger clutched at her throat. "You had your chance, Walker. You walked away."

A muscle in his rigid cheek twitched. "I was twenty-two years old. And I came back."

"That doesn't give you the right to me."

Her heart caught in her breast when he reached out and touched her cheek. It amazed her . . . frightened her a little, even, to see the raw emotion in his handsome face.

"Nature gave me that right, Madeline." He seemed a little heart sore with his answer, but it was his certainty that left her breathless.

Her mouth opened, closed and then opened again. She looked wildly around the tiny room, feeling as if she'd never seen it until that moment.

She lunged toward the door, pulling up short when he grasped her hand.

"I told you I'd make it up to you, but you have to give me a chance. I'm going to be installing some equipment down by the lake perimeter tonight, but we'll be finished by eleven or so. I want you to meet me at midnight down by the gazebo in the gardens. I want to talk to you, Madeline," he added when she dared to glance back at him.

She thought he'd try and stop her when she fled, but he didn't. The hallway was shadowed and silent. When she neared the grand staircase, she heard the sound of Tony's and Hal's voices emanating from the terrace. Something about their casual banter made her suspect they hadn't heard Walker's and her wild coupling. She raced up the stairs toward her private suite like the devil was snapping his teeth at her high heels.

Four

She told Tony she wasn't feeling well when he tapped on her suite door at around eleven thirty that night. She'd showered and put on a sapphire blue low-cut nightgown. When Tony entered, she greeted him while lying in bed reading a book, the sheet pulled up to her chest. She suspected he'd drunk his fill with the Margraves after she'd excused herself earlier. His tread was steady enough, but there was a telling glassiness to his brown eyes. He'd been drinking more lately—ever since he'd become involved in this business of convincing the senate that U.S. banks were at high risk—and it concerned Madeline.

"I'm sorry you're not feeling well," he consoled as he sat at the edge of her bed.

"I just have a headache from spending so much time in the sun today."

"I think you're angry with me, for asking Walker and his crew to the lodge."

She sighed when she saw his downcast eyes. "I'm not angry, Tony. I just think it's an inconvenience and a waste of time."

"But I need Walker," Tony exclaimed. "Above and beyond his help in protecting you until we figure out the identity of this shooter. He's going to make the Aspen Lodge impenetrable, and he'll do the same to my house in Half Moon Bay. He's the best, Maddie. I won't have you harmed. I'd die if something happened to you because of something I—"

"*You* have nothing to do with this!" Madeline exclaimed.

He winced. "You don't know that. I've had nutcases threaten me before. It's inevitable, owning a company like Hallas Technologies. Walker can keep you safe. I know he can."

Madeline interrupted him before he started to once again list Walker's list of honors, accomplishments and commendations, one of them awarded by a former president. She'd heard the list already four or five times today.

"I resent being trapped here at the lodge," she said.

"It's only until the police and Walker investigate the shooting a little more. Abigail would shoot me herself if I let you go after what happened," Tony said earnestly, referring to Madeline's mother. While he talked, he idly grabbed the edge of her sheet and drew it down to her waist. Madeline pulled back on the fabric, but he held firm.

"Let me look at you, at least, since you won't let me touch," he muttered as his eyes roved over her bare shoulders and chest. "You're the most beautiful woman I've ever seen."

"Tony, you're drunk," she said in exasperation.

"It's true," he said simply. He looked sad as he met her gaze. "I wish I'd had the sense to realize it when you were in my bed."

She smiled and shook her head when she saw his expression. "But you *didn't* believe it when I was in your bed, Tony. That's the whole point. There was always something just a little more beautiful, a little more desirable in the corner of your eye."

"I was a fool. There was no one more beautiful, Maddie, just more willing. It was childish of me, to think I wanted a woman to submit to my every whim. You always kept me in line."

"You only think you want me because I never *did* submit to your every whim. If I would have, you would have gotten over me quick enough, as well."

He shook his head soberly. "It was—is—my ultimate fantasy to imagine you submitting, Maddie. Just a little." He gave her an imploring look. "When are you going to marry me? We're not getting any younger."

"Yes, we'll have to pick out our cemetery plots any day now," she chided with a smile, even though she was concerned about the moroseness of Tony's mood.

He looked so crestfallen that Madeline held her protest in her throat when he casually moved aside a band of satin, baring one of her breasts. He stared at it as he spoke distractedly. "I came to a weird realization while I was watching you and Walker sitting side by side this evening."

Her breath froze in her lungs. "*What* . . . what do you mean?" she asked after a moment.

"You used to have a thing for Walker, years back. It used to make me insane with jealousy, seeing the way you two looked at each other. I don't know why I'd forgotten . . ." He trailed off as he touched her nipple with a fingertip. Maddie exhaled and rapidly moved the gown back over her nipple. It didn't surprise her that Tony had forgotten their youthful love triangle. Affairs of the heart for Tony were as common as casual conversations about the weather.

"We were kids, Tony. It was a long time ago. Why don't you go to bed? You promised to take me out on the boat tomorrow."

Tony glanced up at her with dark shining eyes. "You'll always love me, won't you, Maddie? No matter how stupid I am?"

She sighed. He must be drunker than she'd thought. She pushed back a dark curl off his forehead.

"Always. Because you've always been there for me, Tony, you and your mom and dad."

He gave her such a sweet smile she didn't turn away when he softly kissed her on the mouth. After he'd left her room, she glanced at her bedside clock. It was ten until twelve. There was just enough time for her to throw on some clothes and meet Walker. She thought of him waiting for her there in the shadow-shrouded gardens. He'd said he wanted to talk. He'd said he wanted to make it up to her.

She wanted him to try more than she cared to admit.

You've always been there for me, Tony.

Her spine stiffened at the thought. Walker hadn't been there for her when she needed him. All she'd gotten from him was some phone calls, which she'd ignored. He'd said his good-byes, although Madeline refused to reciprocate. She'd rushed out of his arms, not wanting to hear Walker's promises and soothing words. She recalled perfectly the evening she'd gone to his Incline Village apartment and knocked at the door. Some thin, fraying remnant of hope had remained.

It'd evaporated when she heard the hollow quality of her knock. Walker's tiny apartment where they'd shared hours upon hours of joy and rapture was empty.

She shut out the lamp and curled on her side. Her indecision caused a pain of sorts in her belly that she tried to alleviate by pulling up her knees until she rested in a fetal position. Her brain seemed ablaze, making sleep impossible.

The glowing numerals on the bedside clock read 12:17 when she heard her bedroom door click open. She clamped her eyelids shut. It might have been Tony returning to woo her, but it wasn't. Madeline just knew somehow.

His tall shadow loomed over the bed.

"Are you awake?" he asked quietly.

"Yes," she whispered.

He tossed back the sheet. His arms slid beneath her, and Madeline rolled toward him as he lifted, hitting his chest with a thud. His scent—clean, spicy soap and the fresh odor of the pine forest—filtered into her nose. She inhaled deeply. He paused next to the bed.

"Are you going to scream?"

"No," she whispered.

His hands moved slightly on the back of her thigh and along her ribs, feeling the skimpiness of her gown. "Do you have a robe?"

"At the foot of the bed."

A few seconds later, he carried her silently out of her opened bedroom door into the moonlit hall.

He'd said he wanted to talk to her, but neither of them spoke as he deactivated the alarm and then reactivated it once they left the lodge. They remained silent even when he set her in the passenger seat of his car and they drove through Tony's lush grounds and exited the security gate. The tense excitement of a midnight secret mission tightened her chest and tingled in her limbs as he drove through the silent, seemingly enchanted streets of Carnelian Bay and eventually turned onto Route 12, the road that encircled the entire lake. Madeline saw the moonlight shimmering in the dark water.

"Where are we going?" she asked in a hushed tone.

"I bought a house in King's Beach. It's large enough to live in as well as run the business until I rent some commercial property."

"Wasn't one of your staff guarding me?"

He glanced over at her. "I have watch of you tonight."

A ripple of sensation shivered through her, and she pulled her robe closer around her. Neither of them spoke another word until

Walker turned onto a winding mountain road and finally pulled
into a drive. Once he'd put the car into park, neither of them
moved. It seemed the air was so thick with anticipation, she had
trouble drawing breath. He put his hands on the wheel and bowed
his head slightly. Madeline examined his handsome, stark profile in
the dim light.

"I regretted leaving you. More than you'll ever know. But I can't
apologize for who I was then any more than I can say I regret what
I've become. I needed to go and find my own way, Madeline. I was
a kid. I didn't have anything to offer you."

"I never asked for anything but you," she said, staring blindly at
the house in front of her.

He gave a dissatisfied grunt. "You may have had a child's dreams
then, but you're a grown woman now. Are you really going to punish me indefinitely for establishing a career for myself? I couldn't
have done what I wanted to do in Lake Tahoe. I'd have ended up
doing rich people's lawns for the rest of my life, like my dad."

"Do you think I would have cared?" she exclaimed heatedly,
turning toward him.

"No. But *I* would have, Madeline. *I* would have. Do you
understand?"

Her breath burned in her lungs in the seconds that followed.
He exhaled suddenly, informing Madeline he'd been holding his
breath, too.

"It isn't as if I didn't try to contact you. I was miserable when I
heard about your dad dying while I was doing my basic training,"
he said gruffly. "I tried like hell to get you on the phone during
those seven weeks. You were just as religious about avoiding me."

She looked at her hands clasped in her lap through a haze of
tears.

"I suppose you think I'm a fool, still hurting about a boy I fell in
love with when I was nineteen years old," she said angrily.

He put his hand on her shoulder, but she continued to stare at her lap, not wanting him to see her tears.

"I don't think you're a fool. It's hard to know when you're that young that what was happening between us was such a rarity . . . something so special." He stroked her shoulder. "I told you I came back for you, Madeline. Do you really think I'd blame you for being set off balance at the sight of me? I'm fucking thrilled about it."

Laughter popped out of her throat at his wry tone. A tear spilled down her cheek, and she furtively dried it with her fingertips.

"Madeline?"

"Yes?"

"Will you let me tell you now how sorry I am about not being here when your dad passed? I know how much he meant to you."

A spasm of grief went through her. She hadn't realized until that moment how long she'd waited to hear Walker say those words. "I'm so sorry about your dad, too," she mumbled wetly.

She felt his fingertips on her cheek, drying tears that now flowed freely. "I wish you would have taken my calls back then. We might have avoided all this, Madeline."

She shook her head as emotion clawed at her throat.

"I couldn't. It would have hurt too much to hear your voice, knowing you were gone."

"Shhhh," he soothed as he took her into his arms. "I'm back. I'm back now."

After a minute she gained control over her upwelling of emotion. She became increasingly aware of the feeling of Walker's hard chest beneath her cheek . . . the steady, strong beat of his heart . . . the feeling of his chin resting on the top of her head and how he occasionally turned it to kiss her hair.

"Are you ready to go inside?" he asked.

She nodded. The pavement of the driveway felt cool beneath her bare feet. She glanced around the house curiously once he'd let her in the door and locked it behind them. She'd never shown the house but she'd noticed it on the MLS listing for sale. Three bedrooms, a den and a lake view. If Walker had purchased it, he must be doing all right for himself.

He hung his keys on a hook in the entryway. He grabbed her hand and led her upstairs without turning on the lights, moving with a confident stride in the darkness. She thought of what he'd said about how he hadn't felt he could offer her anything as a young man. Part of her had always vigilantly resisted that explanation. Tonight, as she held Walker's hand and followed his tall shadow down a hallway, she examined that part of herself that had blamed Walker for leaving Tahoe . . . for leaving her.

She hadn't wanted what he said about finding his way to be true because then she'd officially have had to let him go.

Had she really been so selfish that she would have denied him his dreams . . . his desire to forge his character into something of which he could be proud?

The full moon reflected off the lake, creating a palette of shifting dark blue shadows and silvery white light in the bedroom where Walker led her. He paused at the foot of a bed and turned to face her. She put her hand on his forearm, halting him when he started to reach for her.

"You're not the only one who owes an apology," she said softly. Emotion swelled in her throat when he said nothing, but drew her into his arms. He pressed his nose to her hair and inhaled deeply. "My father always did say I was a spoiled brat, remember? I think you agreed with him more often than not."

"Your father adored you," Walker rumbled.

"Yes." She pressed her lips against his chest, seeking and finding the flat, hard disc of a nipple and kissing it. Walker went very still beneath her caress. "But he was right to say I didn't particularly like being told 'no.' I wanted things my way or no way."

He spread his hand along her back and stroked her. She spoke next to his chest, hiding her humiliation over what she was about to say.

"If I couldn't have you on my terms then—"

"You didn't want me at all," Walker finished gruffly.

She inhaled and stepped away from him, searching out his face in the dim light.

"If you abandoned me, then I abandoned you just as much," she whispered.

He put his hand on her jaw. "I never forgot you, Madeline."

"I wished I could forget you. When I saw you again, I realized why I couldn't."

Her fingers moved fleetly around his waist and slipped beneath the edge of his jeans. She began to unbutton his fly. She felt powerfully aware of him, his hardness, his maleness, his scent . . . his heat. The moment felt full, tense and delicious somehow. He said nothing when she grabbed the waistband of his jeans and fell to her knees before him. She removed his shoes and socks, then helped him out of his jeans. When he was finally bare from the waist down, she leaned forward and placed a kiss on the satiny-smooth head of his cock. She turned and brushed her cheek against the head, absorbing his texture and heat. His hand closed in her hair, forming a gentle fist.

"Turn toward the windows," he rasped. "I want to see your face."

They both moved in profile to the moonlight. She held the stalk of his cock in her hand, thrilling to the sensation of hard, teeming flesh. She opened her lips and drew the head of his cock into her mouth, giving him a firm, sucking kiss.

"I'm sorry, Walker," she breathed against his cock.

He brushed her hair away from her face before he cradled it.

"Then welcome me home," he whispered.

She closed her eyes and guided his cock into her mouth.

* * *

Walker watched his cock sliding between her lips, held spellbound by her lovely face, excited by the way he stretched her lush lips. He'd fantasized about Madeline's mouth for a decade or more. He'd never known a woman as naturally gifted at giving head.

She polished him with a firm, wet tongue while she worked her way down his shaft. Madeline may be petite and delicate, but she sucked with the strength of a virago. He furrowed his fingers through her hair and gently urged her up and down on his cock.

It was sublime.

He recalled as he watched her why he'd loved having her give him blow jobs when they'd been younger. It was because she gave herself so fully to the experience. She seemed enthralled as she quickened her pace, bobbing her head back and forth, applying a firm, steady suck that had him crossing his eyes. She twisted her head slightly on the back stroke, giving him a teeth-clenching extra jolt on the swollen vein just beneath the head.

"Jesus, you remembered," he murmured as he watched her, touched and aroused that she not only recalled the location of his sweet spot after so many years but that he liked having that area treated to a helping of rough love. She responded by scraping her teeth gently against the sensitive patch of skin on her down stroke. He gasped and tightened his hand in her hair.

"Little tease," he said.

He felt the twitch in her stretched lips as she smiled.

His cock was large enough that he was used to women not taking him fully during fellatio. He found himself fantasizing about full oral penetration in that moment, though, as he recalled all too well that the stunning woman on her knees before him had given the venture a hell of a run in their younger years.

He grunted in tense arousal when she eased him into the

narrow channel of her throat. The semen in his balls seemed to leap at the erotic sensation of being encased in such a small channel. She jerked at his invasion and he withdrew quickly, wincing at the electrifying back stroke along her tongue.

"Madeline," he growled when she took him in her throat again, deeper this time.

He pushed back on her head and his cock popped out of the vacuum she'd created with her steady suck. He resisted an urge to slide his cock back into the heaven of her mouth. She seemed confused as he bent down and lifted her to her feet. The evidence that she'd been so involved in giving him pleasure made something wild and powerful surge in his chest. He wanted to hug her and not let go, fuck her until he filled her with his come, love her until they were both too exhausted to move.

"I'm going to let you finish that sometime very soon, but right now, I want to bury myself in you, Madeline," he said roughly. He lifted her, his hands on her ribs, feeling acutely aware of how small she was, how finely made. She sighed when he laid her on her back on the bed. He stood and whipped off his shirt, his gaze never leaving the moon-kissed vision of her. He bent and lifted her gown to her waist, making short work of the silk panties she wore.

"Open your legs, Madeline. Let me in," he whispered, mesmerized by the sight of her shapely thighs, the erotic span of her belly, the dark, trimmed triangle of hair at the juncture of her legs. When she immediately spread her thighs wide, he muttered a curse that was meant as a blessing.

A groan ripped out of his chest when he slid into her hot, welcoming clasp. It was like being turned inside out every time he fucked her. She was too small for him. She was fucking perfect for him. She squeezed every remnant of rational thought out of his brain.

"I'm not going to last," he said as he pumped. He hoped she forgave him, but the experience of having her give herself to him so freely—first with her sweet, sucking mouth and now with her tight, total embrace—was causing an unbearable tension to grow in him.

"I'm not going anywhere, Walker."

He gave a gruff bark of laughter and put all of his energy into showing her he was there to stay, as well. His exuberance over his task caused both Madeline and the springs on the mattress to squeak and moan. His entire world narrowed down to the feeling of her sleek, juicy pussy pulling at his cock, tempting him until he turned into a wild-eyed animal intent on claiming his mate.

And her face . . . he couldn't remove his eyes from Madeline's moonlit face.

When he felt himself cresting, he jerked his cock out of her, the sensation a little like removing one of his own organs with a dull knife. He pumped his cock with his hand and roared, his semen shooting onto Madeline's belly, anointing her, claiming her . . . marking her yet again.

He wanted to drench her with his come.

When his frenzy quieted, he opened his eyes and saw her belly glistening in the pale light. He touched the side of her body with his hand and groaned when he felt how wet she was. He'd made his fantasy a little too realistic.

"I'll get you a towel," he muttered, moving toward the edge of the bed. She didn't speak when he came back with a warm wash-cloth and a towel to dry her. He cleaned her of what seemed like a gallon of his come, then helped her out of her gown and robe, which had grown damp as well.

He kissed her softly while his fingers moved between her thighs. He absorbed the whimpers of pleasure and shudders of her body when she climaxed against his hand a moment later.

"I'm not going anywhere, either, Madeline. Never again," he assured her next to her trembling lips before he began the process of staking his claim yet again.

Five

Madeline awoke at four thirty in the morning. She inhaled and snuggled closer to Walker. The air was redolent with sex. Madeline smiled as she recalled their soulful, electric lovemaking. They'd spoken quietly to each other in the interims, laughing as they recalled old treasured memories—Madeline being sprayed by a surprised skunk when Billy took them camping at Crater Lake, attending the black-tie Christmas party Tony's parents threw every year, Madeline whispering frequent reassurances to an uncomfortable, out-of-place-feeling Walker . . .

. . . their first kiss at the old Stateline Fire Lookout.

Walker stirred in his sleep and clasped her tighter. She rubbed her cheek against his chest, loving the sensation of power gloved in smooth, thick skin. He was so beautiful to her, with his narrow hips, lean torso and broad shoulders, all sleek and golden, with a walk that was sin in motion and just a tad predatory.

She kissed a flat nipple. She couldn't see in the dark, but she knew it was copper-colored and came to attention whenever she played with it. Like now.

"Again, beautiful?"

She laughed when she heard his muffled, groggy voice.

"No. I don't think even you are that good."

"Oh, I'm more than good enough," he mumbled. She could hear the smile in his voice. He moved his hand and cupped her tender outer sex. "At the very least, eager and willing. I was thinking more along the lines of how sore you must be."

"I was actually thinking we should get back to the lodge," she said regretfully. "Tony would have a fit if he found out I was missing."

He went still. It was the first time the topic of Tony had come up during their stolen night.

"I'll talk to Tony, Walker. About us. I wanted to tell you something in the boathouse. Tony and I aren't engaged."

His head came up like a hound catching the scent. "You're not?"

She shook her head and did her best to describe Tony's and her unconventional relationship, sensing his tight focus on her the entire time. "Something Tony said last night makes me think he suspects something is going on between us, anyway," she said at the end of her explanation.

"Really?"

Madeline nodded, her cheek brushing against a smooth, dense pectoral muscle. Walker touched the back of her head, and she looked up in the direction of his face.

"Let me tell Tony," he said. "I'll do it sometime later today."

"We'll do it together," she whispered.

He hesitated, but then he nodded. She kissed his chest and scurried out of the bed regretfully. "I'm going to take a quick shower. Do you have anything I could put on?"

He laughed and she smiled. She'd forgotten how much she loved Walker's laughter.

"I don't have much in the petite department."

"I'm not complaining," she said archly. She snorted with laughter and darted toward what she suspected was the bathroom when he leapt off the bed and lunged for her.

Walker tilted his ear, assuring himself that Madeline was still in the shower. When he heard the water running, he picked up his cell phone. Jim Stephano picked up after two rings.

"You must have a sixth sense," Jim said in a hushed voice.

"Did you find something?" Walker asked. Jim Stephano was the top expert in his division of the Secret Service for breaking encrypted communications. Tony had been hospitable enough about giving them exclusive access to his personal computers, but he hadn't given them passwords to several files. They'd agreed that Stephano would try to break in to them tonight while the household slept.

"It was too easy," Stephano said. "Most of his firewalls relate to being outside of this room and house. Once we were inside that territory, getting to the payoff was relatively simple, although Hallas had a few good tricks up his sleeve."

Walker was surprised at how heavy his chest felt at the news. Stephano had found what they were searching for. Tony was going to prison for conspiracy to commit wire and computer fraud. When he'd committed to this undercover operation, more than a decade of years had cushioned his regard for a childhood friend. Seeing Tony again had changed that. He may be spoiled and impulsive and foolish at times, but Tony was also a brilliant, dynamic man who had remained loyal to Walker over the years. Walker knew he was doing the right thing. Tony's actions had the ability to affect the stock markets and cause a panic in the banking industry.

But betraying their friendship tasted a lot sourer than he'd suspected it would.

"Tell me what you've got," Walker said.

He listened closely while Stephano described finding an encrypted message from Tony describing the delivery of a piece of software that could give access to certain financial institution accounts. It was followed by a request for five million dollars to be transferred to an offshore account. Jim had even accessed the account number and delivery date of the funds, which came from a known Russian mob front in Moscow called Finansi.

"That's it," Walker said flatly. "We've got him."

"Yeah. And what the fuck? Why would a guy who's worth hundreds of millions of dollars do something to risk his future for five million measly bucks?"

"He wasn't doing it for the money. Not in a direct sense," Walker said. "He was doing it in order to create a panic in the banking industry . . . a panic that would ensure all of those banks would run to Hallas Technologies in order to buy his security software."

Stephano grunted. "The guy's a genius. Too bad he's been using that brain of his to cook up some real nasty business. There's more. Finansi Enterprises, the Russian mob front, sent several requests for additional software, but Tony refused. It appears Hallas's Russian friends are none too happy with him at the moment."

Walker paused, absorbing this news. "Tony must be really sweating about that shot taken at Madeline, then. He thinks his former business partners are trying to tell him he can't stop playing in the middle of the game."

"Just like what you suspected, Walk. Hallas was so desperate to protect Ms. Sayer from his prior misdeeds, he let the wolves right into his den. Course, it didn't hurt a bit that one of those wolves was an old, trusted friend."

The smugness in Jim's voice made Walker cringe inwardly. He heard the water shut off in the bathroom and walked onto the dark balcony outside his bedroom.

"I'm going out with Tony and Madeline on his yacht this afternoon. I owe it to him to explain things in person. You guys be ready to stage Hallas's arrest when we return to shore."

Madeline swam in the sweatpants and T-shirt Walker had given her. She looked ridiculous. Chances were that no one would see her and Walker returning, though. Tony was a late riser, and that meant his staff often kept relatively similar hours. She bent and picked up her blue gown and robe from the carpet. They were still damp. She held the gown close to her face and inhaled Walker's scent. The flash of arousal that tore through her surprised her a little. No thoughts or memories accompanied that surge of heat. Apparently, her body was programmed to respond to the scent of Walker's semen alone.

She was smiling as she walked out the door. Walker was still in the shower, and she wanted to take the opportunity to check out his new house before they left.

A few minutes later she wandered back into the foyer. He'd done well for himself. The house had large, airy rooms, and almost the entire lake-facing side of it was windows. She turned her ear up the stairs and thought she heard the sound of Walker moving around, dressing. She glanced down at her nightgown and robe.

If someone did happen to see them returning to the mansion, she'd prefer not to be seen holding the incriminating items. Walker's kitchen seemed completely barren when she'd inspected it earlier—he still hadn't fully moved into the house—but maybe he had some sort of bag where she could put her nightgown in his trunk?

She grabbed his car keys off the hook and headed outside.

Walker came up behind her a moment later as she stared into his lit trunk and shock settled on her slowly like a leaden cape.

Through the haze of her bewilderment she noticed him glance into the trunk of the car and then at her face.

"I can explain, Madeline," he said.

She flinched slightly like a fly had just landed on her face. She pointed into Walker's trunk. "A Ramo sniper rifle," she said in a leaden voice, her eyes still glued to the inscription on the right-hand corner of the black leather that encased what was obviously a deadly weapon. She looked up at him. "Russian, I think you said it was?"

"I can explain, Madeline," he repeated quietly.

He reached for her shoulder but she stepped back.

"*You* shot at me?" she asked incredulously.

He exhaled in frustration and glanced skyward. After a moment of what appeared to be exasperated indecision on his part, he replied, "Yes. But I'm an excellent shot, Madeline. You were never in danger."

"What the hell are you talking about?" Everything had taken on a dream-like quality—the dark night enveloping them, the trunk with the gun, Walker's stiff expression in the glow of the trunk light, contrasting with the memory of everything that had come before that moment and her newfound sense of hope.

"I had to do something that would scare Tony enough, some-thing that would motivate him to ask me inside the Aspen Lodge with my team," Walker said quietly. He looked over at the trunk and briefly shut his eyes. "It was my idea. I suggested it to my boss. I knew Tony would be upset at the idea of you being threatened in any way . . . upset enough to invite me into his private sanctuary."

"Your boss? I thought you were your own boss."

"I am. Or I will be, as soon as this operation is finished."

"Operation?" she whispered.

He nodded. "I'm technically still under the employ of the Secret Service, Madeline." He looked at her face and nodded toward the car. "Come on. Get in, and I'll explain on the way. It's probably for the best. I was going to tell you later today anyway."

Madeline got into the passenger seat of the car like an automaton. She said nothing as Walker drove through the dark, narrow mountain roads and listened while he explained about his undercover operation and Tony's alleged crime. She felt numb, not saying a word until he pulled back into the drive at the Aspen Lodge and parked his car.

"You said you came back to Lake Tahoe because of me," she said, staring straight ahead.

"I *did*, Madeline. I would have been back here if this shit had happened with Tony or not. I wasn't lying about that."

"But you really came back to Tahoe to arrest Tony for computer wire fraud," she continued, her voice low and flat as if she just received a blow to the head and someone was trying to coach her through the last few minutes while she'd been muddled.

"It's *one* of the reasons I came back. When I saw those photos of you from Secret Service surveillance, it was like a kick to the gut. I may have shot that bullet in order to get Tony to open his doors to me, but that doesn't mean there isn't a true threat against you, with all Tony has gotten himself involved with. The Russian mob is ruthless. Maybe I made a preemptive strike with that rifle, but I was mimicking that exact type of thing they would do to put pressure on Tony for more goods. You were vulnerable, Madeline, and you didn't even know it. I don't regret doing something in order to make you safe."

She turned and looked at him. She blinked twice, trying to see a face that'd haunted her for a better part of her life in better focus.

"How do you know I'm not just going to walk in that house and tell Tony the truth about what you've been doing in his house?" she asked.

His expression grew grim. "Even if you did, it wouldn't change anything. We have ample evidence, Madeline, and it's already been sent to DC. The arrest is going to happen, whether it's right now or later this afternoon. I'd think you'd want me to break it to him in person . . . man-to-man."

"Man-to-man," she whispered, stunned. "You *betrayed* Tony by using your friendship."

"I did what I had to do. You have no idea the type of threat he's risking by his actions. It's one of the mandates of the Secret Service to protect the integrity of the U.S. financial system, Madeline. I'm doing my job."

He started when she laughed, high and scathing. "Your *job.* Heaven forbid something should stop you from doing your *job,* Walker."

He didn't follow her when she got out of the car and ran on bare feet toward the lodge.

Six

Tony opened the sliding glass doors that led to the helm and joined Madeline on the bridge seating area at the front of the yacht.

"The anchor's down. Didn't I pick an ideal spot?" Tony asked, sprawling on the white-cushioned circular couch. He looked like a bronzed Greek god wearing nothing but a pair of ivory trunks. He held a glass half filled with cranberry, vodka and ice. Madeline had noticed he'd been drinking ever since the brunch Alessandro served them at nine thirty this morning. Her desire to confront him about his upsurge in drinking had been quieted by Walker's alarming news.

Tony should do whatever pleased him this afternoon. It would likely be his last day of freedom for a while.

Her throat tightened with anguish. Why had Tony done it, the idiot? *Why?*

And damn Walker. Damn him for putting her through this

agony of bewilderment and loss. She may not want to marry Tony, but he was her friend.

She forced herself to look away from Tony and squinted at the sunlit view.

"It's perfect," she murmured as she inspected the secluded inlet where he'd moored the yacht. Her entire vision was filled with towering pines and sparkling blue-green water.

"I thought you'd like it for a swim. That sun is intense today," Tony said with a smile before he took a strong pull on his drink.

"Where's Walker?" Madeline asked throatily. She'd been hyper-aware of his presence all morning, although she'd hardly muttered more than a half dozen words to him. She'd just become used to seeing him as her lover again and now she was back to regarding him as an enemy.

"He's checking out the equipment on the helm," Tony said, nodding toward the sliding glass doors. "He's like a kid in a candy store."

Madeline narrowed her eyes behind her glasses and peered toward the windows. The glare on the glass prevented her from seeing Walker, but she knew he could see her as he looked out onto the bridge seating.

She felt confused. On edge. Anguished over what Tony was about to endure for his foolishness. His impulsivity. Over and over, she'd considered what she might do to somehow save Tony. But as Walker had said, the evidence had been sent. It was just a matter of time before he was arrested.

She stood abruptly from the deck chair where she'd been reclining. Tony did a double take when she casually whipped off her bikini top and tossed it on the white cushions. His smile widened.

"To what do I owe this lovely gift?" he asked.

Madeline ignored his query. "I'm going swimming."

She stepped toward the ladder that led to the upper deck and the diving board. Tony surprised her by sitting up and placing a hand on her oil-covered hip. He rubbed at her skin sensually while he spoke.

"Take off the panties, too," he suggested in a low, rough voice. "A body as beautiful as yours should never be hidden."

Madeline glanced at the glass doors leading to the helm, sensing Walker's attention on her. On them. She drew her bikini panties down to her ankles and stepped out of them. She paused long enough to allow Tony to rub the oil from her back down onto her buttocks before she headed toward the diving board.

The alpine water cut like ice through her volatile mood.

Walker considered going after her when he heard the splash from her dive, but he couldn't abandon the boat and Tony. He watched from a window on the helm as she swam in the cove, the clear, luminescent waters revealing every detail of her naked body. Fury at her stubbornness mixed with a potent arousal. He couldn't decide what he wanted to do most, spank her bottom pink for letting Tony touch her like that in front of him or fuck her until she begged.

Both options felt equally desirable at the moment.

She swam a considerable distance. Walker was considering going out onto the bridge in order to break the news to Tony since they were alone when Tony opened the sliding glass doors.

"I'm off to the galley. How about a drink, Walk?"

"What are you having?"

"Vodka and cranberry."

"I'll have the same, minus the vodka."

Tony laughed and disappeared down the corridor. When he returned carrying two glasses, he nodded toward the sunlit bridge. "Come out here. I want to talk to you about something."

"I was going to mention the same to you," Walker said, dread settling in his chest.

The brilliant sun immediately chased away the chill on his skin from the air-conditioning. He whipped off his shirt and took a seat at the far right of the surround couch. Tony stood portside, his back to the rail.

"It's about the work you and your team have been doing at the lodge. I know what you've been up to, Walker," Tony began. Walker paused in the action of lifting his drink to his lips. He studied Tony's expression. His dark eyes looked glassy from moderate intoxication, but otherwise he looked sober as a judge.

He opened his mouth to make a cautious statement when Madeline walked onto the bridge, dripping wet, naked and jaw-droppingly beautiful. She paused when she saw both men stare at her. Walker took an uneasy inhale when she looked straight at him and her chin went up in defiance.

"Here's Venus now," Tony murmured appreciatively as his dark eyes roamed over Madeline's body. He put out his arm and she walked toward him, her gaze still on Walker. Despite his rising anger at her, he also experienced a rush of compassion for the hurt and bewilderment he saw in her large eyes. "I was just about to talk to Walker about you, darling, but here you are, beauty incarnate."

Walker watched, his body coiled like a spring, as Tony's hand opened on Madeline's waist and stroked downward, toward her naked hip, smoothing the water droplets that beaded on her taut curves. Despite his fury at seeing another man touch Madeline, his cock thickened in his swim trunks.

For a few seconds, Madeline looked uncomfortable at Tony's caress. But then something seemed to occur to her and her disdainful look returned. Damn her.

He was going to have to punish her again for punishing him.

"What were you saying about me?" she asked Tony, her tone gentle but her expression haughty as she stared at Walker.

Tony smiled as he began to rub her ass. He took a step toward her. His hips thrust forward slightly when he paused, as though he were putting the bulge growing behind his trunks on display.

"I was just about to tell Walker that I want him to assure me you will always be taken care of," Tony said gruffly. "I trust him to do it."

Madeline's eyes flashed over to Walker. He could tell by her distressed expression that she wondered if Walker had already told Tony that he was soon to be arrested. He hadn't, but Tony knew. Somehow.

He watched, a strange brew of emotions building in his gut, as Tony pulled Madeline's naked body against him. He buried his face in the juncture of her neck and shoulder as he kneaded both of her buttocks in his hands. Madeline still stared directly at Walker, but her expression had shifted. He still saw defiance in her beautiful eyes, but he saw tears of compassion, as well, for her old friend.

For their old friend.

When Tony's body shuddered with emotion, Walker stood. Madeline gave him a fiery glance as he approached before she stepped back and reached for the waistband on Tony's trunks.

"Madeline," he said warningly.

"Just one last time," Tony said brokenly. Walker met his gaze and knew for a fact Tony had somehow gleaned what he and his team had done. He might have suspected last night, but this morning, he'd somehow traced their actions. He knew for certain he'd been caught at his foolish game.

Madeline stared at Walker, frozen in the action of pulling down Tony's trunks. "The *only* time," Walker said softly.

Nobody disagreed.

Walker stepped forward. He hooked his fingers in the back of

Tony's trunks, and both he and Madeline lowered them. Tony's erection sprung out of the mesh lining.

With a mixture of regret and intense arousal, Walker walked behind Madeline and placed his hands on her shoulders. He pushed down and she went to her knees before Tony. Walker gently gathered the long tendrils of her damp hair and held the thick strands at her nape.

"Only use your mouth," he ordered tensely as Tony grasped his cock and brought it toward Madeline's parted lips. "I don't want to see you two touching each other."

"I know she's yours, Walker. I think I've always known it. This is just good-bye," Tony murmured. For a moment, the two men locked gazes as Madeline knelt between them. Walker gave a small nod.

He watched as Tony arrowed his cock between Madeline's lips.

It was torture. It was delicious. Walker couldn't decide what it was, precisely, as he watched from above while Madeline wetted Tony with her tongue and then slowly began to work him into her mouth. Since Walker held her head captive with his hand, Tony had to thrust to get friction. He seemed to have taken what Walker said about not wanting to see them touch to heart, because he stood with his legs slightly spread, his knees bent to accommodate Madeline's position and his hands on his tensed thighs. Walker's own cock grew achy and ponderous as he watched Tony begin to face-fuck Madeline with the first five or so inches of his penis.

Tony grunted in pleasure. Walker could see Madeline's hollowed-out cheeks and could just imagine her supreme suck, how good it felt thrusting into that wet, tight vacuum. Tony wasn't as long or thick as Walker was. It angered him to realize Tony could probably achieve full oral penetration with her.

But for some reason, he hungered to see it, as well.

"I want to see you suck all of him, Madeline," he commanded

Bethany Kane

harshly. He blinked a drop of sweat out of his eye, a little shocked at hearing himself speak.

He felt Madeline struggle in the hold he kept on her hair and allowed her to tilt her head in order to accommodate Tony in her throat. Madeline jerked when he breached her and Tony groaned gutturally. Walker pulled back on her head and Tony's tumescent penis slid out of her mouth, the bright sunlight making it glisten. After two more passes like this, with Walker guiding the movements of her head, her lips kissed Tony's balls.

Tony moaned roughly as she kept him completely submerged for several electric seconds. He saw her nostrils flare and knew she was getting air.

Walker didn't know if she'd had enough, but he was on the edge of stopping this. He pulled back on her head and watched Tony's cock slide out of her until she just held the head in the tight clamp of her lips. Tony was so swollen with blood, Walker had no doubt he'd come soon.

Conflict warred inside of him. He wanted to give Tony this gift before he was arrested, but it was torture as well. He was angry at Madeline for purposefully instigating this whole thing with her nude swimming and allowing Tony to touch her in front of him.

He loved her like crazy, but he wanted to punish her for her stubbornness . . . her infernal haughtiness.

He damn well wanted her to suck his cock just as skillfully as she was doing to Tony's right now.

His emotions frothed and bubbled at the surface of his consciousness as he pushed her head back and forth on Tony's cock in rapid, swift strokes. Tony's eyes were closed, his hands on his thighs, moaning in a state of total rapture at being pleasured by Madeline.

Walker's woman.

Whether Madeline wanted to admit it at the moment or not.

Both of them blinked open their eyes when Walker pulled back on Madeline's head and Tony's erection popped out of the tight seal of her clamped lips.

"What's going on?" Madeline asked. Walker grimaced at the sexy sound of her cock-massaged throat. He put his hands under her arms and lifted her to a standing position. Tony didn't look pleased, and Walker couldn't say he blamed him. Madeline had been treating him to a hell of a ride in her mouth.

"She'll finish," Walker said stiffly. He released Madeline's hair, and she twisted her chin to look at him. He met her defiant glance with a hard stare. "First I'm going to punish her for being so god-damned good at it, though. She's going to get a pink ass for being so stubborn."

Tony's eyebrows went up in an expression of surprise and inter-est. Madeline's already pink cheeks flushed crimson. Fury flared in her dark eyes.

"I have a paddle, if you're interested. It's in the bedside table of the master suite," Tony said. He gave a devilish grin when Mad-eline's head whipped around. She made a disgusted sound at what she must have considered to be a betrayal on Tony's part. "Don't be mad, darling. I never used it on you when we used to sleep together, did I? You'd never let me."

"Only one man will ever punish her," Walker said. "Go and get the paddle, Madeline."

Her mouth opened to protest, but then she met his stare. She edged toward the glass doors indecisively, a sullen expression on her beautiful face.

"I'll give you ten seconds. Every second you're not here after that, I'll give you an extra pop," Walker murmured.

Her dark eyes widened. She suddenly spun and raced toward the glass doors.

"I'll be right back," Walker said woodenly to Tony. He went

inside to retrieve something from the pile of clothing he'd left in the upper living area. Madeline returned to the bridge seating area just a moment after Walker returned himself.

She looked beautiful as she stepped onto the deck, naked and mutinous, a polished wood paddle in her hand.

"Bring it to me," Walker said quietly.

He honestly couldn't tell for sure what she'd do in that moment, comply or spit in his face. She found a compromise by stalking over to him, handing him the paddle and starting to walk away. Walker slipped his hand through the loop at the end of the paddle and let it hang. He caught Madeline's wrist from behind, halting her departure. She glanced around in shock when he slid a metal cuff around her wrist.

"I don't know why you're so angry with me," she told him in a fury-choked voice as he grabbed her other hand and bound her wrists behind her. "I'm not the one who betrayed a friend."

"Walker didn't betray me, Madeline," Tony said, sounding a little sad. He'd taken a seat on the surround couch. His cock was still hard and moist, resting at an angle on his belly. "He was just doing his job."

Madeline made a sound like a hissing cat at those words.

"You're the one who betrayed me by letting another man touch you in front of my face," Walker said. He grabbed her arm and led her over to Tony. "Hold her shoulders." He pressed down on Madeline's back, forcing her to bend over in front of Tony. Tony followed his direction, taking the bulk of Madeline's upper body weight while she bent over, hands cuffed at her middle back and her bottom in the air.

His cock tingled in anticipation as he stared at Madeline's bare ass. She didn't typically swim or sunbathe naked—no, that was just a device she'd been using lately to torture him—because her bottom was pale next to her tanned skin. Her ass had always pleased him, round, tight and surprisingly fleshy for her slight figure.

He swung the paddle, giving her a healthy crack in the middle of her buttocks. Her weight went forward slightly at the blow, but Tony braced her. Walker paddled her several more times, the whapping sound of hard wood striking firm, supple flesh making his cock lurch in his swim trunks. He continued until he heard her moan.

He paused and grabbed a handful of sun- and paddle-warmed ass. Tony smiled encouragingly at Madeline when she lifted her head while Walker soothed her bottom. He noticed that Tony's erection hadn't diminished in the least since Madeline had stopped sucking him so forcefully. He seemed to be enjoying the sight of seeing the defiant Madeline being punished. Walker could just imagine what a woman like her could do to a man if he let her.

He stepped back and swatted her plump buttocks again several times, trying to gauge from the sound of her cries and moans if he was causing any real harm. He was trying to make a point, but he'd never cause her any serious pain. He landed the paddle on her ass, appreciating the subtle shiver the blow wrought in the taut flesh. Her ass was starting to glow pink. He was uncertain about the meaning of her low, desperate moan, so he sent his finger between her thighs.

Her pussy was drenched. The moan hadn't been from pain or humiliation. Definitely not. She groaned louder and squirmed against the pressure of his finger.

He dropped his hand and swatted her ass with the paddle, the spankings forceful enough to cause Tony's arms to flex as he held her in position. He paused, knowing he'd been hard, and rubbed her bottom. Her taut flesh radiated heat into his palm.

He stepped back and lowered his swim trunks, grimacing at the feeling of the heavy weight of his cock pulling down on the root.

He fisted his erection briefly, but it didn't give him any relief. He was hard enough to pound wood with the damn thing.

He held the paddle at the ready.

"I want you to tell me you'll never let another man touch you just because you're trying to punish me. You can get mad at me all you want, Madeline, but I won't have you acting like a selfish little brat to make your point."

When she didn't speak, he swung his arm and paddled her briskly. Tony caught her, his cock leaping in his lap at the same moment.

"You always were stubborn, Maddie," Tony told her with a small, sad smile. "I could never tame you."

Walker paddled her again. He heard her moan.

"Say it, Madeline," he warned at the same time he squeezed a buttock in his hand.

She whimpered, but still . . . no promise.

He used the tip of the paddle to spank the captured flesh in his hand. She began to groan and thrash her head, but she didn't speak. Walker grabbed her other butt cheek and treated it to the same focused, stinging spanks.

She gasped raggedly.

"All right. I . . . I promise."

Walker released her buttocks and struck both cheeks with the paddle. "You'll promise to never let another man touch you in an attempt to punish me." She gasped for air and he paddled her again.

"I do. I promise never to let another man touch me to try and punish you, Walker," she squeaked.

"You'll never do this again unless I say so, Madeline," he added grimly, the paddle poised at the ready in his hand. But she shook her head.

"No," he heard her say hoarsely. "It was . . . it was only for Tony."

Tony's face collapsed briefly with emotion. "Maddie," he whispered feelingly as he pushed her hair out of her face. "You always were too much of a woman for me. Always."

Walker frowned at the tender display, even though he was moved by it. So much conflicting emotion stormed inside him, he felt like he was ready to explode. He flung the paddle onto the couch. He hadn't locked the handcuffs. They released when he hit the spring.

"Stand up, Tony," he said gruffly. "Madeline's going to finish what she started."

Tony sprung up from the couch. Walker guided Madeline with his hands on her sun-warmed hips, guiding her into the position he wanted her to take.

"Put your hands on your knees, Madeline. You too, Tony," he added. He didn't think he could stand to see them caressing each other. He felt like lifting Madeline and kissing her until they both melted into hot goo when she immediately did as he asked, placing her hands on her supple thighs. She bent over, her face to Tony's cock, her ass to his.

Surely Walker was big enough to give him these minutes of rapture after he'd betrayed Tony's trust, no matter how justified he'd been in doing so.

"Now take him in your mouth," Walker ordered hoarsely. He saw Tony's face transported by ecstasy when she followed his order.

"Oh, yeah," Tony moaned through a sublime smile.

Walker couldn't take this anymore. Madeline always did know how to dish out her own form of punishment.

He took his cock in his hand—it felt like it was about to burst through the skin he was so aroused—and arrowed it toward Madeline's drenched, tender cleft. They all moaned at once. She was hot and wet and so tight he had to thrust firmly to make way in her flesh. He gritted his teeth, watching as he slid into her and she gloved him like a muscular fist and melted around him at once.

"My pussy," he growled roughly and began to thrust with long, thorough strokes, popping against her pink ass with his pelvis rhythmically. Sunlight beat down on them and Walker fucked the woman of his dreams while she caused their friend's eyes to roll back into his head with her strong suck. Slippery, slurping sounds and grunts of pleasure filled the air as the yacht swayed them, its lulling motions a direct contrast to the frenzied storm building on board.

Walker watched Tony, unintentionally matching his fucking motions to the same rate Tony thrust into Madeline's mouth. She began to keen, low and deep in her throat. It drove him crazy to see the expression of ecstasy on Tony's face as he experienced the vibrations of her bliss.

"Hold her shoulders steady, Tony," Walker ordered tersely. He'd said he didn't want Tony touching her, but she was going to need stabilization with as hard as he planned to fuck her. Tony complied. Her constant keening turned to sharp whimpers as he began to hammer into her pussy. It must have aroused her as much as it did Walker, because Tony's cock slid all the way into her, and Tony cried out in surprised pleasure.

"*Don't* come inside her," Walker commanded as his pelvis smacked against Madeline's ass.

He watched, a snarl on his face, as Tony hurriedly withdrew and turned slightly. He jacked his penis and groaned as semen arched into the air and spattered onto the deck. His arms continued to move rapidly as he ejected his seed. His eyes remained closed, lost in his own private pleasure. Finally, he gasped and fell heavily back onto the couch, panting.

Walker withdrew from Madeline. He felt tight with a potent combination of lust, love, loss and fury. He touched Madeline's shoulder, and she glanced up at him from her bent-over position. What he saw made him caress her, for the same wicked brew of emotions seemed to storm behind her dark eyes.

"Go down on your knees, Madeline." His command had been gentle despite the untenable pressure building in his chest and balls.

She knelt before him. He could see how erect her small nipples were and that her cheeks were even pinker than her bottom.

He guided his cock into her mouth, stretching her lips. Next to them, Tony groaned between pants.

For the next several minutes, Walker was lost in a tossing sea of focused pleasure and cresting emotion. He dominated Madeline thoroughly, not just because he wanted her until it hurt like an unhealed wound, but because she let him. As she gazed up at him as he slid into her throat, he knew that Madeline had accepted what he'd said to her last evening in the bathroom.

"You're mine," he grated out between clenched teeth. Seeing her acknowledgment in her gaze made him bellow in anguished pleasure as he came.

He didn't feel turned inside-out this time; he felt ripped inside-out.

When his thunderous orgasm finally quieted, he reluctantly withdrew and lifted Madeline to a standing position, murmuring to her softly as he kissed her sweat- and tear-dampened eyelids, cheeks and lips.

Seven

She'd lost all remnants of propriety or shame. She'd forgotten her anger at Walker and even her sadness for Tony's foolish, life-altering mistake.

Nothing existed for Madeline in those moments that she was on the receiving end of the force of nature that was Walker Gray. His possession had been fierce, focused and forceful, but behind his sexual mastery, she'd sensed the unspoken lesson he strove to teach her.

Despite the long years of separation and Tony Hallas and Madeline's stubbornness—despite it all—she was still Walker's, body and soul.

And he was hers.

"I didn't come after Tony to hurt you, Madeline. I love you," he whispered gruffly next to her ear as he took her into his arms. He stroked her back and hips and buttocks while Madeline cried softly, her cheek pressed to his expanding and contracting chest.

Walker's gruff voice in her ear and caressing hands made her shiver uncontrollably.

"I know," she replied almost inaudibly. She spoke the absolute truth. The power of his possession had opened her eyes. Walker Gray wasn't the type of man who would have allowed what had just occurred unless love was involved. She understood Walker well enough to know what he'd just sacrificed. She whimpered when she felt his hand between her legs, moving, pleasuring tender, swollen flesh.

A moment before she was about to climax, she felt Tony press against her from behind. They both held her while she shuddered in climax, Walker taking what was his by nature's decree, Tony experiencing for the first and last time what he'd always craved.

Madeline's surrender.

Madeline didn't turn around later that evening when she sensed him approach. She sat at the end of the long pier, her feet dangling off the edge, her gaze glued to the crimson-and-gold sunset. Walker didn't make a noise as he approached her from behind, but she knew it was him, nonetheless.

He sat behind her, his long, jean-covered legs bracketing her hips. He pulled her back against his chest, his arms surrounding her. She leaned her head against him, her eyes fixed on the blazing departure of the sun.

It'd been a hell of a day. Wonderful and awful in equal measures.

"You okay?" he asked, his mouth near her ear as he nuzzled her hair with his chin.

"Yes," she whispered. She reached back with her hand and cupped the side of his head. "I can't believe Tony is in jail. It seems surreal. He seemed so resigned when they took him away."

That wasn't the only thing that seemed surreal. So was the

entire sunlit, sex-drenched memory of being out on the yacht this afternoon with Tony and Walker. It was the memory of her good-bye to a friend she loved.

It was also the memory of her complete surrender to Walker.

Her feelings for Walker were strong enough to overcome the paradox of emotion, Madeline acknowledged as he lowered his head next to hers and pressed against her, cheek to cheek.

"I regret having to do it, Madeline. But Tony needed to be stopped. I was the only man who could do it."

"I know," she replied softly as they both stared at the sinking sun. "I wish to God he hadn't been born so impulsive . . . so fool-ish. The degree of damage he created with his actions—not just real, but potential—boggles my mind. I can't imagine what his par-ents must be going through right now."

"They're gone now. Victor plans to hire the best lawyer money can buy for Tony's defense," Walker said, referring to the Hallases, who had come to speak with Walker and Madeline after Tony had been taken by two members of Walker's team and the Truckee police. Madeline had wandered out to the pier after Walker had regretfully described the charges against Tony. She'd been too hurt by the lost, wounded expression on Victor Hallas's face at the news of the proof against his only son.

"Madeline?"

"Yes?" She turned her chin. His eyes were two perfect mirrors of the fiery waters of Lake Tahoe. An upsurge of emotion swelled in her chest. She recognized the sensation as her love for him, liber-ated. Her anguish for Tony remained, but her feelings for Walker reigned supreme, giving her comfort.

"I wasn't lying. I did plan to come back to Lake Tahoe for you. I could have gone anywhere to start up my business. I'd already made my plans for leaving the Secret Service—for returning here—when all of the intelligence arrived on Tony."

She swallowed thickly, her gaze glued to his.

"I knew it wasn't going to be easy, seeing you after all these years and under these circumstances," he continued gruffly. "But I have to admit, I'd forgotten just how stubborn you can be, Madeline." His eyes narrowed on her mouth. "How beautiful. I didn't plan on seducing you. I couldn't stop myself, though. I did a lot of things that could have cost us this investigation because I was so bowled over by seeing you again."

She gave him an arch glance. "Are you saying you put your job at risk because of me?"

His nostrils flared. "I put everything at risk. My job. I might have ruined everything with you, as well, after what I did out there on that yacht."

Her small smile faded. "You didn't ruin anything, Walker. I'm here, in your arms. I'm not going anywhere as long as you don't."

"I told you, I'm here to stay," he rumbled before his mouth settled on hers. Madeline opened her eyelids heavily a minute later only to see him studying her with fiery blue-green eyes.

"You do understand, don't you," he said, rather than asked. "Why I reacted the way I did out there, Madeline?"

"Yes. I wanted to hurt you, after what you told me about Tony . . . and when I believed you'd come for your job and not me. I'm sorry."

"I'm sorry, too," he admitted. He glanced out at the setting sun. "But I'm not, as well. You'll never know how hard that was for me, seeing you and another man together."

"I know."

"How do you know?" he asked hoarsely.

"I could see it in your eyes. The whole time. I could hear it in your voice. I see it now, as we speak." She touched his cheek and he met her stare. "We did it for each other, Walker. We were acting out our own stuff, our own past. But we did it for Tony, too. What you did wasn't a betrayal of your job. It wasn't a betrayal of me, either. What we did was between us—Tony, you and me."

She leaned up and touched her lips to his lightly.

"Everything from here on out is between you and me, Madeline."

"Yes," she whispered before his mouth fastened securely on hers.